The General's Watch

The Enlightened series, book two

Kiersten Marcil

Vails Gate Publishing LLC

Vails Gate Publishing LLC

Published 2024

ISBN: 979-8-9900942-0-8 (paperback)
ISBN: 979-8-9900942-1-5 (e-book)

Names: Marcil, Kiersten, author
Title: The General's Watch / Kiersten Marcil
Editor: Jodi Christensen
Cover artist: Sevannah Storm
Description: Vails Gate Publishing LLC 2024
Identifiers: ISBN: 979-8-9900942-0-8 (paperback) / ISBN: 979-8-9900942-1-5 (e-book)
Subjects: FICTION / Fantasy / Historical

Vails Gate Publishing LLC paperback edition / 2024

Born in the Original Thirteen Colonies

This is a work of fiction. Although many of the characters' names in this work were inspired by real people from the eighteenth century, the actions, dialog, and progression of events, nonetheless, are the product of the author's imagination. On occasion, the real-life figures from history have been quoted. However, even those brief passages have been lifted out of context and time to create the dialog in this story. As such, no aspect of this story should be misconstrued as factual or nonfictional. Furthermore, any resemblance to actual persons living or among the other dead is entirely coincidental.

Other titles

The Enlightened series

Witness to the Revolution

The General's Watch

~

The Enlightened, Short Stories

"Traitor's Crossing," available only to newsletter subscribers

~

Short Stories

"Muse" appeared in the *Accidental Time Travelers Collective*, volume two

Dear Reader,

Interaction with fictional characters means words were placed into historical figures mouths. While inspired in tone by their letters and known political beliefs (which remain history's and not my own), they are nonetheless imaginary and perhaps even wholly inaccurate representations of the men's true personalities. A mild exception is Polish immigrant Colonel Thaddeus Kościuszko, who referred to women in his real-life letters as "girls." Try not to judge him too harshly. He was still learning English in 1778.

While you read, I encourage you to visit my website, where you can learn more about these unsung heroes featured in this story, find glossaries of the different languages and colloquial terms, and view maps of the region (including the confusing movements of the fictional scouting parties) at: www.kierstenmarcil.com.

Kiersten

To the men and women of the New York, Connecticut,
and Massachusetts Lines

~

Especially my great-great, etc. grandfathers,

Private Daniel Grauberger, Albany County Militia – Sixth Regiment

&

Private Ebenezer Lilley, Connecticut Third Battalion

Chapter One

A dog smashed through the underbrush, somewhere just ahead. Seedpods ruptured after snagging on her golden coat and their stalks jumped back into position, filling the sky with a haze of sickly gray puffs. For some reason, she wouldn't obey my call to come as I chased after her. She let out a yowl and kept darting out of reach, further and further into the withered trees creaking overhead.

From either side, I could hear our respective cries ricochet through the endless stretch of towering oaks and evergreen. Bookshelves erupting from the maze of roots underfoot teetered as we passed. The air shifted, the echoes morphing into the crush of bodies running. Around us, the withered vines, dusty with age; spiderwebs broken and clotted with their victims; plumes of twisting fog; ancient tomes bent and moldy, their yellowed pages coursing after us, caught in our wake—all barren of human life. And yet, the disturbance of breaking branches and crashing leaves carried until I realized the unseen beings weren't running with me but chasing me, closing in, funneling me toward something lying ahead. Something darker and more sinister, like a hurricane thickening, readying to unfurl its violence.

Just as I called again to the dog, gunfire burst through the trees, shattering her side. Her head arched, and her body somersaulted along the ground. My voice cracked as I screamed, floating debris catching in my throat and choking me. But when I reached the bracken where the dog had fallen, a patchwork of stinking mold was stretched beneath the fronds. She was gone.

Soldiers in blue and red exploded from the bark of nearby tree trunks. The noise was deafening as they engaged. Swords clashed. Guns flared, musket balls pierced the ancient books on their shelves, the pages spurting a black sludge where struck. Men yelled, cursing one another—some in anger, some in fear—and the dead slammed into the ground, soaking the earth with crimson pools.

I tried to flee, but rounding a nearby tree, I collided with a soldier who was waiting there. He was young, cheeks full, red uniform coat baggy—one he'd never grown into. And never would. Surprise filled his face, then pain. We both looked down at the muzzle of a gun. Steel from the bayonet extended forward several inches before penetrating his gut. The weapon grew heavy as the boy raised his empty gaze to mine. Color fled his skin, and he slid, lifeless, off the blade's end to the ground.

I threw the thing from my hands and ran. Still, the battle chased me— agony, smoke, and the reek of moldering pages.

There was a break in the trees. The foliage opened, and the cliff's edge of a giant dock materialized. I skidded to a stop, clutching the wooden railing to avoid careening into the ravine below. As I dragged myself upright, darkness seeped from the cracks of a doorway carved into the rocky creek bed. It grew in strength, slithering and grasping like serpentine tongues to devour the trees, stones, iron, the ghostly images of workers, and the hazy outlines of buildings. When it had its fill, the Darkness closed in on itself, swirling into an endless pillar of nothingness looming over me. Death called from within.

"Hold," a man's voice challenged it. Thunder reverberated from its center, cascading over us, rumbling through me. My bones vibrated with its power. Together, we both yelled, "*Apage!*"

Lightning crackled through the Darkness. Blackness oozed outward, thinning from its sides, and the entire thing dissipated like a storm emptied of its fury.

I turned to thank my savior.

The cock of a hammer.

The bluecoat's shot was perfectly aligned, the length of his arm serving as a guide, gun trained on my torso. Before I could ask what he was doing, the flashpan flared. Lead tore through my chest. Fibers burst apart as the musket ball shredded muscle, then splintered and shattered bone, and pierced my heart. My fingers shook as they traced the ridge of the gaping wound. I stared at him and wondered why he would betray me.

Chapter Two

I screamed as the nightmare ravaged me, pain afire within my chest. Then I was drowning from the inside out. My back arched as I gasped fully awake, arms flinging to the sides, desperate. Thick fluid flooded my lungs. Somewhere through the squall rushing in my head, I heard a woman's voice call for help.

Footsteps hurried into the room. A second woman's words answered, garbled and panicking. Hands grabbed at my shoulder and hip to fling me onto my side, a wave of blood spewing from my mouth. It clogged my throat as my lungs fought the invasion. My hair was snatched from my face. It pulled when a sweaty strand ripped from my cheek. One of the women struck my back and yelled at me to breathe. Another burst of blood exited my body, splattering against a wooden chair and onto the floor.

Finally, pockets of air made their way through the fluids. I dragged in a saturated breath, desperate for more. Instructions were given. The other woman rushed to the far end of the room and returned. A wet cloth was forced into my mouth to draw out scarlet clumps. A hand rubbed circles between my shoulder blades. Painful spasms of coughing racked my body until my airway was cleared. At last, I could breathe.

But the pain didn't stop. In the center of my chest, burrowed into my very core, a deep chasm had been ripped open. Something that'd always been there—comforting me, protecting me, giving me strength—was torn away. A part of me had been stolen, and my body revolted at losing a piece of my soul. What remained was an emptiness, raw and cold. And I was afraid.

Chapter Three

The wretched hollowness in me spread over the countless hours' succession of blurred dreams. Firelight gamboled across the ceiling late at night once they'd passed. Tasteless meals and empty daylight scenes flickered by during the brief spells when I'd awoken—a nurse pressing a mug to my lips, bandaging my hands after she'd massaged a balm into the damaged skin. Gentle fingers circled my chest, as well. Each moment more meaningless than the one before. Until *he* came for me.

The door creaked open. Hickory strands tangled around the shoulders of the man standing in the doorway. Rather, the doorway was holding him, his arm collapsing at his side while he slumped against the wood. The white linen of his shirt hung from his trim frame, like a ship's sails flaccid on a dying breeze. Deep bruises shadowed his eyes, his skin a sallow shore to their depths. Although he was struggling to stay upright, his gaze bore into me.

A sense of abandonment burbled in the chasm in my chest. It surged from my core, coursing through me with a feverish iciness, and boiled over as terror. I screamed, and once started, I couldn't stop.

The man tried to calm me; he shushed me and told me I was safe. Despite not remembering meeting him in life or recalling the sound of his name on his lips or mine, I didn't believe him. It took every scrap of energy I had to retreat to the far end of the bed when he stumbled into the room. A hand landed on the mattress, shifting its horizon as he sunk into it, trying to steady himself. He begged, "Peace, please. Allow me to explain myself."

Pain burned in the pit in my chest, as if someone had ripped the fresh scab from where my soul was fractured. It spread like wildfire through my limbs, escalating as he reached for me, fingers grazing my cheek.

"Leave me alone," I shouted.

"What have you in your head, coming in here?" the nurse exclaimed from the hallway. She rushed into the room and hoisted the man's arm over her shoulders, supporting his weight. "Leave her be. Can you not see she is unwell? As are you. You might take to remembering, sir."

She hesitated—the increasing agony in my chest causing me to sob— and was visibly torn between tending to me and dealing with the intruder.

In the end, she chose the burden already draped across her shoulder, practically carrying him from the room. He protested, wanting only to know how I was, what was wrong with me. The nurse's response disappeared into the hallway, muffled by the growing distance. A bedframe groaned at what must've been the man's body being deposited back into its confines.

The nurse returned.

My breathing was coming in staccato bursts. I couldn't slow my efforts. Drawing in too deeply coaxed the lingering fire in my chest to flare. A haze washed over my surroundings, my vision darkening. The fist I was digging into the area over my heart slackened as the spurt of energy drained. With surprising strength, the nurse scooped me into her arms to center me on the bed, back where I belonged.

While she was getting me situated under the covers, I caught her eye. "I don't want him in here." My voice was raspy from lack of use and exacerbated by the fit of screaming. Speaking irritated the soreness in my throat, which led to more coughing.

The nurse's heeled shoes clattered to the far end of the room and back. Her hand slipped behind my head, lifting me while she forced a clay mug between my lips.

"Here now." She set it onto a nearby desk once I'd drunk, exchanging it for a small, clay pot. Whipping the bandage loose from my hand, she massaged a sticky glop into my palm. It stung but eased as she worked the balm into the damaged skin. The fragrance of lemon and peppermint lingered. "Do not give him grief. He only wished to speak with you."

"Keep him away from me."

The woman sighed. "All right, then. At least until you are well."

I wanted to argue, to tell her I would tread every path on Earth to escape him—if that was what Fate required—but I was fading fast. Exhaustion was robbing me of my chance. Besides, how could I explain that the stranger she'd carried away was the same man who murdered me in my dreams?

Chapter Four

Sometimes I watched her sew. I followed the nurse's hand spiriting the needle into a cascade of framed peach linen, piercing the air in a straight path, to stab it back through the embroidery hoop, then tug it downward to repeat the process. Lines of floss, rich emerald in color, assembled one next to the other. Some short, growing longer, then reduced in height again. They wrapped into a second formation, touching the first—end to end—creating unfurled leaves sprouting from future blossoms. The motion was soothing, hypnotic. With each passing hour, day after day, her garden flourished across the linen canvas.

There was some significance to doing needlework, some secret meaning for me. My head would ache at the thought, and I let my eyes close without an answer to what it could be.

One afternoon, the door banged against the nearby desk as she entered the room. The light was failing in marigold shades through the window, deepening into autumnal hues on the walls beside the shifting glow from the fire. She apologized for waking me in such a manner and carried a large, porcelain bowl over to my bed.

"Now, I know you do not wish to speak with him…" The nurse hushed me, her words having churned a nasty stinging inside my chest. "You do not have to—though goodness knows, it might do a world of wonder for you—but he wanted to show you this."

I shied from the bowl she presented.

Still, she insisted, "You should at least have a look. He did say you would want to know for yourself how the poor thing was faring."

Without waiting for further refusal, she sat on the bed and tilted the bowl, slight enough for its contents to become visible over the rim. There was a folded swath of cloth lying in the middle. Resting inside, tucked into the handkerchief, was a pale blue bird. Its breathing was labored, and most of its feathers were mottled with brown. Several scruffy tufts stuck out, loose.

"What's wrong with it?" I asked.

"I know little of birds." She sighed as she studied it thoughtfully. Just then, her charge shivered in its makeshift blanket. The nurse and I exchanged a look, unsure of what to do. "Shall I build up the fire? Would you be too warm?"

She rose, leaving the bowl next to me on the bed, and fed a log into the grate. The bird must've been in bad shape because it didn't cower or try to escape. We simply watched one another, both tired and a little wary.

When the nurse returned, she brought the saucer from her afternoon coffee. It was dusty with the crumbled remains of a corn biscuit, which she offered to me so I could feed her newest patient. Despite the reservations I had about this creature who was somehow associated with the mysterious man, I sprinkled a few of the crumbs into the bowl.

The bird eyed the mess on its bed.

Tap. Corn crumbs apparently receiving top marks, they disappeared; the bird consumed the entire offering as fast as its injured body would allow. At the suggestion it might need water, I was provided with a spoon. It received the water with less trepidation.

It shivered again, nestled itself deeper into its bedding, and closed its eyes.

"Poor little soul." The nurse considered the two of us, then suggested, "What say I leave the bird here with you? Seems to me you could mend together." Interrupting my hesitation, she added, "Mind, until you do fall asleep yourself. I shall move the bowl to the dressing table after that, so nothing should go awry while you are resting."

It was easier not to argue. I curled onto my side to face my new roommate. The nurse drew the covers over my shoulders and gave a kind squeeze before resuming her place at the table. With an encouraging smile, she picked up where she'd left off with her needlework.

The bird peeked through half-closed eyelids at me, attempting a mild chirp. I assured the bird it was safe; we were both safe. After another fluffing its feathers, it scrunched into a tight, downy ball to sleep. I repeated the myth that we were safe.

Chapter Five

Every meal thereafter included day-old bread or a biscuit or cracker or some crumbly treat to feed my new pet. We grew stronger together. The bird lost its raggedy feathers, and the dull brown brightened, transforming into a brilliant deep blue that suggested he was male. He sang to me often, twittering around the room, content to gaze out the window but disinterested in flying away when I opened it.

My left hand had scabbed over, so it wasn't rebandaged. The right—once an angry red, surrounding the blistered skin that'd cracked and split open—was an obnoxious but healthier pink, now softer and whole. It, too, was left unbound to finish healing.

Eventually, I was able to move around the room without help, though I refused to leave its confines. Inside, I was tucked away from the strange man who often paced by my door. His voice sounded throughout the house from time to time, seeping through the floorboards, along with other men in conversation. It cut through me like a knife, straight to the wound in my core where he shot me nightmare after nightmare.

Every morning, I watched from my window as those unknown men left the grounds together to disappear into the woods. I was careful to hide behind the wooden shutter when the stranger would, without fail, catch my eye if I wasn't quick enough. What had I done to become the target of the man's interest?

Like him—lurking outside my room, delaying his daily travels under my window, betraying me in my dreams—the emptiness inside haunted me.

It was late morning when the bird and I were sitting at the table together, picking at the latest attempts from the cook—for me, mushy vegetables in a murky broth. The nurse informed me that, since I was faring better once more, the master was like to let the cook go, and she would see to preparing the meals again herself. The men had already left for the day. Determined not to look and risk being seen, I'd forced myself to remain seated and simply listen to their departure.

The bird hopped around the table's surface, singing with a carefree heart while I finished a cup of weak coffee. Rejuvenated by his indoor recovery, his energy was boundless. Pausing long enough to gulp water from a saucer, he drank too quickly and sneezed a miniature cloud of mist into the air before taking another pass. I laughed for the first time since I'd become ill.

"You look to be improved."

I gasped, my body jerking in surprise. My stalker hadn't left for the day with the other men, after all, and was watching me from the doorway. The bird tilted his head at me, as if confused, and leaped into the air to fly to the man's outstretched hand. While stroking the bird's belly with his knuckle, his mouth lifted into a subtle smile, but his expression grew somber as he returned his attention to me. "Thank you for caring for him. I was worried."

"Don't come in. You shouldn't be in here." My voice betrayed how much he scared me.

His shoulders drooped, as did the rest of him, actually. The man tossed his hand upward, sending the bird into the air, which it took as an invitation to flutter over to me and resume its perch on the table. I eyed it, wondering whether I'd done the right thing by accepting it into my room. The compliance wasn't meant to have encouraged him.

"I will remain here. I will not enter, as you requested." The promise did little to calm the clenching in my chest, a hollow vow coming—as it did—from *him*. "I wish to apologize. I should not have spoken to you as I did the other night."

I gave a tentative nod, hoping it would end the conversation so he would leave. But he continued to stare, his furrowed brows implying there was something else he wanted from me. What would it take to get rid of him?

"It is true that we know little of one another," he said. "Such is not your fault. There have been few opportunities with which to converse at any length, and—"

"Go away," I begged him. Pain had pricked my soul at the first sounds of his voice. Every word made it worse.

"Will you not forgive me? Miss Moore, I am truly sorry." He stepped into the room.

My hand flew to my chest, clutching at the burning sensation inside. "I don't know what I'm supposed to be forgiving you for. Just leave me alone."

"Miss Moore—"

"Stop calling me that. Why do you keep calling me that?"

"How...should I address you?"

Panic struck with full force. I didn't know the answer. Why didn't I know the answer? Why did he?

The air was getting thin. Across the expanse of the bedroom, the lone exit lay behind him. I was trapped. Light-headed, I tumbled from my seat, catching myself against the table at the last moment, before I hit the ground.

"Miss Moore." He rushed over to grasp my arm and seized my head with his other hand.

I bolted to standing, knocking his arm aside. My chair scraped the floor as I tripped over the front leg, desperate to escape. Abandoning its dish, the bird shot across the room in every direction, shrill as it chirruped over what was transpiring. I scurried away from the stranger, my only option along the backwall, where I became cornered by the bed blocking my path.

He closed in, one cautious step at a time, hands extended, speaking calming words as if to a wild animal he was trying to capture.

There was nowhere for me to go.

"Please," I sobbed.

"Bless me! Whatever is the matter?" The nurse was on the far, far side of the bed, too far away to help me.

"He tried to kill me. Please. He tried to kill me," I pleaded with her.

"What?" She searched frantically between us. "Captain Wythe?"

Agony slashed through me, stronger than before.

"Of course not," the man shouted back at her, sounding confused. "Miss Moore?" He was addressing me, but the name meant nothing to me.

I buckled under another wave of blinding pain. He grabbed my sides and guided me to the floor as I crumpled. A rough hand touched my face. He was trying to soothe me, his breath hot on my skin, eyes burning into mine. I fought him the entire way, but I was losing.

A spasm shot through my chest. Blood coated my lips during its expulsion, the sudden surge spraying the man's clothes. He jerked away, shocked. "Fetch Mistress Cloet," he yelled to the nurse. "Quickly, Miss Carroll."

"Don't l-leave me with…him," I begged her, still choking and struggling for air.

He released me, shaking, eyes wide with shock. He was scared. For me, it seemed. Why?

An image flowed from the blanks in my memory. That man—the one pretending to care for me—capturing me from behind, his breath raking across my skin, forcing a knife to my throat, stealing blood with his blade.

I renewed my efforts to flee from him.

"Captain?" The woman's voice trembled.

"Stay with her." He relented and withdrew. Leaving me cowering in a ball on the floor, he rushed from the room, though he kept his gaze on me for as long as possible before he disappeared around the corner. The bird zipped after him. "Remain here," the stranger ordered, and the little bird returned, renewing its frenzied path along the bedroom's ceiling. Footsteps thundered down a flight of stairs. He was yelling a woman's name: Anna.

Like a flash of lightning, the sound flamed into a painful burst through my head. It raced behind a door that flew open in my mind and slammed shut, swallowing the moniker so I couldn't recall it afterward. The ghostly memory of a face once associated with it remained locked within that dark prison.

Meanwhile, the nurse—the woman he'd called Miss Carroll—had gone to the dresser. Water splashed into a basin. Droplets flew behind her during her return, a streaming tail to an Earth-bound comet. Pressing a cloth to my face, she cleared away the rusty sludge from my mouth, shushing me with promises that "everything is a'right." Its coolness washed over me, easing the ache in my head, as well.

I realized the strain in my chest had fled as soon as the man had gone, and found I was able to breathe freely. For the first time since I'd woken, I thought to wonder and worry: "Where am I?"

"Do you not remember?" she asked, stunned. Tears flowed down my cheeks. She swept them away too. "Do you remember me?"

I shook my head and shivered.

She refreshed the cloth and drew it across my forehead, telling me, "My name is Éabha Carroll. Do you remember me now?"

I didn't. I knew I felt safe with her, cared for, but that could've been bred out of the countless days and nights she'd spent nursing me back to health.

Éabha helped me rise from where I was crouched on the floor. Once assured I could sit on the edge of the bed unassisted, she fetched a mug of water, encouraging me to drink. A quietness settled in the room, and the bird ceased zig-zagging through the air. Perched on the window ledge, he hopped back and forth, chest heaving, antsy nevertheless.

The man's voice boomed throughout the house, ripping right through me as he yelled, "How am I to protect her when she is terrified of me? She does not know her own name, let alone where her home is."

Tension vibrated through the walls of the house, to the point where a board's creak made it seem like the walls were creeping inward, ready to strike. Éabha wrapped a calloused hand around mine, and together, we listened. Questions swarmed in my head, daring me to speak them aloud. I was too agitated. Attempts to riddle out where I was, how I got there, and who these people were, stung my mind. Like the man's shouting when he'd stormed off, they were sucked inside me and erased.

Whatever answer the man—the captain—was given stayed downstairs, muted beyond our hearing for several minutes until he gave a final declaration: "Have you seen the terrible pain you have caused her? You had no right."

Heavy boots stalked from one end of the house to the other. A door was thrown open and banged closed, then we could hear him outside, crossing the yard. Not long after, a horse thundered past the side of the house and disappeared into the distance.

Water jostled from the mug onto my lap. Éabha eased it from my grip to replace it on the table, then gathered my hands in hers and held on tight until I stopped shaking. I was again overwhelmed by the belief that I'd just been abandoned.

Questions. So many questions I couldn't hold on to, fractured inside as I was. I focused on what was immediately in front of me: Should I try to discover where he went? Go after him? Or would I be chasing my own death? What was my connection to him? And why did my soul burn while he was near but ache now that he was gone?

Éabha knew what would cheer me—a nice, hot bath. She repeated that of course it would, filling the silence that'd met her suggestion. After patting my hand, she rose to stir the fire. A promise to return once the bathwater was boiled and ready was delivered from where she lingered by the door. The clatter of her heels retreated down the hallway and descended a flight of stairs.

Once we were alone, the little, blue bird plopped onto the pillow next to me. A single tear spilled over, a thinning rivulet rolling down the burning wasteland of my cheek to drip onto my lap. He offered a chirrup, then stumbled as he sought a firmer stance on his downy perch so he could push off and leap into the air. I followed him to the window. Fluttering along the glass, he tapped it with his beak.

My fingers froze on the latch. It was impossible to open… When? When did it feel that way?

A fragrance, more like a reminder than an actual odor I could detect, stung my nose and mind.

Burnt lavender?

The trapped memory was like a hammer slamming against the prison door. It reverberated through my skull, then faded, an echo dying in an empty cavern. It hurt like hell.

The bird twittered at me, bobbing his head up and down. I worked the lock and raised the pane with ease. He bounded toward freedom—hop, hop, hop, hop—and plummeted from the lip of the sill. I watched as he soared, rising above the lilac bush blossoming next to the house. He circled around, forgoing the endless woods, and vanished over the roof. The sense of abandonment grew. He'd chosen the same general direction the captain had taken when he'd galloped off, leaving me in a place I didn't recognize, with people who were as unfamiliar to me as I was to myself.

I collapsed onto the chair by the window.

Thoughts of the man were relentless. The memory of him trying to kill me terrorized me, playing over and over in my mind: the heat of his breath on my neck when he'd caught me, the sensation of him taking in my scent, the strength of his arm holding me captive, the sting of his knife violating my skin.

I couldn't remember him outside those moments or the visions in my nightmares, but I knew with absolute certainty that one day, he would return, and I would die because of him.

Chapter Six

There was a robe in Éabha's hands when she roused me from my frightful contemplation. "The bath is in readiness. I have not forgot," she insisted. "It was a time in the making, what with Glen and all. You would think she had ne'er set her hand to pot… Did you not wish to go belowstairs?" She draped the pink satin around my shoulders until she could draw me to standing and tuck my arms into the sleeves. I let her do what she wanted, unconcerned by her prattle about the selection of herbs and dried blossoms she'd added to the water, meant to ease my cares. I was so lost and empty.

At least until she led me to the bedroom door. When she swung it open, fear opened up with it. From across the threshold, an inferno roared at me, bearing down on me, as if a dragon had torn through the outer walls of the house and unleashed its wrath on me.

Like a furnace—

That invisible force scorching me drove the thought straight through the barrier imprisoning my mind. The pinprick the memory had escaped through splintered under such brute treatment, and the world was plunged into a dizzying blackness as it struck.

I screamed and flew from Éabha's arms, fleeing from the unbearable heat raging at me, flooding me with terror of whatever lay beyond the room. She attempted to soothe me, telling me, "There is none to fear. The men are all gone to the Iron Works. Mistress has left with the children to visit family. It is just us two and the cook downstairs."

She didn't mention the captain.

The unnatural fire assaulted me with renewed efforts, roaring through my skull, hurling her words into the cavern inside and melding the imperfections of my prison door so it was whole again. I retreated further into the room, unable to control myself, all the while confused about why this was being done to me and whether she had said where we were going. The pain lessened as I reached the far end of the bedroom, which was how I knew I'd never be allowed to leave. Not without permission.

Poor Éabha clasped my arms and tried to reason with me, unaware of the agonizing battle I was facing. When my fingernail scraped her hand during our struggle, she released me with a surprised shriek. I fell to the floor, landing hard on my tailbone. Nausea burst up my torso with the jolt.

"Serves you right," she said, her patience clearly run out. She tended to her injury at the washbasin on the dresser, snapping at me, "Have you gone mad, carrying on as such?"

I grasped my knees to my chest and leaned against the footboard of the bed.

What's happening to me? Am I mad? Was I always like this?

Anger dissipated from Éabha's taut expression as she towered over me huddled on the floor, rubbing the silk robe between my fingers, faster and faster. Concern and frustration took its place. "Do you want to bathe? Or has the hauling and boiling of water been for naught?"

I peered around the bedframe toward the open door. The crisp white walls of the hallway beyond the borders of my room welcomed me, quaint and normal looking. Just as I was thinking I must've imagined it, how I wanted to leave, I wanted to take a bath—surely what'd happened wasn't real—the power trapping me inside the room reared its ugly head. Its reminder took the form of a fiery gale affecting me alone, slamming into me and sending me cowering behind the bed, shaking.

"What is it I should do with you, then?" Éabha asked. She didn't chance moving me again, that's for sure.

"I don't know," I whimpered. She sighed and threw another log on the fire, favoring her left hand. Her right outer fingers were bandaged with a thin linen that wasn't there earlier, and I realized she must've burnt or cut herself. "I'm sorry."

"That you are, ma'm."

I think she meant I was a sorry sight.

She stared at me until I apologized a second time, then left me there to "see to the cook before the dinner is boiled to mush like the day before."

That was where *he* found me, an hour or so later, arms and legs wrapped together, leaning against the bedframe. His voice came from outside the room. Still, it pierced me from inside my chest, driving through me when he spoke the name he'd taken to calling me. I held my breath, hoping he wouldn't hear my stifled groan. Footfalls crossed the threshold. The attack intensified as I silently begged him to go away. Tall, black boots rounded the corner, and I buried my face into my arms, knowing I was trapped in that cursed bedroom with him.

"Oh, Miss Moore, I… Come now." He kept repeating, "All shall be well," and crouched in front of me.

I gasped as the pain throve in my chest. "J-just leave me alone."

I didn't trust him. There was something more to it than the nightmare. Something my empty mind couldn't recall but had warned me about when he invaded my sleep. The center of my forehead ached with the effort of trying to remember.

Indecision made him fidgety while he studied me. When he did speak, doubt strained his words. "I can relieve the pain."

There was very little space separating us, even before he extended a hand. I shrank from him, with nowhere to go. The captain brushed a loose strand from my forehead. "God's teeth. You are fevered." He laid a palm there, and the agony slicing through my chest was all there was. "Please, please grant me permission to assist you," he begged, withdrawing his hand. The pain lessened as he did.

Tears flooded his eyes, close to flowing over. I was terrified of him, and yet…it felt real—his concern, distress even, for me. I found myself captivated by him, by the deep pools of his eyes. They were so, so blue. It felt like I was slipping into them, cooled and comforted there. Safe.

I nodded before I could stop myself.

Momentary relief eased his expression, but then he grew serious, concentrating hard on my face. He took hold of my arm, steadying me. The pain in my chest magnified, the chasm in my center ripping open wider. The urge to pull away was overwhelming, even while my soul yearned to be with him. It felt like I was being wrenched apart.

Fingertips alighted on my breastbone. My muscles jolted, resistant to the heat rising there, but his grip crushed my arm as he squeezed tighter. Flames scorched my skin while he pressed his hand into my chest, pinning me against the footboard. Hushed words wove into the sensation, stinging my ears. He was praying.

Another memory assailed me as it seeped through the prison door— the captain yanking me to the ground; his hands gripping my arms, bruising me as he threw me to the side; a gun to my head; me, frantic, searching the woods around me; the weight of him ramming me into the dirt; my mind dissolving as I lost consciousness; all the while, the captain—

I bolted back to the present. Whispering breezed loose strands of hair over my cheek, his dark locks entwined with mine. His fingers were splayed across my breasts, skin to skin. The scent of spice and sweat drifting from the shadows beneath his collar was thick, flooding the mere inches between our bodies.

"Stop!"

"You must allow me to finish," he insisted.

With the blurred memory resonating inside me, I panicked at his words. I shot my fists between us and drove them outward, snagging the captain's arms to break his grasp on mine. But there wasn't enough room for me to flee or strike him with any leverage behind it. His hands latched onto my wrists, dragging me back to the floor. My back was thrust into the protrusions in the footboard as he plunged his fist down the front of my nightgown and his palm slammed into my chest.

My cry to resist choked off as my heart seized. Agony erupted, racing along the fibers of my muscles, taking me to the breaking point. I flung my chin skyward, begging my throat to open. Air was stoppered in my mouth, unable to find its way inside of me, and the world around me narrowed, blurring into an enclosing tomb.

His prayers grew anxious, rushed. Latin filled the room in repeating phrases. Faster still, more intense, melding words into syllables into meaningless sounds.

Until, at last… Relief rolled through me like curling waves on a tropical shore. First in my chest, where the captain's hand was easing the pressure used to hold me. The fire faded, and a different sensation—like spring's radiance—blossomed on my skin. The comforting warmth unfurled, releasing the strain within my muscles. My heart relaxed into a regular rhythm. Fear released my throat, and air flowed inward, soothing the throbbing in my body from the assault. Finally, the pressure in my forehead fled, and I welcomed the freedom my vacant mind offered.

Depleted, my limbs melted while the rest of me floated, drifting toward sleep. The captain was so gentle—as if he were gathering up a precious doll, fragile as spun sugar—slipping his arms around me, lifting me from the floor to unfold my body onto the bed's surface. He drew my hair from behind my neck and shoulders so it didn't catch as he eased my head onto the pillow. Blankets were swathed around my shoulders as a humble shield against any opposing draft. Fingers lightly swept hair from my forehead. A strand from my temple lay between them. He turned it over, brows drawn, while he studied it.

Once finished, he tucked my hair behind my ear with care.

A tingling sensation, like fireflies filling the evening with their summer's jubilee, rose from the path he traced across my forehead, along my temple, to my cheek. There was something familiar about his touch, the way my skin seemed to dance in response.

"Rest," he encouraged me. He backed away, until he was leaning against the wall, then sank to the floor, appearing exhausted himself. "Rest."

His eyes were so blue. Like cobalt. I wanted to lose myself in them.

Chapter Seven

Twittering greeted me. The little, blue bird was bounding toward me, over snowy-white lumps in my pillow. He dipped his head close to my nose, as if purposefully attempting to wake me. My hello was rewarded with another round of morning cheer. It surprised me not only to see him but to experience a wash of gratitude because my feathered companion had returned. The emptiness inside had vanished.

I chanced stroking his breast with my finger and smiled when he rubbed the side of his beak against it in an apparent act of affection.

He jumped into the air as I stretched my limbs. Every inch of me welcomed it, ready to shake off the previous days and be active. I sat upright, feeling the best I had since I'd…gotten sick.

O-kay.

The captain was seated at the table in the far corner. A thin book rested in his hand, one finger holding the pages apart. The bird fluttered to the table's surface and tucked into a generous allotment of crumbs heaped onto his designated saucer. Offering first a passing smile to the *tap, tap, crunch, crunch, crunch, twitter, tapping* in front of him, the man returned to his watch over me. He didn't speak, though. Perhaps waiting to see how I would react to his being there.

"Hi," I said, hesitant, as well.

"Good morn. Are you in health?" His words were spoken with care, as if hoping not to spook me. Given the way our last several encounters had gone, his hesitation was understandable. Unsure myself how I'd react, I paused before answering, in case some horrible memory disrupted the so-far tranquil scene and presented another reason to fear this man. Nothing came. Nothing new, anyway.

The bruising under his eyes had returned. Not nearly as dark as before, when I first—or at least as far as I could recall, first—saw him. I wondered if he'd slept.

"Better." Taking stock of myself, I was relieved to find it was true. The scabs from my left hand were gone, and the flesh lining my palm was almost perfect. My other hand was also dramatically improved and had lost its neon-pink glow. The remaining shade was noticeable, if you knew the skin had once been burned and was on the mend.

Awesome.

The nightgown I was wearing was ridiculous. Its wide, square front was cut so low, it must've considered it an imposition to have to cover my naked breasts.

The captain averted his eyes while I traced my fingers across the center of my chest. Though the wound's impact had battered me mercilessly, I hadn't ever looked at the area that'd caused me such unbearable pain. The skin over my heart was discolored, despite the injury having been done internally, to my soul. It was brutal looking; the exposed, pale skin making the whole thing obscener than it should've been. Deep yellows and greens from a fading bruise spread in a wide circle. Threaded throughout were pink lines, traveling in crooked pathways, like fissures in ice.

I clutched the blankets to my chin, feeling unnerved.

After clearing his throat, he asked, "Do you know me?"

There was a subtle tension in his shoulders, betraying the fact that he was holding his breath while I examined his bearded face and hickory-colored hair, its pleated length tied with a black ribbon. A dark gray suit jacket was left open to frame a matching vest, buttoned high to where the winding loop of a pristine white neckcloth circled his throat, before it plunged underneath the linen vest, its tail pressed tight against his body.

I sifted through the few memories I had available to me. "Captain Wythe?"

"Captain *Jonathan* Wythe," he clarified. It had a slight ring of familiarity once he'd said it, though I didn't know why or what was significant about his emphasized first name.

His watchfulness made it seem like he expected me to say something. "Yeah," I answered.

Our tentative truce was awkward. I wasn't sure what else I could add. "Do you know who *you* are?"

I tried to muddle through the fog in my head. "Miss Moore."

My answer received a nod, though I knew it wasn't satisfactory. It was obvious the name he'd been using was as foreign to me as a distant country.

"Miss *Savannah* Moore. Try to remember."

He waited.

A swirl of odd feelings, too vague for me to grab onto to understand, stirred with the name as he said it. I thought he could be correct, and yet, it didn't fit right. Almost too formal, like I was trying on a ballgown used every once in a while, kept for special occasions. Who I was remained hidden from me.

"Savvy Less…?" The expression had bubbled to the surface of my memory and trickled outward without any real recollection.

Wythe's features relaxed as he said, "Your friends call you that."

"But not you," I realized.

My comment dampened his smile. Frustration, or maybe anger, and something akin to regret replaced it. An attempt to respond set his lips in motion…to no avail. He dropped his chin, then pressed a bent finger to his mouth while he faced the window. I'd say I've experienced less-reassuring admissions, on a great number of occasions, perhaps, if it'd been possible to remember any.

My attention fell to where I was twisting the blanket around my fingers, hoping for inspiration of some meaningful comment. It didn't have to be monumental, just better than empty, nervous replies to my not-friend.

"Do you hunger?" he asked, remarks including even a subpar-but-close-to-adequate explanation about his connection to me alluding him too, I guess. "Breakfast will be served in a short while, though I could fetch you a stimulator."

Dare I ask?

"No doubt Miss Carroll would allow something to refresh you," he continued. "There is bread at the ready."

"Uh, no. Thanks."

"Shall I send her abovestairs, that she might assist you with dressing? If you wish to eat below. You are under no obligation."

"I don't think I'm allowed to leave," I whispered, referencing the doorway.

He followed my gaze, then looked back at me. "Has someone spoken this to you?"

Since the idea of a mystical threshold that selectively spat invisible fire was preposterous, I didn't voice my reasons. I was afraid of what he might think of me. Already, he was eyeing me with concern. What with everything that'd happened, and goodness knows whatever else I couldn't remember, Éabha's exasperated remark echoed in my head, and I wondered if she was right to question my sanity.

But Wythe didn't. Or at least, he was willing to humor me, because he crossed to the open door and laid a hand on the wood frame. His back was turned, so I couldn't read his face when his fist smacked against it, then fell. "We shall leave tomorrow. You look to be strong enough. It is best that our stay here come to an end. There will be no difficulty in that."

Did he actually believe me? That it *was* the doorway preventing me from leaving the room on my own. Except then, the between-the-lines of what he'd said caught up with me. "We?"

"You are under my protection. I am *sworn* to protect you. We travel together until I can safely deliver you to your home."

And pregnant pause.

Because as that revelation crept over me, it churned the bile in my stomach. A lot. Yeah, "home" sounded good. *If* I knew where it was, what was waiting for me. But more than that, I sure as hell didn't want to go anywhere with *him*, alleged vows of protection notwithstanding. The conviction that I'd die because of him was firmly rooted in my mind. I searched for something, anything else to tell me otherwise, but all I could remember were the times he'd hurt me.

"You tried to kill me," I murmured in the direction of his feet.

He didn't argue. Just simply sighed. "Tell me."

Well, that sent a cascade of possible reassuring responses plummeting to the basement.

Does he have to fill the entire *doorway?*

As the seconds slipped by—Wythe's patience appearing endless, though he did inhale as if readying to speak, but instead exhaled deeply and resettled into his neutral silence—I felt myself growing agitated. It soon had me shaking.

"You need not, ah..." His tone lost its initial confidence. "Shall I rebuild the fire?"

He didn't wait for a response but fiddled with the logs in the grate, all the while having gauged my reaction to his progress crossing the room, then at the hearth. An unnecessary task—it was just on this side of cool yet comfortable—still, I appreciated his efforts because it put enough distance between us so I could slip out of bed.

It could've been a dream.

A pair of dust motes lazed on an unseen current in the hallway.

He said I was feverish.

I took a step closer.

What if that was all it was? What if—?

The scorching stormfront roared to life and rushed across the threshold, flooding me with such intense fear, it drove me backward. The pressure backed off after I'd slammed into the bed. An upsurge of bile coated my throat.

"God's teeth," Wythe complained under his breath. I stared at him, wide-eyed, my heart pounding. His hands were fisted to the point where his knuckles were pale. "Let us… Come, let us speak. We must reach an understanding that we might leave this place."

What just happened? Did he know what'd happened?

"Sit with me." He offered a brown shawl from one of the chairs by holding it out in front of him.

Who was he?

"Please." He tossed it onto the mattress, close to where I was standing.

I studied it, while keeping a fraction of an eye on him, in case a memory of its ownership wanted to reveal itself to me. It was either wear that or risk exposing my feminine assets like an Amazonian warrior.

The weave was loose with age. A burble of female laughter echoed through my mind as I fingered the edge. Éabha? The softness against my skin was comforting as I wound it around my torso, as if my body remembered it even though my mind didn't. I clutched it closer.

While I'd been contemplating my severe lack of options for attire, Wythe whistled at my little roommate, who—after eyeing the bread while ignoring the man calling him—ruffled his feathers, sending a shower of tiny crumbs scattering across the table. He flitted into the air, landing on Wythe's bent finger. The captain whispered to his feathered friend, receiving a series of twittering in response, then he opened the window to set the bird loose. One dip, another swoop, and the bird was gone.

Bypassing the chair he'd previously been occupying, which he left pulled out for me, Wythe chose the opposite side of the table, farthest from the only open pathway to freedom. *If* the damn door wasn't such a bastard, that was. Death by supernatural conflagration or the leading man from my nightmares—which of my inescapable tormentors would get me first?

I cautiously accepted, fixated on his deliberate stillness as I lowered myself into the vacant seat. Neither of us moved our chairs closer.

"You cut my throat," I answered the question still lingering between us.

I expected a denial. He didn't give one, instead wanting me to tell him what I remembered. When I described the hazy vision that'd been haunting me, he noted, "I held the blade, which did you some small harm, though not so grave as to take your life."

"No…" Clearly, because we were both there discussing it. Didn't mean he didn't try.

What had happened? I couldn't remember. The scene was jumbled, the images out of order, changing and contradicting one another: his knife slashing my throat, his pistol firing into my body, his bloodied handkerchief smothering my face. I rubbed my aching forehead, lost for answers.

Wythe described how I broke away from him. Very painfully, he added. With his description of the event, I remembered the sensation of driving my fist into his groin and the fear when I slipped down the hill to land at his feet. The image of him pointing a pistol at me flooded my mind.

"You didn't shoot me either," I wondered aloud, pressing my fingers to where the lead ball had torn through my heart in my nightmares.

"Never." He sounded surprised, taking in where my hand had landed. With this realization, the image shifted until I saw him again in the forest, his arm lowering when he first realized I was a woman. Wythe's gaze followed the thoughts across my face as I worked out that I'd conflated the memory to a dream.

As I realized what'd happened—that the altered memory and the dream were tied to the tearing of my soul—I took stock of what I was feeling deep within me. The place was sore when I prodded it mentally, but I was no longer in agony. Somehow, he'd healed that part, patched over it or filled it with a substitute, almost like a wax that was still cooling—a temporary solution that would last, so long as it wasn't tested by proverbial flame. I was incomplete, nevertheless.

Reservations about how such a thing was possible, how he could have done it, irritated me. Someone had asked once—did I know what he was?

Wham. The doorway in my mind snapped shut, cutting off the memory before it could escape and the voice be fully heard. I collapsed forward onto the table; the sensation resonating through my skull as if I'd been physically struck and it'd rung my bell.

Across the void, Wythe's voice called for me. It caught with worry, repeating his demand to know whether I could hear him.

Rather than try to work through the questions playing tour guide in that barren place, I cast them aside, breathing through the pain. My connection with my surroundings grew stronger as I did.

A hand hovered above my shoulder blade, its presence noticeable by a vibration filling the air between us. I slid away, leaning as far back into my chair as I could. Reluctantly, he did the same, studying my face. The concern never dissipated from his eyes; his brows remained drawn together. "We shall say no more."

"Why didn't you kill me?"

"Let this be the end to it. We shall speak—"

"Why didn't you cut my throat?" I wanted to push the conversation forward. Things were falling into place, and I wasn't going to let it go until I could remember what'd passed between us.

He sighed and shook his head, grimacing. "I realized that you were not the enemy."

"How?"

Wythe's face reddened. The surface of the table became very interesting to him. I didn't think he was going to answer. When he did, it was barely audible. "It was the way you smelled."

"My smell?"

"Your hair was perfumed. It smelled of flowers. But your skin…"

"Oh?"

He cleared his throat. "The rest of you had a different fragrance. When I…when I held you in my arms. It was difficult to discern…"

"But?"

"You had recently bathed. Y-you didn't smell like—"

"My perfume saved me?" I laughed. There was a comfortable familiarity related to his awkwardness—how it flushed his cheeks, the embarrassment catching up his words, eating away at his confidence. I couldn't remember where or why it'd occurred, but the sounds of our enjoying one another's company whispered through me. Washing over me, with it, were feelings I once had for him: admiration, friendship, trust.

No, not trust. My trust in him had been misplaced. Why? How?

Wythe had startled when I laughed. His body relaxed, but I watched— as he witnessed in my changing expression—the reminder that something wasn't right between us. His voice was husky when he asked, "What else?"

At the unbidden memory being flung through the prison door at me, I gasped and shrank from the table. He jerked forward, hand outstretched, as if ready to grab me.

"Don't," I warned.

He blinked.

With the same deliberate movements he'd used while treating me like a frightened animal, Wythe pressed his palms onto the table and sat back. He suggested with a nod that I proceed.

The word lodged in my mind was too horrible to speak out loud.

Would the threshold really stop me if I tried to run past it?

"I… Did…?" Perhaps it was better not knowing for certain. There are things we aren't meant to remember. He'd said he was only an escort, not someone I had to live with. Besides, he'd deny it no matter what. Any man would.

But I didn't want him to get away with it if he had. "You were on top of me. You forced yourself on top of me."

"Madam!" His expression was of sheer horror. "Forgive me, Miss Moore. I do not know of what you speak."

I thought he'd stop there, but he didn't. And he denied nothing.

"Tell me what else you remember of…that incident," he asked.

Was he pale because he was being falsely accused, or because he'd been caught?

"You had a gun to my temple. You were pressing me into the dirt." The memory swirled around, refusing to solidify. It sickened me. But I stared him down, daring him to tell me I was wrong or that it was a convoluted dream.

Finally, recognition crossed his face. I raised my brows at him, anxious for him to fill me in and bring me the same relief that returned the color to his cheeks.

"Permit me to… I wish for you to have faith in what I tell you. Permit me a moment to consider." After pressing his bent finger to his lips, a habit of his, I recognized—if only I knew whether it was because he'd done it earlier or I'd seen it before—he said, "Do you recall? You told me once that the reason you trusted me was because I hadn't…raped you, although I had the opportunity to do so?" The *r* word had caught in his throat. He held his breath as he waited for my response.

"No," I snapped, exasperated. Except an image was hovering near the border of a darkened vista. At once, the answer changed. A conversation in the woods. Grubby-white soldiers lined up for revelry. No, not tents. A tent. *His* tent. The one we shared. "Yes…?"

"Think," he encouraged me. "When we were lying—when I was there with you in the woods. The gun, did it fire?"

The prison door was fighting me, making my mind ache. If I could've wrenched my fingers inside my own brain to free myself, I would have.

"Yeah." I realized it had.

"It wasn't pointed *at* you," he reminded me.

It couldn't have been. So, why was his gun by my head? Why did it fire?

"What else?" He urged me to finish putting the fragments back together.

"Your eyes."

"My eyes?"

"They—"

My damn cheeks flushed, I could feel it.

The hem of the quilt was drooping off the far side of the bed, the whole thing having trailed after me when I'd risen and shifted it at an angle.

Studying the exposed knots in the frame was a convenient diversion from those same features, which had widened in surprise.

"What of my—?"

"Never mind," I said.

A smile slipped across his lips and was gone. He turned serious when he asked, "Do you recall what came before?"

I tried, but the world blurred.

"Let us be done," he insisted. "It pains you. I can see—"

"Just tell me. I want to know."

Wythe sighed but supplied me with the answer, hesitantly at first, checking to ensure I was well enough to continue. I nodded along with the telling. Each piece brought the memory into greater focus until the scene played clearly once more.

"You didn't mention the part where I killed the boy with the bayonet."

"Of all the memories," he muttered. "I would have kept that far from you, for your own peace of mind." His saddened expression matched what I was feeling. "What else?"

What about the dream? The pain of being shot came from what was done to me, but Wythe wasn't the one to tear my soul apart. Otherwise, he wouldn't have healed me, right? And there was the rest. I didn't know where the sense of abandonment came from. Or the distrust. Was it just a conflation of my imagination, fear, and regrets?

No, there was something to it. The distrust—the betrayal—was older. I was certain of it.

"I can't remember anything else." I met his eyes, willing him to see more of the truth to the assertion than its missing parts.

It was hard to tell if he took me at my word or not, but he let it slide if he didn't. "You have made good progress. I feared that you would not remember anything. I should not have doubted you." He nodded at me with approval.

"I think the word used was 'stubborn'?"

His smile was bittersweet. "It was not I who called you such."

Someone else, then, who looked at me with the same admiration I saw just moments before. I couldn't conjure the person's face. "But you didn't argue, either." I returned his smile.

"I am certain that you cannot be remembering correctly."

It felt good to laugh with him, even if just a little, but then the niggly voice in the back of my mind reminded me to beware of his charm. He was still a traitor. I felt my face fall.

Something crossed his mind, as well, it seemed. He fidgeted with the cover of the book he'd left on the table. Welcoming the chance to change the subject, I commented, "You're reading Thomas Paine."

"It was you who recommended it."

I didn't remember and, perhaps it was because I was growing tired again, I couldn't make the memory come.

"Your father believed it to be 'one of the most influential writings of the free world,'" he said.

"You know my father?"

Wythe had told me he was escorting me home. Still, the news surprised me for some reason.

"I relay no more than what you have said of him."

My shoulders dropped, disappointed.

An image formed in my mind of an older man with shock-white hair, wild and unkempt on the sides. Full, white beard with random strands of sunshine woven through. A uniform of blue. A pamphlet in his hand: *Common Sense*. He was waving it around, enthusiasm seeping from his very pores, trying to entice me to feel the same excitement about this most influential writing. But no matter how I tried, I couldn't see his face. "He's a major. Or a general, I think." I said, desperate to understand the vision and the circumstances surrounding it.

Wythe perked up at the news. He flooded me with questions, which circled us deeper into the mire. A haze, thick as woodsmoke, clouded the memories. An answer would come, but the images accompanying it were distorted. Each time I relayed what I saw, I had to retract the description because it didn't sound right. "He was with the Continental line. No wait, the militia. There was a crowd, in common clothes, watching the battle. Not uniforms, but I can't see... They're wrong somehow. No, he *was* a general for the army. I remember he wanted a court martial. He..."

There was a bigger piece to the puzzle I was missing, if only I could unlock my mind to search for it.

Wythe was patient, yet—despite our many efforts to jog my memory—we were both left confused, and my headache became unbearable.

"Mayhaps that is enough for one day," he suggested when my head fell from where my hand was trying to hold it upright. Gentle fingertips floated along my temple, leaving a wake that bubbled against my skin, like love's first blush.

I jerked away, my eyes flying open to see Wythe leaning across the table.

"Forgive me. I was merely seeking to…" But he didn't finish and instead chastised himself, muttering, "You are not mine to touch."

His words struck an odd chord. There was meaning there I didn't understand, something deeper than a simple apology from a man wanting to touch a woman.

"Is it any good?" I asked, gesturing to the safer topic of the pamphlet again.

"Do you not remember? You had nearly finished reading it the other day." He lifted a woven ribbon from where it spilled over the edges to show me.

When I shook my head no, he opened the cover, preparing to read aloud from the beginning, but eyeing me while I rubbed my throbbing forehead, he suggested, "It might be for the best if you rested."

A hand was held out to assist me to standing. I froze, staring at the physical contact he was offering so soon after his declaration that I wasn't his. He clamped his hand shut and reluctantly lowered it.

Appearing lost—considering it was improper for him to even be in the room with me unchaperoned, let alone *watching* while I settled into bed—Wythe rocked back and forth before heading for the door.

"I thought you were going to read to me." I surprised both of us. Nightmares and everything else I couldn't remember aside, I didn't want to be left behind—a greater fear I couldn't explain. "Please?"

He checked the hallway, then smiled. "If you wish it."

Returning to his chair, he turned it around so he could face me and began. Though it was agreed—with his hearty thanks—that we would skip the author's introduction. *"Some writers have so confounded society with government, as to leave little or no distinction between them; whereas they are not only different, but have different origins…"*

It wasn't romantic, like reading poetry or a story.

It isn't supposed to be romantic, my mind corrected me.

Why, I wondered back.

Chapter Eight

Éabha was put out when Captain Wythe informed her that he wouldn't be joining a Master Cloet for dinner. "Did you not hear?" she complained. "The men from the Iron Works have come to celebrate the chain's completion."

Wythe assured her, "I shall speak with them, briefly, after dinner. It is that I do not wish Miss Moore to be left alone."

"Seeing as you have passed the whole of the morning in the lady's bedchamber, I dare say you have mended your ways with her." Éabha barged past his post in the open doorway and came to stand next to my blanketed perch midbed. His cheeks breezed through at least a dozen shades of pink on his way toward a fully-flushed red. "Have you minded him here with you, ma'm?" she asked.

"H-he's been fine." I traced the stitched swirl of grapevine on my blanket with my finger. "He was reading to—"

"I was referring to you saying the captain did try to kill you. Do you still think it true?"

"God's teeth, Miss Carroll," he grumbled.

"It is not as though you have any good sense to you." She nodded toward his waistline.

Noticing where she'd indicated, he sighed, then with the same obnoxious, slow pace reserved for frightened animals and crazy women like me, he released his grip on the hilt of a silver knife. It was strapped to his belt, kept hidden beneath his suit jacket.

"Son of a bitch," I gasped.

"There will be none of that," she scolded. "'Tis bad enough the likes of him blasphemes."

"He is my protector, right?"

"That he is. Or so it has been said since you both arrived." She planted a fist on her hip and stared at the man in question who, rather than respond, minded the toes of his boots. Such a riveting, enthralling, mesmerizing, highly polished black.

Her lips twisted into a playful smirk when she added, "I can tell you this. If Captain Wythe is setting aside what brings him here and foregoing the chance to dine with the men below, whilst they congratulate themselves on their cleverness and all, so as to stay here with you, then you can trust that he is dedicated to what is best for you. I have seen naught and no one, no matter how fair and pretty, who could make the great Captain Wythe do—”

"Mayhaps I *should* go belowstairs," he announced.

"You know as well as I that Captain Machin will be wanting to speak with you, especially." Éabha bobbed her head in mock seriousness.

"Indeed. I shall— I…" He cleared his throat.

"What say you to the blue gown, ma'm? You should partake in the celebration, as well."

"Uh." I pressed a hand to my stomach, which was already churning at the suggestion. I wasn't ready to face the ominous doorway and embarrass myself by engaging in another superlative impression of a banshee, not when there was a houseful of unwitting audience members below. Unwilling to respect, or else she was simply oblivious to, my desperate look to Wythe for an intervention, Éabha rambled on, saying, "It looks quite well with your lovely complexion, *becoming* one might—”

"Though she may seem greatly improved…"

Captain Wythe, hero to the cursed and deranged! Well, when you overlooked the deadly concealed cutlery.

"…I fear that were the lady to attend," he continued, "she would make herself ill by trying to be agreeable."

"You shall none of you tire her." Éabha patted my knee. "I will see to that."

"Miss Carroll—”

"I am feeling better." I jumped in, seeing as it was high time I did *something* on my own behalf. "But I think Captain Wythe is right. I don't think I can manage a dinner party." My eyes may've flitted to the Threshold from Hell.

"You would not wish to be left alone," Éabha remarked.

"I'll be fine."

Or shrieking and wailing like Death's herald from Irish folklore.

She touched her fingertips to my shoulder, her lip caught between her teeth with worry. Relaxing the rumpled blanket from my clutches and smoothing it over my lap seemed like a really good idea. Made me far more convincing that way, I'm sure.

After a subtle exchange of head nods between us, she masked her concerned expression with a forced smiled, her hands flying into the air while she proclaimed, "'Tis a great inconvenience having to serve the number of men below without needing the extra work you are asking."

"Truly, Miss Carroll, I appreciate all of your efforts on our account." Wythe's carefully measured flattery was said to her fluttering hands, then her shoulder, then her back, as she rushed out of the room, huffing in pretend exasperation. "You are always so reliable. I do hate to…"

But she was gone. The sound of her calculated exit soon swallowed by the growing din of male voices below us.

Leaving the awkward duo.

"Miss Moore, I, ah…I shall have to forego the pleasure of— Forgive me. I needs must…"

"Yeah, you should go. It's not like you need *me*." Escaping from the far side of the bed, I adjusted the brown shawl around my shoulders, hoping for the comfort it brought earlier.

Thomas Paine had been forgotten on the table. I fingered the pages, fanning them open to where the woven ribbon marked the supposed pause in my own reading. I'd hoped Wythe's reading the pamphlet aloud would bring back further memories, and though I recalled the words once recited, a big, fat blank from my Life Before came with them. Just a vague sense of having never given the subject much thought.

"There is important business, vital business, that needs attending," he said, as if trying to explain.

I allowed the pages to cascade closed, a paper waterfall from my hands. "Well, I'm not going to insist you ignore vital business just because I'm lonely." A cool rush from the tip of my forehead raced toward a hollow pit in my stomach, the embarrassment leaving me clasping my shawl tighter. "Uh, I mean…"

He'd made it clear earlier we weren't friends. Yet the twist in my gut and the parting of his lips in surprise suggested an ill-advised attraction had sparked, at least once upon a time. Double my confusion when our uncomfortable interlude included a hopeful lift of his brows. "Are you…? That is, have you remembered something of significance?"

"Didn't Éabha, sort of, mention an impropriety situation happening?"

"Aye." His face shut down; his feelings unreadable within an instant, locked behind a hard exterior. He bolted toward the door.

Or was I floating further adrift in the wreckage of my memories, off course from where I belonged?

"Don't. I'm sorry. I—"

A hand gripped the wooden frame. His torso rocked out of sight, then pitched backward, into the room again, as if that small part of him was preventing him from leaving. "You speak the truth, even if you do not recall its meaning."

"Okay, is that like a riddle or something?"

"It does not matter if… It is not my place to interfere if you should have…"

"Been lonely?"

He sighed. "Aye."

"I don't understand."

"I will make a final inspection of the general's chain before we depart. I ask that you remain here and rest. We shall leave together once I have returned. Does that suit?"

Objection, nonresponsive.

The random odd thoughts with their bonus baby migraines promised to get old real fast. I pinched the area around my sinuses and asked, "Where are we going? Tomorrow, that is."

"To restore you to your family."

Doubt gnawed at me. His answer hadn't come out smoothly. Something wasn't sitting well with him either. Whatever it was, he didn't volunteer it.

"Where are they?"

Captain Wythe didn't reply, caught up as he was in avoiding my gaze and wrestling with his own thoughts. It was frustrating.

"You ask me to trust you," I complained, "but it's hard when I don't remember you, or why and how I know you, and it seems like you aren't telling me the whole truth."

His head shot upright. "*You* speak of trust?"

"What?" I shied from the sudden fury in his expression. "What have I—?"

"You—" He took a breath and held up his hands, palms forward, as if begging the world to slow down. With controlled focus on each word, he explained, "It is equally difficult that I must decide what is best for the both of us. Before, you were annoyed when I did not consult with you. Now, when I have come to realize that I should hear what it is you have to say— as it is you who knows best *who* your family are and where they may be found—you have been…stricken."

"Well, I'm not going to apologize for my situation."

He sighed and nodded. "Aye."

A merry-go-round of ups and downs, shaking my balance by unexpected twists and turns—that was the ride I was trapped on. It was almost too convenient. Missing memories. We could go around in circles, blaming one another for the distrust between us. If I was the source, well, now I could hide from myself, forget whatever harm I'd done to forge such a fierce reaction in this man.

The prolonged pause, while I worried over whether *I* could've been the cause of my own amnesia, enabled us both to calm down.

"What have you decided?" I asked, cautious of my tone.

He shrugged. "We travel to Moore's Folly, at West Point."

"Oh. You think my father and…the rest of my family are there?"

He hesitated, but to give him credit, he looked me in the eye to say, "The Moores are your husband's family, or they may well be. You did not wish to go there."

I'm married?

The revelation shocked me. Mostly, it flooded me with a profound sadness.

What the hell kind of person am I?

Somewhere—at this place, Moore's Folly, perhaps—was a husband waiting for me to return. Meanwhile, here I was, mooning over my enigmatic escort and his political booklet reading, despite the waves of fear he stirred in me. And now, I felt fairly certain this couldn't have been the first time I'd given into such feelings, or else Wythe's anger wouldn't run so deep. It was hard to look at him after that. "Why wouldn't I want to go there?"

"You said only that you would not visit them."

"Why?"

His head fell, guilt in his expression. "You did not say."

"But you think we should go there? Is it safe?"

He puzzled out the question aloud. "The land of Stephen Moore is readily in use by the army and has been since winter. Construction has begun on the fortifications. There should be no question of the family's loyalty to…" His gaze passed along the contours of my face.

"What?"

The knuckle of his forefinger pressed against his lips, then dropped, and his expression turned colder than when he'd accused me of being untrustworthy. "Once Miss Carroll informs me that you have taken breakfast, I shall come to fetch you."

"But that's tomorrow. What about—?"

"I bid you good day." His hand slammed onto the door latch, and he began to yank it closed.

"Wait, please!"

I rushed after him, but the infernal force of my mystical jailer bore down on me, hard and fast, and knocked the air out of me. Wythe was temporarily moved by the sight of me shaking, huddled on the ground, but some little, nagging voice of his own whispered in his head, made visible by the changing landscape of his features. He grew detached again to say, "For what it is worth, madam, I did travel to where *you* wished to go. It was not hospitable unless one was loyal." He eyed me with something between triumph and suspicion in his stare.

I waited for more, lost and troubled. Loyal to whom? Where did I want to go? And why was he suddenly treating me like this?

He slammed the door shut on all my questions.

Chapter Nine

Male voices carried through the floorboards for most of the day. They grew more raucous as the afternoon waned and the wine was depleted during various loud toasts to one man or another. Although I could hear Captain Wythe's deep voice amid the conversation, his laughter was rarely among the noise.

Éabha brought me dinner consisting of roasted ham with boiled carrots and a sizeable portion of hearty bread. At one point, she stole away for a few minutes to sit with me, thinking she'd gotten the men settled. The visit was short-lived because the roaring celebration escalated before long, and she was obligated to answer calls for another bottle. Meals pass a lot faster when there's no one to share them, so I had lots of free time to finger the indentation on my left hand where a ring once resided and wonder why the man who'd given it to me wasn't there. And where the band that belonged in that conspicuous place might be.

My cursed mind left the riddles unanswered and my head aching. Without Wythe there to prompt me with questions and feed me pieces of the memories, I couldn't free them myself.

Outside my solitary window, the sky had dulled to a light plum, plump with magenta-heavy clouds, by the time the men stumbled through the back door. Hearty handshakes and farewells resounded between them. Once they faced the trees, the dark, wooded expanse curtailed their merriment.

Wythe followed as far as the stone wall to see them out, turning aside with a uniformed man to speak with him, away from the others. Something about their prolonged handshaking as they parted disturbed me. Whatever their secret business, it seemed congenial. The men, though wearing serious expressions at various points, appeared to honestly like one another, so I couldn't understand why warnings of betrayal were screaming in my head, warnings that refused to be silenced throughout the long, dark hours of a restless night.

Unclear visions—foreign places with tall buildings and marble pillars, strange people in unusual and yet familiar clothing, a child playing with toy pirates on the floor—swamped my imagination. The muddy soup of memories and violent nightmares woke me, leaving me gasping from the horrid mixture of fear, confusion, and exhaustion it invoked. Heavy footfalls from across the hall rose and disappeared somewhere in the haze of my drifting off for good. Which meant morning arrived abruptly when Éabha shook me awake. I'd just fallen into a deep and empty sleep as the first hints of dawn's early light bled into the sky.

I donned the billowy, white shirt draped over the chair for me, but had issues with the brown pants. "Doesn't the butt-side open, not the front?" There was a wide panel, held shut by two buttons—one on each top corner, sewn just below the waistband—reminding me of children's pajamas from Old World-style Christmas cards.

"Nay, ma'm. Men do tie their breeches in the back," Éabha corrected me for a second time.

"And as a woman, I…"

For taking a leak in the woods.

"Victoria's Secret?" Another random expression blurted from my mouth to accompany another unfathomable thought.

"Those are the garments in which you did arrive." Her smile perked up on one side. "You ne'er did mention a Victoria. It being so late in the night, as it were, I dare say a secret or two might lie between—"

Wythe barged in while I was grimacing at the distasteful excuse for clothing. "Miss Moore, let us— God's teeth, Miss Carroll. Why do you not have the woman dressed as I have asked? She was meant to have been in readiness before I did return." He scowled at the dishes waiting, untouched, on the table. "Nor has she taken breakfast."

It wasn't until he rounded the corner of the bed, grabbing a cloak from its foot and storming toward me, as though preparing to entomb me within its folds, that he noticed I was wearing a shirt and just a shirt. A sort of squeak erupted from the throat of my once would-be hero, and yet, despite the increasing glow in his cheeks, his gaze remained fixed on my lower extremities.

"Unshaven knees your thing?" My sarcastic snipe earned me his version of *uh,* which if he didn't sound so lost, would've made the *aaaaaaah* sound like he was enjoying the view.

Éabha tested the subsequently silent waters by teasing, "Right fine knees they are, ma'm." Receiving a breathy chuckle from me—not that I should've encouraged her, it just happened—and Wythe being still captivated, she pondered aloud with more conviction, "'Cepting I would have reckoned Captain Wythe had more of a fondness for what lies—"

"Miss Carroll."

Well, that broke the spell. A line burrowed between Wythe's brows. He turned sideways so he could bark at her some more without viewing me straight on. "Have you located Mistress Moore's boots and other missing articles?"

The light-heartedness fled from her face. For the first time since I could remember—granted, it wasn't that far back—Éabha was submissive to him. She apologized, hands clasped in front of her and head bowed. "I swear, I have searched the whole of the house. They are not to be found."

"How do you propose Miss Moore is to leave? Is she to go barefoot?"

Mumble, mumble. "…thought to make a temporary amends, though for certain…" Mumble, mumble, mumble more. "…will not give up the search."

Her words had faded in and out, blocked by a screaming pain in my head, before she hurried to produce a pair of tall, worn, brown boots from under the table. Éabha turned the replacement footwear from side-to-side, examining them for their fitness, and it subsided.

Everything of yours no longer exists, a tiny voice reminded me.

"See to it that they will do," Wythe ordered her, while I was absorbed in the latest oddity of my carousel life. "Let us hope Miss Moore finds herself amongst her kin before the day is done."

"Are these the clothes of a dead man?" I demanded.

"Madam." That damn fisted hand smacked against his thigh. "I have not the time nor patience to debate, yet again, every disagreement that has been had between us."

He slammed the cloak onto the bed and was almost out the door when I threw the pants at his back. "Hey! Why are you being such an ass to me?"

"How dare you?" He snatched the pants from where they'd landed and lobbed them back at me.

"No, how dare you?" I dumped them onto a chair. "It's not my fault I don't remember who I am or anything from before…being sick. If I've done something wrong, how about you try adulting and talk to me about it, huh? Because I haven't a clue what I could've said or done to deserve you being so rude to me."

He bowed his head, straining to temper the anger in his voice. "When you are returned to your family, you may be free of them."

"Captain Wythe." Éabha shook her head at him.

"You're so…" I gave up. Finishing would just fall on deaf, angry ears. Not that my realization prevented Wythe from demanding to know what I thought of him. I faced him as best I could to say, "Confusing."

Body tense, hands clenched, he'd been teed up for a fight, I could tell. It all fell away, and his lips parted while my sad confession hung between us unanswered. The rest just spilled out of me. "I know you said we aren't friends, but I thought…I thought…"

"Tell me." His voice had lost its edge, and he met my eyes—very definitely and only my eyes—as if ready to hear me rather than look for ammunition for his next shot.

"It seemed like you cared, at least a little, about what happened to me. Now, without warning, you just— I don't know, it's like you hate me, and I…"

I gathered the pants and whirled around so he wouldn't see how close I was to tears. Éabha—kind, sweet, fiery Éabha—was by my side in a heartbeat, squeezing my shoulder. Her sympathy lay with me, and she let Wythe know it with a glare.

"Did someone pull these off a dead man?" I obediently stabbed my feet into the pant legs, muttering, "Just lie to me if you have to. Please."

My morning was a mere half hour old, if that. Already, it was exhausting. I dropped onto the far edge of the bed to tug on the knit socks Éabha offered me. I hated how I allowed him to make me feel…what? Hurt? I didn't even know him. Why did it matter so much?

"I am not lying to you when I say that these are not spoils from the battlefield," Wythe assured me.

The wall was the recipient of my quiet "thank you." Needing to bend over to retrieve the boots, I took the opportunity to swipe my palm across my dampened cheek while the bed blocked our view of one another.

Their leather was soft from use. They slid almost to my knees with ease and—I was amazed to discover—embraced my feet and calves as if they were crafted for me. I wasn't certain they would fit, at first, judging by their cavernous opening. The way my feet tingled while drawing them into place made my head irritable, wondering about it.

"Would you please pass me the cloak?" I held out an arm to receive it.

"You have not eaten," he observed.

"Let's just get this over with."

Swift as an eagle capturing fish, Éabha swooped in and stole the cloak from under Wythe's hand. "You must take breakfast," she insisted, her focus intent on him while she spoke, presumably, to me.

"We shall be several hours before we reach West Point." He nodded, murmuring, "If we arrive there at all this day. Miss Moore, I know not what lies ahead. My scout has not returned with a report as of yet. It may be that we will be delayed if danger lies between us and our purpose."

Looking at him felt like watching a ship being swallowed by the sea, the future of so many souls slipping away while I was caught on shore, left to mourn. What I'd learned of him from the brief history of my recollection was that he was the albatross on such seas; his moods tossed about on the wind, turning and changing with the storm.

But now the anger was gone, and his voice carried the same genuine concern his speech conveyed. "Miss Carrol, please prepare a plate for the lady. I shall return soon to escort her from the room."

"You have not taken breakfast either, sir," she chastised. "The journey shall be no less long for you."

"I needs must watch for the scout."

"I shall see to it that any scout who does come will be shown to the parlor. You will know of it straight away." Coffee was poured for me, tea from a pot hidden under a quilted oven mitt of sorts for him. "Always reliable, is that not what you did say the day before?"

"He would never approach the house so boldly as to announce himself at the door," Wythe muttered.

"Mind, you have been right hoggish with the lady. What do you aim to *adult* about it?" Éabha shoved a serving spoon into his hand—which given how thick the pewter was, I wondered if the act would bruise his palm—and charged past the door, out of sight. An injured so-called protector, what fantastic luggage for a journey into the wilds of…beyond the bedroom.

He jostled the spoon several times on his open palm, staring at it. Left with the choice of serving breakfast or risking a dragged-out departure by refusing and chasing after her, Wythe shook his head and slopped something akin to a chunky oatmeal from a small, black pot into a bowl. I searched the overcast sky outside the window, hoping—maybe—the little, blue bird would be playing in the lilac bushes, wanting to be let in.

"Please, Miss Moore."

The bowl was slid into the spot closest to me, and the serving spoon balanced over the lip of the pot. Removing the cloak from the chair, he nodded at the now-vacant seat, choosing to deposit the garment on the bed and take up residence leaning against the mantel. Had the fire not already been rip-roaring away from Éabha's morning routine of freshening it, I suspected from the way he was staring at it that he would've constructed a pyre reaching halfway up the chimney, just to avoid sitting down for breakfast with me.

"She makes force-feeding people seem like an artform." He didn't answer my quiet joke, so I added, "Or an act of war."

"Indeed, she does." He breathed a laugh. After a thoughtful pause, he said, "When first I was brought here, I thought I had known the meaning of hunger." He glanced over his shoulder to smile ruefully and say, "We have become regular companions, Want and I." I nodded, acknowledging the hardship he was alluding to. "I devoured what was given me in so quick a manner, I near let loose my stomach. Miss Caroll…" He chuckled at the memory. "She scolded me with her wit and her laughter, as you have seen done. I made efforts to take little at the remaining meals. The other women pressed and fussed at the economy, yet I dared not shame myself or my hosts by accepting more at the table."

Pushing away from the fireplace, he came to stand opposite me, clasping the chair's back. "In the morn—every morn thereafter—she brought a large tray filled with consumables rather than a simple stimulator. True to her art, to use your words, she won my obedience. She claimed all would go to waste if I did not partake, for she would not serve my refuse to others."

"Smart woman." I chuckled. "I'll have to remember that one."

"You are clever enough without needing her mischief to guide you." He reached for a large roll, splitting it in half. A flair of nerves stiffened my spine when he came to stand over me. I apologized, sorry to see him tense, as well, at my reaction.

Taking a seat across from me, he eyed the portion he'd offered as I set it on a small dish. "Do you not eat because you are unwell?"

"It isn't that. I seemed to recall you liked saying Grace before eating."

"Grace?"

"Oh." The roll crumbled between my nervous fingers as I played with its edges. I searched the sky again outside the window, thinking how the bird would've been happy with the increasingly generous pile. "I thought I remembered you praying before meals."

"Ah. You remember correctly." He laid both hands in the center of the table, palms upward. Tipping his chin in their direction, he invited me to place mine onto his, then closed his eyes and waited.

Strange. My spirit grew lighter, felt freer; an unknown iron cloak burdening my shoulders had lifted. By this simple request to join him in thanksgiving, it was as if my fear couldn't touch us, and in the final fraction between separation and oneness, a vague sensation of similar acts trickled over me. A reminder of another time.

The crackle of the fire and random stirrings from the farm animals outside enriched our homely scene, even while he circled the curve of my knuckle, then drew my fingers inward and pressed them against his palm. A sense of peace settled over us, and our bodies relaxed toward each other.

Once the whispered blessing ended, he hesitated, allowing a thumb to drift over the back of my hand. Like sunlight kissing the water, the warmth of his touch washed over me, rippling across my skin. I opened my eyes to find him watching me. A brief smile met mine, then he released me and dropped his head in thought.

I waited to follow his lead again, not sure if there was something else we needed to do before eating. Rubbing a thumbnail along the rim of a second bowl, he told its empty depths, "You once confided that you were uncertain regarding what course of action you wished to take."

Images of trees sprang to mind. A prior encounter, bittersweet. "I do remember. A little." I nodded for him to go on.

But he didn't continue, transitioning his lonely study from the pewter dishware to his spoon instead. Whatever was to be learned there didn't appear to give him the answers he sought, and he kept the rest of his thoughts to himself.

I startled when he broke the long silence, saying, "Please accept my apology. You deserve to be treated with more respect than I have shown you."

"True. Very true," I agreed.

His focus jumped from the table setting to my face.

"Of course, if you *mean* it," I teased, "you could show me you're sorry by eating breakfast too. Éabha's a great cook and all. Certainly better than the last cook." I smirked and was relieved to see his consternation ease. "But I can't eat two bowls of this stuff myself, and if she finds your bowl unused, it'll be like daring her to triple-load your dish with…with…" I couldn't bring myself to finish the joke. "What's a 'stimulator'?"

"Drink. Or victuals, if one is fortunate. To stimulate the body when one arises. Bread, milk mayhaps, or alcohol."

"Oh." How crude would it have been if I licked my bowl? At least if I had, I could've buried my face within its confines and hidden the burning embarrassment I felt rising in my cheeks.

"Miss Moore? What ails you?" he asked, though the upturned corner of his mouth meant he wasn't worried, just curious.

"It sounded perverse, that's all."

"Indeed?" His eyebrows flew upward. Clearing his throat, he then chuckled. "At times, I wonder if you do say such things simply to cause me grief. Our speech is so dissimilar; I never do know if you are in earnest."

"Why is that?"

"Because, well, you have said you are not from the American states."
"Where am I—?"
"I know not."
Since the wisdom of avoiding Éabha's wrath via fountains of liquor and other bar fare was still mingling in the air, along with the aroma of cooling porridge, I was relieved when he sighed and filled the second bowl.
"But Moore's Folly…?" I asked.
"It is that I needs must go there for my own purposes. Those other than seeking word of your kin." He didn't elaborate further.
Secrets and anticipation of a day-long, possibly plus-some road trip to my mystery husband's undesirable family home, maybe—breakfast side dishes I wouldn't throw out to even the pigs.

Chapter Ten

Captain Wythe placed a hand on mine to still the nervous swirling of coffee in my cup. The tiny black stream that'd been orbiting the channel where the inner wall and bottom met continued on its path, pressed forward by the momentum. Setting the mug down, I watched the remaining liquid thin, almost out of existence, as it flowed across the level surface.

Wythe stood and informed me that he needed to speak with Miss Carroll. After final preparations were made for our departure, he would return to escort me from the house.

There he paused, waiting for a response. His hand separated his suit jacket, a dull earthy-brown this morning, and landed on the hilt of his hidden knife. Although a subconscious act, I was sure—a grounding spot for his own restless energy—it nonetheless stirred the contents of my stomach. I swallowed and followed the line of threaded buttons on his vest to meet his gaze. "Sounds like a plan."

A subtle twitch of his lips hinted at a near smile, but his face tensed as he became visibly anxious. The grip on his blade tightened, his fingers having slipped from the top of the hilt to grasp it fully. I felt myself lean away and cringed inside at the resulting scrape of my mug across the table's surface. All the lovely, ambient farm-life sounds grew harsher, grating even, in those few moments while we held our breath, not moving.

"Scores of sense, indeed," he mumbled under his breath. "Please excuse me. I, ah…" He relaxed his hand and withdrew it from his waistline, allowing the weight of the wool to close like a curtain over the silver weapon. "If you would prepare yourself. I shall be brief."

I pressed my hands onto the table, willing myself to look at him. "Sure."

He nodded, then left. The sound of his boots passing over plank boards continued, changing in pattern as they sounded down a flight of stairs, shifted direction, and moved below me toward the back of the house. A door banged shut.

Wondering at the world beyond my bedroom window, I stood to watch his progress and could make out a black-and-white horse being escorted from an outbuilding by a farmhand. Éabha, who soon followed him from the house, joined the men and handed my moody protector a bundle, which he tucked into a rear saddlebag. She laid a hand on his forearm and spoke to him for a while. Whatever she said was absorbed while he fiddled with the straps rather than face her. From across the distance, it was hard to tell, but he seemed to nod along.

Once she'd finished, Wythe took her hand and gave it a pat with the other. They parted, Éabha collecting the reins to lead the horse toward the front of the house, while he crossed the backyard. A glance at my window as he approached meant gather what-passes-as-courage as ye may. Time for a face-off.

It's like a damn joke.

The threshold didn't appear ominous or dangerous. The door itself was painted this cheerful clown red; loud, almost boisterous, as the color glowed in the sunlight, silkily flowing from the door to the wood of the crown molding surrounding me. It lazed open, and the tune of everyday, normal household life passed through its archway unimpeded. They were welcoming sounds, including the clang of a cooking utensil whipping up another meal in a metal pot and people moving through the unseen rooms below.

But I wasn't welcome.

I didn't know which was worse—the claustrophobic feeling or the nauseating, fearful chill from needing to face that mysterious force. After that, the strange, unknown Beyond. What a privilege it would've been to have met Wythe in the backyard, on my own, rather than waiting like a child for her daddy to escort her from school.

I gathered the cloak in my arms, fingering the extra drape blanketing the shoulder region. Thick wool, dyed a chocolate brown. I whipped it around me, feeling a myriad of sensations echo through me—joy, relief, terror, frustration.

Heavy boots hurried up the stairs. I clasped the cloak shut and waited by the fireplace for Wythe's command. Such a good, passive little ward, wasn't I?

Just enjoy the heat. It may be a while before you get warm again.

The sounds of his footfalls paused at the doorway. I watched the lick of flames over the logs rather than turn. I wasn't sure I was ready.

A draft, cool and moist, as if it'd rained overnight, breezed off his winter coat as he joined me by the fire and took a moment to study it, as well. Already a mild smell of horse accompanied him.

Light at first—like a butterfly tapping against a blossom, then rising, to flutter down onto its surface again—a single finger hovered near me. Or perhaps, it was only the delicate heat from his skin gracing mine, a promise of his touch to come. It glided around my pinkie. I dropped my gaze to discover his hand wrapping around mine.

Wythe cleared his throat. "Come, Miss Moore."

Even with his attention rooted to my face, and his grasp pulling me toward the doorway, pressure—fierce and fiery—bore down on me, driving me backward in fear, separating us. It crossed my mind again that maybe I was on the wrong side of being right in the head.

Wythe reclaimed my hands from where they were death-gripping my arms and brushed his thumbs along their backs. The richness of his voice calmed my trembling, as he warmed a path down my cheek with his fingertips, assuring me, "You have nothing to fear." He lifted my chin to guide my eyes to his. "Focus on your intent, what it is you want."

I gazed into the endless blue striations crowned with gray and was embarrassed to realize I didn't want to go. All I wanted was to stay with Captain Wythe, safe—like I felt in that moment—with him holding me, guarding me from my own fear, and warming me with his compassion.

Somewhere, you have a husband who deserves your faithfulness, I chastised myself.

My heart disagreed.

I forced myself to focus on the idea that one day I'd see this husband again and hopefully remember him. Besides, Wythe had just taken his frustration and anxiety out on me, and somewhere inside him was harbored an anger or resentment. I had only the barest suspicion, with no real supporting evidence, of what the source could be or why. The thought festered, colluding with the memories of violence associated with our history together, from the Before Times of this unnatural house. Apprehension involving the captain gripped my chest and squeezed tighter.

Wythe allowed me to slide backward, out of his arms.

"I know what ails you." He sighed. "I must not speak of it, or it may mean you harm." Silent, he stared, grim-faced.

"Effing shit and a half," I griped. "You're the King of Reassurances, you know that, oh captain, my captain?"

"Hmm. I understand if my words do not calm you." He nodded. "Will you hear and answer what I shall ask of you, without questioning the meaning of it? I swear to you, it is with your best interest in mind."

"Yeah, right. Fine. Ask me, and let's find out," I grumbled.

"Very well. Look at me."

Indulging in a little rebellion, I stared at the auburn patch sprouting beneath his lips rather than obeying, and waited for him to lay the next bombshell on me, which he phrased by asking, "Mayhaps, as you claim me as your captain, we might speak using less profanity?"

"You—" I chuckled, despite myself. "Touché."

He hummed with quiet laughter. "You *can* leave this place," he said, calling my focus back to our purpose. "We shall do this together."

"Together? Even though we apparently keep secrets from each other?"

My uncertainty fizzled the momentary connection he'd worked so hard to build, returning us to our empty beginning. I almost apologized. I hated the tumultuous course we were stuck on. It's not like I had a choice other than to trust him.

Still, he tipped his head sideways to meet my eyes. "Will you promise, once you have departed this house, to never return unless invited?"

I groaned.

Focus on his words, not why.

I repeated the mantra, fighting the twinge of pain from the curse clawing back my straying thoughts.

It bore the severity of a sacred oath, what he was asking me to declare. Without compromise and wholly unbreakable. Every sliver of wood in the house, every particle of its being, waited for my answer. I could sense it— almost like a presence, a watchfulness from across an unknown distance— listening in, demanding my surrender. It was closing in from all sides, drawing sweat from my skin as it made me feverish. It became unbearable to the point where I was forced to agree, for my own preservation. So, I nodded. Realizing that wasn't enough, I swallowed hard and announced, "I promise."

As if it was yanked out of me, the oppression was sucked away—and the fear with it—by a gust of wind, sounding as if it rattled wood, glass, pewter, and flame, though they all held perfectly still and appeared untouched.

And then, it was gone. We were an ordinary man and woman, standing by a cozy fireplace, in a charming rustic farmhouse, nestled within a beatific woodland setting.

I stared at my surroundings, circling to search for a sign of disturbance from what'd just happened, beyond what I'd experienced in my own mind and body. Even an insignificant shadow of proof would've sufficed.

Wythe didn't address it, though he must've felt it too. It seemed as if he knew it was there and understood it all along. Had an outsider observed the way he was gaging my wild trembling with his neutral expression, I imagine they would've dismissed me as a regular neurotic in her natural state-of-being. Instead, he repeated his invitation to go with him.

"I-I…"

"You are free to leave." He offered a bent arm toward me, a model of gentlemanly patience and completely inattentive to the bizarre happenings.

"We, uh…should we put out the fire?" I asked, stalling.

"Miss Carroll will see to it."

Freedom being my sole luxury option on Fortune's wheel, I stepped closer to him. Pausing to exhale, in the hopes that some of the tension in my lungs might be expelled with the forced breath, I then slipped my hand through the crook of his elbow.

Closing my eyes, I noted the passage of heat from the fireplace along my side as we walked, the changing glow from bright to dim to bright again behind my eyelids. Cool air kissed my face as we progressed. My arm was released from his while he wrapped a hand around my waist to alight it on my back, the fingers of his other hand entwining in mine, drawing me forward.

Wythe came to a halt. His breath was warm against my cheeks as I felt him lean in. "Come, see."

I did as he asked and was immediately caught in his stare. Had a waltz struck up by an invisible stringed quartet, we would've been prepared to rise and fall upon the first beats, wrapped in each other's arms as we were. I turned away, hoping the flutter in my chest would calm before it irritated the fissure in my soul much more.

Colonial-white walls stretched at length down a hallway large enough to accommodate us side-by-side, so long as I remained pressed against him. Wide plank floors carved from blonde oak shone where sunlight filtered through open doorways, inviting us toward a stairway at the other end. We'd passed over the threshold without resistance, as if nothing had ever been there.

Disentangling myself from his hold, I followed the floorboards' path to the far end. Below, after the tumble of worn steps, past the painted floor cloth and the heavy wooden door staring me down, my fate awaited me. I laid a tentative hand on the banister, wondering where my courage had gone. He gestured the way, offering me a reassuring smile, and trailed close behind as I descended the narrow stairs.

"Ah, Miss Moore!" A large man exited from a dark-paneled parlor on the ground floor. "It relieves me terribly to see you looking recovered. You gave us quite the scare, my dear." His long, satin robe swayed over a white shirt, similar to my own, and deep-blue short pants. Crisp, white stockings stretched to his polished black shoes adorned with silver buckles.

Wythe nodded, encouraging me to accept the outstretched hand of the stranger who also wore the aura of vague familiarity. I laid mine on its deeply calloused surface, which he blessed with a dramatic kiss.

Like a slumbering princess in a fairytale, my memories of the man awoke—his jovial laughter, the slosh of wine in his goblet as he regaled us with a story, his pleasure as he inhaled the lingering aroma of a hot chocolate pot. They burst through the prison door, rushing toward the forefront of my mind at the touch of his lips. Though not everything. Figures shifted in darkness, conversations garbled where censored, and moments with Wythe passed behind a hazy veil. And there were many gaps. But Mr. Cloet, I remembered. Fondly.

The rush woke the dragon inside. Fire rose from the chasm, swelling and climbing into a towering tsunami. It crashed over me, chasing after the memories not fully revealed by the prison door's release, swirling around them, twisting and melting them into a blur, then driving the pieces back into hiding. The door slammed shut, knocking my world sideways.

A sudden force impacting my body turned out to be a multitude of hands seizing my arms, clapping onto my back, cradling the side of my head, and scooping my knees out from under me. Both men had caught me before I reached the floor, and they fussed while Wythe carried me into the parlor.

"Jonathan, you cannot mean to journey with the lady in such a state," Mr. Cloet chastised, while he snatched stacks of papers from a chair so I could be settled onto its silken cushion. "Stay a while longer. You have not your orders."

"I fear, Johannes, that we must depart." Wythe pressed a hand to my cheek, still grasping my shoulder, even though my equilibrium was falling back in place and I was finding it easier to sit on my own. So long as I didn't stare at Mr. Cloet or try to flesh out more memories of how I knew him or the circumstances surrounding our stay in his home, that was.

"I understand, when we are called, we must to our duty fall in," Mr. Cloet countered. "But surely Miss Moore should remain behind. I swear to you, she would be well looked after. You can be reunited once she has been restored to health." He sent a knowing look over Wythe's shoulder to me, seeking to press on me some message whose context, and therefore meaning, was still suppressed.

All the emotions swirling around inside me about the captain made everything unclear. A brief flash of relief had enlivened me. I was invited to stay, to delay the inevitable, or attempt to avoid it altogether.

Pain stabbed from behind my eyes, slicing through my forehead, which was how I realized the right person hadn't made the necessary invitation. Who, then, was it? And where were they?

Wythe's furrowed brow suggested he was struggling with the offer, as well.

In the end, fear of being abandoned—not to mention of continued torture by just the sight of our host—won. "Thank you, Mr. Cloet, so much," I said, "for all your kindness and your patience and everything you've done for me. I'll be fine. I just need to stay with Captain Wythe."

"Captain Wythe, is it?" Mr. Cloet grimaced.

The subject of our conversation didn't answer, though he stifled his shocked expression within a delayed blink, perhaps at my remembering his friend without further prompting.

"Ah now. What a great, sorrowful thing it is that you should leave us." Mr. Cloet leaned close to whisper into my ear, "There is little I may say to you in your present condition. Know that I deeply regret what was done. Should ever you need counsel, I will be waiting."

I stared, rattled, as he backed away and shoved a hand to his other guest's palm, offering wishes for a safe journey and a reminder not to remain a stranger for long. It forced Wythe to return his broad smile rather than continue to eye me with confusion.

Mr. Cloet assisted me to standing and patted my hand, saying, "You may trust in Captain Wythe, Miss Moore. He has the best of intensions for you," before he released me to my so-called protector's care.

Wythe nodded at him, giving sincere thanks. Looking me over with a rising flush in his cheeks, and once satisfied by my insistence that I'd make it without faceplanting somewhere—I didn't put it exactly that way when I said it, though—he escorted me to the front door.

A kitchen garden in early bloom stretched before us, rows upon rows of herbs, lush greens, and plump flower buds, sweet-smelling amid the aroma of damp earth. The expanse of lavender billowing in the wind made me oddly leery.

Éabha and a speckled horse were waiting for us beyond their realm, outside the stone wall surrounding the property. Mr. Cloet followed as far as its vine-laden arbor to say his final farewells.

Wythe greeted the animal, stroking his neck several times, then held out a stirrup to receive me.

"Wait a minute."

I bypassed him to address the source of swelling in my throat and wrapped my arms around Éabha's shoulders. The perfume of wood smoke and the beginnings of a delicious dinner I wouldn't be there to enjoy lingered in her hair and on the linen of her clothes. All the peace and comfort I could recall—sensations separate from the haunting tide of doubt, fear, and trepidation exuding from the man hovering behind me—were enshrined within the woman I was clinging onto, a woman I might never see again. I was losing my best and only friend.

"Thank you for everything," I said, hearing the catch in my own voice.

She'd startled when I grabbed onto her, but released the reins so she could return my embrace. "Mind you care for him good and proper, ma'm." She squeezed my upper arms, and her mischievous smile filled her face. "For he shall ne'er know the end of it, if he does not do the same for you."

I breathed an uncomfortable laugh, saying I would.

The massive horse shook his coat. Not confident I would come out of this situation with my dignity intact, I drew a fortifying breath and stretched my foot the zillion feet necessary to reach the stirrup. It took a few bounces to build the momentum necessary to mount.

Just as I realized something was amiss, Wythe swung himself up to sit behind me. Rather than address how I stiffened as he collected the reins, his body engulfing all of me, he cleared his throat. The damn saddle was too small. Was it too much to ask for a two-seater? I tried to scooch higher on its incline to put some room between us, but the horrible design had me slip-sliding into the awkward territory of Wythe's lap.

"Erf. Peace, Miss Moore." He shifted his weight from underneath me.

"I didn't realize we'd be sharing the same horse."

"It is how we arrived."

Was it too late to opt for a carriage? I'd build one, if it came to it.

He tilted his head to peer around my loose hair, toward my bowed face. "What troubles you?"

"Well, it's just… I didn't think it was proper for a man and a woman to share the same horse."

He startled me so badly when he broke into laughter, I jumped. The horse whickered a complaint in response to the rowdiness happening above. Wrapping an arm around my waist to steady me, Wythe leaned forward as best he could to pat the horse's neck and begged the animal's pardon. It meant consuming me whole, torso to broken pride.

His voice was full of good humor as he said, "No matter what may happen, Miss Moore, know that I could never hate you, as you accused."

"Captain Wythe, if you were any more complimentary, I might die of embarrassment."

To my surprise, his continued laughter was a heart-warming sound.

Chapter Eleven

Captain Wythe chose a leisurely pace along the dirt roadway, toward the dense woods staring us down, as if in no particular hurry to get anywhere, despite our having a destination several hours away. Just as the trees opened, I checked the clearing we were leaving, wanting one last look.

"What the—?"

It was difficult to twist in the saddle enough to see up and over his shoulder, so I tried the other way, hoping for a better view. The horse grunted as I ducked low, catching a glimpse from around his side.

The captain tugged on my waist to bring me upright. "What is it?"

The forest swallowed the fields behind us; towering evergreens closed in on one another, billowing grasses sprang upward to fill in the gaps, and the sunlight faded as we moved into the shadows of the trees, so it was hard to discern shapes across the distance. I stuttered unintelligibly, lost for an explanation.

"Need I a weapon?" He kept his voice hushed, while remaining erect in his seat.

Doubts of my sanity resurfaced. "I must've been mistaken."

I wasn't.

Body taut, he nevertheless played it cool, and searched the area for danger, moving the minimal amount necessary. His grasp on my waist loosened, and he circled his arm around mine to take my hand. Just as casually, he transferred the leather reins to me, freeing his grip. It hovered above his thigh, fingers wide. I recognized the posture—still, like a falcon studying its prey, ready to fly at a moment's notice. I'd witnessed him doing it before. I must have.

His other hand had reached the knife strapped to the outside of his coat, just behind the small of my back.

"There's nothing there," I muttered.

Casting a glance at me first, he turned to check for himself. The domestic setting we'd left had already faded, and the next act—garish with an excess of woodland scenery—had begun. Whiskers from his beard brushed several strands of my hair aside as he pressed his lips to my ear. "Tell me what troubles you, no matter how uncertain you are."

"I… It sounds crazy. I'm probably just crazy."

"I should like to hear what you have to say, all the same."

Like before, when I'd questioned what I felt, what I'd experienced with the cursed doorway, Wythe didn't seem to harbor any such concerns. His voice was gentle, his demeanor calm and rational, as if what we were discussing was as commonplace as there being air to breathe and water to drink. One glimpse of his expression told me he was serious.

"The house…"

The harder I fought it, the more I trembled.

This can't be real. So stupid. I'm being stupid.

His palm came to rest on his thigh. "What of it?"

Patient as a coach waiting for his pupil to plunge toward the distant waters below, he gave me time to build enough courage to put into words what I could barely make sense of. I could feel his gaze weighing me as I whispered, "It wasn't there. Just…a swampy field. Tangled vines and… There was nothing there."

His muscles settled, though they continued to blanket my body. He assured me, "Your mind is sound," while maintaining his focus on the rocky roadway ahead.

I searched his face, desperate for answers, theories—hell, *lies* even—so long as they gave some modicum of an explanation I could cling onto as being plausible. The space between his brows shrunk as I continued to stare. Why was he unwilling to give me what I needed from him?

I shied away and wished I could run far, far from him—as far as possible—and from whatever unnatural elements formulated his world of fiery prisons, vanishing farms, and soul-mending play dough.

Wythe must've sensed my unease—assuming my gasping for breath while digging my fingernails into the saddle roll in front of me wasn't obvious—because his arm that'd rediscovered the curvature of my waist became bolder. His thumb drifted, rising above the band of my pants. Slowly at first, as if it had floated without purpose from its hold securing me, other than to meander on its own accord. But then, the pad of his thumb hooked around, drawing a new path toward its initial location. Warmth flowed from him, through my linen shirt, washing over me, as he continued to stroke my side in lingering, light circles. The sensation swelled, rolling off his fingers, then palm. It was strangely comforting.

And familiar. His touch—the way it caused my skin to tingle, inspired the essence of who I was inside to dance. My mind ached, wanting the memories of him that were forbidden to be freed.

His chest rose as my body relaxed into him, softened as he exhaled, cradling me, then rising again.

Something about his touch...

The length of my cloak tumbled from my lap, its rustle breaking the hypnotic lull. All the while, his reach—I finally noticed—had passed between the wool folds, under its weight, to embrace the terrain above the swell of my hip. A finger snagged the tip of my hem, displacing the waistband from my skin.

His thumb stilled.

The soothing current ebbed, then faded. Gathering the loose garment flapping aside the horse's belly, he wound it closed around my chest. "Best take care that you do not catch a chill."

I wondered as I regarded his face, tinged a distinct rose color that grew lusher in hue, whether I should worry about how he'd calmed me. Or should I simply accept it, since he'd implied our time together was to be short-lived anyway?

Wythe cleared his throat, as if in preparation to speak, though I knew full-well he did it because he was more uncomfortable than I was. "You are a good woman, Miss Moore. I know that you are frightened. Nonetheless, you have been patient and accepted my efforts to assist you without question. For that, I thank you."

Considering the many ways I'd resisted him, his thanks were greatly exaggerated. All the mysterious, inexplicable happenings surrounding him—I hadn't failed to ask how he'd done any of that out of an innate decency or even neglect. My silence was born, quite frankly, out of being too damned scared to want to know. Deniability meant safety. There was some danger hidden in the darkness of my memory, one my nightmares had persisted in trying to impress on me, and he was tangled up with it somehow. The sooner we reached our destination and were rid of one another, a goal he'd been so determined to reach earlier that morning, the better. The balance of my life seemed to depend on it.

Chapter Twelve

Pine trees…pine…an oak…pine…swayed across my vision as I rocked with the motion of the horse. Side. To. Side. A monotonous passage of wilderness—peaceful and soothing, graced by a soft adagio of birdsong and the occasional woodland critter—drifted by, like a shore to our lazy tide. My lack of sleep from the night before embraced the lull in the weird and suspenseful, and drew me under.

I was on the cusp of blissful nothingness when the sounds of humanity yanked me from my near slumber. Although the view was much as it was before—endless greens and browns, plus overcast skies peering through their thick covering overhead—a multitude of garbled voices and man-made busyness foretold of a camp or maybe a town somewhere ahead.

Captain Wythe acknowledged he'd heard it, too, by drawing his horse to a stop. A brief but reassuring smile lightened his otherwise solemn expression as his attention roamed from the surrounding trees to my upturned face. After another pause to listen, he swung himself to the ground and held out a hand to assist me. Getting the chance to stretch my legs and back after enduring those Highland trails should've been declared a national celebration, because I was ready to sing hymns, I was so grateful.

Once the constraints of the reins and halter had been removed, the horse shook his mane. A dense cloud of dust lifted from his coat, and a leaf bud casing tumbled free with the motion. Unstrapping a pair of messenger bags from the saddle, Wythe then plucked several other wilderness stowaways loose, including a nasty-stubborn burr, and whispered in the horse's lowered ear as he did. Our speckled companion answered with a soft whinny, nodding his head before wandering off into the bushes.

An unexpected sensation rushed through me, resembling what I imagined hot flashes must feel like, but spawning from my brain region downward. With it came the impression of being utterly alone—never mind the local hubbub nearby—topped with a lovely additive of devastating vulnerability.

It seemed my muscles had perfect recall, my magically-induced recollection deficiency clogging up just my useless gray matter, not the rest.

Without meaning to, I shuffled backward, away from Wythe's approach, and landed in a pretty badass defensive pose.

"I will not harm you." His Wacky Wild Woman Whisperer tone was set to maximum impact level. "I am *sworn* to protect you. Do you remember this?"

"The fact that you keep reminding me makes it sound like you're trying too hard."

"You are understandably frightened because you remember so little. Nonetheless, I must ask that you trust me and obey my instructions. I know not whether regulars are stationed in town."

I shook my head. "Except I don't."

"What say you?"

Nervous about what would come next, I held my breath. I was a child, strayed from the path, grasping at my cloak and wondering which wolf would end me—regulars, irregulars, mythical nonsense, or *him*. I hated the both of us for it, not to mention the un-memorable cause of my amnesia.

But this was a truth we'd danced around rather than confront, and maybe it was just plain time. It came out as a semi-whisper. "I don't trust you."

He sighed. "I would speak with you of this, though here is hardly the place. Here, we are exposed, with no information of what lay ahead."

"I get that, but you don't trust me. I don't trust you. How are we supposed to—"

"You have never truly given me cause, Miss Moore."

"To trust me?"

"Nay. It was that I did not know…" Right leg to left, he shifted his weight, focused on the ground. It was with more conviction that he said, "You were made to fear me when you were stricken."

"What? Why?"

What the hell came before?

A hazy memory lingered in the distance, growing brighter, the images becoming sharper, as if the sun was rising over a hillside in my mind, its power restoring the world after a stormy night. The curse fought my urging the scene to come into focus. Biting and clawing, it shredded the image. Still, the memory filtered through its resistance, like threads of fog drifting toward me, slowly weaving themselves together again into ribbons, into strips, into a bolt of cloth containing circumstances I was meant to understand.

Wythe watched, eyes intent on me, and waited.

I ignored the sensation of those claws nicking my mind during its frantic efforts and fought harder, knowing he needed me to remember.

Debris. No. Lavender, gone to ash. Inside the fire that leaped to life at her will. She was there, with me, in the room—

Agony seared through me. She slammed the door on those memories so hard, it felt like I'd been shot through my skull, as if a bullet had materialized from some far away battlefield to single me out. My grasp on those not-so-long-ago moments was lost, and they were banished deeper into the void than before.

Falling. I was falling.

"Enough!"

A summery current washed across my forehead. It flowed through my mind and rinsed away the pain as he cupped his palm there. The relief was immense—how the forest scene shifted from a darkened mass into place, the noticeable feeling of being restored, as if I'd drowned the end of a trying day in a long, luxurious bath. It also left me a little groggy.

More than that, as I forced my limp muscles into action, I felt a subtle hum vibrating through Wythe, its tone plucked from an internal string, as if he were a channel for an aethereal tune. The sensation resonated from his arms encircling my body, into me. It stirred a sleeping part of my soul and calmed the irritation there.

"Forgive me," he said, tucking a strand of hair behind my ear. "I should not have attempted to… The one who bound you must undo it."

"Great. And what happens if that person dies? Will I ever get my memories back?" I gritted my teeth through the pain rebuilding.

"Shh. Do not look to remember."

"But *why* was—?"

The curse bombarded me with renewed force. Everything went gray and shifted on its axis, my insides sliding down an incline while my corpse remained upright.

Spice, a kind I couldn't name but reminded me of hot pumpkin beverages, along with a hint of sweat, dirt, and the unmistakable stench of horse filled my mouth and nostrils. I returned the steadying breath, then sampled another, several times, until my connection between my swimming innards and physical self was reestablished.

A wool landscape flooded my vision as I opened my eyes. Wythe's muscles were rigid; his hands a fraction away from connecting with my shoulders, no doubt at the ready, if needed, to catch me. I lifted my forehead from his chest—could a man's face actually turn the color of sangria, because it seemed like his was on its way—and stepped back with yet another apology on my lips. The shuffling of his feet said otherwise of his insistence, "All is well."

And impasse. Original plan out the window, on the compost heap. Leave it to molder along with whatever trust we'd once had—it was buried somewhere underneath—and shovel a few more sighs on top, because things weren't working out, and the situation just called for it.

"You have taken watch before." It was said as a fact, but still carried the stink of uncertainty. "Mayhaps, it would be best if you waited while I enter town. I shall survey ahead, then return for you once I know it to be free of danger. Would that suit?"

Oh, yeah. Mad woman, in the wilds, all alone—the kinda gobbledygook parents stuff their kids' heads with at night as a cautionary tale: Don't go beyond the borders of town, Little One, or the Savannah with the cursed dragon in her skull will hunt you down and swallow you whole. Classify that as not ideal. Some protection, even if the source whipped up my own personal blend of nightmares, was better than none at all.

Despite my fractured state, however, I recognized how I posed a danger to both of us by my horrifying handicap. "You will come back, right?"

"You shall not be left alone for long," he reassured me, a hint of relief relaxing his grim expression. The quaver in my voice had definitely betrayed how I feared him leaving more than I did him. "Do you recall how to use this?" He withdrew a pistol from the leather bag draped over his shoulder.

"Yeah, it's a gun. You point it and pull the trig-ger." Except there was no trigger. Just a funny ball in its place.

"Can you ready it?"

A spark of recognition flickered in seeing the steel weapon. Curved pieces at the end. Scrollwork carved into the metal. A circled daisy. Details discovered in my past, now reunited with me in my present. Given to me by someone I trusted. A handsome face with blond hair tried to take shape.

"Is it from my husband?" I asked.

"Indeed not."

Mark that as *hell no*. His answer had been downright frigid.

Not willing to play anymore, I shoved the gun into his chest, forcing him to take it back. "I don't remember."

It frustrated him, judging by the grumble in his throat, but he returned the weapon to his bag and selected another item. "Wear this," he said. A silver key dangled from a length of faded blue ribbon.

After my anti-firearms stance, I figured I could humor him about an improv necklace and approached him to receive it.

But the key wouldn't let me.

"Miss Moore," Wythe warned. "This is no frivolous request. Please, do accept this trinket. It was yours."

Try as I might, I couldn't endure it. The empty air around the key buzzed. The closer he came to crowning me with it, the stronger the fury of a thousand fiery wasps stung me, sending me into a swift retreat.

"It will protect you," he insisted.

A ripping sound, from my wool cloak snagging on the rough edge of a tree branch, caught my attention before I felt its grab. I jolted by reflex in search of the source. Wythe captured my wrist while I was distracted and attempted to wind the ribbon around my neck.

"No!"

"You must trust me."

"Please, stop," I cried.

He paused, and he did. Wythe relaxed his grip. For a moment, nothing. Random scratching from wildlife scurrying overhead. A chill wind dying. Then, his palm slid over the back of my hand, and we just stood there, clasping onto one another. Things were supposed to be different between us. Better. More. A lifetime's worth of more.

How long have I known him?

But a barrage of objections swarmed through me, reasons keeping us apart that I couldn't name, not the least of which was the forgotten husband. And the unknown something before the curse that marked him as a traitor.

Yet, here he was. Genuinely anxious for my sake. Fighting with me about how he wanted to protect me with his killer key, yet holding the offensive item as far from me as possible.

We always fight about him taking care of me.

"Okay," I acquiesced. "I'll wear it."

"You are certain?" Concern more than surprise filled his eyes.

"Certainty is a luxury I've forgotten." I breathed a bitter laugh. "But I'll do it anyway. For you."

"Miss Moore." He frowned. "I ask that you do this for yourself."

I thrust my chin into the air. "Bring it."

Cocking an eyebrow, complete with a quizzical stare first, he spread open the ribbon necklace. Just as the cursed bedroom's threshold had bared its teeth when the door swung wide, so too did the assault from the key. One sting multiplied from another, into a dozen, into thousands—driving, stabbing, tormenting me to my core.

"Fuuuu—" I collapsed against the nearby tree, gasping. "I-I'm trying. Really. Promise. It…it hurts."

"I had not realized." Annoyance, or some relative to Ire perhaps, coursed through his body; he nodded, posture stiffening and fists clamped shut. "You must resist what you are feeling."

Our efforts to try again were unbearable. I couldn't take it from him. Wythe's face became pained when I shrieked from his almost-but-not-quite ring-around-my-rosy-cheeked-noggin. He dropped the key into his hand, allowing the ribbon to fold up inside. "I should have done more to protect you." His voice chastised himself, as much as he was offering his angry apology to me.

I clapped a hand on his arm to prevent him from tucking the whole thing away in his bag. "I need you to do it for me."

"To force this upon you, if it brings you pain…"

"You said it's important."

Against all doubts flooding his features—he grumbled at the ground for several shockingly profane clauses while I rested and waited—he relented. "Focus on your intent. Focus on wanting to receive this blessing. On wanting it to be a part of you."

"You've got to be kidding me."

Nice of him to leave that last part out until the final countdown. Soul-mending sealing wax wasn't enough, now he wanted to talk mind-melding with a key?

Buzzing crowded my ears. It rose into a fever pitch, roaring louder as countless needles pierced my body.

"Focus on wanting the protection it offers you," he repeated, drawing closer.

Could you charge an antique with attempted murder?

Pain shot through my forehead, bursting outward so fiercely, I could almost see it. A boiling, desperate intensity that ensnared the key in his hand and circled back into me. It wasn't the key, per se, hurting me. It was the curse in my head, fighting to keep it from me.

I want this key. I want to be protected.

Razor wire slid over my hair, scraped my cheeks, their blades slashing my chest and into my muscles, as if driven through me toward my center. All the while, I was screaming inside.

I want this key to keep me safe. I want Captain Wythe!

A hand clapped over my mouth. Maybe I was screaming out loud too.

Metal spikes impaled my skin and embedded in the narrow divide between my breasts. My heart skipped a beat, then it broke into a gallop, trying to match pace with the vibrations emanating from my so-called protection. Its fire cutting through me was excruciating.

Wythe laid a hand over the key, pressing it into my chest. The world was so loud, swarming against his words, his whispering shrill at first, then softening. Latin phrases. He was praying.

An autumn breeze—soft, carrying the lingering embrace of summer's warmth—flowed from his hand into me. As if tucked into bed after a long restless season, it chased the pain away, and the world calmed, then hushed. A sigh from the wind in the leaves around us, enrichened with the ballad of a distant bird, shushed me, until even those sounds drifted and slumbered again.

Despite all the layers of clothing he was wearing, his heartbeat reached the hand I pressed onto his chest for support. I focused on its rhythm, resting my cheek against the heavy wool. My own relaxed, and the vibrations in the key matched it. Another fragment of my soul melted back into place, easing the ache inside, and the prison door in my mind splintered in response.

"Their influence never lasts for long," Mr. Cloet once told me.

Blue, blue eyes searched mine as I raised my head. Fingers drew a strand of hair from my brow, his thumb brushing the curve of my cheek in turn. He was asking if I was in health. Could I hear him? Worry dampened his eyes.

But I wasn't worried. I was elated. The fear had vanished. The portion of the curse that'd manufactured a rift between us was now broken, and it wouldn't hold me back anymore. Sensations, emotions, desires—all those intangibles that created the fabric of our friendship—flowed freely again.

Tucked away in the woods together, with the thrill of his touch on my skin and the sound of my name being breathed into my hair as he held me, I remembered a sensation like an ocean's wave crashing over me, knocking me off-balance, and claiming me. I remembered falling unintentionally in love.

"Jonathan."

"Aye." It was there in his smile too.

My eyelids fluttered, heavier by the moment. "I'm so tired."

His hand brushed over my forehead. For once, it felt cool. "You are fevered."

Obvious as reality. Thank you, Captain Jonathan. I leaned into the relief his hand offered, but then I was sinking.

"Rest," he encouraged me.

I tried to argue. We needed to go.

He guided me to the forest floor, promising I would be safe.

Chapter Thirteen

Crunching. Close by.

A swish of…fabric, maybe, overhead.

Nope. A tail, flicking against the speckled rump of a decidedly male horse.

"Oh shit!"

A blanket of freshly-cut evergreen tumbled from my torso as I bolted to my feet. My horsy pal snickered. Repeatedly.

"You," I grumbled at the obnoxious beast carrying on at my expense. "Funny. Real funny…"

"Felaróf." Jonathan's voice echoed through my memory. "It means very strong."

Strong ass, maybe.

I brushed myself off and surveyed my unfamiliar surroundings. Dank and dreary, rocks and wilderness without a path. Jonathan had deposited me deeper in the woods.

Frigid or not, I turned my face to the sky, relishing the fine drizzle. It washed away the last of the curse's heat. Hidden beneath my clothing, humming when I focused in on it, was the key. Jonathan's presence resided in its heart. I could feel him, keeping me warm. Safe.

Which was reassuring, because I needed to figure out where the hell I was.

My four-legged canopy neighed loudly.

"I'm not going far," I said, then wondered why I was talking to a horse. It wasn't like he understood me. After I'd wandered several more steps, he lectured me and stamped his foot.

"Yeah, yeah." Strands of his mane were crisscrossed around a prickly. I unwound the thorny seedpod and chucked it aside. "I was just looking for Jon…Captain Wythe."

Excellent. I was minding my tongue with animals now.

Once again, Felaróf beat the ground with his hoof, interrupting my musing. He bucked his head twice. I searched between him and the direction he'd muzzled out, which looked like any other—coniferous.

Thrumming against my palm, the horse's flank—soft and warm, despite the rain and hours of trekking through the mud—vibrated, almost as if he were a giant cat, pleased with the attention that was his due. A sensation that sang against my skin, just as it did whenever Jonathan touched me or—

A firecracker burst through my skull.

Effing witch.

Another explosion had me seeing stars.

Steadying myself against Felaróf's side, I tipped my chin back, allowing pools of rainwater to collect against my eyelids.

Focus on something else. Anything else. Warm baths. Cashmere sweaters. Macchiatos...

My happy mantra ground to a halt with the realization that these weren't luxuries from the Colonies. Warm baths, certainly, but not the other two.

He shifted beneath my weight.

"I'm fine."

But there was a plethora of nothing special in the direction indicated and, honestly, was it really a good idea to indulge the whims of a horse wanting an exploratory jaunt, tingly though he might be?

I chose oak as my watchtower *du jour*. Mr. Speckles lost interest in my progress after all of two branches and began nosing shoots from under the forest's carpet.

"Out of my mind, listening to a horse. Nice of you to help me," I called down.

He ignored me.

The wind shifted so the newly burst spring leaves separated.

Well, damn. Felaróf was right.

A smattering of houses clustered amid a tiny clearing materialized through the opening. Townsfolk, ant-like due to the distance, scurried along the earthy passageways in between. The town Jonathan wanted to explore, was my guess.

Now what? I risked missing him if I went after him. He was a watch-from-the-sidelines kinda guy, and—my luck being absolutely stellar—I'd pick the skid row end of things, not knowing better. Ships in the proverbial night.

How long would he be if he thought I'd be out of it for a while?

The now full-on arctic rain should've been a pretty obvious hint that I wasn't going to be able to calculate the hour from the sun.

Of course, if his idea of scoping things out was getting a beer without me...

I scanned the area, like Jonathan had wanted before our plan was waylaid. An occasional creeping vine accented the otherwise unremarkable woods. A whole lot of don't-even-bother-putting-it-on-a-postcard.

He's a capable soldier, I reassured myself. *Better to wait for him here.*

But how will you know if something's happened to him, Worry taunted back.

Movement. High in the branches, same level as me.

I squinted, in case it was more than my death—pouring by bucket-loads now—displacing the leaves, but couldn't see anything until it hopped closer. A bird. Blue, in fact, with pewter streaks.

Just then, the equine purr-bag trotted off.

Great. There goes my ride.

Attempting to descend from my perch reminded me how cloaks are nothing but fancy, woolen fishing nets in disguise, cast by malevolent topiary to ensnare heights-challenged spies like me. Some colorful language may've escaped my lips while I struggled to free the snagged hem from an offshoot above. Not to worry. The scenery was monotonous. Color was good for it.

Jonathan was decent enough to wait until I was within jumping range to startle me. "What news, Miss Moore?"

"Jeez—"

Fortunately for us both, feline must run in my past lives—I landed on my feet. Mostly. Finding myself unexpectedly on *terra firma*, I held up a muddy finger to stall him and clasped my hands on my knees to take a deep breath…or three. His sudden reappearance had surprised me that badly. "Hi to you too."

"Pardon." He inhaled, then clamped his mouth shut and stepped away.

Oh good. They were both back, my personal cavalry.

"The weatherman lied about it being sunny today."

Jonathan raised a brow in my direction from where he was reattaching his messenger bags to Felaróf's saddle. A stream of water tumbled from his tricorn as he glanced skyward. I envied his drier headgear.

"I don't really have a good sense of time," I said as I joined the odd duo to report my lack of findings. "But I'd guess it's been a half hour since I took watch."

Removing the reins and bridle from the saddlebag while we spoke, he acknowledged my contribution, minor though it had been.

"How about you?" I asked. "Make any new friends in town?"

He hummed, though his amused smile was brief. "Be grateful that I did not. It is as we were informed a few weeks prior. What regulars that had remained moved westward, conscripting bodies to add to their number. They are encamped at the northmost part of Schunnemunk Clove." His head ducked behind the far side of the bridle, out of sight.

"And…?"

"A small band has separated from the whole."

"Somewhere between us and Moore's Folly," I guessed.

"Aye." He continued to fuss with the tack long after it'd been secured. Felaróf grew impatient and shook him loose.

"If you don't think it's safe, we can wait."

"We are less like to encounter trouble while it is not fair. Might you be—?"

"I'm game to keep going, if you are."

Head bowed, he planted his hands on his hips. "There is more."

"There always is," I joked.

He blinked. "Even now." He breathed a laugh. "It relieves me to see so much of your former self restored. You are unflappable."

"Mmm, let's not test that theory, okay?" I returned his smile.

It worked. His hesitation ceased, and he filled me in on the rest of what was bogging him down: The North River lay to the east of town. Between us was the place where Jonathan and I had met—a favored location of the splinter group, within easy passage to Cornwall Landing. Or, last he'd been told. The townsfolk were uncertain.

"Prior to our arrival in New Windsor," he said, "I had use of a scout."

I searched Jonathan's face to see what he was feeling. There was frustration there, but not grief. "What happened?"

"He is undecided as to whether he wishes to continue with our previous arrangement."

"This place was where I wanted to go," I realized. "Before the…before I lost my memories."

"They were not fully restored to you?"

"Only bits and pieces. Not…not when…" I touched the key, unwilling to confront the subject of our fantastical circumstances further. "Why there? I have this hazy memory of you calling it a rendezvous."

He hesitated. "It was your claim not to reside in the American States, though you also insisted that you were able to return home once there."

"Oh hell." Reality sucked big time. "You're afraid I'm a Loyalist." It explained my distrust of him, why I felt he was a traitor, and why he was leery of me. He'd transformed into an unbelievable jerk the day before, when he'd clearly begun to doubt our loyalties rested with the same party. "It's because of me, isn't it? Your scout, he's refusing—"

"If anything, he has not quit me completely because of you." A moment's gratitude filled the fleeting smile given to me.

"But I killed those soldiers. I remember… I can't imagine murdering my own troops."

Or was he a traitor to his fellow colonists?

"At times," he whispered, "duty may require…"

"Well, that would make you an unbelievable asshole, if you were loyal, because you killed far more redcoats than I did that day."

The hand by his hip fisted.

Nice one. Cleared that up.

Stumbling block after stumbling block. Where was this rocky path taking me?

"Let's stop and think about this." I allowed a moment to pass so we could both calm down. "I can't remember what came before, what I was looking for in that place. And not a great idea to wander around clueless where enemy soldiers…?" He nodded, so I continued, "Where enemy soldiers are. Not without some real idea of why." A lump in my throat formed. "You said you needed to go to Moore's Folly. It makes the most sense."

"Unless you had been trying to flee that life," he muttered.

Great.

Felaróf nudged his shoulder. He stilled it by stroking the horse's muzzle.

"We can't keep double-guessing each other." I sighed. "For all the good this is going to do us, with things being what they are, if there's anything I can do to reassure you, or anything you want me to tell you, just ask. I'll do my best to be honest, and if I can't, I'll tell you that too. And I hope you'll be willing to do the same for me."

He shifted his weight, studying my face as he did, and I was glad to see in the upturn of his mouth that he might actually believe me. But then he grew serious and, before I even saw it coming, he grabbed my wrist. Deftly unbuttoning the top buttons of his coat, he thrust my hand inside, pressing it to his chest.

I froze, startled, and stared at our hands. Already, a swell in the atmosphere was gathering around us, being pulled into him. With careful fingers, he divided my cloak, pausing first, as if waiting to see if I would resist, then sought the place over my heart.

A tiny voice warned me to be wary.

"Whatever it is we're about to do," I said, "am I going to be able to decide for myself? Or are you influencing me?"

"You are free to choose."

"And if I say no?"

His face fell. "I will honor your choice."

So much for avoiding the strange and unusual.

"What is it you're asking?"

Blossoming outward, his fingers entwined with mine as our hands joined. Just the sheer brush of his skin electrified me. "The pact is stronger if you look into me."

Blue, deep and wide, welcomed me in, as if I could somehow fall into him through his gaze.

"Miss Moore, as I have vowed to protect you and do you no harm, will you swear that you will not harm me? I do not ask for your protection in return."

"Not that I'm refusing—because that sounds like a fair thing to ask—but so I know what I'm getting myself into…what would happen if we break this pact?"

"Depending on the severity of the act, our lives could be forfeit."

"Jesus, Jonathan." I yanked his hand from my chest. It damn near took my breath away as the force built between us rushed out of me.

"Promises can be broken," he insisted. "This pact cannot, not without consequences."

Yeah, promises could be broken. The memory of such a betrayal ripped me apart; the scene played out in front of my eyes, with all the shock and anger and pain caused when it initially happened. My bed. His paralegal. It left me as nauseated as I'd been on that day.

I backed away, smashing my fists into the stream flowing down my face.

Damn you, Justin.

Expressing regret, Jonathan's touch—light as a petal floating on a secluded lake—glided across the surface of my shoulder. As the tremble of my body worsened, his subtle embrace guided me closer, and he wiped aside the moistened pathway from my eyes. "Tell me what you saw."

Long-ago shame burned fresh along my cheeks.

"I can't." My voice broke. "When the memories come back… You don't understand. It's like reliving them, all over again, for the first time. I… Someday I'll tell you. Not today. Please, not…"

Soft and sad, his smile offered me sympathy. "I will not force you into that which you do not wish to give."

Felaróf pawed the broken leaves, urging us, in his way, to hurry. The rain tapered off, replaced by an uptick in the wind that rustled the branches overhead, throwing droplets to the ground in noisy splatters. From somewhere in the town, a chorus of laughter crescendoed, then faded. It temporarily drowned out a bird's twittering. After the tears ran dry, he still cradled my cheek.

Parting the collar of his coat, I noticed how cold my fingers were as they disappeared inside, the warmth from his body rising to meet them. His breath caught. Tapping my fingertip against a button situated over his breastbone, I took a final moment to consider what I was doing. Energy hummed against my skin, but it didn't accompany the natural swell of heat from his chest caressing my hand, so I felt assured my actions were bred without expectation from him or any urging from anyone or anything but my own desire.

Tightly woven linen stretched across the expanse of his chest. I followed the line of fibers, not as coarse as I would've guessed, and sought his heartbeat with my palm. He released the breath he was holding and drew in another. A hand hesitated before clasping mine. Drawing crescents with his thumb, he explored its shape, and I felt myself falling into rhythm with him, as if the boundaries between us were melting away.

"That day…" The playfulness and comradery were reborn for me—each parry, every laugh, the joy of our friendship maturing into stronger stuff. "…when you taught me how to use a sword."

Cobalt eyes latched onto mine. "You remember?"

"I do." I returned his smile, though part of the memory included surprise at his pained expression, regretting how he'd unintentionally injured me. "When the stick hit me, if this pact had been in place, would it have hurt you?"

I worried he'd resist answering, maybe even pull away at the question. Instead, he pressed his cheek into my hair, nuzzling it aside so his mouth brushed my skin as he whispered, "For a life to be forfeit, the actor would have to seek to take the life of the other, with full knowledge of what is being done. It is a matter of intent. Do you understand this?"

Certainty struck me as undeniable as if it were a physical blow—I was an attorney. Knowledge, intent: concepts we bandied about like currency.

Except women weren't admitted to the bar here. Nevertheless, an image of a jury overwhelmed my ability to see, clear as day, hanging on my words as I thrust a pistol, sealed in a see-through bag, into the air.

"You belong to another." Jonathan's voice called me back, and the images vanished. Guilt filled his downturned eyes. "I have no right to claim a pact from you."

"Why? Do you have to be married to make a pact or something?"

"Nay, ah." He cleared his throat. "I do not seek…*that* manner of—"

"I want you to believe in me again. You used to." *Please let these thoughts, these sparks of feelings, be true*, I silently begged. "We both did. I want that back."

We were so close, the tantalizing scent of spice stirred my senses. I wondered if the taste of mulled wine or holiday sweets would flavor my lips were I brave enough to lift them higher.

When I realized his fingertips had alighted on the hem of my cloak, unwilling yet to draw open its folds, I guided them inside and pressed his palm against the bruised area over my heart. It ached for him.

Nature took control. An instinct I didn't understand, though the innate hunger was anything but foreign. It drove me to his eyes, then into his very being. Groundswells of energy rushed over us from the earth, the trees, and—it seemed—the heavens itself. It enveloped us, plunging us deeper into one another. Our bodies—movement, rhythm, blood, air, all that useless dust brought to a temporary, fleeting life—ceased to exist outside the momentary communion between our souls.

"Savannah Moore." Jonathan's voice resonated through us, the weight of his words bringing me to a precipice from which I longed to fly. "As I do hereby vow to protect you and do you no harm, will you so vow to do no harm unto me?"

"I do. I vow never to harm you, just like you vow never to harm me."

Born out of silver waves, a fire—sacred and wholly familiar, as though it'd once belonged to me and been forged into my very being—flooded into me, raced through me, and consumed me without pain, without destruction. I soared from the height to which he'd led me, alive and light-headed with sheer ecstasy. I reveled in it, allowing our vow to undo me.

Neither fear nor remorse dared disturb the peace I felt when the sensation released me. I was floating, a powdery seed on the wind, at the mercy of an unseen current, yet serene with the knowledge that destiny would bring me home.

Jonathan was drinking me in as my vision cleared, his lips trembling. Warmth from his forehead fueled the heat where it rested against my brow. There was relief, even joy, in his expression. It was impossible not to beam back at him.

Uncertain whether our mouths had touched, I was tempted to ensure they did, but he reminded me that we needed to move on. Tucking loose hairs that'd tumbled out of place behind my ear, he paused to finger a lock from the underside. A queer look crossed his face. Whatever it was passed quickly. "Are you well?"

"Yes," I breathed. "You?"

"Aye."

Reluctantly, I withdrew my hand from his coat and redid the buttons for him. He followed their progress without comment. I allowed myself a final glance into his eyes before I stepped aside so he could collect Felaróf's reins.

Together, we returned to the pathway, falling into step, side by side. A smile passed between us, and my hand reunited with his.

Just before we left the protection of the trees to enter town, Jonathan stopped, saying nothing for a while. I watched, memorizing his features as he surveyed what lay ahead: the crest of a vein in his knuckle while his hand curved around his blade's hilt, how he held himself erect, the random passes of deeper auburn in his hair, how the corners of his eyes crinkled a little while he concentrated.

He chuckled when he caught me studying him and blushed. It was with a serious tone, however, that he cautioned, "Please do not speak of what you know. We would both of us be at risk if any learn of what we have done or suspect that you understand my nature."

An easy request to accept, since I was ignorant of everything he wished kept secret and could barely describe to myself our actions.

Having given his thanks, he exited the forest first. I longed to hold onto him, maintain a physical connection between us, but someone might see. It didn't matter, though. In that moment, I was satisfied. Another part of my soul had been restored to me.

Chapter Fourteen

The sensual afterglow of our pledge lingered. I could feel Jonathan's caress on my body, his presence inside me, despite us walking more than a dozen feet apart as we entered town. I tapped into it, and everything surrounding me was created anew, so much more intense than before. The sunlight filtering through the overcast sky was dazzling. From the beginnings of the main thoroughfare to the far end of town, I could see the minutest detail; concentrate on faces until they were clear, their features crisp, regardless of the distance. Felaróf's clopping along the muddy pathway thundered. Even the tiniest pebble shifting under the horse's shoe declared itself.

Voices became available at will. All I had to do was focus my intent on what I wanted to hear. No conversation was beyond my reach. Plans for the purchasing of acres or else enlisting into service, celebration of a prominent marital alliance, a recounting of regulars hunting along Smith's Clove, recitations from a letter written by faraway relatives, whispering of young people to meet again—spoken as if for my benefit, as though I were a founding member of their society, to whom custom required deliverance of the local gossip.

Aromas woven into the very fabric of the community were readily accessible, as well. I could pick them apart as easily as identifying one book from the next by reading their titles. Smoke and gruel and horse and manure and beer and cinnamon and tobacco and perfume and snuff and gunpowder and leather and earth and rain and grass and daffodils…

It was intoxicating, and its effect didn't go unnoticed by Jonathan. Although he'd entered the clearing ahead of me, then disappeared behind the height of Felaróf ambling between us, a keen awareness anchored me to him. The thrum of energy that, until here and now, couldn't expand beyond the fraction of space between our physical reach was freed from its confines, expanding as our steps naturally fell farther apart while our bodies swayed. His gaze as it sought me out with increasing concern bore an altered timbre to the humming—volume, complexity, intensity, and heat, rising. Our tether lacked any sense of oppression. Instead, I felt elated, reassured by the inexplicable knowledge of his movements, of him, that permitted me to freely explore our surroundings with my newly awakened senses.

A larva twitched between the lathe and plaster of the house closest to the woods. It stretched—

"Let us keep to the tree line so we may pass through undisturbed."

It wasn't so much a suggestion as a command. I turned to protest, eager to absorb the town and devour all the sights, sounds, and sensations...

Glorious. All of him, in every manner, beyond adequate description, other than to simply say, was glorious. Infinite shades of blue, swirling in pools of light, shone from his eyes. His skin breathed life—pure, brilliant, mesmerizing. Ribbons of silver laced and twirled and flowed, rising from the depths of him, mingling with the elements surrounding us, melting into him—an eternal ballet of flame. Beauty personified would've found him breathtaking.

Worry radiated from him as he stared, brows drawn. He hadn't forced the issue, not yet, but he'd have to if it came to it. My conduct was so egregious in its abnormality, an everyday person was bound to recognize it stemmed from more than a personal oddity. Recognizing the danger I posed to us both, I agreed.

Our pace was casual, our passage—veering from the road onto a worn path behind the constellation of buildings—silent. I didn't mind. It meant I could enjoy the world at length without distraction.

"Who's that man following us?" I fiddled with a strap on the saddle as we walked, allowing me to face him and whisper the question.

Impressive—as always—to witness his skill in keeping cool, his reaction consisted of a subtle shift in his demeanor, a sign his mind was alert to what was happening around us. However, his gaze remained forward while he asked where the man was.

"He's keeping pace on the main road. Pale yellow horse. Light-colored hair. Dressed similarly to you... Damn. I can't place him. A friend, right?" Since verbalizing my stream of thoughts had yielded some fruit in reclaiming my memories, I'd hoped for further success. As it was, once the words were out, reservations about the stranger, engulfed in ruby flames, percolated. The reason hesitated in revealing itself, though, remaining tucked away.

Recognition filled Jonathan's face, indicating he'd spotted our follower through the houses, except the tension remained. He stopped us in our tracks.

"Miss Moore, I will explain all when I can. For now, it is imperative that you do as I ask, for both our sakes."

"I look forward to a rousing, lengthy, full-of-details explanation over supper."

"Foolish of me to expect otherwise." The flutter of his smile having vanished, Jonathan gave a solemn nod. "Take my horse. Ride to the edge of the forest and await me there. It is best if I meet him alone."

"Well, then. May I ride you, good sir?" I was only half-joking when I asked Felaróf for permission.

"Wythe!" The man rounded a nearby cottage, ignoring the fact that the narrow, brick path he was traversing—which separated a kitchen garden from a small swath of flower beds, for decorative rather than traffic-related purposes—was insufficient for such a large animal. Fresh sprouts were crushed into the mud under the weight of the horse's hooves.

Felaróf nodded what I assumed to be consent, so I mounted. Jonathan hovered below me to make sure I was well-situated. "Guard the lady in my stead, if you will."

Several additional nods and a whinny were his answer.

Laughter, soldiers, and the threat of enemy attack accompanied a whispered scene in my mind. "A Maiden of Misfortune?"

"Aye. You, my maiden. Make haste." He passed up the reins, clasping my hand to encourage me to lean closer so he could whisper, "Keep to Felaróf. Do not dismount. Or if you must, keep hold of him at all times. It is for your protection that you do."

Sure. Tingly Speckles reports for… Nah, that nickname is crap.

Jonathan squeezed my hand.

Yellow Horse parked in front of my trusty steed. An accusatory finger jabbed in my direction as the stranger said, "Were you not to be rid of this creature by now? What is the meaning of this?"

Another flash of the same memory, overripe with a similar verbal confrontation, rushed through me. "Oh," I said, once it'd released me. "A pleasure to see you again, as always, Affable Alex." And I gave him my sweetest smile just to aggravate him.

If Jonathan hadn't been so distracted by the fight to come, I think the hum that rumbled in his chest might've transformed into a laugh. Sadly, not to be when his alleged best friend was around to harass him, if my memory served.

I wished I could draw upon our secret vow, that cradle of carefree bliss when our souls had embraced, and rescue him from the weight of resignation clinging to him. Instead, I honored his request, and Felaróf and I navigated around Alexander's horse.

Other than letting me know by his grimace how detestable he found me, Buddy Alex barely acknowledged me. At least until he whipped his hand out to snatch at my reins as I passed. In a delightful turn of events, it seemed my self-defense skills were so ingrained into the foundation of my anatomy, missing memories need not apply, because I didn't lose a beat in knocking his arm aside, jolting his balance. Felaróf screamed his displeasure—an experience I couldn't recall ever enduring and hoped would never be repeated. The entire exchange sent Alexander's horse rearing on hind legs.

"Miss Moore," Jonathan yelled. "Alexander, please!"

Yellow Horse backed away, clacking his teeth, despite his rider barking at him to remain steady.

"Come, Felaróf. There's nothing worthy of our time here." I knew better than to clap him with my heals like any other horse. The request was enough to get us underway, heads held high while we basked in the pleasure of having the final word.

"Insolent whore," Good ole Alexander roared after us. Well, never underestimate the dedication of an idiot to making a fool of himself.

"We draw unwanted attention," Jonathan advised him.

True enough. Curious faces were peering across the yard Alexander had trampled, our audience consisting mostly of patrons from the tavern who'd abandoned their favorite seats, though not their mugs, of course. Why would they, when there was free entertainment to enhance the flavor of their beer?

I shouldn't have, but the temptation was too great. From the distant shadows of the woods where Felaróf hid us away, several times beyond the normal reach of human eyes and ears, I opened my senses to spy on the entire exchange between the tempestuous friends. I perceived their words, actions, and expressions with absolute clarity, as if I was still standing among them.

A-hole Alex shooed the onlookers back to their own cares. Once they'd wandered off with varying degrees of disappointment and laughter, he deigned to dismount and wasted no time getting in Jonathan's face demanding to "know the meaning of this."

"Alexander." Jonathan's greeting was formal in tone, sounding as if he was trying to appease his supposed friend's temper.

"We were to meet a week prior. You claimed a delay. One I took to be a difficulty with what the general required. Little did I suspect it was because you were continuing your affair with that bleached mort."

"There *was* a delay that prevented me from leaving New Windsor, but, as always, I am true to my duties. I assisted Captain Machin in overseeing the work's progress until it was possible to leave."

"Is that so?"

"More than that, I continue such assistance, even now, by drawing the regulars' attention from the river."

Awesome. Redcoats on our tail, as if this road trip wasn't killer fun enough.

"What of you?" Jonathan asked.

"You abandoned me to that insufferable, bottle-headed prat. I have wasted many an hour spewing the nonsense from the general's 'baron.' It is beyond my understanding how he expects us to transform cabbage-farmers into soldiers."

"Is that what you do here?"

There was a decided silence between them. Alexander's tone was flippant when he answered. "I follow the example of my fellows and enjoy the amusements life has to offer." Little doubt he was referring to Jonathan's perceived time-wasting.

"Whom do you visit?" My protector-slash-human-lure's voice hinted at anxiety.

"Had you not been amusing yourself elsewhere, I would have introduced you to the lady's cousin."

"She was unwell. I could not abandon her."

Captain Charming dismissed Jonathan's concern with a callous wave of his hand. "The creature would have been looked after and yourself well rid of her. There are greater attachments to be met. Had you come when I wrote, you would have seen I speak true."

"We were both ill."

Alexander's laugh in response was sickening. "You should take better care of where you store your pipe."

Jonathan growled to himself, then walked away.

"Surely you jest." When he didn't stop, Buddy Alex scoffed with disbelief and hurried after him. "You cannot mean to feel for this creature. There is nothing to be gained from the connection between you."

"She is my responsibility."

"A responsibility invented by you." He blocked his friend's path. "Jonathan, none would fault you for disowning it, now you are the wiser to the cost. All that we have, everything around us, all of us lay on the edge of ruin. The victory at Saratoga rallied support, but you know as well as I— what Manhattan wrought upon the spirit of our people lingers still."

Jonathan stumbled backward, as if struck by those words.

"Come," Alexander clapped a hand on his shoulder. "There is much to be done. We cannot fall to the temptations of a warm bed."

"You wrong the lady and me. There is…there cannot…"

"*Frater meus.*" Alexander chuckled.

Jonathan shook his head, visibly struggling from emotion. I held my breath, pleading across the distance for him to keep quiet. Laying a hand to my heart, I wished upon whatever bond there was between us, whatever magic was alive within me, that he would keep my marriage a secret. At least until we had a chance to talk. There were things he needed to know, questions to be answered. Only he would know best how to proceed. We just needed time.

Be silent.

"Jonathan?"

"Captain Grey discovered us in New Windsor."

"What? How?" Even the mighty Captain Alexander Brott could be brought to fear something. It was undeniable in his voice. The very thought was unnerving. I wracked my memory, trying to connect the name to a face from within its confines. Nothing.

"I know not." Jonathan gripped his knife's hilt. "His curse manifested on Cloet lands. By Grace, the chain remained hidden."

"You are certain?"

"He reached me through Cleophes, yet was banished before he could go further."

"Heavens blessed, Jonathan. Did the bird survive?"

"Miss Moore saved him."

"And now you feel obligated to her." The obnoxious tone had returned to Alexander's voice. It ruined any sense of genuine concern he'd shown moments earlier.

"None other than the promise I gave when first we did meet, though I am grateful."

"How?" Suspicion lay heavy with the question.

"How…what?"

"How did the creature save the bird?"

"The woman has a name."

"Of value?"

A fist rapped against Jonathan's thigh. Not pushing the issue, beyond emphasizing his reference to me when he spoke, he sighed and answered, "*Miss Moore* found where he had fallen and nursed him to health."

"You said you were both ill."

"She fell into the pond saving him. She…was injured and lay fevered abed for near a week. Still, she cared for Cleophes."

If a curse from this Captain Grey could reach Jonathan through a bird, did that mean it could reach me? Had it reached me before? I wished I'd known to ask these kinds of questions before I agreed to something I knew so little about.

Mr. Condescending grimaced. "I fear for you, my friend. I have seen how you look at her. What was once a mere distraction has grown into a full campaign to lure you in."

"What difference would it make if she had?" Jonathan snapped at him.

"So, the temptation is there."

"God's teeth, Alexander. I have felt nothing since Cordelia was murdered. Her death weighs on me at every moment. Every woman bears her face. Every voice is Cordelia's. How have you not seen this?"

"You cannot resurrect her, no matter what you do with this Miss Moore."

"Of that I am well aware!"

Jonathan took a moment to collect himself. Mercifully, his need was respected.

"Chastise me no further," he said. "You warned me away from Miss Tuinstra, and now you mock the kindness I seek to bestow upon another. Allow me a moment's friendship with the lady. She will be gone from us ere long, and what little peace I have felt, no doubt, will depart with her."

"Heavens, man. When did I warn you from—?"

"You saw me admiring her and said that 'no amount of land or beauty was worthy of us, unless the lady be one of us.'"

"I never." Alexander's confusion actually sounded genuine.

Clenching his fists, my unfortunate escort resumed his retreat to the woods.

"Forgive me, Jonathan. I did not realize."

Turning back, he acknowledged the apology and asked, "Are matters settled between you and Miss Tuinstra?"

"Her father gave his consent this afternoon. We will announce at supper."

Jonathan paused, nodding to himself. Truly the better man, he offered his hand and, with warmth in his voice, congratulated the future groom. All being restored between them—at least by virtue of the status quo settling into acceptance and good will—Alexander reissued an enthusiastic summons to join the evening's celebration. Though, when reminded of my continued existence, there was a noticeable limit to such good will, in the form of a prolonged absence of an invitation to include me.

Jonathan wished him happy.

"What will you do?" Alexander asked.

"We travel to West Point. There, I hope to see Miss Moore restored to her family."

"So, it is not long, then."

"If you have no other orders, you could assist me. Captain Machin and his men risk discovery if we do not divert the regulars' attentions. Their mission will not go unnoticed, not with so cumbersome a cargo, and they will be quickly overtaken if opposed by more than a few regulars."

"Of course, I shall assist, and before the week is spent, we will raise a glass together at West Point. You will not be alone."

Alexander mounted his horse, bid a final farewell, and rode toward his anticipated festivities. Jonathan sighed, watching his trail long after he'd disappeared. To no one but himself, he said, "I am ever alone."

Chapter Fifteen

Thief in the night, that was me. None of their conversation was meant for my ears, yet I'd robbed Jonathan of his privacy, knowing it was wrong and not caring until the deed was done. Now, I yearned to comfort him but didn't know how. Had he not been stuck in New Windsor, waiting for me to recover so he could truck me back to my cheating husband—was that the life I'd been escaping, as he'd supposed?—his presence at that fancy dinner with desirable women, those superior specimens of substance and political connections and wealth, qualities Alexander deemed important, and enjoyment of maybe multiple other soirees with his Miss Tuinstra… Well, who knows what would've happened?

Instead, he'd remained by my side, stayed by some obligation I'd forgotten, even when the curse drove me mad with fear of him, and the end result was—after discovering some solace, a way forward after the death of this Cordelia—I'd also stolen his chance for happiness.

Ignorance of my sins was the gift I'd thrown away by eavesdropping. "Jonathan?"

He hadn't acknowledged us upon entering the gloom of the woods, and if I hadn't spoken, his lonely shuffle probably would've carried him past where Felaróf and I waited at the path's border.

The devastation in his eyes…

She'd wrecked him, perhaps beyond the repair that was hoped from— what I suspected was more than a casual admiration for—the delectable Miss Tuinstra. Not only did he feel more than the nothing he'd claimed, his grief was consuming him. It scarred him like a pox, in his heavy expression and tenuous balance, as though he'd drowned his sorrows during the short distance that reunited us. And it was visible by the dulling aura of his power.

What if this was the treason he'd committed against me—offered me a haven from an abusive husband, then shown me he was incapable of providing anything other than shelter behind a turbulent, empty affection. After such a discovery of both our weaknesses, why wouldn't he be anxious to see me cared for by another?

"Would you please mount, Miss Moore?" Lifeless, like the rest of him. His voice made my heart ache.

Whatever treachery had come before, it didn't matter. If I knew how to draw upon the elements around us, as he did, I would've drunk in the whole of the oceans, yanked the winds from the corners of the Earth, dug up eons-worth of soil, constructed a pyre mountains high, and lit them all, just to call their power into me and conquer his suffering for him. I was that foolhardy.

"Will you ride with me?"

The question took its time reaching him. When the light of recognition pierced the clouds behind his eyes, he searched until noticing me above him, in the saddle waiting. He pulled the reins forward, out of my hands. Tossing them over Felaróf's head, he tugged, leading the horse onward, down the path.

"Please?" I asked.

"Oh, Miss Moore." He didn't raise his head or even glance in my direction when he spoke. "Would you allow…? I should like to walk. For now."

"Can I walk with you? Unless…you need time to think."

We continued moving.

I buried my own distress, hoping that—somehow—the space to work things out on his own would relieve him.

Evergreens grew dense around us the further south we traveled. The unstable roadway, sticky with bright-red mud that sucked at our tiny caravan's legs, transitioned into rockier climbs that were increasingly difficult to travel. It led us over tidal waves crafted from the terrain, though each climb seemed to bring us higher than before. Occasional chattering of squirrels or whispering of the leaves on the wind, and the ever-present birdsong, kept us company.

Though their scent and minutest characteristics were slipping away from me, the side-effect of our pact's formation lessening. My range of vision and keen hearing were still super sensitive, but not with nearly the clarity as before. Color me depressed. To experience Creation in such vibrant terms, to journey into its inner depths, and then to see the ability come to an end. A match burst into radiance to fizzle out. It brought home the realization that the world was too big and our time in it too measured for us to truly understand everything there was to know.

"What troubles you, Miss Moore?"

Thank goodness. He'd tucked away his grief to focus his energy on keeping watch, which apparently included over me.

"I'm just lost in my thoughts. Don't worry about me."

"That is a road…" He sighed. Abandoning his description of that unknown journey, he considered me while he said, "If you are able to continue, once we reach Butter Hill and go deeper into the Highlands, we should be beyond the patrol of the regulars. We will be free to take a meal."

I checked behind us. If the redcoats were taking the bait, it was with an enormous no-man's-land between us.

"Awesome." I smirked. "I'm thinking…sauteed mushrooms and onions on sirloin, with a side salad, and a pale ale. Lead on, Macduff."

"Hmm. Revenge shall not be mine this day, for this is not Birnam Wood. And in truth, I am glad of it. Though you may bear the strength of Scottish kings, I grow weary."

"Well, I am kinda cold."

Jonathan chuckled. "But no Lady Macbeth. Mayhaps, a fire as our reward."

Bitter and sweet was a favorite combination of mine. It ghosted across my tongue in a variety of past delights as I watched him, a remembrance of artisan brews, rich chocolates, bakery breads, and specialty coffees. Although I wished his smile had been more simply crafted, given all the memories haunting him, I was grateful for its return.

Stroking the length of Felaróf's neck, he clicked his tongue and resumed our journey. His palm remained at its affectionate station, a random *pat, pat* adding to the percussive tune of our passage.

A stone rolled underneath Felaróf's hoof. It disrupted the horse's gait, jostling me. Jonathan grasped the saddle, as if readying to hoist us from a potential fall, although the horse had recovered within an instant. Another few steps, and my body synchronized with the motion of the giant horse.

Barely there at first, the hint of his touch floated between us. As the rocking gait of the horse continued, the edge of his hand came to rest against mine. Still, his gaze roamed the empty spaces between the plump vines clinging to ancient trees. A finger brushed its curve. Before it could float away, the rumbling of his throat a precursor, I wrapped my pinky around his. A rough palm slid over my skin and closed. I rolled my hand over, welcoming our humble embrace as our fingers intertwined. The cold didn't bother me again.

Chapter Sixteen

Rustling disturbed me. It was a lone foot away.

With my eyes clenched and my muscles tensing, my sleep-deprived mind was in a whirlwind, desperate to remember where I was, then where I'd stashed the steel pistol, then moving on to worry about whether it'd still be tucked under the bag Jonathan had given me for a pillow, or would I have accidentally knocked it out of reach during my fitful dreaming.

My mind was set at ease when my companion began twittering.

Yep. Brilliant blue, pewter streaks, cute and stubby tail—Jonathan's bluebird, rustling up breakfast near my face. Granted, the ick-factor of my feathered alarm clock, set to *snap, crackle* as the bug in his beak popped into pieces, was…well, maximum nasty.

"Don't suppose you come with a snooze button." I chuckled, breathing a relieved sigh that my wake-up call arose from the benign end of the spectrum. I stumbled to standing, which sent him fluttering overhead. "Oh, no. It's okay. Come back," I called up the steep incline of the ravine that'd concealed us for the night.

A horse whinnied above me, muted by the lush wilderness that'd ceased to be a pathway several miles prior. My back was aching something fierce, and the horrendous creak from my knees was so loud, it was a wonder the redcoats we'd hoped to avoid hadn't heard.

Riding, I'd discovered—or was it rediscovered?—wasn't my thing. The second Jonathan had selected a location to serve as our hidey-hole, I'd slid to the bottom, where years-worth of fallen leaves blanketed the area, and passed out, exhausted, long before he'd finished constructing the promised campfire. Surrounded by varying gradients of hillside, our humble digs were tolerant of additional light.

Apparently, he'd risen before me, taking care of business—so to speak—or prepping Felaróf for the final leg of our trek to West Point. My own turn with Mother Nature was an issue that was going to require serious attention, so I was counting the minutes. He'd promised we were close. Better mean we could walk the rest of the way, because my inner thighs were protesting from saddle burn.

The far end of the ravine rose straight up, like a giant wall. It was split in the middle, through which runoff from an unknown water source splashed down. A pool formed at the base, but there was plenty of dry, flat space around it within the earthy basin for our temporary bedding. I took advantage of Jonathan's absence to clean up. Absolutely ice cold. My armpits didn't really need... Yeah, they did.

My little friend alighted on my bag and pecked at its weave, then fluttered to the ground, disappearing behind its bulk. It shifted.

"What are you doing?" I laughed, amused by a *whomp*. Its weight was the clear victor, a Goliath to his tiny size. Watching him grasp the flap with his claws, presumably on a quest for better fare than bugs, started my stomach on an audible rant. He paused to eye me, as if wondering why I was making funny noises at him. "Breakfast, coming up," I announced.

Jonathan's bags were missing.

Which was fine. We needed to get packing...

I couldn't hear Felaróf anymore.

After numerous laps within the ditch searching for another solution, my own personal racetrack around Worryville, I decided I didn't have a choice. He'd been gone for too long. And I had to pee, like desperately, but Luck being the fickle gal she was, it would all but guarantee things would return to systems normal in Awkward Central. Meaning, if I attempted anything in our tight quarters, I'd get caught with my pants down.

Crap.

Stop thinking about it.

Jonathan's bird, Cleophes—assuming the little guy wasn't part of a whole flock of winged companions and answered to a different name— flitted along a branch overhead, monitoring my miserable impression of a salamander scaling the incline. As I neared the top, he lifted into the treetops. Several casual swings around the neighborhood later, he settled into an evergreen further up the path and began a light-hearted aria. I chanced peeking over the lip of the ravine.

Quiet. Empty.

I stretched my limited senses until my head ached from straining.

He left me.

No, there were plenty of explanations.

He left.

I slipped, shooting down the incline, the ravine's walls rushing skyward, then transforming into the cold marble of a courthouse, the halls empty. Business done for the day; ours had been the last case by design. Judge Mitola offered a sympathetic glance before vacating the bench.

Papers were scattered in front of me on the respondent's table, blurred by either the haziness in my memory still clearing or the numbness reawakening. My attorney sitting next to me was muttering platitudes and gathering the documents.

Damage done. I'd been powerless to stop it. Our house would be under contract of sale by week's end. Our house. My home. Irreconcilable differences. I'd offered an uncontested divorce. He refused, even though he'd been the one to file. How had I never before recognized his capacity for such cruelty? Justin, with a satisfied smirk, in his latest Armani suit, gloating over his iron-clad prenup, strutted away with his slutty, very pregnant, former paralegal on his arm.

And so, the scene faded.

I slumped to the ground, not really aware of where I was. Mud seeped through my linen pants, cold and coppery. Weathered brown leaves, speckled with fungi, lazed along a pool of water at my hip. It took a moment to remember why. I followed the flow splattering against the ravine wall upward, to the source. The top of the hill was swallowed by dense foliage scrambling among towering pines. But the emotions dredged from the latest replay of my life weren't done with me, leaving me as raw as I'd felt upon discovering I was about to be homeless.

You aren't going to let your ex humiliate you all over again, are you?

I picked my sorry ass up, out of the mire, just like I did the first time.

Chapter Seventeen

The sensation of bathwater swimming with baby oil clung to me as I emerged from the ravine. It tugged at my leather satchel, stretching the hem of my cloak behind me like a cape. Swirls of starlight flowed into place after I pierced the sizeable dome covering our secret oasis. Like the shifting colors on a bubble, the silver waves mixed and danced, resituating themselves to maintain a translucent wall. The view of the distant pool underneath dissipated until a massive obstruction of thornbushes appeared there instead. Not the height of the wall on the other side or the break where the water streamed or even the drop into the ditch itself, though I could still see the silver dome while I stood close by.

Fairytale magic later. Pee first.

Then I'd find Jonathan and rain down something far more unpleasant on him for his unexcused absence…then try not to cry with relief that I'd found him. Was it so hard for a guy to leave a note on the nightstand?

A little way down the path rumored to have been there once upon a time, I separated a cluster of bushes to improvise a covered latrine. Of sorts.

A twig tumbled onto my head.

Cleophes hopped closer, apparently curious about nature's calling splattering the forest floor beneath him. "Seriously. Too curious, don't you think? Give a girl some space." I shooed him.

He flew off. Twittering from across the invisible roadway meant he hadn't gone far.

Oh hell.

Trouble—my dear old frenemy— materialized, sporting three pointed leaves among the nearest cluster of pseudo toilet paper. I pleaded with the doorway to lost memories to pretty please open and send me a lesson on telling apart poison ivy from less noxious plants.

And they had mildew splotches.

Was it Monday? Because, the day was shaping—

A streak of silver lightning flew into my face, hovering in front of me and shrieking. Cleophes, monstrously unhappy about something. He bolted like a shot.

Sure, Mayhem. Join the party.

I made quick use of the leaves and hoped I wouldn't pay for it later. The bird reappeared to yell some more while I was whisking up my pants, then darted back the way he came, deeper into the woods. Deciding he probably knew best, I jogged after him.

Just as I was hoisting myself onto a perch sufficiently out of reach, the first male voice carried. I pressed my back into the trunk, hoping my hiding spot was as imperceptible from the roadway as the imaginary road itself, and balanced my legs along the length of the branch. A funky bump on a log, mid-altitude, in a place called Butter Hill, while possibly cooking up an allergic reaction in my nether region—a month's worth of Mondays.

Friend or foe? Not that accent, appearance, or even uniform was an absolute indicator of allegiance.

One miniature millimeter at a time, I shifted the leather bag into my lap from where it hung at my side. The cool steel within helped ground my trembling fingers, though I didn't dare pull the pistol out. Not right away, anyhow. Sunlight glinting off metal would draw unwanted attention, which prevented me from checking whether it was loaded. Fingering the hammer, I felt a flint in its grip but didn't risk clicking it into place to strike, afraid the sound might carry. Better believe I had it ready.

So frustrating that the side effects of the pact hadn't lasted. I'd have cranked that dial to a hundred-and-ten percent. Still, my mere mortal senses detected two distinct speakers getting closer. Passing behind me. Crunching through the leaves down the path.

One, two, three, peek and…

You're a nasty bitch, Fate.

His Majesty's Best, deep in conversation while performing a half-hearted sweep of the area as they moved. Gold star to Jonathan. He'd fulfilled his mission and led them away from the river, right to me.

One paused, pointing toward something in the opposite direction.

I ducked behind the tree. Pimple on a stick. Chocolate-cloaked cocoon. Whatever they mistook me for, I didn't care, just so long as they ignored the wilderness oddity listening in.

Oh fu—

I glared at my sudden lap warmer staring up at me. Luckily for my feathered friend and me, my shocked scream was internal. Then again, redcoats wouldn't give two hoots about a wren-sized bird. I was the one destined for a cage if caught. Unless they recognized me…

His head bobbed up and down three times.

You've got to be kidding me.

"Cleophes, right?" I whispered.

Single head bob.

"O-kay. How many redcoats we got?"

Three head bobs this time.

"You sure there's three?"

Nod, nod, nod.

Great. After everything that'd happened, why shouldn't I talk to a bird?

I pondered my unusual blue friend, keenly aware that my intel on the soldiers' location was growing staler with each indecisive moment. He tipped his head to eye me.

Why not? I'm freaking nuts.

"I want you to go see what they're doing."

Cleophes didn't budge.

"Please?"

He shuddered and tucked his head into his plumped-up body.

So much for that theory.

I clamped my eyes shut, wishing on the foolish hope that my heightened tracking skills would return. There was a gentle rustling of feathers. I caught the tail end of him disappearing around the tree trunk, toward the location where I'd last seen the redcoats.

All right, progress.

I hoped.

Of course, assuming he did understand and was assisting me, there was still the itty-bitty matter of translating what my little scout uncovered, because I wasn't fluent in tweeting. Head bobs were one thing; I doubted we were going to get far with charades.

If the soldiers had sallied forth, I reasoned, an angry flash of uniforms would've appeared in my periphery, and there was enough vegetation surrounding my pine tower that, if they were closing in, I'd know it before they reached the base.

Nope. They were stuck in park. Why?

I sought the knob of the pistol's trigger and grasped the hammer, ready to cock the weapon if necessary.

"Lieutenant?" a voice shouted down the forest road.

The call having gone unanswered, the two redcoats returned to the area behind me then continued. A careful look around the other side of the tree revealed the man they were waiting for. His hand was raised, smoothing the air, as if gliding over the invisible length of piano keys.

"What see you, Private?" the lone officer asked.

Or he's feeling the dome's boundaries.

His fingers slid upward, along its surface. Silver currents shifted at his touch, flowing in the same direction. Their wake swirled backward to reinforce what'd been disturbed. He shook his hand, as if trying to rid himself of the same oil-like cling I'd experienced. Facing his subordinates, he whisked a handkerchief from his outer coat and pressed it to his fingers. Crimson stained the cloth when he put it away.

One man cleared his throat and stepped forward, the other private making room for him before following his example. The first searched where his commanding officer had been examining the seemingly empty air. He took his time formulating a response. "You can see a fair distance. Naught looks to be disturbed. The trees be solid with no noticeable breaks in the bramble. It is as thickly o'er run as the road we trod."

The lieutenant presented the same question to the second private, who met the eyes of his fellow, then added his agreement. "Oh. Aye, sir."

The confused man hadn't a clue.

"Is it not like, gentlemen, that our quarry did rest here the night?" the lieutenant asked.

A chill ran through me. I shrank behind the tree trunk and clutched the grip of my pistol tighter.

One shot was all I'd have before they could return fire. Though honestly, which was crazier: taking the shot or just surrendering if found? *If* the pistol was loaded, that was, because such useful information was naturally locked away in my mind, waiting for…what? A rainier day?

Aiming for the lieutenant was the smartest course. Assuming it'd work on him, or else I might have serious problems, like of the penny-dreadful variety, requiring holy water or salt or maybe—

My imagination was welcome to shut up.

The first redcoat begged his commanding officer's pardon. "I see not what it is that do speak so."

"Never you mind," he replied. "Manifestly, he is not here. We shall move on."

It took a second time, ordering the privates to continue, before I heard them shuffling onward into the wide, green yonder.

Bon voyage, farewell, and good riddance. They could go on their merry way. I wasn't going to interrupt their progress.

Except for the lieutenant.

Two sets of footfalls, instead of three, floated up to me. Leaving him behind. Still. So still. As if he was waiting for something. I held my breath. A whisper of fabric snagged on bark, almost at the gate of my Highland tower. Another step carried him closer, to linger under my tree. It popped the thread.

Please don't let him see me. Please.

Heat from a rising phoenix engulfed my torso. Biting my lower lip as it exploded over me—scorching along my limbs, sparking the hairs on my body, swirling, raging, plunging through me—I struggled to remain quiet. Myth burst into life, I was awash in brilliant flames, ignited by the silver key thrumming against my chest. A celestial fire reborn.

For an agonizing moment, I worried the silver blaze would spark the gunpowder in the steel pistol and literally shoot me into the heavens. The notion fizzled into the more rational fear of the lieutenant witnessing the living conflagration.

Peace, a voice whispered to me.

A subtle *whoosh*, and the light dissolved, sounding like a puff of smoke bursting free. Or perhaps it was the breath I'd been holding, relieved the searing heat had ceased. I gasped for air and waited.

How could he *not* have seen?

I thought I heard the man hum.

A chickadee called, chirruping its name from close by. The voices of the two privates drifted on the wind as they walked, the men apparently unaware the sound was being funneled our way. One wondered aloud, "Odd, that. Nothing but trees and scrub. Been nothing but trees, rocks, and scrub for a time." The other didn't answer him. "Sure would be nice to make way to camp with the others. Have ourselves proper rations."

"Aye."

"What is it he do search for? Reckon the lieutenant has gone mad. Eh?"

"I reckon 'tis best to say naught on the matter."

They fell silent, each turning in a different direction to search the woods for signs of more practical concerns to the average soldier. Only then did the subject of their conversation address the open air: "*He's mad that trusts in the tameness of a wolf, a horse's health, a boy's love, or a whore's oath.*"

The lieutenant traipsed after them, the sound of his feet tearing through the undergrowth loud as thunder.

Chapter Eighteen

Holy, effing, son of a… Damn it.

He could see the… The lieutenant…he knew Jonathan had been there, left…left something behind. Something that bled him, sliced his fingers like a knife, but favored me. Like it was protecting our refuge, protecting me. It…

Fuck!

Breathe, Savvy. Think.

Okay…

What wasn't clear was whether he could see *through* the protection to the ditch inside. He seemed to know, or so he claimed, Jonathan wasn't there. His "quarry." Which meant he was hunting us, which meant he might return. Or send someone else to investigate.

Either way, our hidey-hole was now a death trap, and I couldn't afford to stay there any longer. If the lieutenant knew about it, I had to assume that—sooner or later—others would too.

Freaking redcoat. Why had he left me alone? If he could see the dome, odds were, he saw the key's magic exploding around me. It was a virtual grand finale of fireworks.

Or could he?

At first, it'd hurt like hell. Until I relaxed, then I could sense Jonathan's presence permeating every aspect of it, enveloping me, protecting me. An invisibility inferno.

Or maybe my unwanted, Shakespeare-spouting guest just wasn't close enough to see it. Assuming his tracking skills didn't extend to mystical third eyes or divining muskets or spiritual garbage or whatever other horrific fantasy stuff was out there.

The ditch still presented as an entangled mess of all things unpleasant, with thorns sprouting from a solid forest floor, lacking any sign of a drop or waterfall. In the southern direction, the triumvirate of British authority were tiny, red pinpricks receding into the woods.

Deciding to chance it, I abandoned my unearthly tower and darted into the foliage closest to our hideaway. Gleaming silver shimmered into sight once I was right on top of it. Hesitant, I tapped a fingertip on its surface, then with more confidence, ran my palm along the barrier's circumference, just as the lieutenant had. To me, it felt inviting, eager to welcome me into its warm embrace, to where I'd be safe. My hand was free of blood.

I dashed inside and slid partway down the incline, beyond view of anyone passing above me on the ridge.

What were my options?

I couldn't stay. That much was clear. Returning north by traversing the nonexistent roadway to search for Jonathan would be stupid—my Gretel to his Hansel, lost in the woods. Or win me an unexpected sojourn at Redcoat Resort. Somewhere on the western side of Butter Hill was the British encampment.

Enough time had passed that I was seriously worried about Jonathan. It occurred to me he might've been captured, and it was the other half of his dynamic duo, Alexander, they were hunting.

Process of elimination left pressing eastward toward the river, then follow it south to Moore's Folly or else hide out on the bank until Captain Machin and his number arrived. Either way, I needed help, particularly if a rescue excursion was in order.

But another option warranted consideration. Guarantees of safety weren't included with the river road. Plus, I risked drawing attention to what was happening there if I was spotted. Jonathan's task was to lead the soldiers *away* from Machin's men and their journey to West Point. Already moving in the same direction was a trio of redcoats. Jonathan wasn't there to stop them. I was.

What was I thinking? Defending myself was one thing, not that I'd been put to the test. To actively hunt down three of the world's best army? Sure, let's wave my steel pistol like a cape in front of the bull, a weapon equipped with this vague memory of a guy called "A Wall" or "The Wall" teaching me how to use it. Plus, there was a definite association of fear at the flash of its flint. I was no match against three trained soldiers, one of whom was apparently gifted like Jonathan.

Not like Jonathan, something whispered. *Like you.*

What the hell?

My extraneous internal monologue went mute.

Excellent.

Supposing the lieutenant had known I was there and chosen to leave me alone…doubtful he'd be so magnanimous as to forgive a second disruption to his journey if I followed them. But if I didn't, and they uncovered the activities at West Point undetected, the British Army would unleash terror upon the Continentals and whatever they were building there.

Or I might very well have become the country mouse he intended to trail back to its nest and destroy the whole mess of us. Which meant I couldn't seek out Machin.

I sighed.

"Did you see what they're doing?" I asked the quiet rustling in the branch above me.

With a little coaxing, Cleophes fluttered onto my offered hand. He bobbed his head up and down.

"Did you see where they went?"

He nodded again, then plumped his feathers to retreat into himself. I stroked his chest to reassure him we were okay. Well, he was. I must be crazy to have contemplated what I was about to do. "Jonathan needs to know what's happening. I'm—"

The bird amscrayed to the north without hearing the rest of the plan; my surprised plea for his return, too late. Add birds to the list of creatures that've abandoned me. Well done, me.

Squeezing the silver key for luck, I tucked it into my shirt for safekeeping and did what every nerve in my body told me was madness. I left our haven behind and pursued the bloody-backed bastards.

Chapter Nineteen

The lieutenant stopped.

I ducked behind my latest post in Fort Woodland. The safest tactic I could devise for *Operation: Insanity* was to locate the Redcoats Three, getting close enough to ensure it was them and not a different trio of bad news, then storm another treetop so I could spy on them, just in case they circled back. Wait, wait some more, until they'd moved out of range again. Repeat. Repeat. Repeat.

The journey took twice as long as necessary, what with the lackadaisical approach the lieutenant had, which seemed to annoy the two privates. They'd find themselves farther ahead and have to stop and twiddle their thumbs, one time releasing an audible huff of frustration. Meanwhile, he strolled along as if it was a bright, summer's day and there wasn't a war threatening to bombard us at any moment.

He did it again. His hand was directing a soundless tune, feeling out the melody on the breeze, a silver ring glinting from his little finger in time to the imaginary rhythm. Its missing white glove dangled casually from his other palm. The movement made my head ache, as if I'd seen it before and the curse didn't want me to know. Or done it before.

If Jonathan had gone this way—perhaps to check in at the fortifications, prior to me tagging along, to see which way the wind would blow with the commanding officers regarding one or the other of us—could that explain what the lieutenant was doing? Could he...*we* track someone like my wilderness tour guide? Home in on Jonathan's powers, magic, aura, whatever?

Next time I was on the ground floor, I planned to test the various theories taunting me and see if I could detect something in the air.

The lieutenant admired the sunlight filtering through the canopy overhead. The curls of his dark hair fluttered against his neck from under his upturned hat. Dark plumage danced on top along with them. Cocking his head to the side uncovered a single lock of pure white wrapped around itself, tucked beside his ear.

Through the entire, insufferable saunter, the lieutenant had kept his eyes front, never searching behind himself—unlike his subordinates—yet he maintained a sizeable distance between us, despite my efforts to creep closer. It felt like he was playing with me.

A rockslide rumbled ahead of us, close enough to be only a few minutes' walk, even by Officer Sunshine's standards. Multiple male voices yelling accompanied it, including a few calling for a sergeant.

West Point.

Privates-Redcoat shot glances at each other before separating to opposite sides of the muddy road and taking cover in the foliage. Since the hidden trail had joined a better-traveled section, I shared their concern about maintaining the center lane on the wide, open highway, what with my own past loyalties being in question to all concerned. The slower of the two struggled to tug back the hammer on his weapon. He'd jammed it, and the clattering from his attempts wasn't exactly subtle. His partner ducked his head and crossed himself.

The lieutenant, on the other hand, snapped out of his musical reverie. "Shall we?" he asked no one in particular.

Sheathing his bare hand with the white glove, he strolled past the two hidden privates, undaunted by the ongoing commotion. The red sash tied around his waist bounced against his side, mingling with the silver cords dangling from his sword's scabbard. Him steering closer to the sidelines than before suggested his otherwise careless attitude was far more deliberate, as was the effect of his hand remaining stationed on the portion of his belt adjacent to his weapon's hilt.

A look of *here-we-go-again* passed between the enlisted men. They dashed onto the road after him, though a sweep of his arm stalled them from taking position in front.

I swallowed hard. It was act now or see Jonathan's mission fail.

C-lick once, *click* all the way, finger on the knob, and...

The blast from the steel pistol cascaded along the rocky corridor. Endless miles of vegetation were powerless against the deafening sound. I was shocked when one of the privates cried out and grabbed at his arm. It had literally been a long shot from my perch.

The lieutenant whipped around, no doubt seeking the source of the attack. I flung myself behind the tree trunk, begging the smoke from the discharge to dissipate faster. A growl and heavy footfalls rushed in my direction. Add in the scrape of his sword letting loose from its scabbard, with no chance of me being able to abandon ship and certainly no hope of outrunning the man, it was enough to make anyone queasy. I fumbled through my bag, desperate to find the tin ammunition case. Targeted vomiting from on high wasn't going to delay his killing me forever.

The gunfire shocked the inhabitants of West Point into a temporary silence. Very temporary. A roar arose almost immediately in the form of orders being yelled and at least a dozen men charging in our direction. Credit to the uninjured private, he did his king justice by firing his shot. Once the size of the welcome wagon became apparent, however, the wisdom of it being better to walk to the American fortress as a whole man rather than receive a complimentary ride there as a dead one led their hands to raise in surrender. Their weapons were confiscated, each man searched and questioned—though the salt of losing my enhanced senses burned, because I couldn't actually witness the encounter, just hear it—then they were led away under armed escort.

Listening from my nosebleed seat, tucked out of sight, I debated whether to reveal myself or wait until the arena emptied. I might be bound for the Continental camp as a friend to the Cause, but the remaining soldiers patrolling below me were on edge. My sudden appearance might not go over well, regardless of how apple-pie, All-American my tale was. Then there was the matter of the lieutenant. Prisoner or not, he rattled me. I preferred missing the opportunity to make his acquaintance.

Anonymity being best all around, I stayed silent and allowed the action to unfold without me. What I wouldn't have given for a cup of coffee…and a muffin, maybe blueberry…and a book…but mostly a muffin. Lacking all those things, I nestled into the folds of my cloak and resigned myself to a lengthy, zero-calorie stay.

A large, brown spider with yellow, banded legs and spots descended on a gossamer thread toward my head. I shied aside, grateful a friendly breeze relocated him onto the tree trunk before his journey brought us face-to-face.

After everything, there had to be a freaking spider?

Its landing zone being an apparently satisfactory location, the spider attached the loose thread to the bark and resumed climbing to repeat the process. Drop, attach, climb, line to line, straight to another, stretching again—remaining in its own little territory—then around and spiraling around, circling inward.

It was finishing its web with a zipper stitch running vertically down the center when another round of boy scouts returned without additional jail fodder.

At my utter wit's end, the nausea from idling on an empty tank having swayed me into believing that being taken prisoner would be a gift if it meant at least a stale biscuit to ease the cramping in my guts, I attempted to climb down. Limited options for shifting my weight while a mile high during that eternity—or so my beleaguered brain insisted—had erased all sense of having an ass to go numb. The rush of blood through my legs reduced them to rubber. I froze, gritting my teeth, and waited for the needlework on my derriere to cease.

Solid ground felt awesome. Going to the bathroom was even better, as was the noise from my clumsy efforts remaining uninvestigated by my Continental neighbors.

The sun had reached the mountain's peak. Clouds tinted like poppies and tangerines basked above in colorful clumps. It was time to make my entrance before the impending night made everyone twitchy again. Squaring my shoulders, I took a deep breath for luck, clenched my bag's shoulder strap for emotional support, assumed a false attitude of confidence, and waltzed toward Moore's Folly like I owned the place.

Chapter Twenty

"Dobry Boże!"

"Shit!" I damn near jumped out of my skin, having stepped into the clearing just as a figure emerged from behind a lone tree. Neither of us had seen the other until his incredible appearing act, smack right into me. His head had been buried in the large document he was rolling up. It smooshed with a sickening crunch as our chests collided and arms shoved our respective attacker away.

"Identify yourselves." Several brown uniforms charged us, long guns drawn; an inevitable chorus line to his startling performance. Their muzzles danced around him once he'd been recognized and gave me the starring role.

"Okay, now. I'm not here to hurt anyone," I said.

Of all the thoughts to have in that moment, my eggs-over-easy for brains had the audacity to worry about whether my palms were filthy from my adventures while I showcased how unarmed I was. Well…not in an open-carry kinda way.

Determined not to drop his document, Mr. Tree Hugger had simultaneously engaged in a strange samba variation, limbs flailing as he struggled to regain his balance, maintain his grasp on the crunched roll, and grab for a sword, each step while assuming *en garde*. A rectangular fur cap tumbled to the ground during his routine. His cinnamon curls rejoiced at being freed and soared into an outer orbit.

Mother of Swords.

My confidence fled toward the safety of the woods without me at the sight of his crazy-long weapon, crowned by an imposingly broad, steel hilt.

The man squinted at me, then embarked on a round trip of surveying my clothes to reexamining my face. His words took a side excursion, lost in a foggy patch until my starved mind found a translation. His accent was that thick. "You is girl?"

"Colonel?" a browncoat asked him.

"Yeah," I answered my curly-haired challenger, the apparent commanding officer.

A voice questioned the guy next to him if he'd heard correctly. Another made a snide comment under his breath.

"*Cisza*," the colonel ordered them and whisked Mother Sword back into its leather scabbard. A delicate pop snapped the dented area out of his document. It was unrolled for a brief scan of its contents. Glancing back at me, he then stooped to retrieve his hat and shook dirt from its dark fur. The crumbs of a decrepit leaf fluttered after.

The soldiers shifted the balance of their hefty guns, appearing uncertain.

"What you do?" He waved a hand at me. "You is man." A snicker drove him to round on the others. "You fear girls? Go, seek for real enemy."

Multiple "aye, sirs" met the command, and the crowd dispersed, curious gawking over shoulders and another snicker or two notwithstanding. Still, the weight of his gaze scrutinizing me as he tucked his paper treasure under his arm kept me on high alert.

He stepped closer.

I pounced on my bag, grasping at the flap to where I'd concealed the steel pistol, which led us both to freeze.

Floating his hands outward, he rotated their empty surface forward. Unarmed. Non-threatening.

So, I mirrored his example, though my offering held little interest for him.

"*Do czorta.*" He frowned at his palms. The sincere regret in his voice broke the heightened tension, and I burst out laughing. They were a fortune teller's delight. Dirt paved the lines in his skin, rendering their pathways obvious. Ink stains ran plentifully along the length of his middle and forefinger. When I demonstrated how we matched, he joined in, amused.

"*Fuj.*" He batted his hands together to clear away some of the filth. "Andrzej Tadeusz Bonawentura Kościuszko."

Completely baffled, I apologized for not understanding.

He explained, "I am called Andrzej Tadeusz Bonawentura Kościuszko. You call Thaddeus Kościuszko."

"Oh boy," I chuckled, embarrassed.

"If it is for best…" He gave me a sympathetic smile. "…you call me 'Colonel.'"

Stubborn as my history reported me to be, I managed—after a few tries with him correcting me—to get somewhere close to pronouncing his last name: "Kuz-*choose*-koe."

He applauded my inelegant efforts, anyway.

"How you is called?" he asked.

"I'm Savannah. Savannah Moore."

Thus, our happy interlude screeched to an abrupt halt.

When I signaled for a time-out, because I was several points behind the serious flurry of Polish and broken English rushing to uncover what he wanted to know, he asked whether I spoke French. The hidden recesses of my mind suggested I did. Memories of poster-plastered classrooms or even associated delicacies or relevant voyages that might've given a vague indication of a *when* or *where* I'd learned it remained imprisoned in my personal oubliette, however.

So, we gave *à la française* a whirl. He was fluent in ways I could never hope to be, but we managed by polyglotting and employing the occasional pantomime.

Kościuszko's concern was the purpose of my visit, which I told him was to connect with Captain Machin. Familiar with Machin, the colonel pressed me instead on the subject of my relationship to the Moores. "Stephen is a Moore of many family."

Stephen… I had a brother by that name. *Crrr-ee-eek.* I cringed at the sensation of fingernails dragging over a chalkboard as the prison door leaked a simple thought before snapping shut again: *Not this Stephen.*

Since that also ruled out a brother-in-law, I assumed—or hoped, really, because the intensity of the colonel's stormy-gray stare was concerning—I said, "Not to me."

Justin had denounced our union. I'd rather eat dirt than claim any association to his family, regardless of whether I was traipsing onto their property. Then again, my battle against bitterness being far from over during this second round of remembering, if there was a connection, I vowed to steal some baked goods. Just because.

"Moore is not protector of you?" There was a gravity to his question. And hesitation. "It is not Captain Machin." He glanced at my chest before returning his focus to my eyes.

"No," was all I was comfortable telling him.

How could he have known about the key, tucked under layers of clothing? Was he like the British lieutenant? The very thought made me shiver.

"Ah, you feel cold," he said. "Let us go to the Red House. It is certain to be warm."

"The *Red* House?"

"You do not know of it?"

"Should I?"

Kościuszko tipped his chin back in thought. "The officers are there. It is they would know when Captain Machin is to arrive. *Chodź.*" A grand flourish of his arm indicated the way.

Successful completion of *Operation: Insanity* having emboldened me, or else starvation making me entirely stupid, I stepped closer as if to pass by. Instead, I snagged his hand. We gawked at one another with surprise.

He whipped out a dagger from under his cloak.

Scurrying beyond his reach—his touch having alleviated one concern—I confessed, "Captain Jonathan Wythe is my protector. D-do you know him? He'd be really grateful you helped me."

A swirling, chestnut-brown firestorm gathered around him. My nerves took umbrage with my severe lack of common sense. "Okay." I held my hands up as a reminder of their filthy but barren expanse. "That was really stupid, but I swear, I'm not here to hurt anyone."

"Why are you here?" he continued in French.

"Like I said. To help Captain Wythe and Captain Machin."

"Are you armed?"

"Of course."

At my offer to show him—recognizing *he* was the closest light source, which might mean a pat down was about to ensue, given how dark it'd gotten—he ordered me to lower my leather bag to the ground, then divide my cloak, which exposed my empty waistband. After inspecting the contents of my bag, including the steel pistol I'd told him was in there, he nodded his head, satisfied. Or less suspicious, I suppose, since the chestnut fire extinguished.

"Captain Wythe, eh?" Kościuszko ruffled the curls at the back of his head, then offered some free advice before he escorted me to Chez Officers.

Chapter Twenty-One

Colonel Kościuszko escorted me across the vast expanse of what was called "the Plain," leading us toward the river. Campfires washed over a sea of tents and decrepit wooden huts, flickering in warm hues. Soldiers—enshrouded in uniforms as varied in colors as state of tatters—kept watch, patrolling a makeshift wall of carefully balanced tree branches bound together with mud. It stretched to both the northern and southern views of the water, effectively cutting off the peninsula of the Plain from the surrounding region. A battalion of wooden Xs, sharpened into spikes, guarded the outer perimeter, threatening to impale enemy riders charging from the woods.

At the northern-most corner, we descended a steep incline toward a shady path that trailed the water's edge. Guards patrolled the rocky passage at random intervals, one of whom insisted on receiving the evening's "countersign" before we were allowed to pass, despite identifying the colonel by name while making his demand.

Though his tone was conversational, Kościuszko continued to question me about my relationship with Jonathan. Picking my words with care—since a vague leeriness haunted me whenever questions about my protector, and now my own past, arose—I shared how we were seeking news of my family but had been waylaid by our efforts to assist Captain Machin and uncover redcoats in the area. When I described my shadowing the British trio en route, the colonel's pace quickened.

"Red House" proved to be an apt nickname for the two-story, clapboard colonial. Windowed dormers in the curved roof suggested a third floor with living space. Matching stone chimneys stood sentinel on either side of the house, and a single-story addition extended to the left. Mountainous walls of trees and stone loomed over the clearing—the demarcation line between civilization and the wilds of the West.

Another whispered password to the guards at the front door bought us admittance. Several aides navigated the narrow halls with volumes of papers, maps, and other documents being put to bed in a side room. Kościuszko led us into a back parlor, where multiple officers had crammed themselves together with too many men and too little furniture. A watery stew was being ladled by a private into whatever mug or bowl each officer had managed to carry with him during his adventures.

Anything that could be called into service as chairs—an old, splintered barrel included—was gathered around three boards balanced on wooden horses. A large fireplace ate up the entire backwall, belching a stifling heat into the room, despite a window being cracked for air. The room shrank all the more as aides squeezed themselves in and out throughout supper, trying to reach their respective commanding officer with some business that was rarely deemed worthy of the interruption.

Revelry plunged several decibels as the colonel and I entered. Confused stares, that took in my mannish attire and less-than-tidy appearance, struggled to make sense of me. One aide snorted as he brushed against me, accompanied by a comical gesture of sorts, if the reaction from an officer who stifled a smirk and waved him off was any indication.

Lone female surrounded by a pack of hungry brass in formal military. My life improved daily.

"How now, Mr. Kościuszko? Have the Highlanders come tae invade us?" Amusement filled the speaker's voice, whose own Scottish brogue colored the remark. It tickled the others, who chuckled at the joke. He was probably the oldest man in the room, somewhere in his mid-forties, with a high forehead that led to more salt than pepper hair. Uniform: blue.

"I bring answer to mystery," Kościuszko replied to his greeter.

"And what mystery was tha'?" He laughed.

"The phantom ally."

At the pronouncement, eyebrows raised. Intentional glances passed among the men, supplemented by a mix of everything from "well, well" mumbled by one man, to disbelief from another. Our greeter, the apparent superior officer, was good enough to send an appraising look my way as he leaned forward in his makeshift chair. The strands of his epaulets kept in perfect dress as they marched back and forth across his shoulders in unison.

With a *well-you-asked-for-it, now-be-our-guest* gesture, Kościuszko invited me to introduce myself. Around the rosy table, roll call consisted of him acknowledging each officer with a gracious gesture of his hand. My story of following the redcoats and firing the warning shot to alert the Continentals was retold, which earned me a seat at the table—a wobbly milking stool, situated where I could be easily scrutinized by all. A Private Lilley squeezed in a wooden box for my Polish escort along the wall.

I was questioned for some time, and I was grateful for it. Torture would've been far less inspiring. My lips spewed information lightning fast, since the reward for my cooperation was a hot meal and cider. Being my first meal of the day, at that late hour, I assured them their apologies for the meager offerings were unnecessary. What little I'd learned of the British movements was shared, along with a warning that none of my information was firsthand, aside from my own bloody encounters. Word of Captain Machin's imminent arrival pleased the room. News of Jonathan and Alexander's didn't generate as much excitement.

As if by simply speaking his name he should be called to duty, Jonathan was announced from the doorway behind me. Anxiety broke through his usual cool composure as he rushed in to address the room. "Sirs, please pardon my intrusion, I am just arrived and—"

"Captain Wythe." I stood to face him. "I'm fine. I'm not hurt."

Shock was replaced by relief, but then his difficult-to-read neutrality returned.

"Do you know everyone at the table?" I asked.

"Aside from General McDougall, I have not been so honored." And a tiny bit of suppressed frustration in my direction, it seemed, judging by the clenched fists being tucked behind his back. Really? A simple note, Mr. I-Will-Keep-All-the-Supplies-While-I-Vanish.

"Forgive me, sir." He bowed respectfully to the man who'd greeted Kościuszko and me. "I thought you to have been at headquarters."

"And dae mae movements displease ye, Captain?"

"I mean no offense, General." Jonathan placed a hand to his heart and bowed again, a nicety that McDougall responded to by staring.

"*We* are always pleased to receive you, General," the man on his left said, filling the silence. The debonair, black hat at his elbow retreated toward the edge of the improvised table when he turned in his place, causing him to brush against it. He was about early-forties with inky black hair and full sideburns, both tinged with gray, that framed his somewhat-recently shaven face. His brown uniform coat still carried signs from an excursion to the riverfront.

"This, if I caught everyone's names correctly," I tipped my chin toward the officer, "is Brigadier-General Samuel Holden Parsons. He's in command here."

"Only, madam, when the good general is not available to us," he said. I apologized, but McDougall waved it off.

Flustered at my political snafu, I then failed miserably at relinquishing hostess duties to the more experienced. McDougall insisted I finish circling the table, so we proceeded counter-clockwise with whom I thought were the higher-ranking officers first. "This is Colonel John Greaton, Colonel

Thomas Nixon, and Lieutenant-Colonel Rufus Putnam." I hoped like hell I got all the officers right. No one contradicted me.

"Sirs." Jonathan gave a deep bow from one side of the table to the other. "It is a pleasure and an honor. I am Captain Jonathan Wythe."

"Oh, we know well of you, Captain. Your reputation does precede you," Nixon said.

"Aye," McDougall agreed. "'Tis braw of the general tae share ye with us."

One of the men *hmphed* under his breath, but since the culprit was difficult to identify and the commanding officer didn't seem to disagree, the slight went unchallenged.

"Do you come directly from the general?" Greaton was curious to know.

"Nay, sir," Jonathan answered. "I come with news of Captain Machin and the general's order for the Works."

Parsons held a palm aloft. "As we have already been informed."

Jonathan paused, uncertain.

Crap. Super spy award…goes to someone else.

"Maybe it'd be a good idea to get Captain Wythe's take on things?" I suggested.

"He will be interrogated," Parsons answered, though the open invitation for such matters to begin led, instead, to a whole lot of eyeballing without questioning.

"O-kay. Awkward." There was only so much throat clearing I could indulge in before I had to carry on. "I'd also like to introduce Colonel Kościuszko. He's the engineer here and has been nice enough to escort me since I arrived."

"You have my thanks, Colonel." Jonathan extended a hand to him. Whatever secret handshake their people had, it wasn't obvious to the casual observer, but beyond a doubt, they recognized each other as kindred spirits, so to speak—their smiles broadened to greater than warm.

"*Pas de tout, Capitaine,*" the colonel said. "*Une femme extraordinaire, Mademoiselle* Phillips. *Vous êtes un homme audacieux qui prend une femme si étrange sous sa garde.*"

"*Qu'est-ce que c'est?*" Jonathan asked him while eyeing me.

Before I could respond, Nixon perked up with all the pomp the rickety, wooden crate he sat on would allow. "Aya, Kościuszko. Can you not learn English, man? 'Tis grating to the ears to hear that infernal dialect upon American soils."

"Best not let His Excellency hear you." Putnam laughed, flourishing the handkerchief he'd been using to wipe at his extended forehead. He tucked it smartly into his fawn-colored coat. "He has taken a fancy to that man… What the bother is his name? He has so many of them… Gilbert du Mortier."

Greaton looked down his long nose at him. "The Marquis de Lafayette?"

"The same."

Nixon snorted at them. He was so tall that when he leaned back, he practically spanned the river into New Jersey.

"Come now," Putnam responded. "He has the recommendation of Doctor Franklin."

"Anyone can have the recommendation of Doctor Benjamin Franklin, if they have the money, the women, or the wine to pay him."

"The Marquis does journey with an impressive entourage," Greaton allowed.

Apparently, the Frenchman had passed through West Point on his way from Albany to rejoin Headquarters at Valley Forge. The escort of seven horses and four "domestics" was still the talk of the camp several weeks later.

Meanwhile, Kościuszko's silent disapproval of the insults was lost under the mix of snickering and simple, thoughtful hums.

Parsons joined the fray, saying, "As I am told, an alliance has been formed with France. Many thanks to Ambassador Franklin. The arms and men as like traverse the seas to rally us already. Of course, we have still the approval of Congress standing before us."

"If 'tis the approval of the Congress tha' is needed," McDougall declared, "we shall see a treaty near the time tha' the beef does make its way tae the men."

"Hear, hear," the other officers agreed. Glasses were raised and drained.

Private Lilley was summoned into the room to bring another "cup of the creature." Knowledgeable laughs answered Parsons' quip: "If it is the best you seek, look to steal from the Crown, for the liquor Congress does not keep for itself is poor quality indeed."

Jonathan was given supper, as well. Reports that the cider was gone inspired McDougall to order a hogshead of rum to be opened and a gill allotted to the men on watch. Jonathan took advantage of the digression into politics to quietly ask me, "Why did you not wait for me?"

"Yeah, and where the hell were you?" I whispered back.

"Hunting. It was my intention to return before you woke." He glanced around the table. "You were protected."

Cautious about how to respond—in case one of the officers should overhear us, despite the growing rowdiness surrounding the virtues, or lack thereof, of the French and our latest ambassador, John Adams—I simply told him, "Our hiding place was discovered."

He blanched. "By whom?"

"Some lieutenant."

"Was he alone?" he pressed me.

"There were two other redcoats, but don't worry. They were captured and brought here."

He appeared anxious, but we were cut off. Nixon had zeroed in on our conversation. "What say you, Miss Phillips?"

Jonathan passed another confused glance over me. I flashed a smile, hoping we'd have a chance to talk in private about Kościuszko's warning before too long.

When I repeated myself, McDougall snapped, "Why was I no telt tha' an officer had been taken? I was led tae believe tha' we had but two enlisted men. Did ye know of this?"

Parsons appeared just as shocked and searched the table for support when he reported he had not. The others also denied any knowledge. My stomach sank.

"There were three," I insisted, watching Private Lilley leave as he was sent to fetch the surgeon. "Two privates and a lieutenant."

"Describe the lieutenant," Jonathan ordered. All eyes narrowed at me. His face registered recognition early in my description. "Lieutenant Porter Sharpe of the Sixty-Third," he informed the officers.

"The Bloodsuckers," Nixon noted.

"*Daingead!*" McDougall slammed his hand onto the boards, sending the menagerie of dishware into an uproar. The officers captured their stock as best they could before the floor became littered.

Greaton faced the general. "How could they have remained all this while without our learning of it?"

"What a time for the militia to abandon us," Putnam grumbled.

"Did no we receive report tha' they were despoiling Philadelphia?" McDougall demanded over the other officers.

"Most have left," Jonathan answered. "A flank company of the light infantry remain, under Captain Grey."

"Now we know how it is that Captain Wythe haunts the Highlands," Parsons put to the room.

Jonathan had been whispering to me that "Bloodsuckers" was the British unit's nickname. His head snapped to attention at the general's scornful remark.

"Where are they now, sir?" McDougall questioned him.

"Last report I had saw the main making to Schunnemunk Clove, driving toward the northern end and pressing men into service for the Crown. But I have seen others in smaller numbers roaming the river region of New Cornwall."

"How many?"

"I know not. I discovered signs of them, but was unable to track them for long." Jonathan glanced in my direction.

"Where, precisely?"

"Bother and 'nation! Why do you listen to the turncoat?" Nixon pointed at my protector. "He is like to betray us to the regulars once he has left us."

I gasped.

Jonathan was polite, but I heard his subtle frustration at the insult. "My information comes from the good people of Firthcliffe and New Windsor. We…" He included me with a tilt of his head. "…assisted the militia under Major DeForest less than three weeks prior and had news of their movements there. You may confirm with any or all, at your pleasure, sirs."

Fire in the hole. A rip-roaring battle between the curse and the information it sought to suppress commenced with a burst of stars shooting through my skull.

Seriously? He'd betrayed the British. Big deal, unless…was he playing both sides?

I gripped my clenched hands tighter against the next shot through my mind.

"What of the woman?" Greaton posed to the others.

"She will only parrot what she has been told." Nixon dismissed me. Uncertainty lingered over a few faces, at least.

Kościuszko reminded us he was still there when he drew me back into the conversation. "How is it you know the regulars and where they go?"

"Mostly from Captain Wythe." I rubbed my aching forehead. "Though I've seen redcoats myself. When I first arrived, at our camp, and coming here. Not a large number. Maybe two dozen, total."

"Where was this?" McDougall asked.

I sighed and admitted I didn't know the region, though I recounted Mr. Cloet's story about soldiers' westward march from a place called the

"Landing." A couple of officers seemed satisfied by the confirmation of Jonathan's report. Near passing grade.

McDougall silenced the rising debate, reminding everyone that all could be confirmed. Or denounced, he declared in Jonathan's direction. Then he welcomed in Doctor Hart, whose insistent ah-hemming from the time of his arrival threatened to leave him hoarse. Doc Impatience reported, "I have met two lobsters, neither of which was an officer. *I* had been informed that one suffered of a ball to the arm, but in truth, the private had barely a scratch."

Freaking bastard. I knew the lieutenant had charged toward me after I'd fired, but having ducked for cover, I didn't realize he'd escaped.

At being dismissed, the surgeon sniffed, then felt the need to add, "Hardly worth the interruption to my backgammon game," and slapped the dust from his hat in the doorway. Eyes rolled. I'd been proud as a new papa about that shot, so I took a modicum of glee in the officers' annoyance. His tune sweetened after McDougall ordered Private Lilley to give him a draw from the hogshead, in light of his service.

Greaton stopped them from leaving. "Are there letters?"

"Nay, sir."

"What of the foraging party, Private?" McDougall asked.

"No word yet, General."

Officer Land darkened.

"There will be naught for the regiments' dinner if they do not return come morning." Greaton grumbled.

"A flock of pigeons has been gathered," Lilley offered as his little ray of sunshine.

"Dismissed, Private."

"Damn'd waste of powder," was the consensus.

Which brought us back to the nerve-wracking point of a lone Brit officer on the loose. Orders were given to double the guard. Scouts would be sent out before dawn, and Jonathan was to join the Massachusetts Fifth to take a watch.

Putnam rose to escort him and give the orders to his unit, but Jonathan stalled him. "Begging the colonel's pardon. Might I join with one of the Connecticut regiments?"

Parsons chuckled. "It seems your cousin's men would be preferred to your own. If only Old Put was here with us to revel in Captain Wythe's compliments."

"Cousin Israel would be welcome to him. I had rather not the responsibility for a turncoat," Putnam replied.

I stood, watching the scene unfold.

An inquiry having been made as to why the preference, Jonathan answered, "One of our purposes in coming to West Point is in search of Miss— the lady's family. She being from Connecticut as a child…"

"And, Captain?" Parsons picked up on the hesitation.

"And all her other family thought to be dead."

"What?" The shock drove me to my seat. Lovely bombshell to avoid mentioning during our previous tiptoeing around my past.

My protector's fatal flaw, however, was stumbling over my newly assumed name. A misstep that didn't go unnoticed by the men, although they'd already risen from the table and were relaying orders to their respective aides for the evening's guard. Putnam seized upon the moment. "Phillips. Was that not one of the officers we did rout at Saratoga?"

"It was," Greaton agreed.

Another round of applause for Madam Fate, who'd just thrust me back onto center stage. Kościuszko's lips were pressed into a thin line, his skin assuming a grayer pallor. Jonathan's brows crash-landed, as well. A veritable horror show that McDougall observed with clear displeasure.

"Jonathan, his uniform was blue." I tugged on my bag's strap, feeling insecure, bordering on desperate. "I remember my father's uniform was blue. He couldn't have been a redcoat."

He nodded stiffly, then informed everyone of my affliction. Excuses of missing memories didn't alleviate the grimacing or grumbling, so he confessed that my father was among the no-longer-living and inquired after the fate of the man in Saratoga. That officer, Major-General William Phillips of His Majesty's Ministerial Forces, was shipped along with all the other prisoners of the "Convention Army" to Cambridge, we were told.

"Perhaps Miss Phillips, if that is her name, should be taken under the care of Webb's men," Nixon suggested. "Just for a time," he cut off Jonathan's protests.

Greaton thought that to be a bit harsh, though Parsons mulled over the idea, rubbing his chin.

"I'd like to stay with Captain Wythe," I said. "I can help with the watch. I've done it before."

Jonathan frowned. "Such would be preferrable, sirs. I would beg you that option over another assuming custody of the lady."

McDougall studied the knots on the table at length, before tilting toward Greaton, who acknowledged the whispered order with a solemn nod and excused himself. Then the general answered aloud, "We are men of honor. It would no dae tae ask a lass, no matter how courageous, tae serve amongst the men. Ye shall be given a room. Aye, General Parsons?"

Parsons deferred to the other general's wishes, then warned me, "There is not a proper bed to be found. Even so, a place shall be prepared for you."

"Anything's better than sleeping outside." I thanked them.

Lilley was summoned. Bedding was to be carried to the attic for me, once Nixon approved his subordinate should be given the task. Room would have to be made among the noncommissioned officers in the barracks. The private's shoulders drooped at the hard labor of having to inform those middling-ranked men of their relocation.

Putnam grumbled something into his mug.

"Should it come tae light tha' Mistress Phillips is naught as she should be," McDougall answered with some impatience, "'tis the barracks prison for *both* her and the Barry captain. Until then, Webb's men must forego the pleasure. There are many eyes tae keep watch o'er them, are there no? If 'tis agreeable with the general, Colonel Putnam, would ye be so braw as tae escort Captain Wythe tae the Sixth?"

Having acknowledged the request, Parsons whirled his hand in a mocking bow. "We, Yankees, shall accommodate you, Captain."

Tallyho! Off the cavalry charged, the evening's orders in their sights.

Putnam barked, "You will accompany me," at Jonathan, who'd pressed a hand to my shoulder and was attempting to whisper enlightening nothings in my ear. "At once," the colonel ordered, already at the front of the house and demanding the sentry open the door.

"If you wish to be so, Generals," Kościuszko offered, "I can attend the girl until the room is ready."

After a polite assurance that it wasn't necessary, he was dismissed. Parsons followed him to the door. It groaned shut.

Click went the lock.

Parsons circled behind me.

The window latch too.

Chapter Twenty-Two

While Parsons finished his circuit of the miniscule room by stirring the fire, McDougall invited me to rejoin him at the table. Like I had a choice. The former tossed a fresh log on the pile, sending sparks flying. A single nod from his superior commenced Act Two.

Round the room he went again. This time to take a post behind my shoulder, from which he leaned forward and grasped my tin mug by way of offering another serving of rum as he smooth-talked me. "You have been through much. What an ordeal for a woman."

Eau de Hudson River, scented with body odor, hovered close. I laid a palm over the mug's mouth, forcing its return to the table, then looked to where his face lingered next to mine, mere fractions above me. "I would imagine war is an ordeal for everyone, sir."

"Ah, yes." The pitcher was placed delicately on the table while he mused, "I am curious. Two hours—no more—had gone, after the regulars were taken prisoner, before you joined us. Why not make yourself known to our men after you fired your shot?"

"Because I didn't want to get taken prisoner, too, and have to sit around, waiting for someone to actually listen to me while I tried to explain that I wasn't a redcoat."

"Oh!" The men chuckled back and forth. "I doubt there would be any who would consider you to be one of the regulars."

"And yet you and your men *are* concerned I'm a British spy."

McDougall splashed another ground cover of rum into his cup. "I think, lass, 'tis rather tha' ye connect yerself with those who possess all the qualities. It does draw yer loyalties intae question."

"General, at the risk of making things worse, please let me explain something," I said. Parsons resumed his watch from his crate-turned-stool. Given permission to continue, I admitted, "It was suggested I hide my married name so I might avoid the very suspicions I'm facing now. But I promise you, I'm not a loyalist or a British spy."

"What is yer true name?"

"Phillips is my maiden name. My name—the one I go by, the only name Captain Wythe knows…" I sighed. "…is Moore. That's why he couldn't remember what to call me. He knows me as Savannah Moore."

"Damnation," Parsons swore.

McDougall, instead, cut to the chase. "Why are ye here?"

"We're assisting Captain Machin," I insisted. "Those, as I understand it, are Jonathan's orders. But we're also trying to find my family or whoever brought me to the Colonies and why."

"Where is yer hame?"

At my confused look—which was related more to why the prison in my brains should give a rat's ass about our respective missions—Parsons translated, "The general wishes to know where you call home."

"I don't remember," I said helplessly.

"So, for all you *remember*, you could very well *be* a royalist spy."

Yeah, I never promised drowning under twenty feet was going to be better than ten.

"Captain Wythe and I both killed redcoats, back before I got sick. You don't trust him. I get it. I don't know that I trust him completely, either, truth be told. But from what little has happened since, I've come to believe he's a good man." I unclasped my cloak. It was too damn hot. "I just can't imagine he'd murder his own men. Or that I would, for that matter. But as you said—you'll be keeping tabs on us while we're here."

McDougall studied me, then issued a small laugh and shook his head. He drained his mug, which he wiped clean with a handkerchief from inside his uniform coat. "I see we shall have tae keep a *close* eye on ye. Ye may outsmart us all, Mistress… What shall we call ye? Do ye prefer Phillips or Moore?"

I offered a humble smile. "I prefer whichever will keep me alive."

Parsons joined in the general's laughter, then asked, "What do you know of the Moore family?"

"I was told a Stephen Moore owns these lands, so I was hoping to meet him to see if he's familiar. Or ask if he knows something about me."

"Perhaps he is your husband?"

"I know he's not my husband."

The tennis match met in the middle; the men exchanged another glance after my out-and-out certainty.

"You are not here to lay claim to the land?" Parsons asked.

"I just want to find my family."

My heart ached over Jonathan's reveal that they were all dead. Our search was destined to be fruitless, wasn't it? What exactly was the point?

Then Parsons served me with, "The Moore family are royalists. That is why the lands of Stephen Moore have been seized for our use. They fled New York Province in '75. The last were removed from these parts in February. What say you now?"

Twenty feet, forty… I was caught in the undertow of something beyond my understanding.

Except, his declaration wasn't sitting right with McDougall, who dropped his head while frowning, but the man kept his consternation to himself. Still, that would explain Jonathan's sudden change in attitude right before we left Mr. Cloet's home, if he'd worked out for himself the possibility that Moore's Folly wasn't a charitable donation to the Continentals.

"I don't know what to say."

Any moment now, I worried, their verdict would land me in the barracks prison.

Tick…tick. Tick…

I rubbed my sore forehead, then folded my hands on my lap and waited for the order to be given.

There was a scrape wending the arch of my forefinger's knuckle. A dried flap of skin stood straight into the air, and dirt smeared the pink skin underneath. The act of noticing the cut was enough to make it sting. My bottom lip trembled. I forced myself to pull it together and met McDougall's stare.

"How dae ye prefer tae be called?"

"Moore. My name is Savannah Moore."

He nodded. "General, ye may see tae yer men."

"I understand, sir," Parsons replied. He collected his mug to throw the last drops into the fire. It hissed its thanks, then simmered down. Issuing a polite bow to the general first, then me, along with a flourish of his hat, he took his leave.

Two little Soldier Boys sitting in the sun; One got fizzled up, and then there was…

Quiet pervaded the poorly insulated house. Numerous feet had already stamped up and down multiple stairwells to claim their bedding, some with less-than-restrained complaints about being removed to the barracks. More than one mention of rats accompanied them. Voices had trickled toward the front of the house, discussion of the aides' daily tasks transitioning to more personal matters. Same was true of the officers who'd returned and retired to the second floor. Every once in a while, footfalls shuffled across the floorboards overhead.

"Ye must be pure done in, Mistress Moore," McDougall said kindly.

"It's been a long day," I admitted.

He grimaced as he rose, slowed by an obvious pain.

"Oft, 'tis no bother." He waived my expressed concern and rounded the table to face me. "I have a mind tae heed yer suggestion of sending men tae Major DeForest for confirmation of yer reports."

"I think you should. Though he doesn't trust Captain Wythe any more than the officers here. I doubt he'll have nice things to say."

The general chuckled. "They are no without cause. Tho', in truth, I have come tae know Captain Wythe a wee bit, and I am of the belief tha' ye may be correct as concerning his fine character." He leaned close. "Ye would no betray tha' confidence tae him, would ye now?"

"Hmm. It's a huge betrayal of his trust." I returned his friendly attitude, smiling. "But my lips are sealed, General."

McDougall hummed for a moment himself, though in apparent thought rather than as part of our little joke, before confessing something else. "General Parsons is no entirely correct. The Moore family are royalists. Tha' said, Stephen Moore is sympathetic tae our cause and connects himself with the Southern Department's militia. Whatever suspicions may surround his family, ye must no be afraid tae be true tae yerself."

Hallelujah. One less worry to haunt me. Perhaps sleeping in a drafty old attic wouldn't be so bad.

I was wrong.

Chapter Twenty-Three

I dreamed of blood.

Armies thundered towards one another, dirt flying through the air. Blood sprayed from the slice to a soldier's neck. It poured from a gaping wound, splattered along the length of swords, soaked the earth. A pile of corpses climbed around me as the bullets tore through them, a scarlet river cutting a gorge into the side of the hill.

I ducked behind a nearby evergreen.

Surprise filled the face of the redcoat waiting for me there. Cheeks full. Spotty with freckles. Just a kid, really. Our focus dropped to the muzzle of his gun. Steel extended forward several inches before penetrating my cloak. Fluid oozed onto the metal, dripping, dripping faster from where he'd impaled me. It trailed warmly down my legs. A musket, sagging as I slid off its bayonet. My blood was lost in the deluge that was drowning me.

I woke screaming. The sight of my bedding had me screaming louder.

A man burst into the attic. His eyes widened as he noticed the stains surrounding my lap. Cries to fetch the surgeon echoed down the stairs, repeated further below. Despite my yelling at the browncoat to keep away, he took a cautious step into the room, aiming his gun around the door, in case danger was lurking in its shadow, I suppose. My only companions were abandoned bits of broken furniture smothered in dust, except where fingers had recently smudged grimy paths.

There it was.

I yanked the flimsy blanket from the floorboards to cover up. I wanted to swipe away the tears dampening my face but couldn't. Crimson hues streaked my hands, painted there during my restless sleep by the dampened straw bedding.

Several excited voices tunneled from the growing crowd at the base of the attic stairs, questioning what was going on and "be tha' the hen a'screeching?"

Pounding footsteps charging upstairs announced General Parsons, who hurried into the attic. Expedient in his quest to suss out an explanation, he relegated me as being "in a state" and questioned the man next to him, whose longing stare at the stairwell betrayed either a fondness for lathe and plaster décor or a desire to flee the country. What little information was divulged consisted of "bleeding an' a-crying."

Parsons ordered the voices below to fetch Captain Wythe or else disperse. In an act of charity—whether his kindness was greater for me or the desperate private, it was a toss-up—he sent the browncoat in search of water and something for a basin.

"Might..." He inched backward to a respectful distance. "...you require any assistance whilst we await the surgeon?"

Hiccups stalled my journey toward calming down, as did a nasty surprise: every brand name muddling up my mind, I recognized, would be foreign to his ears, and every colonial alternative, strange to mine. Why? What was I missing?

Frustrated, I just cried. I was owed a pity party.

The circular surgeon arrived—Doctor Hart came in, glanced, and stormed out. He rounded the doorway back in long enough to chastise me. "You waste the general's time, as well. A nurse is all that is required here." The tails of his coat slapped around his legs as he departed.

Must've been a killer backgammon game.

Parsons accepted my embarrassed apology and, somehow, managed the courtesy of sticking around, commenting on the waterway's traffic occurring out the hall window as a distraction. I reacquainted myself with being rational in the interim.

Good thing the question of my last name was straightened out the night before. Every resident of the Hudson Valley heard the hundred or so times Jonathan yelled each lengthened vowel while he thundered up the three flights. He rushed past the general, appearing not to notice the tight squeeze on the landing. "Miss Moore, what has happened?"

"It might be best if the captain attends to you." Parsons gave me a final, sympathetic glance. "The general, you see. I must assist General McDougall, who is leaving for headquarters within the hour." Then he bolted.

Which left a frantic Jonathan trying to grasp my hands. "Are you well? I was told that you had been attacked."

"It's nothing. Just a nightmare."

"God's teeth," he breathed in horror. He'd caught sight of my fingers. Of course, it was a bigger mistake to bury my fists into the blanket because he was quick to realize something else was wrong and flung it aside. Nausea saturated his skin in new hues.

Embarking on the bucket-filling mission had purchased leave for the beleaguered private from my personal warzone. Sadly for him, leave had just run out. The sight of me huddled on the straw mattress in a blood-soaked shirt while a green-tinged officer knelt next to me, gaping, cut short his sneaking in. Medusa never saw anyone shy from her as fast as the private did from me. Right out the door.

"You there, where is the surgeon?" Jonathan yelled for the poor man. "Miss…woman, lie down," he pleaded.

The private shielded his eyes and delivered his report of the surgeon's brief visit from the landing.

"He would not examine her?" Jonathan's pale complexion sampled a redder shade. "Guard, I demand that the surgeon be brought back instantly, or I shall drag the bastard myself."

To stitch up my protector's palms from where his nails had dug in, if nothing else.

"With a pistol to his head, if need be!" he added.

"Private, don't bother Doctor Hart," I called around him.

Our arms entangled as we wrestled; Jonathan trying to force me to assume the invalid position—which was doubly undesirable because the bedding was getting cold as the blood dried—and me, resisting.

"I'm fine," I insisted. "I just need the nurse to come."

"You are injured," he argued.

"This. Is. Normal."

"This cannot… There is blood."

"Och, here now. 'Tis no place for a man." A young woman with extravagant raven locks entered, carrying a collection of folded rags. She dumped them on the edge of the bedding, laid the bucket of water she'd claimed from the guard at its foot, grabbed Jonathan by the arm to yank him to standing, and sent him packing with strict orders to fetch more wood for the fire. "The lass will take a chill if ye dae not heed, so off with ye." She patted his cheek before shoving him toward the door.

"What a mess is here. Have ye a shift?" she put to me, her voice clearly critical, not of my situation but my male wardrobe.

"No." I glanced at Jonathan, who was lingering by the door. The whole thing was so embarrassing.

"I have garments for the lady." He hazarded a step back into the room.

"Ye fetch her the garments, then. I shall see tae the lass till ye dae return. There is a lad." She shooed him.

Clean clothes really were the best medicine he could offer me. Sighing, he inched the door closed, though we could hear the guard ask if I was going to recover.

The nurse chuckled. "Poor lads. They charge into battle, brawl in the streets, and sing songs tae their drink, but they ken naught of the world without a wife tae teach them its ways." We laughed together, which was a balm onto itself. She softened her tone to ask, "Ye were no with bairn?"

"No." At least, I didn't think I'd been pregnant.

"'Tis a'right, then. Caught ye unawares, did it?"

She listened while I washed my hands, not without sympathy but also with the air of sad familiarity, as if my story of looking for my family with nothing to my name, not even the clothes on my back, was a regular feature of the war's landscape.

A timid knock preceded Jonathan delivering a bundle, which he was directed to leave by the door, which led to another brisk dismissal.

"Well now. Have ye e'er seen such a thing? 'Tis a bonnie color for yer hair." The nurse admired the linen cloth as she unwound a leather cord to reveal his surprise. It was a hunter-green gown, adorned with gray and yellow floral embroidery. Although lightly faded, it was whole and well-made and exactly what I needed. A gray petticoat was wrapped inside the outer garment, along with a shift and stockings that were off-white with age. And—bless him, as Éabha might say—clean undergarments.

And the nurse, who didn't blink at enlisting my bloodied blanket to shield the view of potential intruders barging in on us. After I cleaned my other regions, she clucked her tongue at my ignorance of how best to use the "clout" and much too gleefully instructed me as she handed over the folded rags.

Since my unfortunate nightmarish awakening was my prologue to the delights of the day, according to the meager offering stealing through the tiny attic windows, the nurse ordered a private belowstairs to fetch me a stimulator. She then relieved my protector—who was anxious as a mother hen—from his noisy pacing at the bottom of the stairwell.

"There now. Does she no look bonnie?"

"Ah, it-sh…" He stammered what I imagine would've been an agreement, had she been successful in redirecting his attention from the pile of ruined bedding.

"Where is the wood I sent ye for? Can ye no see the lass is cold?"

That had him back in action, in search of the forgotten firewood.

At least an afternoon's worth was scattered near the trim box straining to call itself a fireplace, its chimney narrowing as it disappeared into the distance overhead.

"There's plenty…" I cocked my head at her.

She gave me a sly smile. "I shall see tae the washing if ye would hand along yer garments."

"You don't have to. I can do it."

"Och, have ye soap then for the washing of it?"

Smooth as silk, that one, and no springtime maid, because of course I didn't have soap or anything else to get by, and she knew it. "A wee extra washing will hurt me none," she teased. "Ye have enough troubles ahead, lass, with calming the likes of himself."

She chuckled and swept from the room, trading places with the put-upon guard.

Damn. I never got her name.

Chapter Twenty-Four

Private Peter Salem of the Sixth Massachusetts—who introduced himself with greater authority and looked lightyears better, now that reminders of my feminine nature weren't as colorful as before—had returned with a shot of gin and a dried cake of bread. Embarrassed to no end, I thanked him but declined. It was a bit early to bottoms up. Except for the bread. That I wholeheartedly accepted because I was starving.

During our awkward chat about what was labeled my "Quakerish restraint regarding spirits," to which he offered a puzzled headshake in trade, Jonathan delivered an armload of wood and intercepted the cup. He slammed back the shot, then relinquished it to Salem.

"Just you holler, if there be trouble," the private told me while eyeing my woozy friend and—presumably having better things to do than monitor the scene already winding up for another dramatic round—took his leave, adding, "Breakfast will be ready by ten of the clock."

Mere seconds after the door clicked shut, Jonathan demanded, "Tell me now. How is it you were injured?"

In exchange for my promise to answer, he got the fire going at a nice, ski-resort-worthy crackle to heat the chilly attic. It took a little coaxing to get him settled next to me. Our sole option consisted of the cushion of dust padding the floor, but near the hearth, huddled together, was the warmest spot.

Assured he wanted to know the truth, I described the intricacies of the female body and its ways. It looked like the gin wasn't sitting well by the time I finished.

"Bread?" I held out a portion. He shifted away and swallowed hard. "Don't you have a sister or someone who's explained all this to you before?" I asked.

Jealousy piped up with a pretty petty remark that Cordelia hadn't been such a bosom buddy after all. Rude. Menstruation *was* a taboo topic.

He shook his head. "I have only a brother."

"Oh. What's his name?"

"He…could we not speak of this now?"

"Sure."

Damn curse. He knew about my deceased family and things my father had said. We'd probably talked about his family at length too. Constant replays weren't going to cure his current agitation, though.

Where was his brother? England, maybe. I hoped still alive, for Jonathan's sake.

"Y-you are well now, are you not?" He rubbed at nonexistent dirt on the pommel of his silver blade. "The bleeding has stopped."

"Uh, no. It'll take several days."

"So," he whispered, "you might die."

Winding my arm around his, I clasped his hand. "I haven't died yet," I joked. A growl rumbled in his throat. He was *not* amused. Then a thought occurred to me. "We've never run into this problem before?"

"I have not known you so long as a month."

Oh wow. What the hell were we doing, cuddled up, holding hands like longtime lovers? Self-conscious, I started to untangle myself from his grasp, but he clutched onto me tighter. After he made several attempts without success to voice whatever was plaguing him, I promised, "You can ask me anything."

"Are..." He swallowed with difficulty. The gin was definitely not sitting well with my anatomy lesson. "Are you in pain?"

Emotion swelled in my chest. Some people might never know, after months or even years, the unfathomable joy that overwhelmed me just then, as I realized how deeply he cared about my well-being. A shuddered sigh wracked my body, upsetting him. "Shh, I'm fine." I leaned my head against his shoulder. "It rarely hurts."

His body relaxed, though his thumb worried at my hand.

We watched the flames in front of us for a while. Flickering shadows jolted along the high ceiling, taking form from the firelight struggling to pass beyond the wooden beams that crossed and joined at angles, to where the sun's rays couldn't reach.

Without warning, his eyes burst wide, and he jerked around to face the closed door. There wasn't any activity on the small landing outside. We'd heard Private Salem retreat downstairs earlier, probably just as horrified as Jonathan about my explanation of the crimson tide.

"What is it?"

His nervous gaze met mine. "Why did you assume a false identity?"

"Don't worry." I sighed, relieved Danger was hanging out elsewhere. "General McDougall and Parsons know my real name."

Then I give him the kiddie version of shadowing the redcoats up to my landing in Brass Central, plus the information gleaned about the fractured

Moore clan—the King-loving relatives versus Southern militia officer, Stephen Moore. Holiday dinners must suck in that household.

Frustration bubbled under the surface of Jonathan's wishing aloud, "Would that you had not been placed in such danger. Still." A smile eased across his lips as he said, "You have done well. I am grateful that you are unharmed. Now that it is day, I shall be free to continue my inquiry on your behalf among the men of the line. Those of the Connecticut regiment," he answered my confused look.

"What about you?" I asked. "Did your scout deliver my message? Is that why you stopped tracking the other redcoats?"

He shifted to where he could eye me better. "My scout?"

"Your bluebird."

"You think a bird is my scout?"

His features were carefully set at neutral as we studied one another. No eyebrow cocked in amusement, or a suspicious meeting of the pair. Switzerland in mask form. So, I was sure. "Yeah, your scout. He was really helpful. He counted the soldiers for me. Told me there were three, and there were. He took off when I said you needed to know what was going on. Well actually, I meant to give him a longer message, but he disappeared before I could get that far."

"A bird?" he questioned me again.

"Yeah, Jonathan. Your bluebird. He even warned me…"

Fingertips brushed my skin. His knuckles traveled the length of my face, lightly tracing a path. They continued their journey, finding harbor at my shoulders, where his thumbs could wander their terrain at leisure. "How is it you have come to know me so well?" he said. "You will be my undoing."

"I would never betray you."

"This I know." He shifted sideways, claiming both my hands this time. "His name is Cleophes. He did come in search of me, though he refused to share his vision with me. Our connection was broken when I, too, took ill. He has chosen not to renew it. As such, I knew only that you were distressed." Jonathan paused and studied me before asking, "How is it he told you the number of soldiers?"

"By nodding his head. I asked a couple of times how many there were. I was kinda worried maybe I was just crazy, but it really did seem like he was trying to warn me."

Excitement was growing outside; men's voices arose, too loud to ignore. Putting a pin in our bitty-birdy spy business, Jonathan crammed his head into a tiny dormer. "I cannot see beyond the trees."

"Try the window on the landing."

"Ah, better. There are several of the Massachusetts approaching the river. I should rejoin the line." He paused, appearing uncertain about me suiting up with my cloak and leather bag to accompany him. "Would it not be best for you to rest, given your condition?"

"No way." I tucked my arm into his. "I'm right as rain."

"Woman." His tone was half warning, half joking. "None but you could seek to assure me of this while referring to the damp."

I laughed. "Oh, don't get me started."

"Have mercy, I beg of you," he teased. "Come…ah, first. A thought."

My thought was to smack him if he concocted some fictional excuse to keep me bedridden. Instead, he confided while smiling, "Take care not to call Cleophes a 'bluebird' where he might overhear."

"Why?" I was bemused.

"He would consider it an insult. Were he to speak to you, he would insist that he is, in truth, black in color. It is the light that causes him to appear blue."

"Okay." I laughed. "So, what is he?"

"He is a *Tanagra cyanea.*"

"He told you that?"

"It is intuitively obvious," Jonathan teased.

"Of course it is. How silly of me."

With the maelstrom of war nipping at our heals whichever way we turned, here was our safe haven—laughing together, comforting one another, facing the horrors side by side. He was rooted so deeply in my heart, I felt I couldn't live without him. By the happiness brightening his smile, as his gaze swept my face, it seemed he felt the same way.

"Jonathan, I want to tell you something about my marriage."

He sobered in a flash and dropped my arm. "Now is not the time."

A burst of cheering outside sounded like a virtual roar compared to the sudden change.

Cupping the air surrounding my elbows, as if wanting to guide me out of the way so he could walk past without our touching, his hands appeared lost. Duty was calling him away as surely as the dark thoughts clouding his face were driving him.

"All right, maybe not the whole story," I said, "but let me ask you something."

"Ask…later," he told the floor as he slipped by me.

"Phillips is my maiden name."

He paused several steps below, glancing back to where he'd abandoned me on the landing. "You remembered your name?"

I closed the distance so I could whisper, "I need to know which is better for you? If people believe I'm married or single?"

"Oh, Miss Moore. You need not worry about what is best for me."

"Yeah, I do. It affects you."

Jonathan's back landed against the wall. The struggle on his face hurt; I felt the unexpected grab in my chest. "Please listen," I said. "I'm not—"

"You told me when we did meet that your name is Moore."

"It is."

"That is all that matters."

He was down the two flights of stairs and out the front door before I could stop him.

Chapter Twenty-Five

Hope came to West Point in the form of Captain Machin and his men. Ships adorned with billowing sails and regimental banners filled the expanse of the Hudson, traveling south of the Red House in a magnificent river parade. They were welcomed by waving and cheering from the gathering audience on the shore, who received a similar greeting in return from those few hands not busy navigating their arrival. The Great Chain lay stretched across the boats guiding it toward the S bend in the river, glistening with droplets that reflected the glory of the sun on its surface; its large, wooden rafts interspersed between them as literal floats to carry this grand marshal. Several more vessels surrounded the fleet, outfitted with mounted cannons.

Those nearest the shoreline dropped sail; their crew producing poles next that they dipped into the water, jabbing at the riverbed to prevent the low-riding ships from striking the rocks. Pairs of oxen dragging carts kept pace with the small navy from the parallel roadway. The end of the Chain, along with the means to secure it in place, were a heavy load for the animals, who grunted as they strained forward. Weapons stayed close at hand by the team's watchful guards.

Jonathan's long stride had created a sizeable distance between us, which was kinda funny because an unfortunate, short-legged browncoat in white pants was forced to trot alongside of him to keep pace.

"Hold there, Miss Philips," a voice called from the front garden as I hurried after them. "You are to remain at the house."

"Captain Machin is expecting me," I yelled back at Private Salem, hoping I'd actually met the officer I'd been name-dropping like a politician with a cause, and tore off after the crowd. Stuff whatever orders he'd been given. I wasn't going to be kept prisoner, not when history was in the making outside.

Silky heels or other girly-girl pumps to accessorize my parlor attire weren't part of Jonathan's gift, which was just as well. My tall boots were better suited for the rocky path. Opening up into a steady run felt so good, I didn't bother to slow once I caught up with him. I blew by, the train of my gown billowing in my wake. It sounded like he chuckled.

Watching the animated expressions of the men and women congregated along the ledge above us, the fervor of their pointing out the wondrous scene, I could feel the excitement radiating from the Plain. A diversity of colored uniforms and peoples, whose homes spanned across the once separate states and even continents, stood united to witness this extraordinary feat. From atop a tawny horse, General McDougall beamed with admiration. His aides, likewise, remained captivated. Over their shoulders, a teal flag floated in the wind, the white letters of "Liberty" displayed for all the Hudson Valley.

"Captain Machin?" I asked the only blue uniform with an officer's epaulet present.

"Miss Moore. Careful."

In one dizzying outburst of my wayward memories, he was promoted from mildly familiar—as he existed when he turned to face me—to restored in my mind. He caught my arm, thus saving me from an embarrassing spill. The curse wasn't generous with relinquishing details beyond a random personal tale and some polite conversation, however.

"Thanks." It took me a moment to recover. "Congratulations, you made it. This is amazing."

"Yes. She will hold. Never again shall the river be taken from American hands." Pride flooded his voice, his entire stance, and expression. The enormous undertaking, occurring just feet from us, was remarkable even to the man who'd spent weeks overseeing the construction of this newest attempt.

The river churned as it wound toward the first bend, threatening to smash a neglectful crew against the rocks. Swells of water sloshed over the lip of the boats at times; they rode that low, burdened as they were with the weight of the Chain, despite the wooden rafts designed to carry the load.

Machin glanced over my shoulder. Jonathan still hadn't reached us, though Salem was lingering in the background, acting natural-ish, as if he wasn't duty bound to chase after me. "I am glad to see you looking well," the captain said softly. "Last we did meet, I was loath to part from you. When I learned you were ill, I feared..." He bowed his head, grim faced.

"I'm fine. We're both fine."

"It relieves me to hear you say so. It was plain he, too, was recovering from sickness when we spoke thereafter. He should have stayed abed longer but would not be persuaded. Nonetheless, that night...honorable though he may be, I have never known Captain Wythe to speak to any as he did to you. It troubles me I did nothing to assist you."

"Jonathan and I..."

What could I say? Feelings aside, I wasn't sure how to describe our relationship, since the argument surrounding his discovery of my married name was now refreshed for me, yet its full significance remained riddled with plot holes.

What's more, I realized, our time together was limited. Any moment, he could be called away or, worse, taken from me. Or me from him. Our arrangement was supposed to be temporary, regardless. He couldn't drag me along forever, an anchor to his personal voyage. If I'd read him wrong, if he didn't feel as I did, eventually…

I didn't want to think about eventually.

"There wasn't anything for you to do," I reassured Machin. "I'm sorry it bothered you."

"Good day, Captain Wythe," he called to the approaching footsteps behind me.

The men clasped both their hands together as they shook, in lieu of patting each other on the back, and grinned like schoolboys on Christmas morning. Machin raised his eyebrows at the browncoat trailing Jonathan. The general wasn't kidding when he promised we'd be watched.

Jonathan shrugged it off and returned to a happier topic. "You have brought her well to port, Captain," he praised his fellow officer.

"As have you, my friend." Machin dipped his chin in my direction, smiling.

My blushing protector cleared his throat. "We each of us attend to our duties. Mine are far lighter, I dare say."

"Certainly fairer."

"All right, stop." I laughed. "If you wanted me to leave so you can have some guy time, you just had to ask."

"You need not go, Miss Moore. We shall mind our tongues." Machin and I chuckled, enjoying the moment. Jonathan…it was hard to tell. He smiled but from far away.

Order up on another round of handshaking, compliments, and admiration once General Parsons and Colonel Kościuszko joined our party. We relocated to the tail end of the cart procession trudging along the towpath. It narrowed into a pimply patchwork of boulders sprouting from the uneven, muddy passage through the trees. At that point, soldiers unhitched the double-ox teams to resituate them into single file. Other workers grappled with the materials to haul what they could themselves while the herd was being renegotiated.

Dramatic indeed in its complexity, especially with irritable animals involved. Must-see activity. Jonathan's tail, whose name we learned was Private Williams, was sent to enlist help from the fort above.

Kościuszko was in his element, examining the quality of the finished product. Churning out his thoughts too quickly, he slipped into French before lapsing multiple times into Polish. In realizing he'd lost his listeners—except Jonathan, who apparently spoke every language ever invented—he began the cycle all over again, after a few halting attempts at English. Together, Machin and Kościuszko calculated the amount of material needed for what ultimately looked like a giant box of rocks—if one wanted to be unfair—that bound the Chain to the western shoreline.

Seizing a lull in his duties after translations were no longer required, Jonathan wandered off, alone, to the water's edge. Being nothing but scenery dressing myself, I allowed him several minutes then joined him. "Congratulations."

A momentary tension relaxed, and he accepted my arm, though his eyes closed and he sighed. "I have done little that deserves your praise."

"That's ridiculous. We're all playing our part in a much bigger picture here. Even if no one ever knows who we are, without any of us, the whole thing would fall apart. Like the Chain."

We grew silent, admiring the view across the river, toward the construction on Constitution Island.

"Captain Machin appeared quite serious when speaking with you earlier. Is anything amiss?" he asked.

Thinking of his apology at Mr. Cloet's house, back before I could remember who Jonathan was and therefore why he was contrite, I decided the conversation didn't warrant repeating. "Not really."

His horrified shock that night, as if I'd shot him when I'd shouted the news about my marriage, haunted me. Shock which the effects of the curse hadn't permitted us to overcome, so far as I knew. He shouldn't have to dwell on it. Not until we had time for a serious talk.

"Today is a great day," I told the river.

Jonathan agreed. "There will never be another such as this one."

Chapter Twenty-Six

Ships multiplied as the day progressed, the first of what turned out to be a four-day venture. Unidentified crafts orbited Machin's fleet, some having traveled a distance from both up and downriver, judging by the rumors, stories, and reports that circulated through camp. Gawkers could be seen lining the neighboring shore, as well. Locals. Sooner or later, one of them was bound to be a loyalist.

Our time out of the action ended, Jonathan and I were called to huddle up with the officers and compare notes on sightings of the enemy. Machin shared his surprise that his men had not openly observed any of the regulars, despite the massive cargo trekking along the Valley's main thoroughfare. Wythe made the goal, with an assist by Phillips-Moore!

Though Machin did hear a bit of gas from the galley pilot at New Windsor, who was "wanting to know how a body was to conduct his business of a'ferrying with the devilry choking off the river and its like." Given the numerous complaints from the Highlands' residents already about the goings-on at the Point, his impression of the pilot would've been funnier under different circumstances.

Matters didn't improve when a woman in a small rowboat hailed the officers, offering to sell us victuals. Private Salem yelled to her, "What might a man get for a Continental?"

"Best you could expect for that rubbish is bum fodder." The woman laughed.

General Parsons thanked her. "But as none have any coin with which to purchase foodstuffs, you had best find another harbor for your bum boat, madam."

We watched with trepidation. She showed expert skill maneuvering around the Chain's installation while still engaging more than one of the regiment's shipmates in conversation, before trying her luck with the bystanders on the eastern bank.

"The guard shall remain at twofold," Parsons ordered. "Captain Wythe, you are to assist with the construction on the Water Redoubt. Private Williams, find Lieutenant Keyes and have him gather as many men as needed. There is to be cannon on the cove to guard the Chain at once.

Someone must cross the river to Constitution Island and organize their placing along the batteries, no matter the status of the construction."

Party over, everyone dispersed, geared up for their assigned tasks. Everyone, except me. I found myself staring at many receding backs, other than my personal browncoat's.

"Dare I suggest you have better things to do than guard my every move?" was my futile quip to Salem.

"No, mistress. I am to attend you while Captain Wythe sees to his duty."

Attend? A load of bullshit if ever there was one.

I longed to accompany Jonathan to the cove, but Salem suggested, "You might enjoy a visit to the Plain. The view is very fine atop the ascent. Many a mile can be seen from there."

"Lead on." I sighed, rolling my eyes. It wasn't his fault I was a woman of suspect in a man's world. I was certainly dressed the part. Once I got my shirt back, there'd be a different discussion, I promised myself.

We retraced our steps along the towpath and turned onto the steep trail leading to the Plain towering above us. While we walked, I asked him to tell me about himself.

"Begging your pardon," he said, sounding skeptical. "Why should a white lady care to know about a man such as myself?"

"Well, if we're going to be spending the foreseeable future together, shouldn't we get to know one another?"

"You do not mean to say, you would make free with tales of yourself?"

"That is part of getting to know one another."

Salem raised an eyebrow at me and shook his head. So, I went first, recounting my adventures of recent memory. Those already on record, anyway, so their inclusion in his daily report to Officer Land wouldn't be an issue. He had to take my hand several times to help me, lest he have to explain all the broken bits of my feminine pride at the bottom of the hill, if my frequent tripping turned into a tumble. All those luscious linen layers made the climb cumbersome. He shook his head again once I'd reached the end of my woodland story and the start of Chapter West Point.

The spring weather had warmed considerably. Uniform coats littered the ground. Their owners worked nearby in shirts untied at the neck, with their sleeves rolled out of the way. Stones were hauled and added, one by one, onto the outline of a future redoubt—basically, a large wall—and then mud was slapped in between. A temporary mixture, I later learned, until more lime could be purchased, should the funds ever find their way so far north. That was the theme of the repeated complaints among the officers during my stay, their personal means to advance payment for the Works having run low.

Staring across the Hudson from the height of the Plain, the beauty of the river took my breath away. It wove into the color-washed valley, stretching into the horizon, and was spotted with tiny, verdant islands. We were at the center of the S bend. To the south, surrounded by craggy walls of insurmountable stone, lay the route to Manhattan, the stronghold of British forces in New York. Northward, the Highlands rose to soaring heights along the banks.

Something sweet drifted on the wind from the grasses nearby. The chirping of crickets filled the air and accompanied the busyness of man and nature in harmony. I gazed into the treetops that rustled at my feet, wondering where Jonathan was in the mix below. Cleophes crossed my mind, as well. His little black—not blue—bird, I mused.

Shielding my eyes as the sun burst through a cloud, I felt a call pulling me north. *Somewhere out there is your home*, it said. *Somewhere beyond Albany.*

"I have seen many things since this war began," Salem said, "but no sight has ever made me feel the blessings of freedom such as when I look across waters and know I can go any distance I want." He removed his tricorn and turned his face upward to soak in the sun. Taking in a deep breath, he told me, "It was not always so."

"Where is your home?"

"Once my service is done, wherever I want." He smiled.

A term of duty, in exchange for release from bondage, probably in place of his former enslaver so the local quota for enlistments could be met. He was one of many who'd made such a bargain.

"And you, mistress? Where are your people?" he asked.

I wished I could return his smile when I answered, "I don't know."

"Lor' have mercy on you."

Wanting to banish the loneliness that crept over me, I turned to face the Plain instead. Immediately behind us lay a solitary wooden hut, standing separate from all the others as if in exile.

"That there is the barracks prison," Salem said, noting the attention I'd been giving it.

I shivered. The decrepit shack was almost my lodgings and might still be, if I ever failed inspection. "Why don't we take that walk you promised?"

"Well now." Salem glanced around the Plain for a sizable pause. A marked off-handedness returned to his voice when he asked, "Seems mighty friendly, that Captain Machin. How is it you did say you know him?"

"We met at the Iron Works, where the Chain was constructed."

"What do you suppose such a heap is for?" He scratched his jaw. "Much too large for hauling ships, I reckon."

"If the officers haven't filled you in on their mission, I'm not about to spill the beans." I chuckled. "But I imagine you already know about the last chain, if you've been here awhile."

"Hmmm." After a deliberate settling of his tricorn on his head, he reasoned aloud, "Colonel Greaton said it was uncordial to detain a lady. A short turn about the Plain might be all right. Let us keep to the riverside."

On the southern tip of the vast acres was a fort in progress. Its eastern and southern walls, those facing the water, stood above shoulder height. The remaining portions were enclosed, stretching in a wave of stonework that crested and fell again, in some places not even rising as high as one's waist. Emphasis had been placed on securing the direction most feared of enemy attack—the river. The barracks inside the fort were near completion, however. Smoke drifted from several chimneys.

It was a tight squeeze as soldiers pushed a cannon past us, pressing us close to a trench that circled the walls. Water was collected along the bottom. It wrapped around the fort, to the Plain's edge, creating a small waterfall that splashed into a second trench on a rocky shelf below, which wended its way parallel to the shoreline before tumbling into the river.

Stubborn as a grousing old mule, the cannon stuck fast in a muddy rut. The soldiers rocked it back and forth, teetering like Sisyphus cursed to roll an impossible boulder uphill to no avail. They drew to attention when Salem and I offered to help.

"Begg'n yer pardon," one stopped me. "T'ain't no task for a lady."

The others acknowledged me politely, but the speaker knew the mind of the group, who all stood erect around the wagon, somehow blocking every portion with their bodies so there was nowhere for me to squeeze in.

I wandered away, frustrated.

Salem's contribution was more than welcome at the boys' club. Together, they heaved and shoved until finally, they achieved what the Corinthian king couldn't and built enough momentum to get the thing over the rut's ledge. Curious eyes passed over me as the cannon was turned into the fort's enclosure.

Partway along the manmade trench, a break separated the undergrowth. Just past the entangled plants' boundary, there was a split in the boulders, as if someone had cracked open a coconut and abandoned the two halves side-by-side. At my feet, the beginnings of a stairway had been carved to lead a brave wanderer down a steep incline, through the fissure, to a naturally formed stone platform. There were only three steps so far. I peered through the cleared growth but couldn't see anything, other than what Mother Nature had placed there. It was a long way down.

"Come now, Mistress," Salem called my attention from my odd discovery. "Nothing of interest to a lady over here. Just noise and the like."

We wandered the perimeter of the Plain, notably away from the interior of the fort or the clusters of other buildings in the encampment, keeping to the outer wall to circle back toward the northern end. Boots shuffling through the grass could be heard patrolling the area on the outside. Soldiers moving in tandem within the walls marked their progress. The Watch.

Several structures' foundations had been outlined along our path, using a hazardous stacking of sticks and logs. One day, these would become a library, military warehouse, storage for the quartermaster, and such and so on, according to Salem's description of the plans. All pie-in-the-sky fiction for the time being and, therefore, worthless intel for the enemy, should I be so inclined to share, I guess. Still, interesting as it was, it aggravated me to see everyone hard at work, including other women, while I was left to feel useless.

Near the finish line of our circular saunter, there was a wide tent in lieu of where a hospital would one day stand. Inside, a different doctor than the crotchety Doc. Hart was setting the ankle of a young soldier who'd slipped on the rocks. My stomach lurched. Brave as a seasoned veteran, the boy "done reckon it will hurt me some," then urged the surgeon to go on and snap his foot back into place. It'd been sticking out at an angle to the side. Bravado aside, he still loosed a muffled yell through the wooden rod clenched between his teeth. After the ghastly procedure, as medicine for his suffering, he guzzled a gill of gin, though he looked woozy from the experience.

I was asked to speak up, having mumbled a description of my savior from earlier that morning. Since every woman back to Eve, it seemed, had served as nurse at one point or another, it was a fool's errand even asking about her.

The doctor commented, "If you did want to express your thanks, you could fulfill a task to which she would have been called."

Grateful to have something to do beyond sightseeing, I silently vowed not to puke on any of the patients if he suggested I attempt any Genesis-era tasks, like bandaging Broken Ankle Guy. Instead, Doc. Pleasant undertook that himself and pointed to a bucket and mug, requesting a refill.

Although it was a fair walk—which was heaven, actually, given the warm weather and gorgeous setting—Salem led me to a stream that ran behind the Red House until it joined the Hudson River, as "it has the best water for thirsting." Enjoying the peaceful waterfall playing amidst the shady backyard, I loaded the bucket as much as I could reasonably tolerate.

Salem swiped the bucket from me to carry it himself, despite my protests, which left me just as useless as before. Chivalrous, maybe, but I could manage more than a mug, thank you. The hill from Hell on Gowns, notwithstanding.

Everyone in the hospital having enjoyed a few rounds on me, the doctor gave his blessing to our serving the soldiers working on the grounds, as well. Our self-appointed duty began on the towpath. Though I would've loved to have found Jonathan right away, I was hailed by numerous men at the Chain's Redoubt, each filthy and exhausted from their labor. Every trip led us closer to where he was stationed, at the Water Redoubt beyond.

"Oh, bless you, Miss Molly," and other similar thanks were my reward for giving them a share from the bucket. After several trips between the stream and the redoubt, and maybe the fourth or fifth time someone called me Molly, I realized that I had officially become a Molly Pitcher. It made me smile…until the unwanted image of a fluttering mauve skirt caught in broken berry bushes overwhelmed my vision.

The rerun sucked, and I was a mess by the time the memory cleared and Salem's face materialized. "Give it here, now." He was prying the mug from my clenched fist.

Construction was stuck on pause, worry clear on the starved faces surrounding me.

"I'm fine," I lied, smearing away the tears with the back of my hand. Water splattered down the side of my gown as I jerked the mug back. Real convincing.

"Let us return to the Officers' House. It is time for dinner, any a'ways."

Loyalty to their duty as their guide, and most definitely to their fellow soldier stuck corralling a damp-cheeked, petticoat-soaked female, the men—en masse—stopped acknowledging me and resumed their sweaty detail. Well, one bluecoat lamented momentarily on my behalf, "the poor brim."

Stewing in an emotional soup, I strode deeper into the cove.

"We shall go no farther," Salem announced, feet rooted in place. "I must insist you return to the house for dinner."

I obeyed long enough to steal the bucket from him. "You can go if you're hungry. I'm going to keep working."

"You have done plenty. Come with me, Mistress."

Fortunately, he didn't seem willing to lay hands on me and force the issue. I resumed my task, not caring whether the rest of my water brigade accompanied me, though I must've looked like a Greek fury storming the rocky pathway, my weapons of divine justice taking the form of a mug swinging in one fist and the wooden bucket slamming against my leg from the other. What few men had waved me over flinched, or else chuckled, as I glared.

As the Fates would have it, Jonathan was on the far, far, far end of the redoubt's hill, shoving a sizeable stone in place. I'd calmed down sufficiently by then, so mythological vengeance wasn't on my mind, but my appearance wore my former intention to wreak havoc. A few browncoats asked if I was a'right.

Jonathan's smile, as he slapped the dirt from his hands and approached, faded. "What troubles you?" He accepted the mug from me but didn't drink, waiting for an explanation.

"Freaking memory," I complained. "It rattled me, and now I'm cranky, and—"

"A memory of home?"

"Several, actually. Half the time, I swear, it's like I'm living in my own head, seeing things I don't understand and doing stuff with people I barely remember." I sighed. "But no. This latest was from the war." I ducked my head, feeling my cheeks burn.

"There is not a man or woman who does not fight the horrors of war." He dipped his chin to catch my eye. "The only difference is how."

"You don't," I murmured.

"Then you have not been paying attention."

He drank while I stared at him, puzzled. Thoughts of his private conversation with Alexander, about how he struggled with Cordelia's death, made me feel guilty. He carried a grief that consumed him. "I'm sorry."

"For what grievous sin do you deem you need apologize? Did you take tea today instead of coffee?" he teased.

"Ha ha." Confessions and hauntings of our past weren't something I wanted either of us to dwell on, so I gave my standard response, "I'll be fine."

"I know that you will be. Here." White linen blossomed from the fingers he held out to me. Another handkerchief from his endless supply. Leaning in, he doused it with water from the mug. "Will you permit me to…?" His hand lifted. "Though…mayhaps you—"

"Captain." The moment between us was broken as Salem tattled on me: "The lady has refused to take dinner."

"You know, I *was* going to apologize to you for being rude." My not-yet-resolved irritability hindered the joke. It probably came off as haughty.

"Was it not your wish that she dine with the officers?"

Jonathan sighed. "You must eat."

"Have you?" I answered, knowing full well he hadn't.

Wooden vessels passing from my hands, to his, to Salem's—he led us in a round of hot potato I didn't enjoy. "Please, give us a moment's privacy," he asked my determined shadow, then steered me gently by the elbow away from the redoubt, to where we'd be out of earshot of the other soldiers. Never out of sight, though. Salem made sure of that.

"Think not of me," Jonathan said.

"That's a stupid thing to ask me," I answered, not unkindly.

He hummed in response. "Your gesture is well-intentioned, though there is none who would begrudge you a meal, least of all me. You give greater insult to the men by not accepting what little their regiments have to offer—as Heaven knows—they, themselves, are in tremendous want."

"What makes me so special?"

"What do we fight, bleed, and starve for, if not to provide for our own?"

"Something doesn't feel right about it."

"Do it for the men, then, if not for yourself." He was only half-kidding.

"My act of heroism is to eat? How noble."

"We each of us play our part," he countered and offered the dampened handkerchief again. I smacked him on the shoulder as we chuckled at his reminder of our riverside conversation, then took a stab at cleaning my cheeks. It was disgusting how much dirt washed off. Even Jonathan didn't want the thing back.

Instead, he lightly traced his knuckles along the side of my hand, saying, "I wish to speak with you. Let us hope this evening, if you would allow it, about the other memories you mentioned."

I nodded in agreement. "There's a lot I want to talk to you about too."

"I shall hear all that you would tell me."

The leaves over our heads rustled. Bright blue fluttered closer. Our feathered scout was watching. Jonathan pressed a hand on my arm to silence me before I could voice my recognition aloud. "Not here," he warned, drawing my attention to where Salem was waiting for us.

I felt like a little kid, dragging my feet as he escorted me from my schooling back to the redoubt and said, "Please heed my request, Miss Moore."

"Fine. I'll go get fat, just for you," I mocked even while conceding.

"Would that it were possible here," Jonathan smiled sadly.

Then he handed me over to my guard.

Chapter Twenty-Seven

We missed dinner, which meant a second apology was owed to Private Salem. The officers loomed over their empty dishes, absorbed with their plans. Their aides had received what little was left, we learned. General Parsons ordered Ensign Allyn to see if the quartermaster could make amends. I begged him not to, blocking the ensign's path through the doorway. "Really. It doesn't seem right." An ensemble of huffed mumbling and wrinkled brows told me how peculiar the men found me. "Please excuse my interruption."

"Hold a moment. Your arrival is rather fortunate," Parsons informed me. "There is some business Colonel Greaton has with you."

A chill ran through me. "With me?"

Greaton nodded. In a gallant gesture, he offered his battered-crate-turned-seat to me, then commanded his aide to fetch a Private Phillips.

I melted onto the crate, stunned at the prospect of finding my forgotten family so suddenly, when just hours earlier it seemed there was no hope. I wished Jonathan was there. Random memories of Stephen had already escaped the curse's cell. Pretty sure my schoolteacher brother was never a soldier, so I figured it wasn't him. Who, then, could this private be? Every moment we waited was unbearable.

Parsons tried to distract me, asking, "Have you seen the Works, Miss Moore?"

"I have." My lap was still damp. I settled my folded hands on the table instead.

"What think you?"

"They're coming along nicely."

"Would you be so good as to inform me?" He smiled and offered a drink from the clay jug sitting in the center of the table. "I have not had the opportunity to inspect the day's progress."

"Thanks, but no." I breathed a laugh. Chances were it was alcohol—the last thing I needed while my head was already loopy from hunger.

"What, pray tell, is amusing?" Nixon chastised my tone. "That the general should seek the insights of a woman. Perhaps you share our sentiments on that score."

"I meant the drink. Though feel free to be straight with me. You want to know how much I know. What I might share with the enemy, if I'm not on the up-and-up, that is."

"General McDougall found your cleverness entertaining. You may not find as much patience here without him."

Three guesses as to who topped that list.

"Sorry. It's how I cope when I'm stressed," I said. "I get it's not a joke. Hundreds of men's lives are at stake. And yeah, I'd be happy to fill you in, if you really are interested."

"I should be," Greaton told the room.

My report of my observations drew eager interest once I got going, though we were interrupted before long. Private Phillips was announced.

A decade easily separated me from the kid that strode through the door. It was a wonder he'd waited for the aide to lead him in, what with his cocky attitude guiding him. At best, he was a baby brother I'd forgotten. His brown uniform hung loose around his lanky build. And it was short, given his height, exposing bony ankles and bare, blistered feet.

I stared, waiting for a memory to seep free from its prison, or even a determined ache from the curse fighting me. Nothing, other than the thought that his toffee-colored hair was too dark to match mine.

Phillips saluted the officers without paying any attention to me. "No letters, sir."

"Private, know you this woman?" Greaton asked.

The kid held his own against his commanding officer, barely glancing at me to answer, "I ne'er did, sir. I was at my post all the night, sir."

Unsolicited denials were as good as a confession. I raised my brows at Parsons to see if he caught it. He frowned.

"Make certain, Phillips," Greaton insisted.

Turning to face the boy when the colonel asked him, I also stood to give him a better look. I already knew the answer, but was dying to hear his. Cock-of-the-walk, he closed in to reconnoiter me with his eyes. Wickedness filled his lopsided smirk, and his response to my breasts went something like: "I surely should like to."

The colonel gasped and cuffed the back of his shoulder. "This lady is Mistress Savannah Phillips."

"I ain't no cousin taker!"

I landed heavily on the crate. Thank goodness the thing didn't break. My whole body trembled with suppressed laughter.

"Well, Miss…Phillips." Parsons looked at me for an answer.

I scrunched my mouth shut, still struggling, as I shook my head *no way*.

Greaton was beside himself. "Out, Private. At once."

The boy's gaze darted from officer to officer, appearing unsure about what'd just happened. He actually had balls enough to ask, "Here, I ain't in a bad loaf, am I?"

"That remains to be seen." His commanding officer grimaced at him. "For now, you are dismissed."

Phillips swore under his breath when he left, but not before he shot me a nasty glare, as if I was the source of all his ills. Maybe he shouldn't have played hooky. We heard an aide snap at him out in the hall, "You have left the marks of your dirty hocks on the clean boards."

His bare feet slapped against the wooden floor as he stamped away from the scene of his sure-to-be future reprimand.

"It seems the Watch was one short last night." Colonel Putnam sniggered.

Since the officers were laughing openly at Greaton's frustration, I felt free to join them. "Don't look at me." I raised my hands.

Greaton sputtered, "That lad draws out trouble from every corner."

Parsons had me confirm what the room had already deduced—I didn't recognize the boy. Still, I thanked Greaton for thinking to ask me.

"I am not certain I have done you a kindness," he apologized.

Ensign Allyn returned with a bit of tepid cheese and dried bread. Not wanting to appear ungrateful, as Jonathan had warned against, I picked up the cloudy dairy byproduct and relayed the rest of my progress report. Reaching its conclusion—which was light on details of the redoubts, courtesy of my previous life flashing before my eyes—I scraped a fingernail along the oxidized edges and found it just as unappetizing underneath. I replaced it on the plate, uneaten. Stale carbs, my favorite.

Putnam pulled out a knife to cut off the outer edges and offered me the fresher interior of the cheese lump while he helped himself to the hardened end pieces. The effort it took him to chew through them convinced my lightheaded mind that my churning stomach was the wiser judge. The lump was later claimed by Nixon.

"Have we a blower at the camp?" Putnam was still considering the question of what the wayward private had been doing the night before.

"General Parsons, really, this…this…!"

The idea seemed repugnant to a couple of the officers, though not everyone joined Greaton's rebuff of the subject. A handful of aides lingered, surreptitiously watching the general for an answer.

Parsons sighed and considered the matter aloud. "Distasteful as it may be, I had rather a single whore we can manage to service the men than a crack who slips herself in and out of the camp. Who knows if such a one would also lie with the enemy and accept greater coin for her information?"

At the question of whether one could be procured, a hovering aide cleared his throat, directing a decided look toward me. I glared at him.

Greaton huffed, appearing offended.

"Worry not," the general reassured me, then turned his own rebuke on the aide. "We would not wish to upset His Excellency by taking that to which his agent lays his claim."

News to me, though I didn't know which surprised me more—learning the general Jonathan had been answering to all that time was General Washington, or that the officers thought he had some sort of claim on me. Surely, the conversation from the previous night about my maiden versus married name made it clear he wasn't my husband.

Wait. Did that mean the room thought I was his blower?

I bolted for the door.

"Please forgive the offense, Miss Phillips," Greaton called to my back.

"I am no one's whore."

My flight from the Red House was slowed for a sympathetic moment—the muddy stains of Private Phillips' footprints on the floor were tinged with blood.

Chapter Twenty-Eight

Rushing from the Red House, I flew across the lawn and broke into a full-out run upon reaching the river path. All sorts of appeal tempted me toward the cove to find Jonathan and bitch at him about the state of affairs.

As fun as it would've been to watch his face explore every shade of red, on and off the spectrum, once I shared the revelation that I'd been earmarked as his personal sex toy, I resisted the urge. Instead, I gathered my skirts, filled my lungs to bursting, and charged up the incline to the Plain. My muscles were screaming by the time I reached the top. They could go right ahead, until I was blue in the face. I pushed through it, weaving my way through the middle of Camp Hut, to put as much distance between me and the officers as possible. The cliff's edge at the far side of the Plain marked the end of the line for my indignant exit strategy.

With all of West Point behind me, I bent over—the dress falling back around my ankles—and clasped my knees to catch my breath, showing all those self-important men which body part they could kiss.

The sun was hovering above the mountains, and the cool of early evening had settled in. Countless boats bespeckled the water, conducting their business. Continental and unknown. Saffron pebbles of sunlight twinkled off the waves and onto the wooden sides of the ships as they bobbed on the current. Soldiers continued to labor under the weight of the Chain, not yet secured to the shore. My anger lessened as I hoped, for their sakes, the enormous task wouldn't require a midnight shift on the water.

A muttering of Polish carried on the shifting wind, without the physical presence of Colonel Kościuszko visible anywhere to give it wing. Other soldiers toiled around me on the Plain, in constant motion like their counterparts on the river below us. Literal bits of the mountains were hauled across the extensive campgrounds. Shovels stabbed the ground, swinging in an arch to fling dirt into large, cylinder-like woven baskets. These were the foundation for earthen fortifications, destined to encircle the entire Plain.

Marching, drilling, building—onward it went. Light in the sky meant darkening their hands with the plentiful work required. The Watch, however, was perpetual.

Closer study as I wandered revealed how many soldiers lacked proper clothing, like Private Phillips. Exhaustion or starvation, or both, clung to them better than the rags and tatters rotting over their emaciated frames. Boots, if they had them, were almost a burden—worn thin, particularly the soles that peeled as the men struggled through their duties. Several bore crusty pustules on their skin; they were recovering still from a brush with smallpox. Yet they persisted, because it was what their new nation demanded of them.

My search for the aethereal Polish phrases led me to the hidden passage in the brush. Greenery and shadows there, deep within the descent through the broken stone. A shower of gravel tripped noisily down the slope as I ventured beyond the trio of steps.

"*Kto tam idzie?*" rose from amid the boulders.

"It's me, Colonel. Savannah Moore?"

Kościuszko rounded the rocky corner. Wearing a linen shirt and short pants, he lacked a way to sheath the dagger in his hand since he was stripped of his other accessories. Even his curls were out of uniform, reaching new heights in the back where he'd scratched his head too many times while thinking. It was an endearing habit, I discovered.

"What you search me for?"

Having worked out that he probably meant *why* instead of *what*, I was about to improvise some nicety about wanting company, in a way that didn't betray my loneliness for allies, but he interrupted. "Forgive me, I am not in clothing."

"That's all right." I laughed. "What're you doing?"

"You would like to see? Or…perhaps Captain Wythe should be made to come. You have not his say."

Swallowing aggravation at the second suggestion in less than an hour that I wore an invisible collar with Jonathan's name etched into it, I said with measured evenness, "I recall arriving here by myself, without Captain Wythe."

"This is truth. If you think he would not feel mad."

Jonathan's opinion could take a swim in the East River with the British fleet, for all I cared.

I shut that thought down in a New York minute and just smiled.

Kościuszko seemed to pick up on the tenor of my reaction. "It would not be very bad." He drawled his words while he noted, "There are the men everywhere."

He disappeared around the boulder again.

Was that an open invitation to brave the triple black diamond slope, in a gown, on my own? Craning my neck to see where he went was useless, so...rock on, I guessed. Turning my feet sideways gave me the leverage necessary to keep from slipping.

The colonel reappeared, half-in and half-out of his uniform jacket. "*Co robisz?*" And nearly took a dive down the incline as his jacket sleeve straightened and his arm shot through, unbalancing him. He steadied himself, then met me to offer his hand for the final portion of the descent and escort me around the boulder to his secret headquarters.

"So much noise. So much men. There is not the place for me to think," he said with some embarrassment.

From our balcony of that stony palace, we beheld another spectacular view of the southern half of the river; the wilds of the Hudson Valley dressed in her spring best greeted us through the trees. A natural alcove was worn into the boulder we'd circled, which was where Kościuszko had deposited his sword, hat, and sketches of his projects. An impressive rendering of the fort and the future surrounding buildings was drawn open. I diverted my gaze.

"Ah." He rolled up the plans he'd been ready to share with me. "I am foolish. Of course, a girl would not have the interest in such a thing."

"It's not that. As a *woman*, I actually am interested. It's just it's dangerous for me to know as much as I do. That's the kind of thing..." I tipped my chin toward his scroll. "...the redcoats would kill to get their hands on."

The fact that his drawing already seemed familiar was also worrying.

He was astounded. "I beg pardon for not think so much. My *raison* is the trust Captain Wythe has in you. Let me assure you." He placed his hand to his heart to tell me, "Never before have I offered to one is not the officer."

"I'm sure. Thanks, though. I'm flattered."

A tapestry of vines wound over the rocks, mingling with the scrub beside us. Patches of buttercups stretched over the tree-laden hill that plunged toward a thin carpet of grass peppered with tiny, white flowers.

"I can see why you like it here," I said. "It's breathtaking."

And the fragrance from the landscape, I found to be just as intoxicating.

"This, I show you." He opened a different roll of paper. "If, as you say, you have the interest."

It was an impressive pencil drawing of his sanctum. He had it all planned out, beyond the three steps already begun. Kościuszko was going to make his own Garden of Eden.

"The stone, it is to be wide." He showed me the sketch of an improved alcove. "There must be a place for a man to sit. Here…" His fingers flew across the page to another stone shelf below where we stood. "…I will have earth to bring for plant. There will be a wall of this height…" He demonstrated with his hand, held at knee level. "…for the flowers. And a fountain!" His excitement grew as he pointed from sketch to landscape. "No man would do it. The Yankees, they slave," he explained, "for the good of the war. But this, this *I* do, for the good of the peace."

Inspiration burst over his eager expression, which he hastened to add to the plans. I watched, amused, as his curls were reorganized while he calculated and scribbled in the latest workings of his imagination.

Rather than risk hindering him by my presence—an engineering tweak to the fountain's mechanism, was my best guess—I shuffled down the escarpment to visit his future masterpiece on the lower ledge.

It was too noisy an enterprise for even his busy mind to miss. He leaped into action and insisted on going ahead of me and assisting, all while flattering my courage and grace of movement in such a place. Given how steep the hill was, not to mention how cumbersome the multilayered gown made the adventure, I couldn't be upset. Well, at least not fairly.

He plucked a leaf from the indentation in the dirt, where he'd outlined the fountain's perimeter, near the edge closest to the river. "Set so as to allow the tiring soldier to see all the many things before him…or her." Backing up, he invited me to do the same. "A panorama of the Heaven, the Earth, the Air, and the Water lay in perfect glory before us." Kościuszko dropped his hands from their demonstration. "Perhaps it is foolish."

"It isn't foolish," I answered his self-reproach and smiled during his embarrassed jumbling of his curls. "It's beautiful."

A flock of geese swooped in from overhead, toward the riverbank below. Their giant wings flapped in majestic sweeps as they claimed the terrain. Waggling their tails, feathers rustling, their noisy chorus picked up in counterpoint to where the daytime birds had quieted.

Without warning, a four-note cry sounded in a tree to our left. Over and over and over and over. Another bird shot from a nearby bush toward a quieter perch below. A famously black-not-blue bird. Peering into the dense branches next to us, I saw brown-and-white mottled feathers fluff up, to restart the endless tune. Reinforcements joined in much louder.

Cleophes fled to the north.

"What on earth is that?" I asked, a little envious of my feathered friend's freedom.

"Ah! How you have not heard before? It is…what the men call…a whip-will?"

"That's a whippoorwill? That's annoying."

"You now have begun to know." Kościuszko spoke with great authority. They were the bane of every soldier wanting a good night's sleep. And every woman, I soon learned.

Against his better judgment—probably the wisest in the end; his initial reaction was to burst out laughing, as if my mad scheme was meant as a joke—he agreed to climb down the steep slope to explore with me. We shoved our way through the thick underbrush until it opened onto the grassy bank where the geese had flocked. It was tempting to charge through them, like kids, to see if we could make them scatter. Once we'd reached a point where it was physically possible to have at them, the size of the birds warned how the geese would be the winners of that game.

Instead, we yielded the field to the gaggle and followed the river toward Gee's Point, the very tip of West Point's lower embankment. Kościuszko described it with extended fingers, outlining the rocky ledge from the Plain that plummeted onto the shore. The bulging outcrop blocked our access to the Point and, thankfully, enemy soldiers hoping to invade the redoubts on the towpath via a southern land route.

Staring up the hill that'd somehow morphed into a cliff from this angle—how the hell were we going to climb that thing, me in a gown and him with a pistol and Mother of Swords strapped to his belt?—I suggested a break. We chose a near-dry rest stop on the rocks to take in the river traffic. A lazy afternoon of watching the latest excitement had passed for the Valley Folk, courtesy of the Continental army, and rush hour commenced for their homeward-bound ships.

"Were you at Saratoga, Colonel?"

"I was," he acknowledged.

"Do you know General Schuyler?"

"He is a man make honor. He is so much to fight for the Liberty. Do not believe lies. I gave the warning—Ticonderoga was in a place of weakness. Cannon was needed on Sugar Loaf Hill. That. That is why she was lost," he complained.

That's right. I remembered the story: Schuyler demanded a court martial to clear his name, having been accused of abandoning the fort in exchange for silver bullets shot into its walls as supposed payment.

"So, you know him well. Enough to recognize one of his daughters?" I asked quietly.

He eyed me. "Why you ask?"

"It's just…a memory came back to me today…of my father." I pictured all the other visions I'd had, including while at Mr. Cloet's house, of the snowy-white-haired man in a blue uniform. "He introduced himself as General Schuyler…?"

Kościuszko stiffened, as did his tone. "You try to…to…*uzurpować*."

I shook my head, because I didn't know what he meant. Frustrated, he bolted to standing, waving his hand at me while he searched aloud for an appropriate English equivalent. "You must not take what is not yours."

"I'm not trying to take anything. I just want to figure out who I am, where I belong."

"Explain what this is you say."

"I can't remember my life. When I do, it's in pieces, and they don't always make sense. But those memories are clear and convincing. Until I realize what I thought was the truth…isn't. You have no idea how awful it is to have your mind fail you. I don't know what to believe anymore."

He calmed. "You have the infliction, is what say Captain Wythe, *oui?*"

"I was cursed, and he can't break it."

Kościuszko held out his hand, as if offering his palm so I could read his future. It spoke of countless hours of dirt and toil. Then he crossed the divide between us, to where I was still sitting, and raised his hand to my forehead.

When he sank onto the rocky seat next to me, the doubt had left his expression. "Not but he who make the curse can break."

Saddened by the sheer hopelessness in his statement, it made my voice catch. "I know."

After a prolonged silence, he added softly, "You look not like the Misses Kayler. Your hair is light. They, dark. Your eyes, green. They have the brown eyes. Miss Betsy, her eyes are…"

A treasured memory of Eliza Schuyler kept him quiet for some time. It shone through the color of his cheeks and happy smile. Embarrassed at having revealed his secret, he ultimately asked me to not share what'd been said. He agreed to do the same for me in return.

The dance of the many boats on that glorious sunset-enlivened river left us content to watch in silence. Yelling from the water killed our respite dead.

Chapter Twenty-Nine

At first, we couldn't tell what the old man's deal was. He sounded hysterical and screeched and hollered for help. Finally, he swiped at the water, and the spray ricochetting off an unknown source several feet away became more obvious. A small figure burst through the chop. It was a dog, scratching and clawing at the surface, and struggling against the rushing current. The man yelled again as it went under.

Except, no one was helping him.

Soldiers gathered above us with weapons drawn. Honor bound to guard the vicinity, the men appeared unwilling to leave their post and risk the treacherous descent to the river. They split their numbers, spreading out around the perimeter of the Plain to keep watch, perhaps suspecting it was a diversion from incoming danger.

None of the other locals were on their way either. He'd rowed far enough away from the Chain, presumably on his way home from a full afternoon of gawking, there weren't any ships nearby. Who knew if they could even hear him?

I turned to Colonel Kościuszko, who confessed his skills were more military than aquatic. Disgusted, I whipped the pins from the bodice of my dress. He babbled some nonsense about the wisdom of such an act as my gown tumbled to the grass.

"Someone has to help," I snapped. Shedding the rest of my attire down to my shift, I rushed into the water and froze partway.

Crap, it's cold!

But the animal was shrinking from sight, helpless against the current carrying it downriver, much too fast for its distraught owner to catch it. An entire fortress of soldiers, and its best hope was me. Just what I deserved for complaining about my limited opportunities for heroics.

"Stupid is as stupid does," someone, somewhere in my past once said. I resumed course, taking the plunge as soon as the water was deep enough. The current shot me forward, the river being swollen with winter runoff. Better to work with it than fight, so I swam toward the animal on a diagonal.

A gunshot cracked through the air. The water exploded several feet in front of me, where it struck. Who the hell would shoot at a dog?

Behind me, I could hear Kościuszko; a mishmash of languages echoed off the face of the rocky wall. Jonathan screamed, "Stop!"

If they don't shut up, every redcoat within miles will be on us.

I scanned the nearby shore for unfriendlies. The trees whizzed by, their rushing shadows blurring whatever lurked inside, watching.

I lost sight of the dog. It'd gone under somewhere ahead of me.

What had once been my limbs deadened into logs in minutes. Already, I was aching and stiff from the remnants of winter clinging to the tide. My legs bore the worst of it, having taken a beating earlier during my Olympic flight from the Red House, not to mention scaling the rocky cliff with the colonel.

Shadows slithered over the water. Really inconvenient time for the sun to slip behind the mountain. Was ten more minutes so hard? I reached for a dark clump.

Are there eels?

I swiped my hand back.

No. Snapping turtles. I'd...

My thoughts blurred; the cold was getting to me.

I grabbed at the clump. It was a branch.

Boat... Where's the boat?

The retreating daylight stole my perception of space and location. Shouting echoed everywhere. I tried to stand. A swift and vast emptiness churned beneath me. Treading water sped me along the current's trajectory, whether I liked it or not. My shift snaked around my legs during my efforts, binding them. Paralyzing cold crashed over me, and I was sucked into darkness.

I forced my legs to kick through the numbness. Once, twice, and broke the surface. Jonathan's voice reached me through the roaring of the growing rapids, shouting out my location.

Something brushed against my arm. I jerked away.

A whimper.

The dog. Its mouth snapped at the air, as if it was gulping its last breath, because unable to paw at the water any longer, it was swallowed by the river. I snatched at the miniature whirlpool. My fingers passed over fur.

Shit!

Too late, I realized how much danger I was in, when I—too—was snagged by the undertow.

Black...

Where...?

Panicking. Can't. I'm—

My shoulder smashed into the surface of a boulder as the rushing water forced me into its submerged base. I was dragged around the edge, raked across a jagged bit in the process, toward an unpleasant end. My fingers scratched over a piece of it, then were wrenched loose.

Down I went, captured by the pull on the far side. A squishy mass slammed my stomach. The impact jolted my mind into high gear. I grabbed onto the thing, then pushed, pushed as hard as my weary legs would let me against the rock. But the undertow prevented us from going anywhere. Fatigue wasn't helping.

Light, brightening from a tiny pinprick out of the gloom, welcomed me. A memory of swimming with my family at the lake warmed me. My parents waving to me from the dock. Laughter from other families trickling along the water. Floating on the breeze, the smoky blend of grilled meat. There was lemonade waiting for me. Come and have some. But I didn't drink lemonade. I was a mermaid. I could swim through anything. Kick like a dolphin, the way my parents taught me.

Watch me, Daddy!

Summer sun glittered off the water, blinding me. Was it…?

It wasn't the sun lighting the way. It was a key, awash with a brilliant, silver light, urging me to escape the watery depths surrounding me.

No, I'm not going to die.

I drew my legs together and beat them as hard as I could. Following the key straining against the ribbon around my neck, I dolphin-kicked over and over until I burst through the river's surface, gasping. The warmth from the memory faded as the evening air struck me.

Voices sounded. I reached overhead, trying to hold the mass above water. They grew closer, letting me know where the shore was.

Cold. Freezing cold. I wanted out. My limbs were leaden. The thing in my arms was so heavy. I had to get to…

Follow the voices.

My soles scraped against a solid patch. The river dragged me past it. Men, closer. My feet collided with the ground again. This time, I found my footing and stumbled to standing. The air burned; it tore at my frozen skin. I dropped, exhausted, into the water, where the wind couldn't bite me.

Pressure struck my shoulder. Hands. They grasped my upper arm. Yanked me. My other arm was seized. I was dragged forward. A dripping mass was pried from my grasp. Soldiers were barking questions. Loud. Unclear. Muffled.

A weight wrapped around my shoulders, causing me to stumble. I was hauled upright. A damp cloth with a hefty lump in it was pushed into my arms. Hands held its weight from underneath. Garbled shouts from the distance answered the voices surrounding me.

A whimper. It was a dog.

Why do I have a wet dog?

I tried to rub it with the cloth. The scrap fumbled from my deadened fingers. All of me shook. It was so cold.

Why did my dad take me swimming at night?

Rough hands grabbed my face. Words formed out of the harsh sounds being flung at me. "Why would you do that? Are you mad?"

Those hands scrubbed against my arms.

Warm. I heard him say warm.

I liked that word.

Chapter Thirty

Things were kinda hazy, beginning right around my sunset drowning and resolidifying into the present duress in the attic bedroom. A fire was stoked until it roared, an inferno to the curious who poked their heads in, wiping their brows, but too intrigued by the commotion to leave. Hands raced over me, flicking aside my collar, shoving up my sleeves, my hem. A voice cataloged aloud the torn skin, bleeding scrapes, river slime, and other trinkets relating to my madhouse excursion.

Jonathan.

He was welcome to keep the snail caught in my stocking.

Swaddled first into my blanket and cloak, I was engulfed by his greatcoat next. Whimpering arose from my chest, under the layers, during the jostling. A dog. The little bugger made it. With his fur matted against his body, trim and trembling—more puppy than adult—I worried about how the effort of holding such a small animal was exhausting me.

A dictator to our tiny corner of military might, Jonathan grew hoarse ordering people around. He snapped at anyone who dared delay in their response, including Colonel Greaton, who'd come in to survey the situation. Born out of pity for me or Jonathan, and I imagine the general goodness of his heart, the colonel didn't scold my frantic protector for forgetting who outranked whom. The reprimand he received was for not pouring out the spirits he'd promised to see delivered moments earlier. Had Greaton actually left the room to fetch them first, the grief might've had some teeth.

Private Salem, however, heard the worst of it.

"Were you not assigned as guard to her?" Jonathan berated. "Is your duty so oppressive that you care for nothing, other than where she goes, and not for seeing her safe?"

That was where I drew the line.

It was Salem whose attention I captured, and he pointed out my efforts to interrupt. Abandoning his authoritarian manner, Jonathan flew to my side and leaned close to hear me repeat, "Stop." He was drawing breath for a full-throttle tongue-lashing, no doubt, but I said, "Comfort me."

Confusion knit his brows.

"Like before."

"Get out. Leave!" He chased our audience into the stairwell. "None is to enter, Private. None." Slamming the door behind him, he rushed back over. "Tell me what it is you need."

"When you cast your spells on—"

"They are not spells."

"You healed me."

"God's teeth." His head dropped.

Skirted around the issue, alluded to it, agreed it was secret—we'd done all that, but never had we acknowledged the truth outright: a power, beyond what an ordinary man possessed, resided within him.

The door creaked open. Private Williams had apparently lost whatever debate had been brewing outside, because he raced into the room, a wild look of fear in his eyes, as if the three-headed beast of the underworld might lunge for his throat. He deposited an offering on the ground—a safe distance away, lest he become one of the deceased, I suppose—and fled before Jonathan's wrath could be unleashed again.

Ironically, Colonel Kościuszko was the one spared that day. Membership privileges of the Mystical Boys' Club. He narrowly avoided the fleeing private crashing into him as he entered, bold as Hercules on his quest. My wayward clothing and accessories were returned, though—with his apologies—many of the bodice's pins had been lost.

Retrieving a mug from the imaginary altar on the attic floorboards, he laid a hand on Jonathan's shoulder and whispered. My overtaxed protector huffed at the news. Kościuszko merely shrugged.

"Here." Jonathan shoved the mug to my mouth, forcing a thick, spicy wine on me.

I gagged and spat it out.

"Drink, woman. Please."

"Alcohol."

"It will warm you."

"My skin." Another physical exchange disturbed the puppy, who gave a pathetic whine. "Stop." I buried my face into the blanket. "It'll just kill me faster."

Jonathan slumped backward, landing on the architectural structure he abhorred the most, which was liberally coated with mud.

Confident my patchy recollection of the medical explanation wasn't going to remedy the moment, I snuggled the puppy, debating what to say. Misfortune's Mutt nestled deeper into my side. "I couldn't just watch and do nothing."

Head hung over the abandoned mug in front of him, Jonathan stared into his open palms laid across his knees. "Is this to punish me? Are you punishing me?"

Kościuszko met my shocked look. Lips pressed tight, he hovered, silent.

I hardly knew how to answer. "Why—?"

"I will delay, Captain." The colonel certainly bought us privacy in a hurry. He was exit stage *now* in a flash.

Curious eyes peered from behind the swinging door. They disappeared as he whipped it shut. Multiple sets of footsteps marched downstairs.

"Jonathan?"

"For forcing you to go to dinner," he mumbled.

"What?"

"For stopping you from assisting the men."

"No."

He looked so lost when he said, "For not delivering you to your home."

I reached out to him. "I would never hurt you like that."

"Your hand is ice," was his excuse for bending over to warm it with a kiss. Except then, his voice caught. "How could you be so foolish?"

I flinched at his sudden change, though he was distraught more than angry. It was hard to tell whether my words reached him when I whispered, "Someone had to save the puppy," because he didn't wait to lay into me.

"Regulars seek to take our lives. Hunters track our movements. British ships could, at any moment, make their way upriver to bombard us. Are there not dangers enough that you must purposefully throw yourself into harm's way?"

"Please." The ache traumatizing my lungs was worsening. Could rigor mortis set in before a body expired? "If I promise to listen…lecture me later?"

"Attended by regiments, still you make mischief for yourself." Both hands gripped my face. He searched my eyes, as if struggling to understand a secret message written there.

"You really think I'm selfish, don't you?" The realization stabbed at my center. It felt like I might burst.

"Oh, Miss…" He pressed his forehead to my chest, hiding the dampness collected on his cheeks. "Heaven, help me."

Nutmeg tickled my nostrils, my tongue, as I nuzzled into him and breathed in his scent. In my mind, I tasted the pleasant sting of it, how it sharpened autumnal desserts with a luxurious richness. Perhaps that was the fragrance that rose from him, garnishing the air between us.

Starting at my temples, his fingertips soothed a slow, gentle trail around my jaw. Happiness, laughter, sunlight—they blossomed from his touch, bringing summer's glow first to my face, then fluttering down my neck. I invited the sensation in—embraced it—allowing its warmth to penetrate me and still my body.

That little bit having achieved so much, I was able to breathe easier.

Lips apart, he stared, face full of wonder, as though he couldn't fathom the depths of his reach. "How…? I sought to calm you, nothing more."

Tearing aside the layers to uncover me, he hesitated before caressing my brow, sparking alive the line of muscles of my throat. Tracing my collar bone with the barest of touches at first, his fingers skimmed across its path, lengthening so his palm could glide along my skin. I gasped as he found harbor above my heart and it skipped a beat. Cupping my cheek with his other hand, he gathered me close, burrowing into my hair and reciting a Latin prayer into my ear like a whispered balm for my soul.

If the world stopped spinning, and all its inhabitants ceased to be, the radiant tranquility he wished into being for me would resonate through time. Peace and splendor, everlasting.

As the frostiness infecting me from my polar plunge melted and the shivering died down, my body relaxed, and I relished the spicy suggestion flavoring the heat rising from him. Light as a breeze kissing the water, barely stirring its surface, I touched my lips to his temple. He shifted alongside me until a sigh floated over my mouth. The moments passed as we stared, our breath flowing and ebbing together, wedded across the fraction of space.

An authoritative throat clearing interrupted us.

Colonel Putnam.

He considered me, too exhausted to vacate the bedding by the hearth to greet him. Then he addressed Jonathan, who rose to stand over me, palm to hilt. "If you are finished alerting the neighbors as to our presence."

Jonathan inclined his head without apology. The neighbors damn well knew we were there long before his tirade.

Putnam continued, "General Parsons has orders for you. The activity this day on the river has drawn much attention. It is time we knew for certain where the enemy lies. You will meet me at the fortress in a quarter of an hour to join a scouting mission. I suggest you prepare provisions."

Another mission, so soon after he'd arrived. Another unexpected harbinger of the obstacles separating us. My eyes met his. Worry filled them.

Putnam offered a brief smile at the yip from my furry bundle, before saying, "Captain Machin and Colonel Kościuszko are included in the party to journey to headquarters. They have both requested you accompany them.

As you will be indisposed, the lady may attend in your stead, should she be well enough. If that is agreeable to you."

"My thanks, Colonel. Might I give my answer once I have discussed the matter with the lady?"

A surprised laugh escaped him. "As her guardian, we naturally shall defer to your *discretion*." As he reached the door, he paused. "Be assured, the lady will be well attended, whatever your decision, Captain."

Jonathan thanked him again.

From standing at attention, he dropped to his knees the second Putnam disappeared around the corner. How he wasn't bruised was beyond me.

"You will stay here. Please, Miss Moore."

"You don't want me to go to headquarters?"

He sighed. "If you truly wish it. It is said the officers celebrate the recent treaty with France. You would find a proper dinner there. That said, I implore you not to go if you are unwell."

Recognizing Worry made a terrible second—dueling with Duty, and all its travails, was best won when his sights remain on his mission—I assured him, "I'll stay and rest. You won't recognize me when you return; I'll get so plump on whatever banquets they offer here. Assuming the food's edible, of course. It hasn't all been edible." My bravado faded around the last part. Besides, our respective guards' voices had reached the base of the stairwell.

"No more mischief, I beg of you. I shall not be here to watch over you."

"Jonathan." I sighed rather than argue. For his sake, I promised instead, "Trouble and I aren't on speaking terms anymore. You'll see. I'll be fine."

"Aye," he muttered, sounding like he was trying to believe it. "Give me the key."

Bit by bit by bit, the silk ribbon peeled in unsteady bursts from where it was pasted to my skin. He balled it into his hands, along with the key, and whispered as if imparting his confidences to the firefly glow building between his fingers. When he finished, the key reemerged as a shining star in his grasp. Though its glorious light wasn't what captivated him. A finger dragged across the soiled ribbon wilting from his palms.

"I'm sorry."

"It matters not," he answered dully.

Of course, it did. It was a poison in my mouth I wanted to spit out—how I regretted ruining his memento, even sympathized over Cordelia's murder—sentiments I couldn't express because I was meant to be ignorant of their significance.

Instead, I squeezed his hand in thanks as I accepted the key from him and restored it to its place. A faint blue line stained my skin, outlining where it belonged.

I shifted the dozing puppy and groaned. The little beast was like a boulder, hampering my ability to sit up. Oh, the lies we tell ourselves.

"Please." Jonathan clasped my shoulder. "You must sleep…so that you might heal."

"You're going to want your coat. It's still cold at night," I reminded him, "and I have a roaring fire with a stronghold's worth of wood stockpiled here, just for me. Thanks to you."

"Mayhaps, it would—"

"Of the two of us, you need to keep up your strength more. You're the soldier. I'm…I…" I didn't know what I was in that mess.

A simple "thank you" passed his lips, and he helped untangle the layers cluttered around me, possibly because it was the most expedient way to get me tucked back into bed. "What more can I do?"

"Nothing," I answered his humble inquiry. "Just…"

An arching willow branch rose and fell under my thumb, an unusual emblem for a coat button. Lost in the blue sea gazing back at me, I wished I knew how to comfort him in return.

Thoughts of Alexander's warning about my being a distraction were a rude interruption to our final moments together. I released his coat collar. "I don't need anything. Okay?"

He brushed a lock of hair behind my ear, continuing to stare, as if drinking in my face, memorizing every curve, the quality of my complexion, so he'd know if I'd heeded his advice and rested. Then he offered a regretful smile in return for mine. A resigned hand stroked the puppy's head before he stood.

From the doorway, he said, "You are incorrigible, Miss Moore."

"Always and forever."

"You are also most extraordinary."

"Good," I answered sincerely. "It means you won't forget to come back for me."

There was absolute surety in his voice when he vowed, "I will come back for you."

Chapter Thirty-One

The sounds of Colonel Greaton shooing the puppy from the breakfast dish he was trying to lay by the bed woke me. Soon, it became a game, and the colonel was swept up in it, teasing the dog with one hand, over to the other, to keep the little beast's attention away from the bowl. Yips and barks tracked the playful path of Greaton's arm, and my furry roommate stretched his front paws low to the ground, butt raised high in the air, waggling it along with his tail as he prepared to leap.

It was the first real look I'd gotten of the creature I'd risked my life to save, the both of us having been swathed like mummies once we'd emerged from our evening dip in the rapids. What a shaggy, white fluffball! Excluding his head, which was ebony colored—like the poof of his tail— and muzzled by a single powdery band. A giant, dark splotch decorated his one side, and another rode on his back.

I laughed and wished them a good morning, then wolfed down the porridge. Even sludge tasted like perfection to those starving.

"Good day, Miss Phillips, as it is past midday," Greaton greeted me in return, though his attention remained on the imperative task of tickling the dull red swaths poking out from behind the puppy's ears. The surname thing was an issue that required caffeine before tackling, if at all.

Glancing at the sunlight brightening the filmy windows, its source far beyond the limited view from the attic, I realized he was right.

A hint of soreness grabbed at my joints, though by his spell or magic or whatever Jonathan wished to call it, I'd been blessed with a deep and dreamless sleep that'd left me otherwise refreshed. Clearly, the puppy had gotten over the worst of it, too, if a little shaky on his XL-sized paws, and yipped as the colonel stood upright.

"Shall I take charge of the dog?" he offered. "You could dress…er, finish your breakfast in peace."

After everything I'd endured to save the hairy ragamuffin, I was reluctant to let him out of my sight. I sighed. Probably best to resist falling for the adorableness, though. Finding his real owner was added to the afternoon agenda.

Run out of steam, he flattened into a fur puddle—each leg splatted in every direction—and turned his head to the side quizzically as Greaton called, "Come. Come now, pup. Has he a name, Miss Phillips?"

"I have no idea."

"Come along, little dog. Let us go out of doors."

Scrambling to all fours, he backed away from the sound of the door creaking open. His high-pitched bark echoed through the cavernous attic, and he leaned forward again, frothy tail flopping, gearing up for more play. Called a third time, he whimpered and ran to me instead.

Scooping the puppy up, I ruffled his head. "Go on, silly boy. It's okay."

Enthusiastic kisses washed my face.

"It appears you have made a friend, Miss Phillips."

"Yeah, it does." Setting my little buddy loose again, I was prepping a fabricated recitation of my great expertise in managing dressing and dog sitting simultaneously…except I saw him sniffing around, pelvis lowered.

"Ah now." Greaton saw it, too, and grabbed him. "That settles the matter."

The puppy struggled and yipped, but was total soup in his arms once the belly rubbing began. Laughter traveled down the stairs as the pair made their exit.

Still damp and—ugh, reeking like river piss—my shift required intimate relations with soap, or else Jonathan's gift would be ruined. At least, it better be a gift and not a loan. For the love of all that was sacred, I hoped the dress hadn't belonged to Cordelia. That would've been worse. Thinking of the grief that weighted his body, the vacant tenor of his voice when he said the damage to her ribbon didn't matter, made me a little sick to my stomach.

Private Salem's eyes widened as I reached the second floor, wearing my original pants and shirt. "You rightly do not suppose to be seen in such as that?"

"Yeah. I rightly, actually do."

"What should Captain Wythe say, were he to see you?"

"Since he's the one who gave me these clothes, he'd probably say, 'Looking good, Miss Moore.'" All right, he'd die of embarrassment before those words were uttered, but a girl could pretend.

"Surely not." He was aghast, not skeptical, I noticed. "What say you wait here while I search out some proper garments for a lady?"

I served up a sly smile, then waltzed right past him. "You can feel free to stay here if you're embarrassed to be seen with me."

"Well now, I do not think I could do such as that. My orders are clear. I am to attend to you, and…" I stopped when I reached the stairwell leading to the first floor and waited for him so he could finish his speech, which was delivered dead into my eyes. "I will not be shirking in my duty again, no mistress."

"Please don't call me mistress." I laid my hand onto his, where it clasped the banister. "Look, I'm sorry Captain Wythe yelled at you so much yesterday. I hope the other officers didn't give you grief too."

Salem looked down to where my hand was resting on his, brows raised.

Friendly and forward. Great way to dispel the whole whore rumor. I relinquished my grasp and apologized. "*Did* I get you into trouble? What is that called? A 'bad loaf'?"

Shaking his head, he answered, "It is kind of you to take notice, all the same."

"This being kept prisoner thing and being told what to do—"

"You are not a prisoner, Miss Moore. I would that you not think of me attending you in such a way."

I tilted my head and tried lightening my tone. "Kinda hard when none of the other women have guards."

"None of the other women accompany an officer."

For real?

True, the officers' mess bore the many hallmarks of a frat house in full swing whenever I'd joined the party as the token female of the bunch. If he was right, the sorority of women I'd witnessed on the grounds were the family of the average soldiers, living in the same freezing huts as the men, instead of enjoying the relative penthouse of a third-class lodge like me. Or else, they were crammed into the humble, crowded barracks where Jonathan and the other lower officers had been stationed. Once more, Imposter Syndrome grinned its ugly teeth, making me self-conscious about how much preferential treatment I'd received.

Salem rubbed his chin, intrigued by my subsequent apology. "T'ain't nothing to forgive."

A mental stew for me to chew on until Jonathan's return.

We caught up with Greaton on the Plain, where my fluffy ward was doling out kisses to any of the boys-turned-soldier willing to ruffle his fur or sneak him a bite from their meager supplies. He tensed, paws spread-eagle with anticipation, as the gravest of foes appeared—a stick, waving close, closer to his face, and needing attack.

"What gives, doggo?" I called to him. "Little traitor."

His head snapped to attention. Two enthusiastic barks later, he was bounding over to me, loose hairs flying from his swinging tail. My empty hands received a thorough wet greeting. "I'll have to name you Sir Licks-a-Lot." I tossed the puppy's ears around while I smooshed his face, returning his affection. It sent him leaping in circles, yip yapping.

Lo, the enemy stick was captured in my hand, and he leaped at it. A second attempt was interrupted by a man's raspy voice saying, "The mite has a name."

Fickle Furball darted over to the speaker and jumped at his knees, tongue flapping freely. It didn't take long to realize that the man—who introduced himself between a phlegmy cough and a shaky squeeze of my hand as Heinrich Grauberger—had come to reclaim his puppy. His recounting of the dog's rescue to everyone within earshot was grossly exaggerated—as worthy of publication in a propaganda rag as the Boston Massacre drawings, I thought—but he was so grateful, he refused to hear any downplaying of the dramatic scene he "ne'er did see before, and I have seen me a thing a'plenty, let me tell ye."

And tell us, he did. At length.

Pup-meister didn't mind, occupied by the gathered soldiers, though legitimate excuses of having duties that needed attending kept a regular rotation of those permitted on puppy leave. Greaton was about to abandon Salem and me to the man's epic stories from the prior war, which was feeling more and more like the Seven*teen* Years' War, but Grauberger clucked his tongue at the colonel. "'Pon my word. Is this all the soldiers have for wearing? Thought my Daniel was a bowyer. *Jongen* always had a notion for telling lies. When he was younger, mind ye."

"Who is Daniel?" I asked, just to be polite.

Good thing I had nothing better to do. The question probably would've kept me there all day, had other matters not intervened. As it was, we learned his son, the aforementioned Daniel, had joined up with the militia out of Albany. Papa Grauberger was proud though "Distressed! mark my words, to think he or his fellows should be in as dire a straights as I do see here this day with all the nakedness about."

"Sir, attire notwithstanding," Salem protested, "it is not fitting to talk of…lacking garments when there is a lady present."

"Begging the *dame's* pardon, but I cannot but wonder whether one dressed such as herself should have a care, seeing as she has no proper stitching."

Greaton made a more insistent effort to leave, but Grauberger wanted a word with the commanding officer of the post. "I have a mind to share with the man."

"The officers are quite engrossed—"

"Ye cannot mean to say…" The old man closed in on the colonel. "…that my a'knowing who was the pilot that did betray ye all to the King's Men is not of interest? Steering the filthy lot of 'em 'round the…" Here, he stumbled over his tongue, landing on something like "shove-da-freeze."

"Of course, we shall make time for you." Greaton bowed his head, gracious as a maître d'.

"Now, ye have a care to yer manners there, Bose. She may not look much of one, but ye would be a fool if'n ye do not do as the *dame* here tells ye." He pointed a stern finger at the puppy, which sent him cowering. A sympathetic side rub set him right, and he trotted off to snatch his stick.

Grauberger considered the animal and tsked. "I 'spose the mite is in good hands."

I assured him, "Oh, yeah," just in time for the little beast to hack up a bit of the stick he was gnawing on. It didn't stop him, and Danger Dog went right back at it. I laughed nervously at his owner and tried rolling him onto his back and tickling his belly as a distraction. Stick demolition took priority.

Puppy sitting otherwise settled, the colonel escorted the old man in the direction of the Red House, while Salem and I tag-teamed wood chucking. Mostly Salem, though, who seemed to revel in ruffling the dog's floppy ears during breaks in describing the intense action he'd experienced at Breed's Hill. A mistaken place for a stand, since the American rebels had been in a hurry during an overnight maneuver to prevent the regulars from seizing Bunker Hill. When the third wave of British regulars had crested the American breastworks, he recalled a moment of horror among the men, who'd stared in shock. "The day is ours!" naval officer Pitcairn had exclaimed, until Salem fired his musket, ending the British major.

"What were those things Mr. Grauberger was talking about earlier?" I asked. "If you can tell me, that is?"

"*Chevaux-de-frise.* It is them over yonder," Salem answered, pointing to the makeshift wall of the Plain. "What lies along the barrier."

It took me a moment to remember what lay outside the wall. "The giant spikes? The Xs?"

"Yes, indeed. Except those the ships were running are sunk into the river, over a ways, at Plumb Point. Got themselves metal tips. The ones in the river, that is. If the old man is true and knows which of the locals aided the lobsterbacks last autumn, it would be a world of help, knowing which of the ship pilots can be trusted. I hazard to say, we have come to rely on them that lives here for our victuals and information."

The gravity of his statement settled us into silence for a while, which was fine. The swarming activity buzzing around us was decent company.

About the time my stomach growled loudly enough to be noticed—the puppy, Bose, launched his paws into my belly, requiring me to stand out of reach—I realized the old man had been absent for an extended period. One suggestion from Salem was all it took to convince me we should go back to the Red House to scrounge something for dinner. Besides, the officers might require a rescue from Grauberger's lengthy yarns, and I had some feminine issues needing attention.

Guilt was such a bastard. It occurred to me, as I dusted myself off, that room service for the soldiers hadn't exactly showed up. Just me and Salem, running rounds the day before.

"We can look to the men once we have seen to ourselves," Private Mind Reader said. "There is no harm in strengthening yourself first, given all that you have been through."

"And we wouldn't want Mr. Grauberger to have to go searching for us. He'll want his dog back," I offered as further justification. Jonathan's comment, that I'd insult the regiments—if not the entire Continental army!—should I fail to gratefully accept their help, was a ringing endorsement for the plan.

I still felt bad.

That settled, I scooped up what was left of Bose from where he'd flopped, out cold and unflinching while I got him situated in my arms.

Salem shook his head, chuckling. "My master—my former master, mind you, when I lived in Framingham—had himself this one dog. He was a right smart dog. Lor', he had a mean streak to him too. Good for drawing out game from the field, but ne'er could be trusted for long with it. Had to bag it quick, or the beast would take to it and refuse to give it o'er. Got myself bit more than once, I did."

Surprises abounded upon our being welcomed into the officers' backroom. Grauberger had left West Point more than an hour earlier. He was to return sometime the following day, or the day after, or thereabouts, as crossing the river was an uncertain thing, what with the marshes and cowboys a'loose and ships being wrecked under the waters, he'd reportedly said, in near-unending detail that didn't bear repeating.

Bose was mine to mind. Such presumption might've rankled me, had the dog not been so darn cute, and it wasn't like my dance card runneth-over while Jonathan was performing his duties elsewhere.

Zilch from the scouting parties.

Not that I should pay it any mind, I was quickly reassured. It was like the men would be gone for several days before they made their reports.

"Dinner is soon to be brought to the table," General Parsons rushed to change the subject. "Why do you not join us? I should like to make amends for the slanderous insult given you before."

Salem gathered Bose from my arms while room was made for me at the table, but once the hullabaloo of reorganizing the woodland-rejects-substituting-for-furniture settled, I discovered that yay, I'd finally shaken my guard, but also lost my puppy in the process.

My concern about their disappearance was brushed off. The soldiers had their own messmates with whom they ate, as was only appropriate. Read that: there wasn't enough to go around. I snuck a serving of bread into my leather bag, to make my own amends.

Although it masqueraded as "dinner," I wasn't sure it was worthy of such a grand title. The bread was stale. Shocking. However, the main course—the one and only, really—was worse. It was an excessively salted fish the officers called "shad." That was how it was stored and woe be he who tried to prepare it any other way. Whenever efforts were made to soak the fish clean, the local otter and mink always managed to steal it, leaving the soldiers empty-handed.

It burned the entire way down. Gin being the single option on the drink menu to counteract the monstrous seasoning, needless to say, I got more than a little sloshed that afternoon.

Chapter Thirty-Two

Gunfire cracked throughout the Highlands and continued blasting away for several days thereafter. Some rounds were in the distance; others, infinitely too close. Before the skirmishes began and threatened their fun, however, Captain Machin and Colonel Kościuszko traveled to headquarters in Fishkill. An invitation was extended by each man to accompany them as their guest, and as much as their stories of the food, music, and laughter made me regret not going—they had actual beef!—their apparent hangovers when they slunk back to camp were hardly enviable. My gin and shad looked like child's play by comparison.

Kościuszko seemed particularly irritated by the camp's daily racket, gritting his teeth whenever anyone spoke to him with any volume. How he managed the thundering of his horse's hooves on the stony roadway into West Point was a mystery. It was when a cart of building supplies overturned next to where he'd been standing, reviewing the progress of the new fortress, that he lost it. A slur of what those of us who observed the calamity could only guess to be profanity-dressed-in-Polish-best led his charge toward the *chevaux-de-frise*, to find some peace in the "battlefields of the forest!"

General Parsons, as star witness—and, of course, the commanding officer—ordered the rest of us to let Kościuszko be. Whether in deference to the colonel's situation or as a result of sheer shock at the usually congenial man's reaction, I don't know. But not without signaling for one of his men to trail our curly haired friend. "For his protection," the general told me.

I resumed my self-assigned Molly Pitcher rounds. Private Salem disliked my insistence in fulfilling the role, particularly as my own agitation grew—this shot ricocheted terrible memories onto me, that shot might've been the one that ended Jonathan. At one point, our debate got pretty heated. Duty called for the men and other women. Cowering in the attic bedroom was not going to be mine. Truth be told, I caved. For a few hours, anyway. Being confined, with worrying as my sole occupation, drove me and everyone around me nuts. As such, Mighty Molly won.

Useless as drying laundry in the rain, so too was attending the "meals" with the officers. However, being my constant shadow day and night, Salem deserved mental health moments away from me. How could I refuse going and deny him the break? Imagining succulent dishes of sweets and savories, swimming in heavy sauces, was distracting but almost as bad as trying to ignore the plentiful dishes of plain air on the table. Every remaining hand was needed within the confines of West Point, which left few to scavenge for food. The return of General McDougall and his entourage from headquarters wasn't burdened by supplies.

No one had any definitive answer as to where the redcoats were encamped. Each regiment had contributed a number of scouts, and all but two had returned. They'd spread through the Highlands, journeying along a different compass point, and all had encountered representation from the enemy, one small band at a time. Redcoat recognizance parties, as well, it would seem.

Putnam was snippy about the disappearance of his men. Who could blame him? News of their wellbeing was just as absent, yet the gunfire alarmingly present. Greaton sympathized over how the dinnertime-without-sustenance conversations rattled me, even though his men were MIA too. I did my best, truly I tried, to hide what I was feeling—one day, I vowed, I'd be so Switzerland with my expression, I'd rival Jonathan—and insisted the officers plan and plot and discuss as needed. My flippant threats to leave so they could get back to business made them resume course. My grim silences never fooled anyone.

Breathing space was granted to me when I visited Felaróf. He was agitation personified—or animalified, I guess—while enclosed with the ordinary animals. Restless and complaining, he was often found wandering the Plain, having mysteriously liberated himself. Tying him with any thought of keeping him contained was as futile as hoping the sun would rise in the west. My suggestion to just let him do what he wanted was ignored, since orderliness and discipline must reign in all things military, no matter how inexperienced the three-year-old Continental army was with its rulemaking.

Then, one day, Felaróf was gone. There the night before, screaming about the latest efforts to subdue him; by morning, vanished with the evening star. The Watch was chastised severely. I suspected my sorrowful sigh while I'd stroked his muzzle and slipped loose the leather strap that final night, questioning where Jonathan could be, might've played a part. It was, of course, a suspicion I never shared.

My nightmares devolved from unpleasant pastimes to downright abysmal horror shows. By the end of the first week, I was checking every bleeding face and broken body that returned to the Plain with the scouting parties. Each restless night, their corpses reappeared—more gruesome, shattered in impossible ways—littering the battlefields of my imagination where, reliable as the darkness's arrival, a redcoat waited behind the tree. The only difference from dream to dream was whether I killed him or the boy killed me.

Little Bose managed more heroically than I did. Day One, he was full of nervous energy. He huddled at my legs throughout the heaviest exchanges. Within a few short days, he was a pro. His head perked up at the first shots, and he barked during the reprieves, as if he was telling off the enemy for being so loud. At night, he accepted my clutching him to my chest and burrowing my face in his fur. A lick or two of my hands sent him yawning back to sleep, long before exhaustion carried me under too.

Without warning—perhaps as an omen, or as a means to torture us—the breakfast hour passed one day, and the gunfire ceased. The minutes ticked by toward midday, on to dinnertime, then evening, and the absent-supper seating. After the prolonged days of blasts erupting, exchanging, echoing off the mountains, the relative quiet was alarming. Either the redcoats had been beaten back or eliminated from the immediate vicinity, or they were regrouping for some serious, take cover kinda havoc—reasons unknowable from within our barricaded peninsula.

War raged at West Point, as well. The dinnertime disputes were impassioned as the officers fought over whether more men should be risked to scout the area or the shifts doubled on the construction of the fortifications in preparation for a possible attack.

The receiving of reinforcements was hopeless. General Washington was anxious to retake Manhattan. His mind had turned to calling upon some of the regiments to participate, though the officers had written back that it was impossible to spare the numbers he would need so early in the post's construction. Rumors that the British might evacuate Philadelphia were also circulating, an opportunity for an offensive attack too tempting for the Continentals to ignore and, therefore, allow for further assistance to be called northward. And everyone seemed hesitant to call back the militia, unless a large-scale assault proved imminent.

We were on our own.

There was a bright side to our plates being empty, I realized one evening. The table was pounded so many times, an aide had to slip between the shouting officers to save the watered-down gin from disaster. Food would've been strewn by the ruckus and wasted.

Unable to take it anymore, I trailed behind the aide to wind my weary way to the third floor. Bose seemed content to go wherever, particularly if it meant being carried up the steps that were still too big for him to manage. He draped a paw over the edge of my arm, his tail beating against my shoulder while his tongue lolled out of his happy, doggy grin.

Whine, whimper, and pounce, though, once in the attic bedroom. The sun had set on my throwing the slobbery ball the soldiers had made for him out of a ratty, old shirtsleeve. I laid in bed, exhausted, and watched as he plucked the twine to unravel his toy all over again. It was his favorite game, after fetch.

My hand sought the silver key. I held it against my heart, wishing Jonathan was there. Hoping he was alive and safe.

Chapter Thirty-Three

Dirt showered over the armies as they thundered against one another, a whirlwind of colors clashing as I ran through the melee. Blood sprayed from the slice to a soldier's neck. It poured from a gaping wound, splattered along the length of swords, soaked the earth. A pile of corpses climbed around me as the bullets tore through them, a scarlet river cutting a gorge into the side of the hill.

Hell unleashed its fury, driving me to the ground as an explosion burst in front of me. Through the ringing, I heard him—Jonathan, calling for me. I bolted to my feet and raced along the shoreline, his voice drifting as I tracked it into the thick of the fighting.

'Round the evergreen I went.

Cheeks full, sunburnt, spotty with freckles—the redcoat was waiting for me. He was always waiting for me. Our focus dropped to the muzzle of his gun. Steel extended forward several inches before penetrating my gown. Fluid oozed onto the metal, amassing faster as I felt the blood drain from my body, before I slid off the bayonet's end.

He stood over me, satisfied.

Just a kid, really.

Coldness wormed through my skin. Death was coming for me.

My cheek relaxed onto a pillow of browned weeds. Through the hazy darkness stretching over my vision, I found Jonathan. His sword parried an attack, flinging it aside. The men paused, tired, glaring at each other. Blood ran along the edge of his opponent's sword, tumbling to the ground.

Jonathan glanced over the man's shoulder. He gasped and stepped forward, distraught by my dying breath. His enemy took full advantage and plunged a sword into his stomach. All the while, as he fell against the man's chest, Jonathan's blue, blue eyes remained focused on mine.

I woke, screaming, hearing his voice calling my name, feeling him clutch my shoulders as I crashed into the waking world.

It wasn't him.

Private Salem released me once I was able to repeat his name back to him.

Like every other rough morning, he held out a mug, and true to myself, I rejected the weak gin he offered. The morning stimulator was a habit I fought, because once I drank my way down that path, I was afraid no recovery program in the world would save me. As part of the routine we'd stumbled upon, an alternative mug was provided that always held water, since milk and bread were forgotten possibilities. "You are needed downstairs."

It wasn't morning. The sky bled dimly through the attic windows. I'd fallen asleep before the sun had set, after the latest fictional meal with the officers.

"Why?" I asked.

"I know naught, except you have been summoned."

Bose's head smacked into my chin as he scrambled from his station against my stomach. He scampered to the far end of the room, his nose twitching at the draft from under the door.

Dread slowed me. If Jonathan had returned, Salem would've just told me. But bad news…such was the burden of officers to deliver it themselves. A foodless supper, which bred a killer headache, now this.

"Best to know what lies ahead, Miss Moore, whichever way the wind is going to blow us," he said.

But I didn't want to know. Let the violent storm rage for everyone else in that forsaken place, blow itself to the ends of eternity, for all I cared. While I remained in the attic, ignorant of Fate's blustering, Jonathan was still alive for me.

Salem was all kinds of against taking Bose outside, leaving me by myself, small and quaking and lost, but the dog was barking and darting back and forth, his signal that he was ready to do his duty. And I needed time.

"Do not you leave this house alone, Miss Moore."

I agreed, so he gave in.

The monotonous, nothing motions of changing my clothes steadied me. I was going to face the news on my own terms. A mirror would've been nice. I couldn't remember the last time I'd seen a reflection of myself. Would I even recognize me?

I clasped the silver key hanging loose against my chest, longing to touch Jonathan's power hidden there. Warmth wrapped around my hand, embracing me. It helped.

Half a dozen heads were clustered close together over the table in the officer's mess. Tension wove their hushed debate into a tapestry of overlapped hissing. I clutched my elbows, allowing my thumbs to drift over the linen gown Jonathan had given me, and tried to pick apart the various threads in their conversation.

General McDougall noticed me first and leaned back from his position to invite me to join them. Reservations were required at the full table, and none of the fatigued officers rushed to offer their seat. The nightmares plaguing me had an audible effect that woke the second-floor dwellers, as well as myself. A moment before we reached awkward, Colonel Greaton called to an aide to fetch my usual stool.

Without waiting for its arrival, McDougall acknowledged the newcomer whose back was to the door, saying, "Lass, I believe ye are acquainted with Captain Brott."

Good ole' Alex. He didn't face me, didn't acknowledge me, and most assuredly, didn't relinquish his first-class barrel seating either. "We were made to wait for a woman?"

Someone cleared their throat. General Parsons narrowed his eyes, suppressing the frustration screwing up his brows. Actual insistence by a superior officer was required before Alexander shifted his ass over to make room for me.

Leaning forward, McDougall rested his forearms along the table to emphasize the preface he was about to give: "Certain information need be telt but once."

Alexander's back stiffened.

Gazes aplenty—sympathetic, stern, subdued, but not his—tracked my careful lowering onto the milking stool that placed me between Parsons and Colonel Putnam. The colonel handed me a mug of gin. It'd been recently washed; its sides were cool and damp on my palms.

At any moment, it felt like I might float away. It was all so surreal.

A steadying breath later, I faced McDougall. He passed the proverbial torch to Parsons, who nodded before informing us, "Several of the Massachusetts Third have returned. This is known to Captain Brott. They intercepted his approach." Parsons paused, as if choosing his words before he directed his news to me. "We await the report of the final unit."

"I'm…glad to hear your men made it back safely, Colonel Greaton," I said.

He offered a sympathetic smile, knowing from our conversations together how I must feel. "It is good of you to say, Miss Phillips."

"Phillips?" Alexander snapped and scowled at me.

McDougall availed himself of the privilege rank gave him to ignore the remark. "Not all have returned safely. There were casualties, and the preliminary report does no bode well for the Fifth."

"What has this to do with Captain Wythe?"

No one spoke, so I answered, "He was with the Fifth."

Alexander sputtered, disbelieving. Grim faces at every corner, especially Putnam's, whose men he'd personally chosen for the unknown fate.

"W-what do you know?" I asked.

Parsons topped off his mug and spoke to its watery contents. "Colonel Greaton's men went to the aid of the Fifth. They learned that a nest of regulars had been uncovered. Before Colonel Putnam's men could send for reinforcements, they were betrayed by the son of a local farmer. By the time word reached the Third, the fighting had nearly ended. Greaton's men forced the regulars back into the mountains. The wounded have been returned. The rest…are still being accounted for."

Parsons raised his mug to drink but paused over its lip. McDougall was holding his own aloft in silent tribute. Numb—*this is not happening*—I joined the other officers in following his example. Thinned to almost spring pure, the gin burned against the lump in my throat anyway. I imagine everyone in the room felt the same awful, empty anger and loss. An aide halted in the doorway at the solemn toast but didn't enter.

Alexander bolted upright. The barrel rolled out from under him. He kicked it, which sent it careening into the wall and ricocheting into the wooden horses. The impact rattled the table's boards, forcing the officers' hands into action to keep the whole thing from falling.

"Ye have no been dismissed, Captain," McDougall pointed out, right before he could escape the room.

"The man shall hang for his betrayal," he yelled.

"He did, and the farm was confiscated by the militia," Nixon informed him.

Alexander banged a fist on the doorframe, which he fought to still by leaning his mouth against it and pressing it into the wood. Fury inflamed his skin, ruby licks of fire rising off him. His eyes closed, lips moving in silent prayer.

Why couldn't this have been some horrible fairytale, like the hero bound on a quest to solve an impossible riddle, when all along, the answers remained at home? I'd scream "the end" to the skies, and Jonathan would reappear, the both of us the wiser for his journey.

Firm resignation stiffened Alexander's expression. Rolling back his shoulders, his exit of the room was again stopped by the general. "Ye shall have charge of Mistress Moore, Captain."

His eyes passed over me. "She is nothing to me."

"You were Captain Wythe's brother-in-arms, were you not?" Parsons picked up smoothly. "Is that not what is said of you?"

"General," I started.

Alexander finished, "The bitch is a filthy spy. Keep her at your own cost."

My shock at his complete lack of compassion didn't silence me as he'd probably hoped. It infuriated me. "*You* are the only spy in the room, Captain Brott."

"Captain Wythe may have been bewitched by you, but I am not so—"

"Tae accuse one of being a spy is a serious charge." McDougall grimaced at us.

"Yeah," I acknowledged. "I—"

"Mae words were for Captain Brott." The general stared him down. "What proof have ye?"

"The proof lies before you," he answered. "She tempted Captain Wythe to her bed to lay his secrets out of him. There she sits, a drab dressed in an expensive gown, taken from his purse. Drinking at an officers' table by the side of its general, and you lay bare the movements of our soldiers for her to report back to the enemy."

Greaton croaked maybe a syllable before Parsons cut him off with a raised hand. "Should you care to rethink your words, Captain…"

But he refused to back down.

Voice fair and impartial, McDougall turned to me. "What say ye?"

"All the nights you left our camp." I glared at Captain Asshole. "The time you abandoned the militiamen, despite your agreement with Captain Wythe. Where did *you* go? And how is it you arrive safe and sound, when so many of our soldiers were wounded or killed by the enemy?"

Oh yes, I remembered Captain Alexander Brott, in full color, surround sound, and with curse resistance-free clarity. The pompous, arrogant douche bag who never gave me a chance and was willing to feed me to the wolves. No amount of grief could excuse his maniacal dickishness. If Jonathan was gone, then any need to keep the peace, for his sake, had died with him. Such niceties as even thinking of the bastard as "Friend Alexander" were embargoed from my mind. And better believe, I'd spit fire and weave whatever lies I had to, before I *ever* allowed Brott to see me hanged as a spy without a fight. Hell, I'd wrap the noose around him and take him down with me, if it came to it.

Then, without warning, he rushed me.

I shot out of my seat, as did the other officers. Everything was in an uproar as the table's boards were overturned. An aide flung his papers on a chair outside the door so he could hurry in to assist. He missed, and the entire stack crashed to the ground, scattering with the shifting air of so many bodies charging into the room.

Putnam situated himself between us, catching a grasping fist in his shoulder in the process, while Salem and another aide forced themselves into the small space to surround the outraged captain. Bose appeared, barking furiously at their feet and hopping back and forth between the commotion and me. Greaton and Nixon, trapped as they were behind the upset table, were squashed against the wall. Nixon surprised me by being the one to shout, "Captain, if you cannot contain yourself, it will be the barracks prison for you."

Threat enough for his tastes, apparently. Brott-hole quieted, though he threw Salem's hand off his arm, glowering at him. The colonel wasn't stymied by the deadly glare and returned to shaking the puddle of gin off his uniform coat. Neither was Bose, who continued to growl his own insults at the captain.

"Colonel Putnam," McDougall ordered, "Gang and find a man to serve as Captain Brott's escort."

"Mark you," the self-righteous ass replied, "I have orders from General Washington I intend to keep. I make way after breakfast, once my horse has been fed and watered."

"Insubordination is punishable by lashes," Nixon informed him. "You dare—"

"Captain Brott will be shown tae the *lower* officers' barracks. See if there be any wha might be willing tae share his bunk," McDougall said. "Discussion about the braw captain's fate can bide. As for the captain's horse, it will be boarded and watered, but mind ye. There is no food. For the men either."

"There was a half dozen sheep being driven onto the grounds as I did arrive." Brott scoffed.

The general paused. "They are tae serve another purpose," he said coolly. "Colonel Putnam, would ye be so kind?"

Rather than demonstrate any sort of remorse, the petulant Brott ground his teeth and followed Putnam's rigid show of going "this way, *Captain*."

With the renewed understanding that I wouldn't leave the house unescorted, Salem accompanied them, until Putnam could devise other arrangements. Nixon shed his coat for an aide to take so it might be laundered. Others hurried in like a swarm of worker bees, seeing to the tasks of reassembling the makeshift table, gathering the flood of papers, whispering to their respective commanding officer, and refreshing the pitcher of gin. Its former contents were decorating the floor.

Parsons gave a half-minded laugh at the mug clutched in my hand. "It seems, Miss Moore, you were the only one quick enough to save their drink."

"That's because I was going to break his nose with it if he got any closer." I crouched to quiet the pawing at my gown.

Parsons' full attention was on me when he chuckled. "Of that, I have no doubt." He returned my stool to its rightful place, welcoming me to resume my seat.

Maybe drunk was the way to go. The universe could have this night…in trade. I had a nominee who deserved more daylight hours on this Earth.

Most of the gin from my mug had abandoned ship during the brawl. Everything was such an effing waste.

Bose happily resumed his post as my official lap warmer, exhausted after his campaign as guard dog. Greaton was about to sit, as well, on a freshly dried crate when an aide barged in. "Sirs, several of the Massachusetts Fifth are returned. All are wounded or," his gaze darted to me before he said, "dead."

"Captain Wythe?" I hurried to ask.

"I know not," was the reply.

"Remain, if ye would," McDougall addressed my anxious look. "There is tha' which must be discussed and should no wait."

Greaton offered to go in my place, to search among the wounded, but was also told to hold. The general was generous enough to wait for my consent, then issued his next order to the aide: "Inform Colonel Putnam of his men's return. Ye are to learn the names and report back at once." Once the aide left, he accepted Greaton's offer, saying, "I desire a full accounting from the men of what has occurred. If there be any tha' are able."

Nixon was also dismissed, with the request to close the door behind him. Bose tipped his head at the squeaky hinges and returned to Snoozeville.

Once everything was settled, my patience was commended. "'Tis imperative tha' we ken at once what ye dae about the matter of Captain Brott."

"Very little," I admitted. "I don't know why he left our camp when he did. It happened twice. Both times, it was the night before he and Jon— Captain Wythe were supposed to leave for a mission. I know he took the road into a nearby town. I don't know which one. It was just a thought that occurred to me once, how he might be a spy. In all fairness, you should know—he was dating someone and recently got engaged."

It took a little language clarification, but the general nodded. "How did ye come tae learn this?"

"I heard him telling Captain Wythe."

A thin swath of Bose's fur lifted into the air from my nervous petting spree. Shaking loose stragglers free first, then placing my hands flat on the table's surface helped quiet them. A tiny snore lured them back.

"Know you the lady?" Parsons asked.

"They called her 'Miss Tuinstra'…?" The name was not familiar to either officer. "Jonathan was in love with her too."

A statement that was met with disbelief.

Should I find her and tell her, I wondered. Would she even care? Or would she shrug it off with mild sympathy when she inevitably learned it from the man who'd stolen her from Jonathan?

The significance of having to tell someone, anyone, about his death was… But there wasn't anything definite to tell at this point.

"I'm sorry, sirs," I said. "You're right. Calling someone a spy is a serious accusation." Around went my thoughts of a possible explanation, born and departed without being voiced. It really didn't matter, given the gravity of my selfish snipe.

"It was Captain Brott who first did call *you* so," Parsons observed.

"That doesn't make it right for me to do the same thing."

McDougall considered my apology and turned a silent inquiry to his second-in-command. Parsons was of the opinion that "Captain Brott is insufferable."

"His Excellency has made better choices," McDougall said to his cup. "It places me in a delicate situation, lass. Insubordination. Reckless disregard for the welfare of another. Such actions canna be tolerated. They must be dealt with, lest they spawn further insurrection. Yet…I canna act quickly against His Excellency's agents. It requires thorough consideration and politic persuasion."

Silence awaited my response.

I shrugged. "Do whatever your conscience tells you is best. I just ask that I be allowed to avoid him while he's still here."

McDougall was a little surprised. "Have ye no opinion on the matter?"

Responding with care, I answered, "Captain Brott has always claimed to act in Captain Wythe's best interests. He hasn't liked our friendship and has been very blunt about it."

"To call you 'spy'? Does that not excite your blood?" Parsons asked.

"Of course, it does. That's why I was willing to make him explain his running off like he did. But that doesn't mean I'm game to weigh in about possible punishments. Whether he's really a spy…I don't know."

McDougall leaned back on one arm, rolling the bottom of his mug on its edge, back and forth. "He shall gang unpunished in the end. Ye ken tha'?"

Parsons protested. "Abandoning one's post is a serious charge in and of itself."

"Captain Brott was no under our command at the time. Tha' is a matter for His Excellency."

Nothing frustrated me more than people getting away with hateful behavior towards others; however, being a miserable prick wasn't proof of espionage. A court martial on that BS would be over before it started, and—I reminded myself—grave consequences befell those convicted. Aggrieved as I was, a noose was unwarranted here.

"I understand," I told them. "What questions do you have about his accusations against me?"

"Och." McDougall chuckled. "The lass speaks of a most serious charge as though she were a merchant engaging in his daily business."

"Indeed," Parsons answered him. "Tell us, Miss Moore. Of what do you dream each night?"

He threw me. "Excuse me?"

"What is it that haunts your dreams, that has you cry out at night?"

Bose groaned in his sleep at the increased fur removal. I swallowed and stretched my fingers against his side, feeling the race of his tiny heartbeat under my palm. "The War. Things I've seen. Men I've killed. The first…boy…I killed."

"Ye dream of killing men?" McDougall diverted his eyes.

"Sometimes. Soldiers. Sometimes, they kill me," I confessed. "And Captain Wythe."

The generals exchanged a look, then McDougall nodded. How many men had he ordered to a fate of death? How many haunted his dreams?

Parsons spoke again after a respectful silence. "We have not yet extended our thanks for the many hours you have given to serving our men. It has not gone unnoticed."

"I don't like sitting around doing nothing. Especially with everyone else…" Parsons gave me a funny look, while McDougall continued to roll his mug. So, I said instead, "You're welcome. Sirs, if there isn't anything else, I'd really—"

"Aye, of course," McDougall answered. He finished his drink in a large gulp. "General, would ye gang to the hospital, as well, and assess the state of any tha' has returned. By His Excellency's example, a general should see tae the men."

As we exited the backroom, Parsons snagged one of the passing aides. "What is this of sheep being brought?"

The aide didn't know, but another—having heard the question—approached to say, "That man what was here before. All a prittle prattle, he was, about the state of the men." The two aides laughed at the description. "Though, he was knowing about the royalist pilot."

"Old Man Grauberger?" quizzed Parsons.

"Aye, that be the man."

A sharp turn of the general's head started the first aide on his way, but he stopped, remembering a dispatch to give Parsons. He paused long enough to pet Bose, who was snoring contentedly in my arms. The general tore it open and scanned the page while he asked the remaining aide, "To what purpose did he bring them?"

"Why, said they was to feed the men, sir. Rather old buggers. Had plenty to say about them. The men, that is. Said he did not like to think of his…David, was it?"

"Daniel," I prompted.

"His son," the aide continued, "to starve. Hoped Providence might move some soul in Albany to do the same for the son and his fellows. Beg pardon, sir. I thought ye did know it, or I would have told ye sooner."

"Never mind that now. Best let the general know."

The aide saluted Parsons at the dismissal.

"What about his dog?" I stopped him from hurrying into the backroom. "Did he say when he was coming back for Bose?"

"Oh aye, he did say something about that. Did not quite understand what he meant at the time. He said Little Bose was for the 'river *dame.*' Reckon that is meaning yer the *dame.*"

"Indeed. Carry on, Sergeant," Parsons ordered.

The aide disappeared down the hall behind us, and the general and I exchanged a shocked look. It was a surprising turn of events, by all means. Internal calculations as to how far the meat could stretch occupied his muttering during our exit of the house.

Twilight was full upon us, and the skies were awash with stars. Surveying their number, he laughed and shook his head. "Once more, you have served the men well. I doubt such a gift would have been made, had it not been for you."

Parsons tipped his hat in thanks, then gestured for me to lead the way.

Chapter Thirty-Four

A leg without an owner was carried from the hospital tent in a basket, all of which was unceremoniously dumped outside the entrance until it could be properly disposed of. The sight, coupled with the wailing from inside, were guaranteed featured roles in future nightmares, to say the least. Bose dipped his head at the haunting noise to growl, the fur on his neck rising.

General Parsons was aware of my many visits over the nearly two weeks since Jonathan had vanished and the corpses started returning. Nevertheless, the hospital was no place for a lady, he insisted. Setting the struggling puppy on the ground as a means of stalling, I took a deep breath. My stomach performed a triple pike dive, the wrong way, when the stench belching from the tent's flaps hit me.

But knowledge for myself of Jonathan's condition was the best defense against denial, so I vowed the wounded wouldn't be decorated with upchuck for their service and started toward the opening anyway.

Colonel Greaton burst out, finding himself up close and personal with me. His surprise was short-lived. Hundreds of people occupied West Point, but secrets about the goings-on there weren't kept for long. He'd referenced, in roundabout ways, his concern over my unhealthy pastime during our more private conversations.

"The news is best not shared where we are," he said. Another thought passing over his features led him to offer, "Why do I not escort you back to the Red House, Miss Phillips? I can speak with the general after that. It is late, and there is nothing to which you would want to be a party."

"Sounds like there's something you don't want to tell me, Colonel."

"Captain Wythe is not amongst the wounded or dead, so far as any know."

"What *is* known?"

An unconvincing response of "not a word" accompanied his head being bowed.

"Colonel," I begged him.

Parsons ordered a nearby private to escort me, saying, "I shall hear the report and let you know that which is pertinent, Miss—"

"I'm not going. You will tell me the whole truth and nothing but the truth."

So, help me, God.

Someone chided Bose more than once to "keep 'way there, you."

Freaking unbelievable. Why are dogs the grossest? He was open-mouthed sniffing the amputated leg.

"Bose, come here." My hoarse yelling, then charging after him to try to scoop him up, sent Spastic Mutt darting in different directions. The edge of my gown snagged the body basket, spilling its contents. It nearly had my stomach copycatting.

Downward-facing dog, tail flapping carefree, he lapped up our unintentional game.

A gentle hand closed around my elbow. Parsons' sympathy burned in my chest as he said, "Come, it is my duty to see to the men. Colonel Greaton will escort you to the house. We shall hear his report with the general, away from the ears of the camp. Yes?"

He meant the both of us.

Greaton stood at the ready, his face full of compassion. A sweeping glance around the grounds showed the Plain's inhabitants were settling by their fires for the night. Some sewed. Others cleaned their weapons. Two men were debating whether to boil down their last candle to make soup. Their wistful eyes glanced at the makeshift enclosure for the work animals, the source of not-so-distant baaing. A small group pooled together their supply of tobacco to pack a clay pipe. The Watch, ever on patrol, kept tabs on us all and the surrounding area. Everyone tensed whenever another wail carried over the grounds, fully aware of the suffering in the hospital and our inability to do anything about it.

Bose found occupation among a group of teens, who were playing Monkey in the Middle with a bit of rag. The linen comet streaked between them, so they could take turns teasing him. He snagged a piece. Every once in a while, one of the boys—whose features were beyond pale, from his hair to his complexion, and rounded out with bluish eyes—would slip Bose something from a pocket in a cupped hand. The puppy scarfed it up, thanking him with an enthusiastic round of yips and jumping. At the general's request, the boy eagerly agreed to dog sit Bose until someone sent for him.

"Have a pup kinda like this one," he told us. "Back home. Only 'tis blacker. Does not mind much neither." His buddies ended the homesickness that crept into his eyes by slapping him with the rag to resume playing.

"I will not keep you long," Parsons promised me. "Colonel, you shall be kept abreast of any developments regarding the health of your men."

Dipping his chin to us, he then turned to face the hospital tent. The journey of his hat from its perch on his head to being tucked under his arm was the slowest in recorded history. Duty could afford him no further distance.

"It is no bother to escort you," Greaton assured me, despite my offer to let him return to what he needed to do.

Reaching the Plain's edge, I hesitated. How dare the river sparkle, alive with the reflection of starlight riding its waves?

"Please tell me the truth," I asked. "Is Captain Wythe dead?"

"There are reports of his movements. None have seen him dead. Take comfort in that. Now, come. The rest must wait for the general."

This is ridiculous. What has this man done to me?

A great deal of my life remained shrouded in mystery, yet in all the spotty memories—painful or otherwise—Grief was a companion I couldn't recall, and I wished it would take the hint regarding its too-early arrival.

As we rounded the curve in the river path, the façade of the Red House peeked through the thinning trees. Greaton paused. He glanced at me, then began examining the Hudson, or so his eyes suggested. His thoughts seemed adrift.

The decline in waterway's traffic created a sharp contrast to the bustling highway it'd been when Jonathan and I first arrived. Now, travelers weren't allowed through unless they carried a pass from the governor. British supply lines from Canada had been effectively cut off, thanks to the installation of General Washington's Watch Chain—its christened nickname by the men—as were the hopes the Crown had of dividing the United States.

"Miss…Phillips, I know not what arrangement you had with Captain Wythe. Let me assure you, I dare not flatter myself that the passions you have shown of late toward his welfare would ever flame for me. Nor should they. But…should you find yourself alone in this world, I would be only too happy…" Nervous laughter colored the colonel's cheeks. "That is, it would be an honor to serve as your guardian."

Women aren't allowed to support themselves here, I recalled telling Jonathan. *They have to have a husband.*

Greaton was clearly older than me, his dark hair already thin and graying. The pronounced center peak was trimmed short into a tuft of bangs, allowing the longer sides to be combed in waves, flowing forward before looping back into a lengthy braid. The area under his eyes drooped darkly, though perhaps it was the stress of war and lack of sleep rather than his natural appearance in happier times.

Still, in his late thirties, he was decent-looking, kind, and had concerned himself with my well-being from pretty much the beginning. If I had to submit to another man's oversight, his friendship meant it might not be burdensome.

"Forgive me."

"You haven't offended me," I cut off his apologies. "That was the nicest thing you could have said to me just now."

"But you cannot consider it."

"I've been so worried about Captain Wythe…I haven't thought about what would happen to me if he *is* gone."

Was I ready to abandon my quest to find my forgotten family? Would there even be an option if I couldn't remember enough on my own, without Jonathan there to guide me?

Words cluttered uselessly in my mouth.

"I have upset you. You need not answer now, of course," Greaton said. "Know that you have a place. If you would give a thought to the matter…?"

"I will." I breathed past the lump in my throat. "Thank you."

Settling me in my usual seat in the backroom, the colonel excused himself to find us more gin. It might very well be necessary for when Parsons returned.

Chapter Thirty-Five

What the officers had learned from the many fragments brought back by the Third and the Fifth was explained like this: Captain Wythe's fate was unknown. At his suggestion, or maybe it was orders—no one was certain, because none of the officers had returned alive—the Fifth had traveled along a deer path, due west, toward the Clove Road. Water was a'plenty on the other side of the mountainous walls surrounding West Point, lying halfway through the roughly six-mile journey. So, the men felt themselves unconcerned by his guidance.

The Clove within sight, they turned north, always keeping within the safety of the trees. However, they divided first, such that each wooden area tracing the road's progression could be searched, also at Wythe's suggestion. They ne'er went so far west as Schunnemunk mountain, believing the regulars to be north of it. The two halves of the scouting party were near enough as could communicate with a series of birdcalls that he and one of the enlisted men knew and could agree upon.

Murderer's Creek saw the death of peace. It stretches from the North River westward, past Brewster's Iron Works in New Windsor, until it cuts a sharp path to the south. The Clove Road led the men in parallel to one of its capillaries.

But fickle as any female—present company excluded, I was told— Murderer's reverses direction, choosing a new course, where the outlet and Creek join. This winding passage, Wythe thought, was best to mark, arguing members of the Sixty-Third were reported to be clustered to the northern end of the mountain. They would need water for their animals and men, Murderer's Creek being a likely source.

Captain Goodale, on the other hand, wanted to return south to a junction they had passed, at which point, farther west was the route he desired. A different waterway favored the north, as its infamous fellow, which was found on the opposite side of the highest peak. Regulars would seek the protection offered by the culvert within Schunnemunk's shadows. He was certain of it.

Wythe disagreed, arguing that should they come upon the regulars whilst inside the rocky channel, they would become trapped, with no escape other than a direct retreat.

Goodale countered that coming at the regulars in that manner meant the enemy could not swarm in from all sides. They would be forced into a narrow defense, which would even the field, should the Fifth find themselves outnumbered but in a position to engage.

The debate became bitter and recklessly loud, though the resolution was kept between the two captains once they regained control of their volume. The sum total of it saw Goodale going south with half the men and Wythe traveling north with the remainder. It was presumed they would meet on the northern side of the mountain, perhaps to surround the regulars.

Only one of them that laid in the hospital tent came from Goodale's men. All others, including the captain, be dead. He knew not what became of Captain Wythe and those that followed him, but for one, who had arrived at West Point already deceased. That poor bastard lay in the cot beside him. "God keep him."

It was speculated by the survivor that Wythe had led them into a trap, alerting the regulars to the location of the others. Why else should he have been determined all should answer to him? To what other purpose could a body have but to lead them to ruin?

Such was the report of the sole survivor from the Fifth.

The story from the Third differed, and so the theory of Wythe's treachery could not have been entirely correct. More than one man reported it was a Tory family who had betrayed them. Fortune favoring the Third, their orders had sent them along the North River's roadway—an easier route, thereby they covered more ground. Across Murderer's Creek, they went so far as Hasbrouck's Mills in Newburgh.

What information Wythe had supplied of the regulars' movements, given upon his arrival at West Point, was confirmed within the tavern halls of those few towns visited. The men needed to retire during their dayslong journey, mind you. Such was the best place for gathering intelligence. Finding nothing of the enemy, they journeyed west, then searched along a different route meant for their eventual return. But first, the Third had an eye toward Vails Gate, to see if any lobsterbacks might remain in the forest.

By sheer Providence, a scout sent in the direction of New Windsor to raise the militia encountered them, not a mile after they had set out. They changed direction immediately and quick marched. Not knowing the source of the betrayal, they rested for an hour on that very farm, though one man claimed some wickedness he did see in the eyes of the senior he took to not liking. Having caught their breath and all in readiness, the Third resumed their march.

Confusion came at a fork in the road, whereupon hearing the sounds of a skirmish, they chose the southern route to find themselves the rescuers of the Fifth, the portion led by Captain Wythe. With no one able to dispute the claim of rescue, it must be supposed so for the time being. Only one of Wythe's men returned, and he—as told before—was waiting on the Plain for his final resting place.

The others being fit, Wythe's Fifth and the Third did unite. They had hoped to refresh themselves first. The northern tip of the mountain, so as to find their fellows, was what lay ahead of them.

That was not the way of it.

A scout did appear, returned from his earlier orders around the southern part of the mountain to seek the aid of Goodale and the rest of their number. An awful sight was said to have unmanned him. By all appearances, regulars had entered the culvert from behind and engaged Goodale's Fifth, who were greatly outnumbered, being but half a dozen. He'd hurried to raise the alarm for reinforcements.

There, the story paused.

"Who sent the scouts?" I asked.

Why, Captain Wythe, of course. He sent two of his men: one south for Goodale and one east for the militia, for they had discovered the lair of the enemy. Within the safety of the woods, Wythe's Fifth awaited greater numbers that they might attack. Lo, those did not arrive in time. Damnable betrayal by the Tories, who'd alerted the regulars to their presence. Gunfire was exchanged. Yet, somehow, Wythe and the three men who remained did survive, victorious, not counting the fourth who perished.

But the story continued…

Wythe, now aware of Goodale's distress, determined the journey around the southern tip of Schunnemunk to arrive behind the British would take too long, because the road tarried over the mountain itself for a time. Fastest was for the men to circle the northern approach and enter the culvert there. They would simply have to enhance Goodale's numbers and see the fighting done together.

For all their racing without catching their breath, it was not enough. When they did arrive at the field of battle, desolation of Goodale's men lay before them, the Bloodsuckers having quit the place and taken their wounded with them. The survivor of Goodale's Fifth, now in West Point's hospital, was discovered buried under a messmate.

"Captain Wythe?"

"Is the gin too thin? Perhaps more."

"What happened to Captain Wythe?" I insisted.

We had not yet come to that.

Goodale was not among the number that littered the ground. Indeed, the ensign did count the bodies and reported a Private Napthali Campfield also to be missing.

As there was no means to return all the dead to West Point, they must consign themselves to the mountainous pass for their resting place.

"So, why does the guy in the hospital say he's the only survivor?" I asked. "Because it sounds like others survived."

It was explained that his story had been told before those of the Third. He had awoken, lying in the Tories' dining hall with the militia's surgeon digging in his shoulder for a ball that could not be found. At the man's insistence, he was reunited with his regiment rather than lie another moment on the table that fed traitors.

But let us go back, for here is the last of what was known from any who returned: Wythe, the three survivors with him, and the Third debated what was to be done. Rest was needed, and the wounded man required a surgeon. Remaining in the culvert was too dangerous, especially as Wythe claimed to have seen signs that the regulars had also entered the passage from the north, thereby surrounding Goodale on both sides.

All made haste to the farm where they had thought themselves welcomed before. Crimes against Liberty being done, so Justice demanded her vengeance, and our men were to be her instrument. Two lobsterbacks were discovered hidden in a cupboard, having arrived with Judas's reward for the sins committed by the family before, in sending their son to the regulars' camp. They were slaughtered at once, the family with them. The youngest child, being a girl and but two years of age, was spared and delivered to the neighboring farm.

My shock that the regiment would do such a thing was quickly corrected. It was the militia who had arrived before the regiment to uncover the malicious betrayal. One of their number was distant kin to the villainous family. He suggested the fate of the little girl and asked to lay claim to the farm in the name of the militia.

The request being granted, our men found themselves in a fine situation, since the furniture was commendable, the number of buildings suitable to offer protection from the elements, and there was a sizeable store of foodstuffs to provide for the survivors, despite it being early in the season. Some of the more plentiful root vegetables had been sent along with those who returned to West Point.

"But what about the Fifth?"

Well, now we come to it.

Dawn arose, and the militia being in possession of two deceased lobsters—who, having been missed by their commanding officers, it would seem—meant the enemy came in search of them. Discovered before they could do harm, the Third and Fifth gave them chase toward the mountain. The regulars had the advantage, whereupon they could fire their muskets at our men, who were easily exposed on the flattened roadway, while the lobsters had nature's stonework for their fortress.

Wythe, being the ranking officer, ordered a cease fire. Once all was quiet, he instructed them to fall back. He, alone, would remain to ascertain where the enemy did go from there. Those of the Fifth, being brave—as well as any, truth be told—refused to leave him to his own defenses. The powder being low, and another of the Third having taken a ball to his knee, it was decided.

Not all liked a man, whose reputation was tied to the enemy, to be in command of three who might be easily captured if led into a trap, but the men of the Fifth would hear none of it. Wythe was said to not press for one way or the t'other.

All did as the captain ordered. The Third and the militia returned to the farm. Those of the Fifth remained. Nothing was heard from them again, except for an exchange of gunfire shortly after the breakfast hour, that—when investigated—left all to wonder as to what had occurred. This was more than four days prior.

Such was the totality of what was known about Captain Wythe and his fate.

Chapter Thirty-Six

Colonel Putnam had joined us midstory. Keeper of some details gleaned during his hospital rounds, he supplemented the narrative where General Parsons and Colonel Greaton's information was lacking. Upon reaching the finale of Jonathan's command, he glared at me. Dreadful fates formulated in the firestorm of his imagination, judging by the unsteady expression that dared me to speak.

In the end, Putnam slammed back his gin, took another for good measure, then asked to be dismissed. "My men deserve the victuals that have been brought, and I fully intend to lay claim to them."

General McDougall thanked him. "'Tis a generous offer tae assist the quartermaster in o'rseeing the foodstuffs so as tae divide it fairly amongst the regiments."

If repercussions were as fleeting as a leaf's dying flight, I imagine Putnam's boiling point would've spilled over. Being a man of honor and otherwise reasonable, from what I'd observed of him, a coolness of conscience dissipated his anger. The tempest in his expression faded. Reality was cast from a cold and ugly, gray thing, lacking all the simplistic rosiness that time's distance places on matters: every officer had offered up their men to War's altar. It was misfortune that caused his men to sacrifice the most.

Though he'd never voiced any vitriol, Putnam nevertheless apologized for wishing me ill, for which I quietly thanked him. A solemn nod preceded his departure.

Then everything stilled. A heartbeat passed. A breath, then two, then more. The log in the grate crackled and split, then carried on with burning. The front door creaked open and shut with formal military precision, then each man carried on to the next task. Life continued throughout Moore's Folly, and we, in the room, sat and kept watch over those empty yet precious moments.

"Perhaps you should retire for the night, Miss Moore," Parsons suggested.

Greaton filled the silence by adding, "I shall send Private Salem to fetch Bose, unless solitude would be best...?"

"No," I whispered. "Please bring him."

"Might there be other assistance you require?"

I sat. And I waited. But nothing happened. The expected tears never came.

Next I knew, a draft brushed my cheeks. The narrow hallway surrounded me, the backroom receding into the distance. Without any recollection of leaving my stool, I was clasping Greaton's arm and being escorted toward the stairwell.

A white handkerchief with the initials "J.G." stitched into the corner was offered to me.

J for John. The man who now assumed responsibility for me was named Johnathan.

My skin turned cold.

Chapter Thirty-Seven

Dirt showered over the armies as they thundered against each other, a whirlwind of colors clashing as I ran through the melee. A blade flashed in the sun, zinging past my cheek as it flew. It struck another in my wake. Blood poured from a gaping wound, a scarlet river cutting a gorge into the side of the hill. Hell unleashed its fury at me, choking me with a dark haze, bitter from ash and smoke.

"Miss Moore!"

Swords and guns, fists and gore—none of it mattered. I had to find Jonathan. I raced along the shoreline, his voice fading as I tracked it into the thick of the smoke.

Nearing the evergreen, I slowed. The redcoat. He was waiting for me.

My focus dropped to the muzzle of my gun. Steel extended forward several inches from the barrel. Pledging my actions to a cause I couldn't recall, I raised the weapon and drove around the corner of the tree with it, circling, circling...

The boy was gone.

"Miss Moore!"

Gun smoke crumbled, like shattered glass tumbling in bits and bursts. Across the battlefield, I saw him dueling with a man in red, parrying an attack. The men paused, tired. Blood ran along the edge of his opponent's sword, dribbling onto the ground.

"Jonathan!"

He stepped forward, distracted by my desperate rush toward him. The man took full advantage and plunged his saber into Jonathan's stomach, drove it further, until it caught on bone. Fluid pooled on Jonathan's lower lip. Coldness wormed through my skin. Drips spilled over in a long line from his mouth. Death was coming for him.

"No!"

Blue against blue, the depths of his eyes—once rich and bright—faded, and the light that shone through them dulled. His stance softened, and he slid from the sword's end to the ground.

His opponent watched from above, black curls fluttering in the breeze. I thought I heard the man hum. One leg rising, then the other following, he casually stepped over Jonathan's body and strolled along, as if it was a bright summer's day.

I screamed.

All the while, the man in red tuned me out. To him, I didn't matter.

But when I reached the place where Jonathan had fallen, only a patchwork of stinking mold was stretched beneath the fronds. Whirling around and around, I couldn't find him. Barren woods. Skeletons of trees. Darkness.

Gone was the smoke, swords, blood, sound…

I was left alone.

Chapter Thirty-Eight

Calling out sick bought me sympathy but not solitude. Private Salem still charged up the attic stairs, tasks for the day at the ready. Breakfast needed to be eaten. Bose wanted out-of-doors. The fine weather was ripe for minding. Perhaps find some new scraps, since the latest drool-sopped toy needed replacing. There was so much frivolous, invented need, as if a day of isolation, my hands idle, might conjure up deeds more wicked than sulking in bed. It was the darker thoughts they feared.

We don't even know that he's dead.

I took a stab at Molly Pitcher duty, except after a single round—Salem actually forked over the bucket, so I must've looked like Davy Jones's latest plaything—Colonel Greaton "needed" my thoughts on the Works' progress, putting an end to any useful physical labor as a distraction. He meant well.

Concerned looks, sympathetic eyes, and regretful shaking of heads followed me everywhere, feeling like claws at my back trying to tear down my determination not to scream Jonathan's name into the Highlands and demand he return.

Irony was as cruel as her cousin, Fate. A real dinner awaited us at the officer's table, thanks to the dead loyalists, but my appetite was wanting. Extreme hunger and stress being equal catalysts for nausea.

Greaton enlisted Colonel Kościuszko as his second-in-command of Miss Moore's folly, having been snagged by the nurse of the day to attend one of his private's final needs. I offered to assist. So many men had clutched my hand during their own passage, calling me "nurse" or "Molly" or even "*Mutti*," what was one more? He wouldn't hear of it.

Occasional rays of sunshine seeped through the thick smear of clouds, highlighting portions of the landscape in a yellowed hue. The river was no less beautiful. Pasture regions were flooded with color where countless flowers bespeckled the wild portrait of the Hudson Valley in bloom. I studied the river's course, trying to imagine—as Salem had—that I could travel anywhere I wanted on those waters. Watching the waves narrow between the mountains, then wash onto the horizon, I waited for the North to beckon me home. It remained silent.

Having lost myself to the prison in my mind, had I become so bound up in Jonathan that my chances of recovering my sense of self or freedom were gone?

A nearby stalk of tall grass buckled in front of me. My itty-bitty scout fluttered onto a stronger piece and snapped open the seed husks to devour their hidden treasure. A brisk shake sent the husks flying from where they'd clung to his beak. At the sound of his name, he startled then eyed me. A quick peck scored him more grass seed.

"Cleophes."

The way he ducked his head, it almost looked like he was wilting with frustration, which maybe he was, but the maneuver preceded him rising into the air and accepting a perch on my finger.

Kościuszko had been in hard-core caffeine-esque mode, describing with tremendous enthusiasm an idea he'd cooked up to build a little cabin in the woods to be his headquarters. He paused to remark, "I do not know your people had gifts with the animals."

Huh. Guess I made the club, our secret identities now an open book between us.

"I don't." I drew a lonely finger along my friend's black-not-blue chest. "He's Jonathan's."

We turned at the sudden rise in voices. Someone shouted, "Send for Colonel Putnam." Three men in brown were being welcomed by their fellows near the Plain's entrance. A horse, laden with supplies, stood aloof from the excitement. Because it wasn't any simple beast of burden.

Racing over to the starry, black horse, I pressed my palms onto Felaróf's flank, grateful for the familiar sensation tickling my skin. I scanned the un-uniform uniforms and the multitude of cheerful faces gathering to celebrate the browncoats' return.

Three. Three men from the Fifth went with him.

One slowed long enough to answer my question about Jonathan's whereabouts, saying, "I do not reckon to know, madam," before being enveloped by the happy reunion.

Felaróf rubbed me with his muzzle. A moment later, he bopped me, snorting at the bundles strapped to his back. Dust kicked into the air as he shook his mane, his response to my anxious question: "Where is he?"

Slumping against his neck, I fought the frustration stinging my eyes.

"Ow! Damn horse."

He'd bitten me.

A burlap sack nearly plowed me over, its weight a surprise as it slid free from where it was tied to the saddle. A man took it from me. The rope on the next bundle wouldn't budge. Why did this day have to suck? Hands grasped my shoulders to turn me around, but Salem's words sounded like mush in my ears. His muttering continued, aimed at my retreating back.

My feet carried me to the break in the Plain's wall. A blond-haired bluecoat I'd seen on my rounds many times, but who was too shy to exchange pleasant nothings with me about the weather, etc., jerked his head to the guard next to him. Together, they lifted the *chevaux-de-frise* out of the way. Footsteps trailed after me from a respectable distance while I wandered into the mouth of the forest and stared down the dusky road.

Sunlight struggled to penetrate the dense canopy. A solitary rabbit bounded into the thick undergrowth nearby. His white tail flashed between the brush and was gone. Cluster after cluster of knotted bark and twisting branches, shaggy with scores of weeds and vines, surrounded me. Clutching the key at my chest, I wished my sight to go farther, all the way, to show me where he could be. Details sharpened, his presence floating into my hand, but the metal turned chilly. I couldn't lose the last remnants I had of him, so I imagined myself pushing against that rising heat and forced it back into the key.

The end, Jonathan. I'm calling it. You can't just disappear.

Wrapping my arms around my middle didn't stop the dread from creeping in. War was a hungry beast. Did we really think we were immune from becoming lambs to its slaughter?

Carefree dancing broke out on the Plain, but I just couldn't make myself rejoin them. The world was a cacophony of voices, cheering, animals braying, banging, stamping feet, nose clearing, crying, singing, and all the other sounds that'd been simple background noise before. It irritated inch after inch of me.

A tendril of warmth caressed my face. I tipped my chin heavenward to welcome the breeze washing over me. It smelled of spice. The memory of fingers stirring sensations from my body, electrifying yet serene, took my breath away.

Then his voice carried on the wind. The voice that'd emboldened me, driven me across bloody, nightmarish battlefields, yet haunted my waking hours, was calling my name. I opened my eyes. Stormy gray irises met me. Kościuszko, watching me.

My momentary peace vanished, and my head fell. Once again, my dreams had bled beyond the boundaries of sleep, exhausting me more than the broken hours wearing me down. I'd imagined Jonathan was there.

The colonel tapped a finger to my nose. "Look."

Following his gaze…

Jonathan. There he was, on the forest road, approaching the gate, slowed by another man leaning on him heavily. Their matching epaulets jostled against each other as the men hobbled toward us. The unfamiliar officer had a twisted ankle. Another browncoat, a private, escorting them, relaxed his grip on his pistol.

A joyful holler arose from West Point. Soldiers rushed past us to greet "Private Campfield. Captain Goodale!" Men wound their shoulders under the captain's arms to assist him. The rest clapped and cheered all the way back to the safety of camp. Their voices faded, and then the Plain came alive with three "huzzahs!"

Jonathan hadn't moved. Neither had I. We stood, staring at one another. Life around us continued, but we were frozen, lost after weeks apart.

Time and distance, stuff inconsequential in those moments, vanished. Inches separated us now. Society's rules and regulations about appropriate conduct between the sexes could take a massive leap off a cliff. I didn't care. I threw my arms around him, pressing myself into him, grasping his hair, reveling in the heat rising from him and the potent fragrance of a man in serious need of a bar of soap. Alive, it meant he was alive. Those long-absent tears moistened my cheeks, smeared onto his. I clutched onto him harder, afraid he'd melt away and I'd find myself adrift in the lonely attic without him.

Hesitant at first, his hands alighted onto my shoulders, then they brushed along the curve of my arms. Unable to stay on tiptoe any longer, I slid down his chest and buried myself into the folds of his coat. Deep into the stinking heart of it. The gentle current of his exhalation against my skin was a balm to all that emptiness and grief I'd been fighting. His arms drifted around me, embracing me fully, and his body melted into mine. He nuzzled my hair, and the cool draw of his breath inward glided over me.

This was the first time he held me close without a purpose, not to heal me or guide me by the arm or scrunch together with me on an extra-cramped saddle. More than a few stolen moments with hands and fingers intertwined. We shared ourselves for the undeniable sake of giving comfort. I wanted to consume the relief he offered me from the torment of the last two weeks, to drink in everything about him.

Abrupt, like a strike of lighting, his muscles stiffened. His hands grabbed my shoulders to push me away.

"Are you hurt?" Damn it. Nothing had caught my eye before. From his face to his chest, to his arms and downward, I searched for injuries. "Where are you hurt?"

He seemed whole, aside from a sizable but bloodless snag on his sleeve.

His hands stilled mine from their recon mission flying over his body. A stilted pronunciation of my name brought my attention back to his face. Voice louder than necessary, he advised, "You need not have worried."

"Did you hit your head or something? Of course I've been worried."

After so many days of fearing and so many nights of dreaming about how I'd lost him, it was hard to make sense of him. What was he thinking?

"Captain Machin was told all." He glanced past my shoulder toward the scuffling sound of someone shifting their weight behind us, then intoned, "I have kept my word."

I ignored the unsubtle scoff behind me. Jackass.

"What are you talking about?" I asked the guy directly in front of me, avoiding my gaze.

"Of where we did meet. He was well-advised regarding how to return you there and why you were to be escorted. He would have found you a proper guardian in my place to assist you. So, you see. Your worry was for naught."

After everything that'd happened, after everything the weeks had wrought on me, my body took over and drove me to the one response it felt deserving of such a cold accusation that I was being selfish. I pulled my arm back and punched him as hard as I could.

Chapter Thirty-Nine

The punch was perfect. I should know. My thumb was in exactly the right place. My fingers, hand, wrist, and arm aligned with textbook precision as I drove my fist into Jonathan's jaw. Despite the violent deconstruction of my little finger from battling redcoats during an earlier encounter, that wasn't where the pain struck. Like a match sparked to life, it ignited in my soul. Flame blazed up my torso, and when it reached into my head, my jaw burst into a wash of fire and ice. The force of the punch, intended to wound him, slammed my face to the side, twisting my body around as the power of our pact returned my harmful act onto me.

The earth rushed up to crash into my chest, driving the air out. Nothing came back in, just a wheezing gasp.

Voices roared alive. I think Mr. Sensitivity tried to reach for me. Fingers passed over my shoulder, anyway, but then Captain Brott was nearby, yelling at someone, who was yelling at Jonathan, who was… Sporting arenas are quieter. Dirt shot along the forest floor from all the stampeding male-life in my prone vicinity, stinging my eyes and coating my tongue.

Desperate hands flung me over. Jonathan pressed his palm into my chest, and heat flooded the muscles stuck on pause. Air overwhelmed my lungs in a sudden gust of wind, and the dirt caught in my throat flew out in a spasm of coughing. I dragged in another wheezing breath, sounding like a grossly overstuffed teakettle spilling its guts.

Colonel Greaton's voice demanded, "How could you strike a woman in your trust?"

Excellent. The racket had reformulated into English. Lucky me.

Forcing myself to sit upright was an arduous task. Seasickness on land, what a wild ride. The world darkened, and bursts of light—like fireworks before they explode—flared toward the periphery of my vision. Or was it cannon fire exploding through my body? I tumbled backward and felt like I was sinking further after I made land-ho.

Jonathan's fingers skimmed my injured cheek on their way to cradling my head, except he was dragged away. "You must take me back to her. Miss Moore!" His pleas having been ignored, he called to Colonel Kościuszko instead. "See to her, please. We have invoked the *Votum Fecerit*. I would take the payment. It was mine to bear."

Brott's voice chastised him for being a "damned fool," then shouted, "The viper struck *him*. I saw it done."

"How dare you?" Greaton hissed. "I shall see you both whipped."

Colonel Putnam's calmer voice ordered, "You, there. And you, Private. Take them both to the barrack's prison until General McDougall is prepared to deal with this." Another onlooker was sent ahead to the Red House to alert him.

Woah. My world did a full dusk-to-dawn rotation as someone drew me to sitting.

"Sirs, I can bring the girl to her room." Kościuszko grasped my bobbling head to steady me, thank goodness, because I swear it was ready to fall clean off. "Miss Moore, you will allow this?"

Focusing on the gray swirls in his eyes helped, but the concept of speaking was feeling pretty synonymous with puking.

Putnam and Greaton towered over us, the first trying to convince the other to accept the offer.

"She is agreed," Kościuszko interrupted them.

My temporary, self-appointed guardian paced in small, jerky circles while grumbling, but he didn't argue. Private Salem, who looked loaded for bear at Kościuszko's insistence that finding a dog for "the happiness" was best, scowled but fetched anyway.

"You must stand." Leader of that proud movement, my Polish friend could stand all he wanted. I was ready to desert him for horizontal grounds, which left him to carry my limp weight by wrapping his arms around me. "We come, Colonel Greaton," he announced.

Once our tentative left, right, left caused everyone else to advance beyond earshot, he asked, "You trust in me?"

Words were still woozy inducing. Nodding was right out. I wondered if we could agree on one upchuck meaning yes and two for no.

"None but he that make the *Votum Fecerit* can take payment," he whispered. "This I cannot heal, but I mask the injury so one cannot see. *Rozumiesz?*"

He was remarkably tender as he cupped my injured cheek with his palm. Warmth drifted from my temple to my jaw, spreading like a seabird's wings over my skin. With it, the pain eased. Once he took his hand away, though, the relative coolness of the air renewed it. A headache that'd been brewing as a dull storm in the distance began thundering loudly, along with a lightning-quick agony that locked my jaw into place. And my head would just not stop spinning. Swell. The pact had given me a concussion.

"Let us return to the Red House."

"Jah," I mumbled.

"It is for after you is rested," Kościuszko promised.

Chapter Forty

The shrill whippoorwills, those baneful birds of West Point's finest, were mere crickets compared to the discordant shouting from the officers. I couldn't hear Bose's battlefield bark—his special reprimand of enemy activities—until Private Salem was practically on top of us, rushing to the Red House, his arms overflowing with boisterous puppy. Once inside, Private Fluff-n-Stuff scolded the occupants, while Salem tag-teamed Colonel Kościuszko in steering me toward the stairwell.

"Captain Wythe has broken no laws, nor regulations," Brott-hole thundered from the backroom.

Crap and a half. If I left Jonathan's fate in the hands of such a despicable defender, they'd invent new ways to kill him before supper. I dropped to the floor, toddler temper-tantrum style, forcing my escorts to adjourn our proceedings. At least, until I could gather enough energy to call, "Jah—!"

The yelling ceased when the accused answered.

The bread of our military sandwich were left in the awkward position of trying to explain their intentions to an infuriated Colonel Greaton, who'd stormed into the hallway to investigate. Bose was crawling into my lap, yipping at my face, while Salem was grasping my hand and elbow, and Kościuszko had encircled my waist.

"Jon-a-than."

Hey, a full word. Swear me in, Judge.

Greaton squatted in front of me, scouring the four corners of my face. Surprise eased his angry expression. "If you insist upon it," he agreed dully.

Kościuszko whispered into my ear, "They will not see," before Greaton took over as limp lunchmeat handler.

"Briefly," was my newest escort's warning once he'd lifted me to my feet…and caught me as I continued reeling past vertical. Instructions to Bose to, "Quiet now. Stay," might as well have been directed to a cat. My determined furry companion jumped against my legs, howling. It took Salem rubbing his chest, plus producing a new rag to wave at his nose, to calm him. An anxious whine still carried, crying after the train of my gown.

An unfamiliar voice exclaimed, "This whole situation is an outrage. Captain Wythe is to be commended for his bravery."

Rounding the corner, Greaton insisted to the speaker, "Any man who beats his ward, including an officer, shall be punished, Captain Goodale."

The captain's attempted response was overpowered by Brott's protestations, which were fixated on the verbal carnage of my reputation. Such profanity—though I'd like to think the topic, as well—rekindled the free-for-all of high-volumed opinions.

General McDougall rose from his spindled stool. Its harsh scrape across the wooden floor muted the other officers. Except Brottworst, who supplied one last swipe to denounce the "witch on a colonel's arm." Such a guy.

Under cover of the various disapproving reactions, Jonathan asked him, "Are you mad?"

Seriously. Projecting much? Wisdom was inherent in clamming up rather than risk exposing the reality surrounding the two men.

A fearful glance turned to the persecuted, being me, before focusing again on the general.

Parsons surveyed the room. "Gentlemen, there is a lady present."

Guess who the odd man out was in acknowledging his reminder. Even Colonel Nixon appeared to feel differently from the malicious Man-Who-Cried-Witch, and the officers rose to their feet.

Parsons collected the milking stool that'd come to reside by the fireplace. My own personal hot seat. "Here," he offered his hand while settling it at the table.

"I don't need help…General."

"You look rather unwell," he replied to me.

Jonathan shifted his stance, growing pale. A bluecoat seized his arm, forcing him to stand still. Rope creaked from around his wrists during the process. "Please, General McDougall," he begged.

"You dare?" Greaton chastised. "*After* you have raised your hand to the lady."

That sent Brott off again, insisting Jonathan was "too softhearted to discipline" what became an impressive line of slurs. The nicest label he used was "whore."

"Please desist," Jonathan said, which almost shocked Brott into silence. Almost.

His vitriol turned on his supposed friend. "Can you not begin to see the extent of your foolishness? You have allowed this Mab to captivate you. It places us *and* our mission in jeopardy."

"Shut your bone box," Nixon rumbled at him.

"What, exactly, is yer objection tae the lass?" McDougall asked.

Brott appeared baffled. "Is it not obvious? She holds Captain Wythe in her sway. *And* all of you."

An authoritative hand was held aloft to silence everyone voicing their thoughts on the subject. "Tae what end?"

"Why, to steal his fortune." He waved his bound fists at me. "She seeks to elevate herself above her station, bolstered upon Captain Wythe's good name."

"Have ye other complaints tae lay before us?"

"She has bewitched him and should be punished."

The way Brott leaned in to hold McDougall's attention, ruby flames flaring around him, just raised all kinds of hypocritical red flags. Would he really try to influence a general with his power? Jonathan seemed wary, as well.

Parsons' waved hand cut through the midst of the staring contest, thus interrupting whatever misdeeds were afoot. "The day before, she was a spy. This day, a witch." His observation was met with several thoughtful hums.

Jonathan risked attesting, "The lady is neither of those things, sirs."

McDougall blinked, then indulged in a steadying drink.

Brotten's face fell, dumfounded. "Why should my testimony be taken so lightly? What more proof does the general require?"

Unable to withstand weight on his injured ankle, Goodale groaned and resituated himself against the wall. McDougall apologized for the delay, but the captain insisted, "Pay it no mind, General, though I should like to be heard so I might see to my men and visit the surgeon."

"Take this." Putnam offered his subordinate his own crate to sit on.

"That is generous of you, sir. But had I paid half a mind to what Captain Wythe did advise, I would be standing straight on my own two feet, with my men at my side. No, sir. I welcome my punishment and shall bear it as a man ought."

"Yer brave words shall be heeded," McDougall respectfully answered the speech. "We are most interested in yer report, if ye can bide a wee longer. The lass is also injured. We must address what concerns—"

"General? Sorry to interrupt." It took a lot of effort to force out my interjection. My stomach was doing a great impression of a barrel careening into a ravine. "The captain's injured. I'm not."

Parsons shushed the muttering around him. "You are not?"

"The captain first."

"You most assuredly are unwell, madam."

Hesitant, I glanced at Jonathan before reminding everyone, "I haven't slept or eaten well in days. I'll be fine."

As much as it was a contributing factor, I regretted saying it. Trying to think through a concussion was like traveling through a blinding snowstorm—my visibility was restricted to what was immediately ahead— so I couldn't foresee my next roadblock, which would be choking down the stew Greaton commanded be brought. A bowl was ordered for Goodale, as well, and—since the waitstaff was here—Putnam insisted on something for the captain to sit upon.

"This is preposterous," hissed Brott.

Bullseye. Clean shot, right through my headache.

"Perhaps ye should retire, Mistress Moore," McDougall suggested. "Ye are peely-wally."

Was that English?

I couldn't work it out.

Jonathan begged him again with a simple, "Please."

"Could we do this without Captain Brott here?" Scrunching up my eyes hurt more, if that was possible.

"By all means." McDougall sought assistance from Nixon, who sounded relieved, nearing gleeful, about ordering the guards to escort Captain Obnoxious to the barracks prison.

"Woman scorned" was an expression demoted that day, reserved now for moments of blissful nonchalance, compared to his fury. He elbowed one of the ensigns during the ensuing struggle. The battle of wills reached a stalemate at the door, where the enlisted men became bottlednecked during their efforts to remove the unwieldy captain.

"You have no grounds upon which to hold me. If I do not arrive at General Washington's headquarters, others will be sent in search of me," he threatened. "What will you do when he learns of your treachery?"

"Ensign Allyn," Parsons responded, "be certain to give the captain his writing set and paper. We should not wish for His Excellency to wonder about the goings-on at the Works. Of course, we shall include your report with ours, Captain." A snap of the general's chin indicated political playtime was over, and Brott was hauled away.

"General, sir—"

McDougall silenced Jonathan, saying, "The same rope need no swing for ye, Captain Wythe."

My alarmed gasp set in motion a sensation like oil slicks slapping against my skull. It had me withering in my seat. Greaton was horrified. "Miss Phillips, what is the matter?"

Exhaling slowly—long odds of me making it to overtime—I pried open the lead flaps that'd replaced my eyelids. "Captain Brott was telling the truth. I did punch Jonathan, and now my hand really hurts."

"Will ye show us?" McDougall challenged, with diplomatic politeness included, naturally.

Looking to Jonathan for guidance, I hoped he was tuned in to my wishful thinking. He frowned; however, a subtle nod bade me to precede.

"You're taking over as doctor now?"

The general wasn't amused by my poor humor and displayed an open palm to receive my false evidence.

"What say you, Captain?" Nixon asked.

Jonathan ceased whispering and said, "I simply wish that the lady be permitted to retire rather than endure further interrogation."

Another round of covert nodding encouraged me, so I gingerly acquiesced. Engagement rings have received far less scrutiny. The surprised officers crowded around—what appeared to be—my swollen, reddened pinky and ring finger.

"Well," Nixon commented. "One should understand the proper maneuvering of fisticuffs before attempting them."

"I know how to throw a punch," I snapped. Yeah, chalk that up to concussion brilliance. "Sorry, sir. It isn't from hitting Jonathan, per se. My hand was already injured. I just keep forgetting to stop using it on idiotic men."

Mr. Man clamped his mouth shut, choosing wisely to look repentant.

"Should it be so," Greaton insisted, "it is no reason for Captain Wythe to strike you in return."

"Jonathan's never hit me. He's sworn to protect me."

Okay, he needed to stop rocking on his feet and realize even ordinary human folk could understand the idea of promising to protect someone without suspecting magic was involved. Because I was about to heave-ho if he didn't.

"Your loyalty is commendable, Miss Phillips." Greaton shook his head. "But you, for certain, were. I did see you fall."

Parsons received a signal from his fellow general and urged me to move in the direction McDougall indicated. Lest I be excluded from the encoded-orders gift exchange, I guess, Jonathan slipped me a surreptitious nod, so I allowed myself to be escorted toward the fiercer light emanating from the fireplace.

Bouncing his attention from my one cheek to the other, Parsons asked, "Where did you see Captain Wythe strike her?"

The colonel grimaced. "Her face. It must have been." He rose to reexamine what he'd already witnessed for himself in the hallway. "She was flung about and fell upon her front."

Doing my best to anticipate which segment they wanted to review, so I could preemptively turn my head, helped me avoid their grasping fingers from guiding me. I doubt I could've withstood the gentle care of an antique dealer handling the masked damage. "Pain" didn't begin to cover the experience.

Catching Jonathan's eye again, I saw the whispering the others missed while distracted. It almost got me manhandled.

He cleared his throat. "She swung her arm around wide," he said, addressing the open accusation. "It knocked her to the ground, yet still, she landed her fist solidly across my jaw."

"Rubbish, complete and—" Greaton stopped, confused.

What a spectacular illusion.

My glee in Jonathan's abilities, I knew, was wicked and wrong, but I couldn't help it when I saw what hadn't been there moments before—the hint of discoloration burgeoning above his beard. By moving closer, one could find, within the full growth, the early stages of a fabulous bruise swelling around his jawbone.

A master thespian—or maybe his embarrassment was real, considering my fist had slammed clean into him without his flinching—he shied from the attention, hiding the fictitious injury on his cheek. Nixon grabbed his chin, causing both Jonathan and me to gasp, and showed the other officers.

Guilt caught up to me. "I shouldn't have punched you. I'm sorry."

Nixon released Jonathan, who exhaled sharply at the rough handling.

'Round the table they settled, the mystified spectators of our fantastical exhibition.

Game, set, but the match was not yet won.

Chapter Forty-One

Now what? Jonathan and I remained standing, separated by the table and our current troubles. "Your supper grows cold," he noted.

Captain Goodale had finished his and was not-so-secretly enjoying the unfolding drama. "You do live under the cat's foot, Captain Wythe."

Oh, please. One bad act doesn't a modus operandi make.

Having a role to play in the masquerade, I took my place at the table setting and dragged the bowl closer. It hurt like a mother, but opening my jaw only as far as necessary to squeeze a spoon in got the job done. Thin and made of perhaps three ingredients, the stew was bland as paper. The first few bites rocked my stomach. Then, I couldn't shovel it in fast enough and groaned when the joint cracked.

Jonathan launched into an attempt to circumnavigate the table, but Greaton blocked his passage. Several minutes of quiet meditation passed before McDougall startled me, asking, "What do ye gain from an alliance with Captain Wythe?"

Confused, my gaze darted between the two men. Jonathan tried to shake his head without being detected, but the general was waiting. "His protection," I hazarded to guess.

Neutral Nelly in the one corner.

"Tha' is no about what I inquire," came from the other. "What is it tha' Captain Brott accuses ye of seeking from him?"

Bed and leaving Jonathan to tidy up was gaining some serious ground on Good Idea Hill.

"If," Nixon suggested, "we were to remove Captain Wythe from the room—"

"Don't. Please, sir," I begged him. "With all due respect, isn't that between me and Jonathan?"

"Not when *Captain Wythe's* fate is in question." Greaton emphasized his correction of my address.

"As it *is* my fate," Jonathan said, "question the lady no further. I shall answer for myself."

"Your fate affects me too," I reminded him.

His voice grew glacial. "It is good of you to admit that which guides your actions."

"You really are that thick? We all thought you were dead! Is it so hard to believe I was upset because I was afraid I'd lost you?"

Greaton shot to standing. The room went bug-eyed still, staring. His body stuttered, jerking in one direction, then the other, unsure where to go next. Color flooded his face, and he raced toward the door, tripping over Goodale's leg in the process. Fortunately, it was the uninjured one. He stalled out in the exit, then blurted, "It is true. The lady had not a thought of herself or what would become of her until…until her future became a topic of concern amongst us."

Noticing the general's raised eyebrow, he flung his fists downward and cursed, "'Nation," before tearing out of the room.

I tried to follow. Calling his name saw him pause, but then he snapped at the guards to "look sharp." He didn't glance back as the front door was closed behind him.

Left hovering in the backroom's doorway, I was torn over which relationship required more damage control. Since the room continued flying forward, even after my body had crash-landed into the doorframe, the choice was made for me. I braced myself against the wood and answered the outstanding question. "Captain Brott didn't know I'd been married. I guess he thinks I'm fortune hunting."

Chasing after the colonel had been a bad idea. The world wouldn't stop tumbling around me.

"Miss Moore," Jonathan said quietly, "my heart…belongs to—"

"I'm not asking you to love me!"

"You are not?"

"No."

"You—? Then…what?"

I breathed a laugh. "You're the most amazing man I've ever had the privilege of knowing."

His brows lifted in surprise. "How can—"

"But you're supposed to be getting me home, and…well, you said I'm not from the Colonies. If you're right, I'm never going to see you again. Or anyone from here. I'd have to be some kinda monster to want you guys to fall in love with me. Do you really think I'm that cruel?"

Dumbstruck, he turned aside. Our classy, little tiff left the rest of the room squirming too. To varying degrees. Nixon looked bored.

Was he for real? Why would Jonathan claim his heart belonged to someone else? To who? His dead girlfriend? The oh-so-wonderful and engaged Miss Tuinstra?

Stumbling toward the fireplace, I slumped onto my stool and faced the corner. Throw a dunce cap on my head, and the rest of the world might think I was just another sad cautionary tale—there sits a fool drawn in by silky caresses and warm smiles that whispered of something hotter, then shown the error of her sinful ways.

A spent log crumbled apart, reduced to red ash. Only McDougall, at the head of the table, could see my determination to drive my teeth into my bottom lip rather than allow myself to cry.

Parsons supposed, "It must be a notable fortune for Captain Brott to take such a *brotherly* interest in the matter." The familial term was flavored with sarcasm.

"I doubt it," I mumbled.

"Ye doubt what?" McDougall leaned closer. "The fortune or the friendship?"

"Both, truth be told."

Amused, he cocked an eyebrow. "Will ye elaborate?"

Why not? I turned to stare down Jonathan, whose embarrassment couldn't have been greater than if he'd been stripped naked, just as his personal life was about to be. Fair or not, he'd struck a nerve—the one I kept hidden because it ached from time to time—and I was going to make him wretched for it. I was that cruel…except, not really. He'd exposed the damaged line to *my* heart, soothed it, and made me almost believe I didn't have to leave these shores. I'd imagined rebuilding my life with him.

But my body was in agony, and he'd run me through the ringer for the last two weeks. Every nerve was aflame, so emotional was all I had left. My vengeful assessment started by addressing the fact that: "Captain Wythe has a brother. If the brother inherits, it's doubtful his fortune could be that great."

"These are uncertain times," McDougall egged me on. "What if the brother were tae die? Then Captain Wythe inherits, if none else stands between him and the fortune."

Jonathan groaned. "Surely, this coarse conversation is unnecessary."

But the generals and I weren't finished with him. Parsons jumped in and insisted, "The allegation does not include you alone. Exploitation of we, the officers, was also declared to be at work. It is best to understand the lady's mind."

His interest probably lay more in the direness of Jonathan's wallet and its susceptibility to foreign influence than my actual interpretation of primogeniture, but whatever.

Determined to prove my innocence, I continued, "His situation would mirror what it would be if he were the eldest."

"And what is tha'? Pray, tell us," McDougall asked.

"He's from England. His inheritance is, likewise, probably in England. Land, money, property. Everything of greatest value resides in the very country he betrayed to fight for us. If his father had half a brain, he would've disowned Captain Wythe by now. Otherwise, his father risks being labeled a traitor like him and could bear the punishment in his place."

"And Colonel Greaton?"

"General, I..." Sickened, I needed a moment to choke out the words. Even then, the men hovered closer, across the table, to hear my humbled mumbling. "I'm mad at Captain Wythe, so I don't mind embarrassing him right now. I'm sure I'll feel awful about it later, but...I'm really not comfortable... I think the situation with Colonel Greaton speaks for itself. He was being charitable. I was surprised when he...said something to me about what if... Would you please ask him in private? He's done nothing wrong."

Finding it difficult to face Jonathan after the humiliating dissection of both our situations to a room packed with his superiors, I welcomed the cup of gin Parsons slid over as a distraction. No wonder the officers drank so much. Faceplanting in my mug meant missing any possible return judgment. Though I still owed more to the ring of brass staring at me, I realized. "Captain Brott's got it all wrong."

Lamest summation ever.

"Remarkable," Parsons said. "The whole disagreement could have been resolved earlier had he been informed of the lady's circumstances."

His comment was directed at Jonathan, but I was the one to answer, "Except it's not that simple."

Nixon snorted. "Why should it not be? Surely a pompous coxcomb such as Captain Brott can be made to understand the connection of marriage."

"True, but I'm not married."

"What?" Jonathan breathed.

Parsons glanced at the others, confused, before responding, "You did tell General McDougall and myself that Moore is your married name."

"It is. It was. But I'm not married anymore. Not for a few years, I think."

"Why…?" Jonathan struggled to transform the sounds he was making into his eventual question: "Why would you not tell me?"

Seeing the hurt in his expression, I fought to keep any blame from creeping into my voice as I answered, "I tried. You wouldn't listen."

From that moment onward, fireplaces became my favorite feature; their dappled bricks full of reds and browns and oranges, the rolling grain of a wooden mantel, the sheer avoidance offered of a face gone pale with shock and grief. Fire witnesses so much useless destruction, doesn't it?

A creak of the floorboards sounded the rhythm of a familiar gait moving towards me.

"Must we do this here?" The exhaustion in my voice silenced his approach.

I was a shadow in his presence, as he hovered over me. He made me feel protected from the forces working against us, yet suffocated for the sun, like a blossom on the leeward side of a mighty oak. In my periphery, I saw his bound hands reach. An uncertain finger drew a path in parallel to my arm. The silver flames surrounding him crossed the divide between us and caressed my skin. It spoke of a calm surrender after a long and lonely journey. I would be welcome in his arms.

Suspended by that moment, I was lost. I didn't know whether it was time to give in.

"Ye had best step back," McDougall interrupted us.

Jonathan inhaled. If he had the answers, I would've devoured them and accepted them as mine. Instead, his sleeves brushed noisily against the front of his coat as his arms fell, defeated. His footsteps retreated to his prior post by the far wall, and the decision was deferred for some other occasion more hospitable to confused souls such as ours.

Another fresh tear burst apart as it collided with the glamoured hand cradled in my lap.

"Ye are excused, lass," McDougall said.

"Thank you, General. But I'm not leaving until I know Captain Wythe will be set free."

Nodding his head to tell me, "Verra well," he then requested Goodale regale us with his adventure.

It sounded incredibly heroic and was spoken with great admiration for Jonathan's capabilities as a soldier. A wonderful recounting of rescue from the British camp, judging by what little made its way through the fog.

Our ruse was so extensive—having convinced our audience to accept the truth of our actions and dismiss the mysterious wrongness affecting it—

had we forgotten to stop and, as a result, conned ourselves regarding the heart of the matter?

After the general pronounced Jonathan innocent and went so far as to ask his pardon, I bolted for the door. Jonathan was inadvertently prevented from cutting off my escape by the bluecoat unbinding him. For some unfathomable reason, Parsons came to his aid just before I could round the corner to freedom. "Miss Moore, will you hold?"

It was a narrow, cavernous hallway, lengthened by the exhaustion in my body and my spirit wanting to cross it yet feeling overwhelmed by the effort it would take. Leaning against the backroom wall, I "held," as the general had asked. Pain took that as an invitation to rejoin me. All I could do was stare and wait for him to finish.

"Have a care with the lady," he warned Jonathan. "She is a lovely creature and has proven herself a woman of value; a woman deserving of your respect, Captain, for whatever time you are graced by her presence. She certainly has earned the respect of those whom she has served here."

Touched by his speech, I thanked him. Then, I begged to be excused.

"I shall come to speak with you directly," Jonathan promised.

"Why bother?" I answered.

I conquered the hollow passageway and stared from the base of the mountainous staircase toward the second of three floors, an impossible journey. The motivation that spurned me onward was Nixon advising Jonathan, "Speak to her not, man. Go and bed the lady! Perhaps then we shall all get a good night's rest."

Chapter Forty-Two

Forever in Private Salem's debt, and I was gladly invested in that. He rounded the banister and spared me the necessity of requesting help from Jonathan. An accounting of the many things left unsaid, each of them having accrued interest since the moment we parted, was business for my executor, as far as I was concerned.

"Miss Moore."

Ascending the stairwell two-by-two worked if folks got cozy close, so our third wheel was relegated to the rear. Though the timeless act of ignoring The Great Unwanted remained lost on Jonathan.

Granted, the concussion had magically transformed my ear canals into stoppered wind tunnels, so I probably missed a couple variations; however, after enduring him wearing out my name with increasing insistence—especially once we'd reached the second floor and he could rush to my side—I was done. "You know, you insult me every time you call me that?"

"I…what would you have me—?"

"Savvy, please."

He seemed almost regretful when he said, "I cannot."

"Right, because how would you keep your distance, huh? You're a man of honor. That's what you care about. Just fulfilling your promise to get rid of me."

Bose howled above us, his claws rattling the attic door.

"That is not true, Miss…Phillips."

"Oh, shut up."

Salem steered us past him and around the corner. As he swung open the door separating the second floor from the third, I thought I was going to cry. Hell doesn't lie below us. It's a flight of stairs that keeps going up and up and up.

"Come now, mistress." Salem cheered me on. "You are nearly there."

"She does not care to be called 'mistress,' either," Jonathan interjected.

It was good to know that feeling like roadkill couldn't diminish my ability to reduce him in size with a dirty look.

Okay, deep breath…

One step.

Two…

Someone could collect my corpse later; I had to sit. My head was spinning faster on its axis than recommended. Leaning against the wall didn't help. Worse, actually. Tilting its alignment made it worse. But the draft from the stairwell cooling my cheeks stemmed some of the nausea.

"Allow me," Jonathan's voice rumbled from close by.

A shuffled duet included Salem cutting in, saying, "You should receive the lady's permission before you take such liberties."

Guess it was time to pry my eyelids open and monitor the boys.

Jonathan was like an ice sculpture struck by August sunlight. His classical features were frozen, then his arm, that was cast out in front of him, melted. Clearing his throat, he gestured with a cupped hand and raised eyebrows.

"Were you planning on seducing me?" I asked.

"Byrlady!" He threw his hand into the air when he swore.

Appalled wasn't a great reaction from him, according to my ego. Shocked. Just go with shock.

He stepped forward, saying, "I would—"

"She shall be well-guarded, sir." Salem pressed his chest into Jonathan. "Naught to fear."

Private taking on a captain. Medal of honor to him, because that bump actually knocked Jonathan backward.

"It is for her…" He glanced at me, then back nervously at Salem, which became understandable once he said to me, "You are in pain."

I sighed. "I know what you're offering."

Off-kilter was going to have to do. I collapsed again against the rough stairwell wall. Good news: I missed the nail protruding from the lath.

Whomp. Bose wanted company, and the bedroom door was paying the price for our delay. It upset the monster pounding at the back of my eyes.

Although I couldn't see it, Jonathan's worried study of me was palpable in a way that was almost as comforting as if we had touched. Strange. For weeks, his absence was like a hole in my chest, being gnawed wider by this pest called Time, but then—suddenly, finally—he'd returned, and I wasn't sure how we fit back together again.

"Might I have a word alone with my ward?" he asked.

Assuring it was all right with me first, Salem agreed to step aside. "I shall not be going far, lady. My sights will be on the captain the whole while." And his hand dangerously close to his pistol, I suspected.

Jonathan's exhaled commentary of our chaperone, whose footsteps stalled midway along the second-floor corridor, included a mild whistle. "I could not have asked for a better man to guard you in my stead."

"Yeah, he's a good guy. Though you did chew him out before you left, remember?" Runner-up prize to me. I managed a half smile without my face falling off.

"It was wrong of me." A playful quirk of his brow accompanied him saying, "What success can any man be expected to have, against so great a charge as yourself?"

"Ha ha. If you're trying to get back on my good side, you have a funny way of doing it. Have a seat." I meant to point at the step below me while issuing the invitation. My hand flopped in its general direction. How awful would sleeping in the stairwell be? Some of the aides did, for lack of room at the inn. Salem too, outside my door.

The natural brush of Jonathan's shoulder against my bent knees, as he eased to sitting sideways at my feet, brought the puzzle closer to completion.

"You…" His voice was so small. I lifted my head, and fraction by measurable fraction, I wilted toward him to hear him say, "Your thoughts were, in truth, of me."

"Not tonight." What the hell was he thinking? I grabbed his arm for balance. "I've got nothing left. You understand?" Next, his cheek. "Everyone needed me to be strong, especially when… Why couldn't they just let me…?" Our foreheads met. "I don't want to be strong anymore." Sparks electrified the space between our mouths. They knew where the final piece belonged. Damn it. "You exhaust me."

Body and spirit. My defenses were crumbling.

"You were never far from my mind, either." He dove his fingers into my hair and smoothed away my frustrated tears. "Please allow me to assist you."

"No." I lifted my face from his.

"Whyever—?"

"You'd have to take the pain back, right? Experience it for yourself. You couldn't just heal me, could you?"

He glanced around the corner.

"How did you know that?" he whispered.

"Colonel Kościuszko said you were the only one who could 'take the payment' and, well, I need you whole," I reasoned.

Skeptical at first, he shook his head and grumbled. "There are times your mind is much too troublesome for your own good."

I laughed. Sort of. It was more of a reverse gasp, posing as a laugh. The backhanded compliment was actually appreciated. "I deserve it, Jonathan, for breaking my promise to you." And, were I honest, for giving him flack when I was fully aware that Brott was scowling at us, in the woods, probably making Jonathan feel like a scoundrel for getting physical with a woman he believed to be ball-and-chained. "Man, I just wish I hadn't hit you so hard."

"You did not." He hesitated. "The pact visits the harm upon the transgressor twofold. That is the payment, added to the cost of the pain."

"Okay, you could have lied to me and let me think I have a wicked punch."

"Of that, I can attest to be true."

Jonathan gathered my hand, drawing it from his lap—I noticed—to cradle my arm against his chest. When had my cheek nestled into his shoulder?

"I'm still mad at you."

"I would not deny you that, if it comforts you," he said.

The bustling of the Red House and its daily trade vibrated through the woodwork. Compared to our quiet companionship, sitting alone together in that enclosed space, the small city in motion made for a pleasant soundscape. Rather, Jonathan sat, and the watery mess that was left of me found solace resting against his body.

Pressing his thumb into my palm, he roamed its circumference several times, massaging the muscle, then he traced a line along each of my fingers, exploring one pathway, over to another, then revisited where he'd started. This simple gesture—devoid of magic, caring and wholly human—quieted the bedlam in my head. It was also lulling me to sleep.

"Jonathan, will you do something for me?"

"Anything."

"Relieve Private Salem tonight. Stay with me as my guard."

He groaned.

"You know the officers expect you to," I pointed out.

"Their intentions are not pure."

"Well, certainly not the activities Colonel Nixon was condoning."

"I will not compromise you in such a manner. Private," he called out to Salem.

"But you'll stay, right?" Tiny prickles from his beard kissed my forehead. "Please," I whispered. "I'm scared."

"Dreams?"

I felt his face turn to the side.

"The lady cried out, every night, since…" Salem's report stopped there. I hated how it probably guilted Jonathan, but no stitches for snitches in this instance. Such tattling was a gift.

"Very well." Jonathan agreed, then convinced my other reluctant protector to swap sleeping arrangements.

Bose burst through the attic door when Salem opened it to collect his bedding from where it was stored inside. The puppy's scampering sent him skidding into the wall and plopping onto his furry rump, hind quarters knocked askew. He gave his head a quick shake, tossing loose plaster into the air. A sniff of the stairs led to a snort of dust boogers splatting onto the floor. Undeterred, he lapped it up and bobbed his head at the challenging top step, studying its depth.

As we passed by, Jonathan's eyes skirted over the narrow, chilly landing that'd been Salem's bed. Height equated a rough night ahead, if he stayed out there.

"Would you be offended if I slept in my dress?" I asked. "I just don't think I can manage fumbling through all the pins and ties to find my way down to my shift."

"I cuh, ah…" An instinctual offer to help was quickly choked back before the words escaped. At least, that's what it sounded like from the awkward sounds he made. Instead, he answered, "Nay, Miss Mmm—"

"Lor', make me not to be a fool this night," Salem muttered as he disappeared downstairs.

Laughing hurt. It was so worth it.

Bose charged inside the attic and yipped at the blanket being flapped into the air and spread over me, then he divebombed on top.

"Should the dog be removed?" Jonathan wondered aloud.

Explaining that his being "my teddy bear" meant Bose was my companion each night, I tugged at where he'd flopped against my stomach to snuggle him closer. Teddy Pup didn't mind and stretched his front paws out wide, accenting his mighty reach with a gratifying grunt. One patted the blanket in appreciation of Jonathan scratching behind his ear.

"And a fine guard you are." He smiled.

After a sloth-paced building of the fire to roasty-toasty for us attic dwellers, Jonathan stood and stared across the void at the matchstick-sized landing.

"You could sleep in here," I offered. "At a respectable distance, of course."

"It would not be proper."

"It's huger than the tent we shared."

"God's teeth." He chuckled. "Does nothing trouble you?"

"Well, my head," I teased. "My nightmares… I'd feel better if you stayed."

Jonathan knelt beside me. "Whether apart or by my side, you shall be kept safe."

Chapter Forty-Three

Something in the air wasn't right. A stickiness I felt on the inside rather than on my skin. The sun pierced the canopy of leaves in a twisted haze of stormy yellow, flashing sickly hues, then dissipating. Nearing the evergreen, I glanced upward, toward the sound of rope creaking in the stillness. A large brown spider dangled from a branch overhead. Its dried legs crinkled inward as its carcass swung. Death had already trod this path.

In a violent outburst, the wind ripped across the landscape. The silk thread snapped, and the body was flung into the withered grass. A flurry of leaves slammed against me, slicing my face and neck. I threw my hands in front of me, and the wind assaulted them, as well. Whirling around to avoid the worst of it, I felt the hairs on my exposed skin rise. Something wasn't right. Cluster after cluster of knotted bark and twisting branches thronged for miles; every direction identical, no matter how I turned. Where were the soldiers, the smoke, the noise?

I was all alone.

Except, I wasn't. There was the man in red. His black curls fluttered delicately in the gale, unperturbed by the ferocity of its roar. Blood coated the edge of his sword and dribbled onto the ground. One leg rising, then the other following, he casually stepped over a lump protruding from the weeds and strolled along, as if it was a bright summer's day.

Unbidden, my pace fell in step with his.

A uniform of putrid green stank—the obstacle he'd passed, the aged remains of a soldier. It crumbled from the viciousness of the wind.

An impossible distance stretched between us. He was farther ahead than his lackadaisical saunter should've allowed. Desperate to run the other way, I was nonetheless lured by the same temptation that carried him forward—a need in my soul, tethered to an ancient calling.

As the pathway shrank, it grew cluttered with older, more decrepit corpses. Not all of them were soldiers. The frail fibers of a faded lavender gown fluttered over the last gray flakes just before they released from weathered bone. Near her feet was a child.

Rumbling startled me. Tiny pebbles bubbled from the ground.

The man froze. His sword whipped to attention, blood coursing from its tip along the steel blade toward the hilt. It was unnerving how he turned his head a fraction to the side—slow, even slower—as if afraid the motion would be seen, as if afraid of what was coming. His hand disappeared to his chest to remain hidden.

A presence, menacing and cruel—one of pure evil—tore down the path, hurtling from behind us. Dirt shot along the forest floor, flinging particles into the air. Its passage disturbed my skin, causing it to ripple across my body, like it was being pulled and might actually peel off. The redcoat gagged on the debris. A foot fell back, uncertain.

Pressure drove hard into my chest.

I gasped awake to find a wet nose bumping my own. Bose hopped off me when I bolted upright. Round my topsy-turvy realm went, tumbling down an imaginary hill. I caught myself before smacking into the ground from my lightheaded plunge. Clouds of dust gusted across the floor.

Forcing my internal core to chill via some serious meditative breathing first, I found Bose desperately huffing and pacing the line of the attic door. He charged at me to bark, then raced over to rear up onto his hind paws and scrape at the wood. So much for the sympathy of animals.

Darkness clung to the world outside. Hours remained until it would be free of its spell. I groaned. My fur baby *had* been sleeping through the night.

Yowling was added to his growing insistence, so I hurried to answer his cries, though I was waylaid by the rocking and rolling churned up in concert with tugging on my boots and cloak.

Not expecting the door to go very far, I eased it outward a crack. It swung all the way, drawn by its unimpeded weight. Yeah, great. And at the base of the stairs…

Where, by the ever-loving deity's teeth that he swore on, was Jonathan? Private Salem?

Crap.

Or my truest, most reliable companion—the steel pistol. When my brain function was operating at full capacity, I kept the leather satchel strapped to my side, but the concussion was gumming up my tired mind, and I'd forgotten it. Very little light emanated from the remaining embers in the hearth. A ghostly shaft struggled to pass through the window's divide into the interior. The area beyond their feeble reach was swallowed in blackness, so the bag remained hidden from plain sight.

Bose dropped his front paws down the first step. He whimpered as he tried to navigate the process of bringing his hind legs with him. Before he could take a nosedive, I crouched to gather him in my arms. The sudden action almost sent me plummeting in his place.

Okay…

My sitting on the top step to deep breathe stability into my horizon made him impatient. He growled at the lower level, then scraped, pulled, and pushed his way free to renew his efforts. Piddle cleanup wasn't my idea of middle-of-the-night fun, so I hugged him close again. He stopped struggling once the puppy-lift kicked into gear, heading in the right direction. Thank goodness, because it meant I could balance him on one arm and avoid slaloming down the staircase by grasping the wall studs for support with the other.

After we reached the ground floor, Bose refused to be carried. He tore toward the front door and searched the space underneath. It remained shut when I knocked. Doorman slipped off duty for a little private canoodling?

Just don't be one of Greaton's guys. The poor colonel doesn't need the apoplexy.

Moonlight peeked through the panel windows into the hall. It shuddered on the river, the wind knocking the water off course. Bushes and weeds rustled and scraped their fingernails against the wood siding in its wake.

But inside the safety of the Red House, the muted sounds of snoring drifted through the floorboards and among the lower-level rooms where the aides were crowded together. One man muttered contentedly to the woman of his dreams. Their lazy exhalations tempted me to go court my own attic bedding.

Unfortunately, my merciless, little fiend was scratching feverishly at the door.

"Shush."

The latch wouldn't budge.

"Ow."

I glanced around me, but the men remained dedicated to their slumbering.

All right, there wasn't any reason it should've burned, yet the latch felt like it was fresh from the furnace. Determined to escape, for the sake of a poopless evening, if nothing else, I wrapped my hand with my cloak and rattled the metal until *POP!* the latch burst loose, and the door flew open.

Bose hopped to it, clawing at the empty air with his front paws. The unnatural barrier holding him upright shimmered where he struck.

What is going—?

Just as I reached to touch it, he tumbled through. Stunned for the briefest of seconds, he shook it off, then bolted onto the river path.

"Bose. Bose!" Gathering my skirts, I started after him. A hand grasped my arm, tugging me back toward the house. "Jonathan, I—"

Except it wasn't a person stopping me. Silver strands looped around me, his presence within them as real as if he was standing there, reaching across the barrier and urging me to stay.

A chill crept up my spine. Something in the air wasn't right.

"Bose?" I called over my shoulder.

The last of the moonlight flickered…

Gun. A gun would be super swell right—

…and vanished behind a heavy swath of clouds racing the wind.

Where was the Watch?

Bose yelped.

Oh hell. I have to find him.

Plucked loose, as if by the thought, the silver threads separated from the protective energy coursing along the exterior of the house. They enveloped me, murmuring sensations warm and enticing, as if Jonathan had embraced me against his body and was offering anything—everything—I desired, if only I would remain in his sanctuary, kept safe from what was happening.

But the absence of Bose's barking disturbed me. I couldn't abandon him.

Silver tendrils brushed my cheek on their journey toward my heart, where they melted into the key residing there. *You are incorrigible, dear maiden,* they whispered.

Incorrigible and dramatically stupid.

An unexpected ally presented itself as the howling wind picking up speed. It concealed the rustling of my gown, the clattering of rocks that slid under my boots as I ran, the increasing catch in my breath. Never mind whatever other noises lurked behind its wailing.

Two paths, one choice—I'd reached the fork in the road.

"Bose, please."

He didn't answer.

A warning sounded, rattling the parts of me that yearned to climb to the Plain, where hundreds of soldiers with weapons were encamped. Something sinister skulked within the shadows of the trees ahead, slithering toward the Chain's foundation. I felt its wrongness, repulsive like sap caked against the underbelly of my skin. Which was why the river path was where Bose had gone.

Grasping the key at my neck, I tried to ignore the stream of fearful tears clinging to my cheek. A reminder of Jonathan's hand warming mine rose from its metal.

Scraping my foot forward, I traced the crooked break of a boulder and felt out the safest route. Angry waves slapped against the rocky shore below, ready to punish any mistakes.

The terrain jutted out in a miniature peninsula that obscured the redoubt. Step again, over a rotten log. One more, around the bend.

Moonlight fought to pierce the cloud cover and lost.

Trees loomed over the narrow ledge between the cliff rising toward the Plain and the drop into the river. The wind didn't dare follow me into the bowel of the shoreline where the Chain's end was buried. Still, my heartbeat pounding in my ears and the churning pain in my jaw overwhelmed my senses. I paused, trying to adjust to the hungry shadows devouring the cove.

An animal growled, low and deep in its throat.

Reaching to the barren space at my hip reminded me I was unarmed.

Barking transformed into the sounds of scurrying. I had to move faster.

Toward the top of the redoubt's incline, I found Bose backing over the crest. His white fur reflected what little light reached us. He stamped his foot and took a stance, growling louder, hackles raised.

As it materialized out of the gloom, the evil menacing Bose made my skin writhe, just like in my dream. I extended the key in front of me. It trembled from the shaking of my hand as it dangled from its ribbon. Silver threads swirled around its shape, lighting the stony enclosure surrounding us.

Holy effing bastard.

Malevolence wore the form of a soldier in a mottled brown coat, red lapels smudged with filth. Random fragments of dirt belched from the uniform's crackled folds and scattered along the ground. They tremored above the surface of the rocks at his feet, never stilling. The reek of copper emanated from the smoldering black haze encircling his body. Hands—the color of withered carob pods—opened and shut, clenching at the air. His head turned in bursts of effort toward the redoubt. Shuffling to the base of the wall's construction, he peered over the edge.

Bose launched into enemy-chastising level barking.

The soldier shifted stiffly to snarl—which drove the puppy back a few steps, whimpering—then ran his hands along the top of the redoubt without touching it. Leaning his chest forward in an unnatural curl to inhale the river below, he pressed his palms with deliberate force onto the stone wall. Puffs of dust polluted the air where he struck. His feet heaved upward, crunching his body into a crouch on top. Crooking his head to the side—*Where the hell is this guy's spinal column? His head's almost parallel to the freaking ground!*—he surveyed the foundation where the Chain connected to the shore.

I rushed over to collect Bose and whispered, "It is Time. To. Go."

The soldier snapped his skull back in place, then turned in bits and jerks in my direction.

Oh no, no, no, no.

Do not look into it, a voice cautioned.

Staring at the far edge of the path, I backed away.

The soldier was doing just fine in my periphery. He lowered one leg to the ground with complete disregard for how his skeleton should've limited the contortions of his body. The other leg lurched after. A ripping sound accompanied his hands as they separated from the wall. Impelling his body into the appropriate posture, the soldier trailed after me. He devoured my scent with a rattling intake through his nose, then let the breath burst from his lips in delight.

Bose struggled in my arms, his barking reaching a fever pitch.

Cue that treacherous bitch, Fortune, screwing me over—the train of my gown caught underfoot, introducing my backside to a boulder in an unhappy way. Bose took full opportunity to wriggle from my arms. He stationed himself between me and the soldier, his body jolting wildly with each insistent bark. Then he crouched low, readying to leap at the thing that clearly wasn't human.

Fearing he'd be killed, I dove forward and grabbed him by his chest. The sudden maneuver triggered the ill effects of the concussion, and the world shifted out of sync, leaving me dazed.

Flames burst from the key, the metal searing my skin as its light cascaded outward. Grabbing the ribbon from my neck, I thrust it in front of me. The thing mimicking a soldier had its face a mere foot from mine. It hissed at the silver light and shrank from the radiance. Its dark aura retreated faster than the filthy husk attached to it, and the stench of copper burned my nostrils.

Hands gripped my shoulders from behind and yanked me off the path. "*Z drogi!*"

Not about to argue with the colonel, I scrambled out of his way. Bose darted after me, guarding the space between me and the creature.

"*Acuero ut fulgur gladium meum.*"

Mother Sword flamed to life, a reddish-brown brilliance engulfing the steel being released from its leather scabbard.

"Ego reddam ultionem hostibus meis."

Energy thrummed through the elements. It surged around Kościuszko, wove into him, shone brighter. Every glorious inch of him was breathtaking in its beauty, like an evening star penetrating the stormiest of nights. He strode forward, unafraid; his sword leveled in front of him, blade prepared to engage its prey.

The limbs of the false soldier snapped. A grinding noise of stone on stone echoed within the cove's boundaries as they relocated to the side of its body, the joints of its ankles bent in the wrong direction to support its weight. The thing drove its fists into the earth and tilted its head back unnaturally far from its flattened torso. A grotesque tarantula rather than man now, it glowered at the power collected in Kościuszko's free hand and snarled.

Kościuszko circled his arm, then pitched a shaft of light at it. Particles of dirt broke away from the black aura as it flooded the ground, leaving its physical shell to skitter along the stony path, untouched by the light soaring over it.

The debris whisked together into its horrid, arachnid-like shape. Drawing a raspy inhalation first, the thing roared, shooting a thick cloud of muck at us. Bose yelped and scampered behind me. I flung myself over him, hoping to protect him from the shower and avoid the worst of it myself. Why couldn't this just have been a puppy poop run?

Light blossomed around us.

Filthy scraps from the devilish spew burst into flame where they connected with a chestnut-colored globe shielding us. They guttered into darkened ash that floated to the ground, harmless. Kościuszko hummed with satisfaction.

But the thing hadn't waited to see the outcome of its attack. Its dark aura seeped into the dirt, and the broken husk tremored against the earth's surface while the evil raced beneath us. Dirt shot along the pathway as it passed, tossing particles into the air as it fled.

We laughed, overly pleased with ourselves.

Because wrong. We were so wrong.

It circled around, gathering up steam, and charged.

"Watch—"

The dirt assaulting us choked off my warning.

Kościuszko whirled his sword overhead and, with both hands grasping the hilt, drove the tip deep into the pathway as the evil reached him, shouting, *"Nox ultra non—"*

A shooting cyclone of gravel exploded from the ground. It soared about a dozen feet or so into the air, imprisoning him in its center. His incantation was smothered by the swirling pillar plunging hellward, taking him with it.

"Colonel!"

I grabbed his sword swaying in its earthly sheath. Staggering under its weight and the incredible dizziness in my head, I slashed at the place where he'd disappeared.

A sickening snicker emitted from below.

Bose growled nearby. Searching behind me, I found him snarling at a darkening patch of soil to my left. A long, withered, clay arm erupted from the spot and seized my leg. I screamed as I fell backwards. Kicking the damned thing just seemed to encourage it. It hauled me faster toward the rupture in the ground, Kościuszko's sword dragging noisily with me.

Silver flames rushed from the key along my body and into the clay hand, causing it to smoke. Fissures crackled down the creature's arm. Soon, charred flakes were sizzling and sloughed off, thickening the air. Otherworldly fury reverberated underneath me, and its damaged fingers melded into a solid mass, crushing my leg.

Courageous to a fault, Bose raced over and bit it.

It bit back.

Squealing, he stumbled backward, whipping his head around. Grime coated his mouth. He collapsed, whining in pain, and pawed frantically at the gritty tendrils snaking through his fur.

"That's my puppy, you evil piece of shit!"

Powered by my ingenious battle cry, it still took both hands to fly the sword into the air so I could drive the point straight into the possessed arm. Black silt sputtered from the wound. It released me, and the entire thing disintegrated, the bits sucked under the earth's surface.

Two more arms punched through.

Oh, if this monstrosity has multiplying limbs…

Lucky thought to have as I ripped the sword loose and hesitated over amputating them into a zillion pieces, because I recognized in time the ink-stained cuff. I swung around onto hands and knees so I could grab Kościuszko's sleeve, pulling with everything left in me. His face emerged, gasping for air. Wrenching the back of his uniform coat, I helped drag him from the pit that was still trying to guzzle him down. We fell when the rocky pathway vomited him out, splattering us with pebbles.

The ground shifted.

Time out, mother fu—

We retreated from where the dirt was slurping together, bit by bit, amassing upon itself to rebuild the false soldier. It stank of copper.

"Do not look at the eyes," Kościuszko shouted.

No problem. My head was whirling so fast, staring at the inside of my own eyelids was a-okay with me.

Getting all touchy-feely with my surroundings, I dragged myself onto the leafy incline. The pain from the fall made my snail's pace an utter delight.

At the sound of him grunting, I rolled over and saw him snatch Mother Sword to slash in a wide arc at the monster reaching for me. The weapon sliced across its stomach. It hissed, glaring at the dust trickling from its manufactured body, then it sneered as it raised its hollow gaze to challenge Kościuszko.

Blazing out of the darkness, silver haloed the thing's body. A hand wrapped around its front to tear a shining blade across its throat. Kościuszko lunged forward from where he was kneeling to thrust his sword into its belly, joining his voice to Jonathan's. "*Nox ultra non erit, quia Dominus Deus illuminabit illos!*"

The false soldier spewed muck into the air, black silt oozing from its throat and stomach. Then the entire being crumbled apart, collapsing in a shower that melted into the soil and was gone.

Chapter Forty-Four

A gentle breeze floated across the water, drawing the gloom apart into inky wisps. Moonlight returned to the river valley, and nature restored itself to normal posthaste. Frogs burbled their mating songs from the riverbank. Splashing from an occasional fish, or turtles popping their heads above the surface, added to their increasing numbers, as did the obnoxious call of the local whippoorwills.

"Too long has it been, I have been called to the duty." Kościuszko laughed.

Jonathan clasped hands with the colonel and chuckled, as well. "That is why we seek in pairs."

"I heard you say you will help me." He waggled a finger at Jonathan. "*Psia kość!*" A disgusted eye noted how dirty his uniform had gotten from the encounter. He slapped silty puffs from his sleeve into the air.

"In my haste to follow…" Jonathan swatted at the dust. "…I neglected to evade one of the Watch. The fool enjoys his duties of commanding the officers to recite the countersign, as any other, too well. Had he taken any longer to 'remember' whether I did speak the proper phrase, I had a mind to report him for his forgetfulness."

Their comradely celebration when the colonel suggested a name that proved to be right was so boisterous, one would think a banquet of steaks had unexpectedly sprouted from an olive garden. It was interrupted by a howl.

"Bose." I crawled to where he was hunkered in the grass, scrubbing at his mouth. Pitiful puppy eyes rolled upward as I stroked his fur and tried to console him. There was so much blood, smeared along his muzzle, his paws, the ground. "Help me," I cried over my shoulder.

"God's teeth," Jonathan breathed. "How are you here?"

"You knew I left the house."

He stared, dumbstruck, as if I'd claimed I was freshly arrived from another planet.

"Just… It's okay." My super pup reverted to a fur baby and buried his head in his paws, whining. "Come on, Bose, please."

"What is this now?" Kościuszko knelt by my side.

Relaying Bose's role in the unfathomable action, I begged him to do something.

"Ah, how daring is your little dog." He touched a lone finger to the puppy's side, as if testing a doorway for a concealed fire within, then slid his palm across the filthy fur.

Jonathan's exclamation of "Alexander!" extinguished the rising swirl of light around the colonel's hand. Unexpected Third Wheel—as the pair's matching shocked expressions seemed to indicate was his designation—was storming the redoubt's incline, golden dagger in hand. "You have been freed," Jonathan said. "What a relief, truly."

Such a profound relief, it inspired him to subtly position himself between us, I noticed.

Captain Jackoff scowled. "Ever fools, those who bask in glory rarely know what must be done in the shadows to bring them success."

"Such is our lot." Jonathan pivoted, maintaining his Monkey-in-the-Middle status as Brott roamed. "There is nothing for it this night. You had best return before you are missed. Even His Excellency would be hard-pressed to defend the escape of one held prisoner."

Brott-hole, however, ignored the warning, electing to survey the ground where the monstrous soldier had perished instead. Behind his back, a subtle tip of Jonathan's head indicated where I was cradling Bose. His intended audience grimaced at Johnny-Come-Lately shifting the blackened silt with the toe of his boot, the golden blade poised to spring into the action he'd missed.

"Give me the animal, *d'accord*?" the colonel whispered to me.

Okay…weird. Rather than speak to me, with his usual joie de vivre brightening the path between us, he stared beyond my shoulder. Empty shadows and rough terrain breaking into the cliff walls of the Plain, that was it.

During my distracted check, his careful arms gathered Bose and rested the puppy flat across his chest. "*Chodź piesku. Pozwól mi cię zobaczyć.*"

Creepy, crawly feelings irritated the patch between my shoulder blades. By his overall actions, he was the normal colonel everyone knew and loved. Affection seemed to guide his hand petting Bose. He was fluent in soothingness as he spoke. Fluff Puddle was certainly content to let him do whatever. It was Kościuszko's caution—how he handled Bose, like the way he avoided looking at me—that was troubling.

Brott ceased playing with the dirt. "It is done?"

"It is." Jonathan nodded. Moving almost too deliberately, he gestured toward the river to ask, "Will you assist me with the blessing?"

"Oh, now you wish for my assistance?"

"What? What mean you?"

An accusatory finger pointed at Kościuszko. "You did seek without me."

"You were indisposed."

"You left me to rot."

Yeah. Regardless of anyone's apparent inability to keep frat boy locked up. Although it was just a hum, Jonathan—for once—let it be known he wasn't having it.

Brott's glower fell upon me. "What of the creature?" And his knife pointed out the subject of his accusation, which for some crazy-ass reason wasn't the evil dead.

"Miss…" Jonathan's shoulders fell as I was drawn back into the discussion. Any other time, our ongoing name debate might've bordered on amusing. "Are you injured?"

"Um, no. I mean, my back hurts a little." A bit more, really, but I wasn't feeding his worried expression with that. "Nothing serious."

My gown was hurting lots, though—yards and yards of filth, a sizeable tear along the seam where the skirt joined the bodice. I snuck a guilty glance his way, hoping his appraisal hadn't caught it.

Brott protested, which Jonathan shut down and frowned at me. "Allow me to look into you," he demanded.

"W-what?"

"It is imperative that I examine you."

The uncomfortable, nervous itch between my shoulders wormed into my chest. It was way worse than his Wild-Woman-Tamer approach, the way he closed in on me—gaze locked on my feet rather than meeting mine, just like the colonel. His grip was firm on his knife, the sharp edge darkened by an unnatural tarnish. Dried leaves crunched under me as I shied away.

"Peace now." He raised his palms, his weapon balanced between his thumb and forefinger so it wouldn't fall.

With deliberate slowness, he shifted it to his other hand to pass it to Brott, who rebuffed him. "You would relinquish your blade?"

"You are *Frater Meus* to me. I am well-protected with you here."

The confident words weren't white flag enough. "Do not be so foolish."

Jonathan sighed, frustrated.

Severely lacking in calmness-invoking skills right then, he didn't sheath his knife, which would've done worlds of good for easing the tension.

Instead, he backed to the far side of the redoubt and placed it in the grass. Brott rolled his eyes and started towards me.

Jonathan grabbed his wrist. "She cannot harm me, even if compromised."

A cliff's ascent separating us from the soldiers on the Plain, magical men encircling Unarmed Me, a single treacherously uneven rocky ledge as an escape route—so not fantastic.

"What's going on," I asked.

"We must ensure that the Possessed did not taint you."

Gaze plastered on the ground, he knelt in front of me. Scratch that. All three avoided my gaze like I was a pariah come to town. At least Kościuszko paid me the courtesy of trying to reassure me while he was studiously tousling the dark splotch on Bose's back. "Fear not."

Jonathan leaned forward, reaching for me. I whisked the key from where it was dangling loose and showed him. "I still have the protection spell."

His hands enclosed mine. "It is a blessing, not a spell."

"What's the—"

"You will feel no pain, Miss."

Without warning, without permission, Jonathan ended the delay and seized my face. He raised his eyes to mine, and I gasped, instantly caught.

It was different from when we formed the pact. The glory of the elements didn't arise with the act. Rather, I felt him plunge into me, driving through my body with a force like a blazing ocean, searching with intensity. The sensation swept through my head, into my chest, to crash through my limbs, flooding every hidden recess, saturating the essence of who I was with his spirit. Although it frightened me—the intensity causing me to writhe within myself—it was exhilarating. I wanted him to stop, as much as the sheer pleasure of it urged me to cry out.

Before it overwhelmed me, and I lost myself to it, he withdrew; the tide rushing out of me, leaving me breathless. I couldn't move, caught on a stagnant sea, where the air didn't stir and the light couldn't reach.

At last, as I felt the numbness fade and my physical self resolidify, I became aware of him, inches away, surveying my features. He smoothed a strand of hair behind my ear. "Are you well?"

Around the merry-go-round spun on its dizzying course, my thoughts rising and falling with the turning of our fortune together. I think it had the undesired effect of me nodding.

"The lady is pure," he pronounced over his shoulder, then his hands clasped my elbow and waist to draw me upright with him. Lightheaded and a little drunk on the traces of power lingering within me, it took longer than normal to regain my balance.

Once ensured I could manage on my own, he nodded, and a smile flitted across his features. But then he turned away, crossing to the opposite side of the path where his knife waited, leaving a sizeable opening between us.

"You did not finish." Brott rolled his dagger in his fist. "A witness cannot be allowed to live."

Jonathan paled. The colonel pressed his lips together, silent.

After all those broken moments, missteps and misgivings and misunderstandings I'd never overcome, now the inglorious prick claimed a chance for revenge and closed the distance. "I shall do it."

"Jonathan?" A boulder at my back marked the demarcation line to the cliff.

My self-proclaimed guardian bolted in front of him. "Alexander, hold."

"You know the law, Wythe."

"That law is of the Old World." Kościuszko approached the duo, all sunshine over an insignificant squabble. "Here, we build a new one."

"This does not concern you." The blade pointing at the colonel's face dropped. Brott's attention snapped back to Jonathan. "You slew the Possessed in full view of a human."

Kościuszko eyed them both, confused. Really bad time to realize I'd neglected to mention how the tempestuous brothers-in-arms were in the dark about my questionable status within the ranks of humanity.

Jonathan, meanwhile, scowled. "There was little choice. It had already engaged us."

"Our people's fate is not to be gambled away by ignorant tongues," Brott said. "Those that hunt us have not left us to find peace in this new world, *have* they?"

Whatever its meaning, the intended hurt found its mark. Jonathan withered.

"Captain Wythe…?" I took a hesitant sidestep toward the path. "You know I won't tell anyone."

Kościuszko nodded. "The girl and her dog seek the *bestia żywiołów*. They find it before us."

A grayish wave washed over Jonathan's pallor, but then he lightened his tone considerably. "The lady poses no threat, then."

"She is not one of us," Brott insisted.

"That is of no matter," Kościuszko answered.

"Of course it matters. We cannot protect others when we, ourselves, are exposed." He turned on Jonathan. "It is the law for a reason."

Laws were supposed to be fair and balanced, knowable to everyone and applied equally. Wasn't that what we were fighting for? What possible society were they seeking to install that demanded my death, simply because I'd witnessed the destruction of evil? As Jonathan stared at the two of them, an amalgam of horror and disbelief, and Kościuszko scrubbed his curls, looking grave, I realized theirs was a cause that should never be brought to fruition.

Jonathan's shoulders dropped. His head followed.

His buddy straightened, reeking of smug satisfaction, and stepped around him. He clasped Brott's arm, and the two men stood—the one, frustrated; the other, lost.

Kościuszko tried a different tactic with the man I once trusted. "You make the girl forget. It is done before. *D'accord?*"

If only it was an option.

Our carousel ground to a halt, the music of our journey souring upon reaching this final moment.

"Please don't do this." Gravel crunched under my boots as I stepped onto the path. "Jonathan?"

He sighed.

I thought our last stop would see us embarking on another ride, something just as dizzying yet wonderful. Instead, a hand settled on his sword's hilt. He raised his head to face me, pools of regret dampening his eyes.

"Help!" I tore down the pathway, screaming. "Someone help me."

"Stop."

Stones slid under me as I ran, spilling from the ledge into the river below. Footfalls chasing after me weren't far behind. The front corner of my gown was dragging from being torn. It caught underfoot. I stumbled, smacking into the cliff wall, and screamed again. Muffled voices from the Plain overhead alerted the camp of the noise.

Bose's barking at our backs cut short.

Thundering boots hurried toward the cliff's edge, men's voices yelling in confusion, calling down at us, demanding to know if someone was there.

The bend. I had to escape the tree-covered cove so they could see me.

A hand seized my arm, yanking me to a halt. Swung around by the sudden force of it, I let my fist loop with the motion. The unplanned move meant I caught Jonathan in the ear. Might as well have been brawling with myself. Fiery sparks burst from within my soul and charged through my skull as the pact reverberated the pain back on me twofold. Dazed, I stumbled as we collided.

Memories of a man called Sensei urged me to focus on leverage, a push-pull maneuvering to knock my opponent off-balance. Driving my fist into the soft part of his shoulder, I tore my other arm backward.

Sensei was a genius.

Finding myself free, I shoved against Jonathan's chest, propelling myself away from him. But the pathway kept circling long after I picked a direction to flee in, and I fell, unable to get my bearings. Arms ensnared me before I plummeted from the ledge. They dragged me into the shadows.

"Over—" I screamed to the soldiers, who were calling out for my location, but I choked on the rest of the words. My body couldn't take any more abuse, and the stew from supper erupted from my stomach.

"Shh." Jonathan's voice was shaky as he swept aside loose hair and held me. Another wave of vomit splattered onto the ground in front of us. It felt like my insides were rolling outside of me, twisting my shape the wrong way.

"There, now." His lips brushed my ear. Passing his hand along my damp brow, he continued to soothe me, cheek pressed against my head. "Breathe."

For the briefest of moments, the Earth slowed. The contents of my skull ceased swaying, steadied by his arms wrapped around my waist, his body encasing my back. My head lolled to the side, and I spat out the remnants of supper cluttering my mouth.

Voices shouted from a distance, "Search the river!"

Dragging my eyes open renewed the panic. Brott was almost on top of us, drawing back his blade to strike. My impaired effort to scream was reduced to a gurgle. Coherent thoughts vanished. My ability to comprehend their words, expressions, even body language—anything and everything— was sacrificed to the basest of instincts: fight or die.

I crumpled forward. Jonathan's grip on my middle tightened, and he leaned closer. Becoming every bit the viper I was accused of, I struck, flinging myself back as hard as I could. His head dodged out of the way, his face avoiding the worst of it. My chest received the payment of the blow. But the motion also knocked him off-balance. Taking advantage, I swung my leg around, twisting my torso to hook my foot behind his knee. We both went down when it buckled.

Someone else could worry about the intricacies of an explanation, because I sure as hell didn't care just then, but there was enough intent in his actions for our pact to revisit the pain on him. A chill swept through my side, swirling in on itself until it was sucked away, taking an initial snap of agony with it, though his weight landing on top of me still knocked the breath out of me.

Clawing at the stones underneath my hands, fingernails tearing into the crevices for leverage, dragging my belly over the broken pathway, feet kicking against his limbs entangled around me, I failed to free myself. Fists yanked at my wrists. I was tugged upward.

A hand stifled the guttural sounds ripping apart my throat. Smothered as I was, I still regurgitated enough spit to coat the hand. It jerked aside. Another wave of nausea consumed me as the stench of vomit was smeared across my face. Thrashing, yelling through the moistened palm with what failing strength I had, I struggled against the being that'd gathered me in its arms.

"Savannah! Be still."

Shocked, the fight left me, and I collapsed, entirely spent.

The hand covering my mouth relaxed, then lifted. A moment later, his knuckles passed along my temple. I felt the tips of his fingers—dry and rough, but also warm and alive with magic humming under the surface of his skin—spread over my cheek to cushion my face. A familiar fragrance drifted through my hair as he cradled me to his chest and whispered, "I am trying to protect you. Please, believe me."

A cool breeze washed over us, drawing with it the heavy scent of the river—fish and mildew, battling a hint of sweetgrass. And spice.

Wrapped around me, as if he could banish the rest of the world with his embrace, or else conceal me from it, his body trembled alongside mine.

Sounds materialized out of the haziness. Men, yelling about the wayward captain missing from his cell. And his weapons.

"They seek for you," said a shape stationed between us and a figure with a golden dagger.

"Lady, are you there?" another voice called from close by, approaching the next curve in the river path.

"You had best return," Jonathan warned.

"Finish this," the figure demanded.

"Worry not."

An angry grasp tugged on the sheath attached to his belt so he could thrust his knife inside. He growled a sigh, twisting his neck until the joint cracked, then squeezed past us, whispering. Flickers of the world beyond the cove bled through his body, finding substance as he dissolved from plain view.

"They come." Kościuszko, the shape left standing near us, deposited a bundle into the grass. Leaning into my face, he said, "He sleeps. He will not remember this night." The colonel scratched at the curls on the back of his head, troubled. Sounds of soldiers crashing through the brush were almost at the bend. "Conceal yourselves. I will undirect them."

Rocks, the river, dropped. No, it was me that was lifted, my surroundings seeming to fall from underneath me as Jonathan hoisted me upright, grunting as he did. There was no struggle between us, my body a somewhat distant thing from what little of my conscious mind remained, unfeeling, as he staggered off the pathway, towing me with him.

In the leaves at our feet, limp limbs sprawled in crooked angles amid a rocky bowl, an unconscious Bose lay with a pink serpent lolling from his mouth. Helpless to save him, or even myself, I think I whimpered, because Jonathan muttered a long string of nonsense.

Kościuszko rushed toward the soldiers as they burst through the tree line. "A woman, she scream for help. We must go to her." He was pointing at the opposite shore.

The leader held back to consult with the colonel while the others spread out along the path, some heading further into the woods towards the second redoubt. The rest circled around, dividing aloud the task of readying a boat. Although there was barely any underbrush to hide in, we went unnoticed during their search. The guard with Kościuszko reversed course, leaving him behind, unsuspected.

Though I'd seen the spell work, known how it would erase us from the tapestry of human existence, with those Latin phrases still echoing through me, the knowledge that Jonathan was free to kill me and no one would know—not even if it was done a foot away from them—broke the final connection I had to myself. Death was a visitor I couldn't refuse, and I'd known with absolute certainty Jonathan would be the one to invite him in.

I know I laid in the grass. Their blades cut across my vision. But whether I fell or was placed there was lost, a useless specter within the corridors of time. Noisy stamping of feet was absent, even when they must've rushed past me in the blur. If he spoke, Jonathan's words didn't reach me across the hazy tunnel of gray. In its center, water lapped against rocks, muted by the distance, until they blurred. Floating on the foggy surface, a single piece of down rode the waves. It flowed up and over a crest to roll along the other side. Glimmers caught on the tiny black strands that danced in the air and glowed blue. There should've been music.

Chapter Forty-Five

Woodsmoke perfumed the air. Charred logs crackled, a large heap of hot ash under the andirons. Dark crisscrossing beams above. Dust motes floated in the sunlight streaming through a miniscule window.

The attic bedroom.

I raised the bowling ball tethered to my neck. A lagging sensation of the walls and floor wobbling out of sync from the rest of me struck. The concussion hadn't spared me yet, which meant I was alive.

Ghostly meetings, from the long-ago time of Before, revisited on me tales from trauma survivors whispering their experiences. In those haunting memories—singular in their recall of a lone impression, like the spinning of a coin on a table, yet devoid of all other aspects, as if kinder beings had banished the horrors from their minds—I recognized the same phenomenon had stripped me of the pain, fear, and ability to remember the final portions of my encounter at the river's edge.

A soft rumble from the vicinity of my belly turned out to be Bose nestled into me. Two oversized oven mitts for paws stretched forward in his sleep. Stroking him while trying to resituate his head so I could examine his mouth woke him. He extracted his chin from my hand, then shook his ears around, before plopping back into sleep mode with an irritated puppy exhale. I allowed him his snooze, grateful his injuries appeared minimal.

But why was I alive?

A quiet survey revealed, as a bonus to still being ensnared within this mortal coil, I'd been tucked into my uncomfy bed. Wearing my shift. Without the rest of it. Absolutely cringeworthy, the thought of someone manhandling me while I was unconscious—slipping pins from my bodice; drawing the front panel open to expose my torso, which was pasted with the crusty, white linen; then peeling the sleeves from my skin; untying ribbons to ease two layers of petticoats from my waist.

Unfortunate nervous reflex before brains, my fingers closed around the key at my neck. It was duller than before. Colder. Its…"blessing" running low.

An enormous mass was sprawled against the door. Jonathan, his hair unbound, stripped to his undergarments, was rolled onto his side and using an arm as a pillow while he slept. And he was blocking the way out. A vague silver haze hovered above the contours of his shape.

As far away as possible wasn't far enough. The air in my lungs froze, and the cavernous distance collapsed in an instant. A wild scan of the room flaunted what I already knew to be true—there was no escape. The windows were too small to squeeze through and too high to jump from.

There had to be options. Where was my leather satchel?

Shit.

Or my clothes.

Jonathan groaned. A hand flew to his side.

Dust. There was dust everywhere. A trunk on the far, far end of the attic, near him. Logs piled by the hearth, none within immediate reach, though. A mad dash, maybe, to grab one before he could stop me. Then what? Considering how our previous scuffle had gone, the ability to take him out and get away was delusional at best.

"Shall I rebuild the fire?" he asked, clutching his knee as he stumbled to standing.

Shrinking from his approach was enough to ground him to a halt. A rise of surprise in his expression cascaded into dismay throughout his body, especially when I refused to meet his gaze. Once so stunning in its brilliance, its alluring beauty was captivating for what I now knew to be unholy reasons.

Determined to master the rising panic in me, I measured my shaky exhale by the whack of an axe splitting wood in the yard below. A hapless struggle that was noticed. "I deeply regret all that you must be feeling. It was never my intention to harm you."

"You should've let me go," I snapped.

"I feared…" Clearing the huskiness from his voice paused his excuse. "…that I would not have been the first to find you again."

Crack. The axe pierced another limb.

Possibilities raged through me. If it *was* the truth, our fight was a catastrophic misunderstanding; his role as my protector applied in some misguided, poorly calculated way to ensure he was guardian of my whereabouts, at all times, throughout the danger, without me knowing freedom from his oversight.

Crack. It struck harder.

Moments of naïve blindness—stuffed with woeful, wishful desperation for goodness in such an unnatural existence as his—might be ticking down if he was lying. If I guessed wrong…

"Are you cold?" he asked. "Shall I—?"

Thwack. I heard it crumble apart.

The "no!" I barked in response caused him to flinch.

"Forgive me. I…" His head fell. "Forgive me."

He drifted into the far corner to collect his pants from where they were suspended from a crossbeam in the rafters. Not ready to trust him yet, I refused to look away. He fingered them for a prolonged while, testing the fabric.

Why should I trust him? Truth or garbage, it was meaningless. Eventually, the laws of his secret society would catch up to him. To me. And his constant, sickening deferral to Brott-hole would be tested again. What if multiple members of their Protect-the-Ignorant, Kill-the-Rest Order attempted to assert a similar influence? I'd assumed Jonathan was the hero in our story. Loved him like an innocent princess wanting rescue. What if he wasn't actually strong enough, the way he blamed himself for Cordelia's murder?

Unable to take the dizziness any longer—the reeling in my skull had reached ocean-in-a-storm level, regardless of whether my body held steady or turned port to starboard—I revisited the lumpy horizon of my straw mattress. "Where is Captain Brott?"

Cheeks clad in shame, he faced the wall rather than ask for privacy, and stepped into his pants. "He returned to the gaol. There will—" A sharp inhalation led to a grab at his side. "No doubt…be many questions…as to why the guards believed him to have gone missing."

Instead of voicing that it served the murderous bastard right, I asked, "Does he—?"

"We have not spoken since the events by the river."

Which meant he didn't know whether Jonathan had killed me or not. At least, I hoped so. Who knew what the men were capable of?

"And Colonel Kościuszko?"

"He—"

A rhythmic rapping on the door prevented him from filling in the missing gaps. "Good morn!"

Bose perked up at Colonel Greaton's voice; his tail thumped against my chest. Jonathan slipped on his coat, wincing as his one arm rounded into the sleeve, and moved closer. "Are you well enough to receive him?"

It took me a moment to respond, "Yeah." His skin had downshifted to a less-than-healthy shade for a heartbeat there.

My fluffy yogi master downward-dogged it, pawing at the floor as he demonstrated his skills, then reverse stretched, and bounded to the door, barking and reaching for the latch.

"Savannah." Jonathan wrestled with his words as he spoke. "I must ask that you be good enough to not reveal what occurred last night at the river, and…I pray that you will grant me the opportunity to try to restore your faith in me." When Greaton knocked a second time, calling for me, he hurried to finish. "If you feel that you cannot, I beg you not to betray the others. Let it be only my fate that you decide."

Asshole clothed in nobility. What the hell was I supposed to do with that?

The contours of his body shrank.

I didn't have an answer. I was too damned overwhelmed by things I couldn't begin to wrap my head around. Why should he get one from me?

Grimacing, he rose, unsteady as if seasick, and opened the attic door. Bose bolted onto the landing, yapping at a startled Greaton.

"Good morn, little dog." The colonel laughed at the excitement prancing at his feet. Returning to his purpose, he scowled while taking in Jonathan's hasty attire and loose hair. "Miss Phillips?"

"Colonel. My thanks for bringing breakfast for the lady." Jonathan stepped aside. "Mayhaps you would care to join us?"

A whistle called Bose's attention away from his attempts to go downstairs by himself. A firm command to, "Come," saw him trotting over and plopping his rump by Jonathan's feet, tail wagging.

"How quickly you have trained the pup to mind," Greaton said. "Most admirable."

"Others have done the work, sir. I only reap the benefits." Captain Humble Pie nodded at the bowl in the colonel's hands. "I should warn you, the lady took ill during the night. She has just woken, so I have yet to learn how she is faring."

Concern puckered Greaton's features. "She was not the lady injured, was she? Mr. Kościuszko did tell…*us* that he had looked in and seen she was safe abed. Did you not speak?"

"What has occurred?"

"Therein lies the matter. No one knows. It was thought the distress had come from along the riverbank. Since none was to be found, and there were those who supposed the trouble to have arisen from the eastern shore, some few men were permitted to cross in search. But with a scarce number of houses, it did not take long to survey those that could be visited so early. All was in tolerable order. Another party left after dawn to speak with those same families who did not answer their door. They are to search the marshes across the river, as well, lest some maiden lost her way within their watery maze."

"I pray the poor lady is well."

"As do we all, Captain."

They maneuvered around their personal beefs with each other with impressive tact, I had to admit. Meanwhile, Bose had wandered over, such mundane matters yawn-inducing to him, and commenced washing my face in exchange for pets.

Jonathan had glanced in my direction when he voiced his prayer for the "poor lady," which drew the colonel's attention over to me, as well. "What ails her?" Greaton asked.

"It appears to be a malady of the stomach."

"Well gracious, man. What did the physician say?"

"In truth, the lady is very proud and permits few to come to her assistance. It is why I am grateful for the friendship that you have shown her in my absence. And why, if you will pardon me, I must impose upon you: Would you be so good as to speak with her about the matter?"

I shuddered. His story manufactured a plausible explanation for why my nerves were in ruins and my appearance an undoubted wreck, beyond what restless hours of nightmares or the officers' condoned lovemaking would generate. Plus, the compliment completely sucked in Greaton to take his side, the exact sin of manipulating the officers Brott had accused me of. It was both clever and maddening how easily Jonathan twisted the truth so he could fool people. And he wanted me, depended on me, to maintain such lies or else risk his fate and, thereby, ability to guide me home.

The colonel was not-so-secretly pleased at being called to my service. "Of course, I shall make the suggestion. We cannot allow the lady to go without the proper care of a physician. I confess…" He sort of shrugged while he confided, "It had been my hope that your return might restore her spirits. They have been quite distressed. A lady does not care for her guardian to be so long absent."

A moment of similar hopefulness came and went for Jonathan. Any concern for our future together had been tarnished by what'd happened during our recent misadventure, and I witnessed its reminder within the deflation of his whole being with far less indifference than I desired. Those were my hopes dashed too.

But Greaton saw none of that, turning to address me instead. "How fare you? Oh no, please. Do not rise." His invitation arrived too late to prevent the surge of dizziness that flattened me. "Captain Wythe, you must collect the physician," he insisted. "Miss Phillips, you look very ill indeed."

"You certainly know how to charm the ladies, don't you, Colonel?" A breaker of stomach acid crashing over my tongue hampered my ability to rise entirely above the storm while teasing him.

"Ah," he chuckled, embarrassed. "Well now, what a relief to know you are not out of humor, as well."

Managing a small smile in return, once my excessive bodily fluids had stabilized, my eye inadvertently caught Jonathan's. Grief was written across his face. I felt it swell in my chest, as if our pact was inflicting a two-prong attack on us.

Forcing myself to look away, I told Greaton, "I'd like to try eating something first. Maybe that'll settle my stomach."

Jonathan whistled for Bose, who launched from my side towards freedom. A final melancholic glance from him darkened the moment, then he slipped through the attic door.

"Where are you going?"

Alarm was a tenor I needed to excise from my voice.

Jonathan sounded uncertain about how to respond to it too. "I shall not seek the surgeon without your permission." Then he started closing the door again behind him.

"Don't. Please."

"You…wish me to stay?" The glimmer of hope returned.

Round and around my emotions drove me, from fearing him and how he'd used his abilities to influence me, control me; turning the corner toward abandonment, where I was left unprotected from his kind; circling to the unexpected reminder that I could use him in return to empower myself; returning to the desires I was denying my heart from expressing; back to fear, questioning if his magic might be addictive, while he was nothing to me but a vehicle for its fleeting delights.

Greaton grew uncomfortable, eyeing the silent passage between Jonathan and me. He rallied himself, saying, "I had sought to gain your opinion, Miss Phillips, on some matter brought to you before… If your guardian would permit it, of course." The last part was tacked on, begrudgingly.

The hope vanished. "If the lady wishes it. I shall enlist one of the aides to take Bose to the camp, then remain on the stair so you may speak freely. Would that suit, Miss?"

"Where is Captain Brott, Colonel?" I rushed to ask.

Greaton's brows raised in surprise. "Why, he remains within the barracks prison. Had you heard otherwise?"

Freaking concussion brain. I struggled for an appropriate response. "He hasn't been brought to the house to be questioned, has he?"

"Nay. That will…the poor pup grows anxious to be out of doors." He was distracted by Bose dancing back and forth and whining on the landing. "Have I your permission to speak with you as Captain Wythe suggested?"

Where did the ride end? It just kept spinning.

"I will be brief." That damn reassuring tone Jonathan used was far too effective for comfort. "And if the colonel will permit it, I shall tell any who would seek to order me from the house that I am acting under his orders to remain."

Yeah, my heart really needed to cool it until there was a reconciliation of Me to my sense of self. It was impossible to judge others with blanks instead of context in my memories. Some distance was what the doctor would prescribe. Time heals all wounds, right? So, I ignored his questioning look for approval. "You have my permission, Colonel. Besides, I owe you an answer to your proposal."

Jonathan paled.

"Oh, well…" Greaton blushed. "It was not so much a *proposal*. In truth, I did not intend to speak with you about…" After a brief acknowledgment of the hovering occupant in the doorway, he leaned closer to say, "With the return of Captain Wythe, it would not do for him to think that—"

"It isn't his business what I do. I make my own choices."

Shocked by my cavalier answer, the colonel flashed another awkward glance in the direction of the landing.

"Have I your permission, sir?" Jonathan muttered.

Greaton threw his hands up. "Very well. You may do so, but only if asked, Captain."

"Aye, sir. If I may…before I go…" He retrieved a dark lump hidden within the shadows. Or at least, the shadows that were there until he left the room. Crossing halfway to the bed, he asked, "Would you be so good as to give this to the lady? I know she would not wish to be without it."

My leather satchel.

Having delivered his pseudo olive branch, he scooped up Bose, who'd already made it past the first few steps on his own. The crotchety stairs remained unnaturally tightlipped about his presumable passage downstairs.

Digging into my bag, the one he'd concealed from me, turned up the steel pistol. He'd given me a weapon. It struck me as an empty gesture. I couldn't kill him with it. Not without harming myself.

Or, you incorrigible brat, I chided myself, *he's giving you the means to defend yourself against others more sinister.*

Assuming he'd left me cartridges.

He did. Plus, spares.

Of course my "guardian" would want to see me armed, Greaton's grim acceptance seemed to suggest. I'd arrived at West Point on my own, after all. He knelt beside me and, once certain he'd regained my full attention, insisted, "You *were* the lady in distress. Tell me, what has occurred?"

"Colonel—"

"One of the Watch did swear it was your voice he heard. If you are injured, I demand to know it."

"Do I look injured?"

The question tripped him up.

Though I'd invited him to review my many features with the remark, I confess, I was surprised by the unexpected warmth rising through my body while his eyes drank me in. I wound the blanket around my chest to cover up. "Captain Wythe was telling the truth. I was sick in the middle of the night."

Accepting the bowl from him freed Greaton to place some square footage between us. While I spoke, I drew careful spirals through the porridge, watching the sludge reshape itself to my will. "He took care of me when I threw up and stayed with me, despite the way everyone's assumptions about his presence here bothers him."

Well, wasn't I the star pupil, using the same techniques as Jonathan to paint him in such a good light? All the shades of truth blended into a simplistic scene, far more tranquil and innocent than the subject. Whose soul was that canvas sold for, I wondered.

I slashed my creation with the spoon. "Would you do something for me?"

"I should be only too happy to assist you. What is it?"

"Free Captain Brott."

Greaton wasn't expecting that one. Judging from the quiet shuffle on the stairs, neither was Jonathan. The colonel heard it, too, and stormed to the door. "Captain Wythe. You shall be permitted to join us in short order." He then slammed it. Pointing a finger toward the accused outside, he strode back to the bed. "If he is forcing you to make such a request—"

"He isn't."

"I swear to you, Miss Phillips. If he is, there will be a price for it."

"He isn't," I promised.

"Captain Brott has earned his fate. He shouted at his superiors, disregarded orders. He injured a colonel during his attempts to attack you. To call you 'spy' and 'witch.' Do not take such accusations lightly. I must warn you, not all the officers are as assured of your good nature as they ought to be."

Okay. Disconcerting, but not entirely surprising. It also wasn't my biggest problem. "Sir, it's because of Captain Brott's conduct that I need you to let him go."

"Damnation! His words…to be sure, his words, if believed… Madam, this is without reason. Such a man should remain imprisoned for his efforts to cause you and your reputation harm, not released."

"General McDougall's already said he can't take any action against Captain Brott."

"That is preposterous."

"Brott's gone on and on about being expected at General Washington's headquarters. If he were made to leave immediately, then I'd be safe from him until Captain Wythe and I can take off for our next mission."

"Y-you are not staying?"

The peach bloom across his cheeks during our mutual recognition of his detour was sweet. I wanted to wallow in it, in the relief at having something normal right then, like being flattered by someone's attraction. His was a normal life.

"I'm still trying to find my family." Dismissed that temptation mighty quick, didn't I? "They're not here like we'd hoped. So, Captain Wythe and I need to continue searching for them." Stabbing a lump that was caked to the side of the bowl, I played out all the possible outcomes of my next request before choosing an approach. "Please, if you would do this one other thing?"

"What is it?" Greaton shook his head.

"Don't let Captain Brott know I'm the one who asked."

"My dear lady. Again, what you say lacks in reason. Should the general agree to this idea of yours, the captain should feel himself relieved. That you were his champion, do you not think it would lessen whatever disdain he may have felt for you before?"

"You don't know him very well, Colonel. I think it would have the opposite effect, and he'd hate me more."

The question was: would Jonathan get on board with the plan? The gauntlet had been flung at his feet—defy the laws of his fantastical fraternal order and cast aside his long-standing friendship. For me. Was my life worth it to him?

"Do not distress yourself," Greaton bade me. "Rest is what you require."

But I had to know if he was willing to do what I wanted. "You've been such a good friend. Please know I'm grateful. I…want to tell you something, but it's a secret, and it's really important it stays that way."

His expression softened. "I assure you, you can trust your confidences to be kept safe."

I paused there. Despite how far apart we were, with a closed door separating us, I suspected distance, iron, and wood couldn't prevent Jonathan from hearing every word. The breath he was holding filled the room with tension only we two could feel.

"Miss Phillips?" Greaton prompted me.

"Captain Brott believes I'm already gone. That can't change."

"And am I to say Captain Wythe has fled with you?"

"No. I…had the opportunity to leave in the middle of the night, without Captain Wythe. That's the story he invented, so you guys can work out the details. But please, please do this for me. Captain Brott must believe I'm gone and no one but Jonathan…Captain Wythe knows where I am."

Appalled, he jumped to his feet and paced several times, muttering while he verbally meandered to his ultimate determination. "Absolutely not. Remain here. General Washington shall hear of this."

"My life depends on it."

He stumbled backward, staring. "This…you…" He sighed. "When?"

"When, what?" I asked.

"When do you depart with Captain Wythe?"

"As soon as possible." With or without him, I vowed to myself. Machin could tell me the way.

"If you should feel compelled to make such a request… I am sorry, lady, but this is not the best course for you. Captain Wythe and Captain Brott are said to travel always together."

"None of us arrived together," I pointed out.

Appearing unconvinced, he lowered his voice to add, "There have been rumors that they are assassins. Surely, you do not believe yourself to be safe with Captain Wythe?"

Once, perhaps. Dare I again?

Of course, a confession to anything being amiss in that corner would send Greaton charging on the nearest horse for Valley Forge. "Given the delicate nature of my circumstances," I hedged, "Captain Wythe is still the best person to act as my guardian. He swore an oath to protect me and help get me home."

"Of this, you are certain?"

One slash, two slashes, a curl like a stroke across someone's throat. I stared at the smiley face I'd carved into the congealing porridge. "Yeah."

Give me top marks in the art of lying.

Chapter Forty-Six

Colonel Greaton stormed to the far end of the attic. At the last moment, he jerked to a halt and asked to be excused while he conferred with my "guardian." Leaden disdain for the word, so fickle in its assignment, was hurled downstairs. Wishes that I would eat and rest were delivered in a gentler tone.

To have had Jonathan's abilities just then, to will into crystal clarity from across the drafty expanse of my makeshift bedroom his heavy sigh, the colonel's hissed words, the hidden nuances to their verbal interplay. I contemplated stumbling to the door and listening the old-fashioned way—the human way—but Madam Chance vowed the stars would align so it would fly open into somewhere that hurt. Dragging my sorry derrière upright alone sent my wheels reeling, which made it abundantly clear that, since everything hurt to some extent, it wouldn't take much skill for someone to find the right place.

Greaton did not like it. No, sir. He did not like it.

Heard at full volume from my humble straw mattress by the fireplace. That and the colonel thundering down the attic stairway, leaving me alone with my preternatural warden, who was hesitating outside. A *thunk* landed against the wall during his solitary reflection.

Eventually, a tapping on the door preceded Jonathan's cautious reentry. He was good enough to ask, "Have I your permission to enter?" and then once in, "Might I close the door so we can speak in private?" He eyed me with concern. "Will you not rest?"

"Don't worry about me. I'll be fine." Grasping onto the chimney because a tornado was twisting my head off, but just fine and effing dandy.

"Thank you for what you did for Captain Brott."

"I didn't do it for him."

His hands fidgeted while he studied the floor. "Then, please accept my—"

"I didn't do it for you either. I did it for *me*. Someone has to save my life. That someone is me, apparently."

Because that's what the petulant part of me insisted—it was my actions that saved my life. If I hadn't run, if I hadn't screamed, my blood would be soaking the same rocky soil as the evil creature's. Brott was only stopped because the guards were closing in on us.

"Savannah."

"I think you were right to call me 'Miss Moore.'"

An albatross in a vicious storm, he was stunned into silence. His despair almost moved me to regret everything and attempt to start the morning over. I had to stay the course. "Are you going to do what I asked or not?"

"Colonel Greaton seeks a private audience with General Parsons. We shall know his answer soon." He ran his fingers through his hair, perhaps trying to gather his thoughts together along with the loose locks. "It was shrewd of you to make such a request."

"Yeah, well. I learned manipulation from the best."

"I…do not know that word."

"Influence. Control. Make me do things. Keep me prisoner—"

"I have never sought to…" He sighed and unclenched his fists. "I have only, ever acted to protect you."

"Everything you do manipulates me. The way you're smooth-talking me now. The way you touch me. Hell, I can't look at you without y-you… Take this."

I swung the ribbon around my head. It caught, pulling a strand at the back of my neck. A cluster of dried grass was clogging up the tiny knot where the hair circled in on itself and the filthy ribbon in confusion. Even the damn key wouldn't release its hold on me.

My topsy-turvy emotional ride broke down, trapped on the point of how Jonathan had forced himself inside me just hours before. I'd been helpless to stop him, and what was worse—a part of me liked it. The pleasure of his power working through me was better than sex, and it *was* addictive, I decided. That made it dangerous. He was dangerous. I had to remember that.

"What?" I retorted, more absorbed with my stifled sobs than his muttering.

"I did not take your memories," he repeated.

Oh hell no. I hadn't considered that.

Searching through the sensations from that night—concentrating hard on the force of his grasp imprisoning me, the strength of his body subduing me—they were wrought with physical pain, nausea, fear, cold…but lacking the heat that rose whenever he used magic on me. Nor did my head ache from trying to remember. Which meant…he *hadn't*, despite the injuries he'd endured, too, during our struggle or the fact that his life depended on my silence, even then. Any memories stolen were what my subconscious sought to protect me from.

But I wasn't willing to grant him an inch. It was so much easier to focus on the anger. The anger, I could control. Dish it out with all the vitriol I wanted until everything boiling over inside of me was spent. But the fear? The hurt? The uncontrollable need to believe him, to race into his arms and beg for forgiveness for doubting him? It was too much, and it was winning. The key tumbled from my hands.

"Where are my clothes?" I whispered.

Across the chasm between us, while I stared at my feet rather than meet his gaze and risk being seduced again by his power, a sense of longing bridged the divide to my lonely shore.

At last, he relented. "There."

Shadows on the far side of the fireplace lifted, as if the sun had swept into the room and brushed them aside. Draped atop the crossbeam was the green dress. It'd been cleaned, and the torn seam repaired. From the dampness, tiny sparks fizzed against my cautious fingers.

Freaked out by the dissipating spell, I snapped at him, "I want my real clothes."

"Please rest," he begged me.

"You took my gun. You hid my clothes. Are you planning on keeping me captive?"

Why didn't I just listen to him, or his spell or whatever, when he wanted me to stay inside? I almost wished he *had* taken my memories. Then things would've been all right between us.

The very thought disgusted me. How could I wish away knowing exactly what he was, what he was willing to do in the name of protecting his people? Or the look on his face when he realized he was going to allow that bastard to kill me?

"I merely want what is best for you." The desperation in his voice made me wonder if he was wishing he'd taken my memories too.

"Who the fuck are you to decide what's best for me? Your job was to get me home. That's it. Instead, you've dragged me all over. You nearly got me killed."

Not caring anymore, I tore the ribbon free. The knot of hair clung to the blue silk. When Jonathan tried to reason with me, he didn't get beyond, "Miss," before I threw the key at him as hard as I could. His hands flew up, sending it bouncing off the wall with a noisy clatter.

"Damn it." I cursed the pain howling at me for such a stupid move.

"You have injured your shoulder?"

Beneath my shift, a pale but undeniable bruise colored the soft region between the bones. "Since defending myself means I get to feel all the pain, I guess it's no surprise you don't remember me shoving my fist into you while trying to escape."

Could Colonel Greaton have seen that? He didn't say anything.

Abandoning yet another source of worry, I returned the linen neckline to its place.

"If it gives you any comfort," Jonathan said, "I do believe my rib to be cracked from the events of last night."

Staring at the spot where his hand had been glued since waking, I asked in total disbelief, "I'm supposed to feel better because you cracked *my* rib?"

Guiltily, Jonathan admitted, "I suppose not." A knuckle grazed the length of his jaw, indicating the fictional signs of his missing injury. "I will gladly take the payment. I never wanted you to suffer."

Tempting, sinfully sweet in its allure: to be able to defend myself, kick ass rather than capsize—forget that, even just to walk!—without the sickening jolt of my surroundings catapulting out from under me whenever I moved my head… Strike two, because he almost broke me. "Don't you dare touch me."

Loose waves tumbled across his shoulders as his head bowed. "Is there nothing I might do to…?" His hands sank to his side.

Wow. Wow, wow, wow, was he pale. Far beyond shock or grief, as if with just those words, the pact had revisited on him all the nausea and fear the sleepless nights and the concussion were compounding on me. Murky plum burgeoned beneath his eyes, separate from the phony bruise where I'd punched him. The stretch of his collar bones bursting through his shirt, particularly around the open collar, was pronounced.

"When's the last time you've eaten?" I asked.

It was kinda terrifying how death valley he looked. Options for wilderness gourmet hadn't fit into our conversation yet. He'd only just returned to West Point the day before. Because of the debacle surrounding our reunion, he wasn't offered supper.

"Oh," he remarked with quiet surprise. "Do not worry for me." A bittersweet smile accompanied his thanks. Albeit a temporary truce, a heaviness seemed to lift from the room. It was, admittedly, a welcome respite.

Asking again about my clothes, I searched the crossbeams near the gown. Like any passing storm, however, the eerie stillness that lay amid our swirling disturbance dissolved. A looming presence closed around me as

Jonathan reached over my shoulder toward the rafters for an out of reach bundle.

"No, please!"

Flying, falling, tumbling—I was plummeting from the height of the Plain, past the ledge where I'd fought for my very life, landing not in the rush of the river but onto a barren surface, hard and unforgiving. A cloud of dust engulfed me. Hands clasped my arms. Instead of capturing me and yanking me into a viselike prison, after the end of a lingering groan, they loosened. Across the expanse of his reach—his body separate from mine yet offering an anchor to ground me—by his careful touch while I cried, Jonathan gave me the choice to flee or, once ready, accept and seek solace within his embrace.

"I swear to you, I will defend you," he promised.

Pressing my palms against my eyes stung. Too much dust. "I saw your face. You were going to let him—"

"In truth, I do confess it, I did not know what to do in that moment or how to stop Alexander. But I swear to you, I swear on my life, I would never have allowed him to kill you. I...I am..." Sucking in a sharp breath, he leaned backward, releasing my arm and grabbing at his side.

"You need to see a doctor." The benefit of sliding out of his reach meant I could keep tabs on him. The bundle of clothes by his knees, anyway.

"I bloody well will not be seen by the surgeon when I cannot convince you to do the same."

"The problem with that is people think I'm just sick to my stomach or have a sore hand."

That's it, I coached myself. *Focus on a plan. Corral what you're feeling into something actionable.*

"If we let a doctor examine me," I said, "he's going to realize I'm lying to him, even if he can't see the injuries. You, at least, can explain away a cracked rib and get help."

"God's teeth." He shook his head, perturbed.

"Please. Though..." Incredulous as I heard the words escape my own lips, I realized it was time to be brutally practical. I swiped my face dry with my sleeve rather than accept his outstretched handkerchief. "A concussion can last weeks, if not months."

"You are not taking the payment," he answered in no uncertain terms.

"You won't be able to defend anybody like this, least of all me."

"With your plan, Alexander will be ordered from West Point at once. You shall be safe from him." He tossed the bundle to me so I could dress.

"You don't really think he'll just leave without talking to you first? He'll hang around until he can corner you and make sure I'm dead." Realization dawned on Jonathan's face. "He knows about the pact, right?" I asked.

"Aye." He frowned.

"So, he's going to expect Colonel Kościuszko to have been the one to actually kill me." My reality just sucked rose-colored crap. "What does the colonel have to say about this whole thing?"

"That you saved his life."

Jury was still out regarding what exactly the hellish fiend was that we'd fought or the scope of their supernatural abilities, so the only answer that came to mind was, "He would've done the same for me."

"He did."

I paused in my effort to slide my pants over my hips. "What do you mean?"

"After we returned…" He raised his eyes to the roof, meaning the Red House. "…the colonel spoke passionately about how your life should be spared. He believes it a sin to harm the same innocents that we are entrusted to protect."

"Oh fuuu—" Grasping onto the stone chimney to one-handed climb to vertical, while clasping onto my waistband and battling my avalanching equilibrium, was as abominably difficult as it was painful. My shoulder especially disliked its sudden introduction to the craggy formation of the chimney's corner. Slow, steady exhales through my pursed lips distracted me from the throbbing. "He still…" Sort of. Circling my arm behind me to reach the waistband's ties hurt way too much. "He still thought you should wipe my memory."

A tentative lift of the linen ties at the small of my back, then a tiny tug, wound them together. Through the rift between us, the coolness of a draft graced my skin, but the warmth of his breath and the vibration of his power kept their distance. "I think his purpose in suggesting such was to convince Captain Brott that you were not a threat to us."

"You mean you."

His fingers froze. "I never—"

"He was trying to convince you." The reminder of his resigned expression, the regret, crashed over me again. After the knot tightened, I bolted around the fireplace to the far side, beyond his reach. "Would you please send for Kościuszko? I think he's the best person to protect me today."

"Miss—"

"Send for the colonel. Freaking mother." It felt like I'd kept circling toward him while my body remained flattened against the stonework. "We need…to make sure they haven't spoken since last night. You've got to be the one to talk to Brott, and then please see the doctor. The colonel can protect me while you do that."

"I cannot."

"What?"

"I cannot." Apologetic, he shook his head, then lifted it.

"Can't or won't?"

"He will know that you are not dead if I do speak with him. A pact, such as ours, dies when one of its members is no longer living."

"But…" I wracked my brain for a solution. "Can't you just tell him you were injured when you were fighting with the Fifth and last night made it worse?"

He sighed. "Such an injury I could heal myself."

"Oh, well. It must be nice to be you."

"At times." His meager smile dropped when he realized I didn't find him funny. "This is not one of them." Perhaps it was from watching the expression on my face, but his voice turned severe again when he reminded me, "I shall never permit you to take the payment for this pain."

Oh shit!

"Can you read my thoughts?"

"That is not among my gifts."

Panic percolated in my chest. "Can Captain Brott?"

"I know of only one other. Nay, you need not fear." He sought to soothe me. "She no longer poses a threat to you."

Something about what he said rang familiar. The firestorm assailing my gray matter certainly supported a working theory.

Surrounded by multiple assailants on my corpse, it was harder than usual to drive off the curse's ill effects. One ache distracted me from another, which then shifted elsewhere. Eventually, my imagination relieved me, and I regained a steadier grasp on reality. Remembered luxuries, like the buttery embrace of my favorite cashmere sweater, melted away, and the attic bedroom sharpened into focus. The warm comfort I'd found materialized into Jonathan's arms.

"Your people suck, you know that." Though how sincere could I really have sounded while clamped onto him?

Laying down again promised to be heaven, once my condemned body stopped falling, despite him already gathering my blanket around me. Grabbing the floor to find where bottom was helped.

His voice was strained as he answered, "My people are entrusted with the protection of mankind."

"Are you kidding? Your *people* stole my memories. They want me dead. Do you have any idea how much fun it is to be tormented, just like it was the first time, witnessing someone die or being abused by my ex-husband?"

"The memories from the woods?" A gentle brush of his fingers drew aside a strand of hair from my cheek. "What did he do to you?"

There was every reason not to trust him. What with everything that'd happened between us, add to that the suppressed uneasiness still haunting me from long before our arrival at West Point… But watching the man kneeling by my side, respectfully folding his hands onto his lap, who was suffering from his own past and current torments yet nevertheless vowing again and again to help me… How my heart begged me to open myself to a renewed faith in him.

Instead, I asked, "Would you please send for Colonel Kościuszko?"

Without further argument, he set aside any pleas to reconsider and, just as he always did, granted me what I needed most—he allowed the pathway toward forgiveness to crumble. I felt its divide in his broken answer. "Of course."

Stifling a groan, he rose, one careful shift of his weight at a time. A twitch of his hand was redirected from his side to grab his knee.

The whine of the door's hinge paused halfway as it opened.

"Not all wish you ill, Miss."

Tendering a weak smile, he left.

Chapter Forty-Seven

General Parsons agreed with the plan and was only too happy to be rid of the headache that was Captain Brott. Perhaps by giving him what he wanted, it might lessen the noise sent to His Excellency. Beggars can be dreamers. He also took some relief in knowing the enigmatic Captain Wythe wouldn't be a concern for much longer. Such was the news Colonel Greaton delivered to Jonathan, along with the general's anticipation of a fond good riddance. Dissatisfaction with the whole affair was expressed, as well. Or so it was relayed to me.

The conundrum of how Jonathan might face Captain Cock without betraying the fact that our pact—and thereby pesky, little me—still lived, likewise, had been resolved. Summons to the backroom for the expulsion would occur in short order. Jonathan had been granted permission to be present, after another masterful rendering of humility, implying how he was nervous about a potential confrontation over him not departing with his former buddy.

As fortune would have it, a personal friend of General McDougall—a fellow officer of some celebrity—had arrived two days prior, though Jonathan had been too…busy since his return to have crossed paths with him to know who he was. And though I'd been introduced in passing, I'd also been too…distracted to catch the name of the lopsided general limping around Moore's Folly. Most of the man's time was spent laid up in the barracks. To be nearer the action, being the alleged reasoning. Barking at his aide, who was also injured, was a favorite pastime, as well. Or at his private doctor, who was staying at the Red House but journeyed to and from the Plain, back and forth and back again, just to attend them. Apparently, renown afforded one unfettered pissing and preying upon the obedient nature of lower officers.

All I knew of the visiting invalid was he'd arrived from a sojourn in Middletown, Connecticut, where he'd been recovering from "his most dreadful wounds tha' he did receive at Bemis Heights," as McDougall had explained in introducing him, and then drinking to his good health, and then to his honor, and then to the promotion he most assuredly deserved but was awarded to lesser men. "The Heavens be all tha' ken the Congress and their mad ways."

At present—Jonathan informed me—the duet of generals was inspecting the Great Chain and the newest fortress before McDougall's guest would depart for Valley Forge. Though it wouldn't have surprised me to learn they were both limping around West Point, given the destruction to the stores of alcohol. One of the rare benefits of being a woman was, other than a polite nod here and there, no one paid any attention to me, and aides were excellent sources for overhearing the gossip of other aides' officers. But never their own, of course. Rumor had it the generals made a sizeable dent in the rum and wine to ease their respective sufferings once the other officers had called it a night.

Jonathan continued to explain the arrangements as follows: Brott's pass through the no-man's-land of southern New York would be signed, sealed, and shipped off, with him as part of the esteemed general's entourage. Such a privileged escort, complete with armed guards, was expected to discourage him from lingering in the Highlands, or else word was to be sent posthaste to Parsons through a reliable private entrusted with those secret orders. That would be an end to it, and plans could be made.

Though with the subject of peace between Jonathan and myself being but a whisper in the wind of possibilities, *what* those plans might entail was equally insubstantial. Just that they would—I was emphatically ensured—be based on my wishes having been heard and my approval given.

Ah, but one more thing. Leaving nothing to chance, he asked if I would excuse him, so he could compose a letter to convince Brott that all had gone as…

Sparing Jonathan the turmoil souring his enthusiasm for our machinations, I agreed, letting it slip I understood what he was trying not to say. The letter would be delivered at the time of Brott's audience with the Generals Three so our backroom dealings might be kept hush-hush. An immediate banishment would prevent any mano a mano. Jonathan would decide, depending on how things went, whether to see the party off from there.

A full afternoon separating us, in any case.

Upon completion of the inspection, Parsons planned to entreat McDougall to accept so convenient a deliverance of Brott elsewhere, and in such an auspicious manner as might smooth over any unpleasantness as grudge-taking. Other than those necessary to see the deed done, the inhabitants of West Point would hear the fictional tale of my evening departure with the natural progression of wagging tongues. Silence regarding my continued existence was a small price to pay, it was supposed, for the gift we offered them.

Since the inspection had already begun, Jonathan estimated he had less than an hour to compose something to give Brott. After more internal turmoil, relief flooded his face. "Mayhaps you should decide, not I. Shall I remain here while I write, or would you prefer I take up my task elsewhere?"

Albeit the chance of Captain Carnage deciding to rid himself of the burden of imprisonment and seeking Jonathan in the attic bedroom was slim, the prospect was blood pressure-raising enough to encourage my hasty decision. "Stay, please. At least until Colonel Kościuszko gets here."

"As you wish." Unrelenting in his quest for forgiveness, he smiled and hazarded an alternative path, saying, "This will permit me to give you the letter. Your opinion of its contents would be greatly appreciated."

All right, he earned that small victory. Small, miniscule, barely worthy of notice in the grand scheme of things, I swore to myself. My ludicrous heart was still at war with my dizzying suspicion and fear. His excessive efforts to defer to me—like a prancing lapdog, licking my hand and begging for scraps—made me leery. Deference wore a similar garment to Manipulation.

With nothing better to do than try to outlast the concussion, I closed my eyes. Attrition warfare on my unfortunate state held some promise, so long as I didn't move my head, though a tiny throbbing was advancing from the bridge of my nose and picking up steam. I pinched the spot, wanting to cut it off. It would not wear me down.

Jonathan commented from where he'd set up shop on the attic floor, "I wish it were that Bose could be brought to serve as your 'little bear.' He seems to be a great comfort to you."

I loved the substitute endearment. Simple and cute.

"It's probably for the best. A puppy traipsing through the woods isn't exactly stealthy, so we can't keep him." My practical statement of *that's just how things are* shifted without my meaning to into a lament. One needing to be suppressed. There was only so much torment Jonathan deserved. My regrets were my own.

"He is a fine dog," he mused. "Would that we were settled somewhere, that he might be trained first. I have seen many a dog accompanying officers and other soldiers."

"You seem to have a way with animals. He listens to you."

Jonathan set down his quill and addressed the fraction of pleading, saying, "It is my gift to communicate with the creatures of the air and earth, but it does have its limits. A willful puppy is similar to a small child. He still needs to learn to mind and why."

I bit my lip, regretting my indulgence in such a serene yet foolish hope. "For all we know, he can't go home with me, anyway."

"Ah, Miss. I did not wish to upset you further."

"It's…what it is."

After a thoughtful pause, he said, "He does seem happy with the lads from the Connecticut. The aide that did bring him to the Plain said they were only too pleased to have his company."

A bittersweet smile brightened the divide.

Pulling the blanket to my chin, I risked rolling onto my side. "I'm going to try to get some rest until the colonel gets here." Yep, my innards kept somersaulting.

"I am glad. I will ask him to take care not to wake you."

"No, I want you to wake me. I… There's something I have to talk to him about."

"Oh?" His tone almost managed breezy and unconcerned.

"Nothing you need to worry about. He's been a good friend."

"Such as Colonel Greaton?" Forget living under the cat's paw; there was bite to his unsubtle accusation. "I beg your pardon. That was not an appropriate remark."

"You think?"

Contemplative hums were historically plentiful with him, perhaps as fruitful as his endless supply of handkerchiefs. Our current exchange was no different.

Delicate scratching commenced, soft and too inconsistent to be actual writing. It turned out he was tapping the end of his quill to the page. "Have you decided?"

"On…?" Did I miss a question somewhere?

"Whether you will marry him?" The black feather floated above his page, caught midair as he held his breath, as if waiting for my answer to crash over him.

The whole artful exchange had just happened earlier that morning, but what with drafting our plans and so much said in between, my show of rejecting Jonathan felt forever ago.

Receiving an honest recitation of how the so-called proposal had gone lightened something in him, especially after I shared my suspicion that Greaton was offering a guardianship, nothing more, despite the obvious attraction. His brows loosened, and he worked much easier.

At least, in terms of the passage of his thoughts onto paper. Regular shifting of his weight, often accompanied by a stifled groan or a brisk gasp, which he hurried to amend using a pronounced throat clearing, as if that might erase the evidence of his discomfort, made me wonder whether I could fool the doctor into seeing only what I wanted him to. It would be worth trying if it convinced Jonathan to be seen, as well.

Kościuszko arrived, armed with a lap-sized box. So, the internal debate was tabled.

His wooden treasure unfolded into a writing desk, housing his own collection of parchment and supplies. "Miss Moore, I am happy you is good."

Read that: not among the *Dead Gals Tell No Tales*.

Despite a longing glance at his traveling imaginarium, he agreed to assist us and gave us his cliff notes of the riverside epilogue. Captain Brott was persona non grata in his book. They'd not spoken, and the wrinkling of his nose at the very idea made it clear he hoped never to have the misfortune again. Once informed by Jonathan that, "The lady will sleep and seeks only the comfort of knowing an Enlightened man is here as an ally to protect her," Kościuszko was all in.

Giving his letter a final flourish, Jonathan then polished it off with a dusting of powder. Face glued to his page, he hurried toward me, oblivious to how his sudden speed unnerved me. "Uh, nope." I cut him off. "Colonel Kościuszko's got it."

"I feel certain, truly…" Jonathan glanced between us. "…that you should see for yourself what is contained within the letter."

"Just give it to the colonel. He's more than capable of helping you."

"Well, ah."

One would think he was preparing a foreign treaty upon which the balance of the world depended. He gave it another quick once-over before presenting the dramatic manuscript to the colonel, who found the whole interchange odd and chuckled. At least, until he read the thing. It dangled from his fingers, listing in my direction, while he muttered to himself in his native tongue. Thankfully, he didn't press Jonathan's agenda on me. It got several more reads, which led to suggestions.

They were still debating the kiss-off communiqué when Private Williams knocked and announced the generals were gathered and ready to dispatch Captain Brott. Mention of haste being appreciated was added as an addendum. General McDougall would not wait for long. His guest was due to leave within the half hour.

As it turned out, McDougall was soon to be relieved of his command of the Highlands Department and had his own affairs to pack up before "Granny Gates" arrived. Not much love for his replacement, one might suppose. Though the general was said to be delighted to return to the action, where men of honor belonged. General Parsons remaining at West Point being just as honorable, of course. "No doubt, the anticipated assault from Hudson's River is gaunnae be soon, and the action brought tae this verra doorstep without the inconvenience of having to ride out tae greet it, while Gates keeps hisself holed up at Headquarters in Fish Kill, per the usual." Those were McDougall's reported remarks on the subject, anyway.

"Aye, I know," Jonathan snapped at Kościuszko about some error in his final copy and struck the passage.

Williams rolled his eyes. "If you please, sirs."

Another cloud of powder was blown into the air, left to hang in the sunlight. Then he and Private Williams flew out the door, and the wait began.

Or so he was meant to believe.

Chapter Forty-Eight

Their thundering footsteps no sooner rumbled along the second-floor landing than I threw back the covers and began bombarding Colonel Kościuszko with questions. "Is Captain Brott still in the barracks prison?"

"I suppose it to be so. I hear him abuse the guards for want of water as I come to the house."

"Can your people see each other when invisible?"

"Why is it you want to know?" His curious expression landed on my boots being whipped on. "Is it not for sleep with you?"

"We're going for a walk."

"Ah." Tapping a rhythm on his neglected desk, a mournful sigh as he stared at it augmented the tune. He rose from the sunny patch on the floor. "I shall send the word to Captain Wythe."

"No one needs to know. It's just going to be us."

"This you judge is best—to keep he, who give protection, from know where he is to find you?"

"I don't trust Captain Brott to refrain from using his influence on Jonathan, so I don't plan on being here when that happens or letting either of them know where to find me."

Sympathetic to his other obligations—and Kościuszko's curls, which deserved a reprieve from his frenetic meditation—I suggested, "Bring your stuff. You find me a comfy place, away from the Red House or the camp or anywhere Brott might look for us, I promise: no exploring, no dips in the rapids. I'll rest, quiet as a mouse, while you work."

"*No cóż.*" He waved his hand in a vague, humble circle. "I know not one live here to give us the shelter."

"Don't worry. It looks beautiful out. A sunny bit of grass will be just fine. Somewhere peaceful… away from all the noise and the men."

Awful. Now, I was shamelessly manipulating others, though it did restore Kościuszko's enthusiasm as my ally. Oh well.

Bedecked in my cloak and leather satchel, I clasped the steel pistol hidden in my bag, stunned by an inelegant wrinkle. What a pretty, pretty scene I'd fashioned: just the two of us, all alone, far from human help.

"What is for waiting?" he asked.

"Do you…still believe I shouldn't be killed?"

"Do you believe *I* should?"

"Why would I?"

"Because I am *Strażnik Ludzi*," he pronounced with pride.

"I don't know what that is."

"You know not the words, but you know what I am when we meet. And you know it of Captain Wythe."

Members of things magical, mysterious, and, at least one of them, murderous—got that. Beyond…?

"I could never kill you." Not in cold blood, I knew that. Not without provocation.

"But you have the fear of me, *oui*?"

He was kind, even while challenging me to deny what I felt. And puzzling. His eyes invited me in, fascinating like thunderclouds brimming with rain, but their draw wasn't nearly as enticing as Jonathan's.

"Yeah, I'm scared of you." I spoke my careful thoughts aloud, gaze averted. "And Jonathan. But you've been a good friend, and…" Pleased at my slow discovery, I met his warm expression, smiling myself. "…you saved my life. That has to mean something, right?"

"I want you fear not me. But come." Kościuszko gathered his writing desk, then held out a hand to me. "It is necessary, if we leave, with no one to see."

Warmth and fuzziness in our happy reunion aside, touching my fingertips to his palm, sensing his power thrumming against my skin, I found myself gun-shy. He accepted my hesitation with ease and grace, as he always did. "There is more that is for say, but it is for out of doors."

True, considering an entire secret world had just reared its ugly head— literally from the ground—to reveal a glimpse of itself when it threatened to swallow me whole. Far more terrifying than anything I could remember. Where to begin unpacking that? Did I even want answers from him?

Kościuszko shook his curls from his shoulders. Undeterred, they closed ranks around his cheeks once he'd finished.

Although it sprung upon his first recitation, *"non me videbit oculus,"* there was still enough time to wonder at the progression of the Latin spell or blessing or prayer—what have you—blossoming from the region above his heart. Light unfurled across his chest, entwining his limbs with chestnut ribbons, flourishing over our joined hands, and erasing him from sight. As the flames coiled up my arm, their brilliance and heat running along my body, glimpses of the dusty floor grew clearer through them until I, too, vanished.

"If you speak, I alone will hear," he said, "but it is for good if we go quietly. *D'accord?*" Since he couldn't see me nod, though I had, he jumped right into his next incantation. "*Nos ex Deo sumus non qui non est ex Deo non audit nos.*"

An uncomfortable dampness formed along my palm, the second lick of flames nourishing the heat already consuming us. Once the light soaked into us, the universe kicked the volume up a notch or so.

The colonel tugged me with him, to where the spell's amplification permitted us to listen through the closed door and realize that the stairs— actually the entire second floor—were vacant, except for a single officer puttering in his room, somewhere mid-hallway. It sounded like Greaton.

Muted by Kościuszko's touch, the *pop* of the attic door's latch remained mum, and the usual protest from the heavy wood having to make way was suppressed. Nor did the stairs speak of our descent to the second floor.

It *was* Greaton we'd heard, grumbling about "such deception," though which lie fed his frustration was swallowed by another "'nation." We continued past his door undetected.

The floorboard, as we wound around the second banister, kept its squeak to itself, even as the board's edge dipped under our weight and rubbed against its neighbor.

A general hubbub had arisen among the aides on the ground floor. With two generals preparing to depart from West Point within roughly a week of one another, an unruly captain to see off, bills pouring in from the neighboring merchants while the officers awaited Congress to send currency of any value, oversight of the continued construction of the United States' best hope for disrupting the British supply line from Quebec, and the growing threat of a naval attack from the direction of Manhattan—there was a lot to scurry around about.

We remained on the bottom steps to avoid being trampled, though at one point, we were pressed against the wall as an aide dashed upstairs. His nose flew from its place in the letter he was ensconced in, turning over its owner's shoulder. The cuff of his sleeve has snagged against something unseen on Kościuszko. It disengaged on its own, releasing him. Or so it appeared. A little paler, the man shuddered and crossed himself, then continued at a quicker pace.

At an ebb in the stream of rushing aides, the colonel squeezed my hand, which I assumed was his signal to dive in. We rushed to the wall closest to the door.

What the freaking hell? I grabbed onto Kościuszko's arm, hoping he'd seen them too. A gentle pat on my hand answered me.

Redcoats. On the river path. Approaching the house…escorting Brottworst, their hands clamped onto his elbows.

Angling my head so I could peer around the sidelights' window frame—and apparently through my companion, because my forehead smooshed into an otherwise undetectable resistance—I discovered the guards lazing against their muskets, which remained planted butt end on the ground. One of them hailed the trespassing duo, who returned the proper countersign. Our men didn't appear the least concerned. They opened the door wide, welcoming the procession of one redcoat marshaling Brott-en, the other shoving him through.

A yank on my arm led me to the threshold at the first available moment, right before the guard could reach for the door's handle. Fortune wasn't who antagonized me this time. I ducked around the guard's arm without a problem. It was Jonathan's protection over the house that refused to let me pass. Caught between the colonel's grasp and the silver cords imprisoning me, I grimaced as the door was slammed into my hip by the guard. The jolt almost knocked my sweaty grip loose from Kościuszko's.

Perplexed, the browncoat banged the door into me several times. I threw a hand up to block it. If Congress wasn't doling out trivialities like sufficient food and clothing, the likelihood of me getting a disability pension for a hip dislocation due to insistent door swinging was nil.

"Can you not close a door?" The second guard laughed at his bewildered fellow.

"'Ere now. Ye be one to talk, ye loiter-sack. The bleeding bugger be jammed."

Slamming Door Enthusiast circled the "bleeding bugger" and repeatedly swung it while staring at the frame, in case something was amiss with the hinge, I suppose. His buddy snickered, making himself busy by tracking a river otter scampering along the grassy edge to find a shallower drop into the water.

During the ribbing between the guards, the silver cords ballooned outward, solidifying into a glass dome blown from the doorway's mouth. Stubborn, budge-free, and irritable. Silver lightning crackled against my palm as I pressed against its surface. A suggestion that we call the whole thing off was muttered in my direction from the vicinity of Kościuszko.

Closing my eyes, I focused my thoughts, hoping to impress them onto whatever aspect of Jonathan existed within the barrier. *I have to go. It's the best way to keep me safe.*

With careful, steady effort, I inched forward.

It fought me, flaring its dissent, but as I repeated how he'd promised to protect me, how leaving with the colonel would ensure my safety, it surrendered to my will. The dome stretched outward, drawn from the house as I continued.

Hands clasped onto my cheeks; Jonathan's presence embracing me so tightly, as if he was actually there, I felt the exhale of his breath across my face. *How shall I bear it if misfortune steals you from me?* it whispered.

The would-be engineer of doorways, having uncovered the nothing that was wrong with the hinges, exited around me. He waved it back and forth—his thoughts as loud as if he'd spoken the *one, two, three*—to lead off a heavy slam. Our connection snapped, and I stumbled at the sudden release, the concussion revolving the Earth faster than my body. Kościuszko rescued me before I was jostled too far off kilter.

The guard didn't have an ally to keep him upright, and he shuffled backwards to land smartly on his ass. His fellow browncoat laughed so hard, tears streamed from his eyes. Then he caught a stitch in his side, for which the grounded guard might've taken his turn in receiving some satisfaction, were it not for the aide who threw open the door and chewed them both out for disturbing the officers in their "most serious business."

Given the hefty guffawing over a toast being put to the backroom, the officers hardly seemed disturbed. That task was left to me, and I took it to heart, wondering why the banishment of Brott from a military base, while he was still present and able to argue, should be met with so much boisterous good cheer.

Kościuszko's voice broke my consternation. "We had better leave."

With a jerk of my hand, he guided me northward along the river road, away from the Red House, the camp beyond, and Captain Brott-hole cheering, "Here, here, General."

Chapter Forty-Nine

We followed the river road in silence. The day was deceptively cool. Thin traces of clouds lazing along the tips of the mountains filled the bright blue of the early afternoon sky. The addition of my cloak had been an afterthought, but I was grateful for it as the breeze pulled off the water to filter through the shady pathway.

At a random break in the tree line, we paused so Kościuszko could admire a slender, orange-patterned snake sunning itself on the rocky shoreline. He relinquished my hand to squat down and study its face. A deep-red tongue flickered to test the air, as if taking measure of the danger we posed. It darted into the weeds.

When his hand fell, so did the connection allowing his power to circulate between us. It rushed out of me, leaving me chilled. We were once again visible to the outside world, should any of the Hudson Valley care. The curved passage we'd rounded earlier protruded into the river, concealing us from view of those at West Point.

Kościuszko rose to standing, then followed my line of sight to where a small boat was bobbing by itself on the water. Its sail was tied against the mast, and the ship's sole crewman eyed the way south. He brought a hand to his mouth, and when he pulled it away, the core of an apple showed in his palm before he drew his arm back to heave the remnants in the direction of the Great Chain.

The massive barrier was hidden behind the S bend, requiring a river wander to navigate the sharp turn to discover it, where they'd also find themselves caught in the current, unable to steer out of the line of multiple cannons' fire.

But clearly, this seafarer was aware of its presence or, at least, of the hundreds of soldiers laboring on the land surrounding it. He leaned over the side of the boat, splashing water onto his wrists. After shaking them dry, he rolled up his sleeves and, with a final look southward, got to work hauling ropes that extended overboard into the depths beneath. Smacking tails against the surface of the water foretold a successful haul of fish as he reached the end of the line.

"He know not what you is," Kościuszko commented, his voice casual while his attention remained on the fisherman. "Captain Wythe."

"You…you make it sound like I'm not human." I felt so small, so unready, as he measured my answer. The multiple missing parts of myself weren't enough? Did I really have to acknowledge there was an unfamiliar expansion pack to my existence?

While he seemed to find me odd—which, why shouldn't he? I'd revealed my unnatural abilities with reckless abandon during our initial run-in, when I'd grasped his hand to sort him into the Jonathan-esque category—he must've believed me. His simple reply was, "You is more."

"Well, is it possible…maybe, I'm like you?"

It was a childish hope. My encounter with the British lieutenant in the woods pretty much proved it, how it brought to life a voice inside me, declaring with unflinching certainty that my extra-ness made me more akin to him than Jonathan and my present companion. I dropped my head, disappointed. "I'm not, am I?"

"You have not the *Iskra Stworzenia*." Kościuszko smiled, his sympathy and gentle understanding encouraging, even while he voiced what I knew to be true. Magic thrived within them, an inherent something that I lacked, though I could witness their channeling it—from the elements, through themselves—while others couldn't.

Unable to work out a translation, he raised a hand in front of us. From the center of his palm greeting the skies, a spark appeared. It spun, sprouting threads of reddish-brown flames that flowed along, then encircled his splayed fingers. Swirling around his entire hand, the light grew, a heavenly body blazing brighter between us.

A powerful yearning I'd been struggling to deny, emboldened by Kościuszko inviting me to touch what he held there, overwhelmed me with such force, it frightened me. I desired his magic, wanted to possess it for myself. It erupted from a hidden chasm and irritated the broken parts of my soul.

I withdrew my outstretched fingers, ashamed.

"You see, *oui*?" At my silent admission, Kościuszko rotated his hand, palm to back to the cupped source of magic, seeming to examine what was displayed there. "I many a time wish to know what the *Iskra Stworzenia* look like."

"You don't know?"

He drew his fingers closed in a wave, compressing the core of light within his fist. It seeped through the spaces between his fingers, the color swelling stronger, a sailor's delight flaming through his skin. Flicking open his grasp loosed a fiery puff, like smoke from a candle that bursts to life again because it wasn't fully extinguished.

"It has a feeling," he said, "but my people see not."

Kościuszko released his hold on his power, and the light faded away.

"What about when we were fighting the…best…something," I asked. "By the river? Could you see what it was?"

"The *Bestia Żywiołów*? *Nie*. It is for know, for feel. Here." He rapped a fist against his heart. "What is it you see when you seek it?"

"I wasn't. It wasn't like I *wanted* to go head-to-head with some kinda raging clay monster." I bit my lower lip. "I just wanted to save my puppy."

Still, I shared everything I could, leaving Kościuszko fascinated by how I instinctually knew the thing was evil. Sap was the descriptor he understood best, the sicky-sticky sensation, which turned out to be similar to his own internal warning system. And by my description of the dark apparition hovering around the shell of the earthen soldier. To him, it was only a man of "great evil."

Copper funk and rickety movements? The excitement fled from his features. "This I not see. It is for tell Captain Wythe."

"His Royal Brottness wanted to kill me just for being there when you killed the best-ya thing."

"Captain Wythe give you protection. Why you fear to tell him?"

"Humans…regular humans can't see these things. So he's gonna know I'm…what? *I* don't even know what I am."

"You is not as them that seek us," he admitted. "They seek to kill us, as we seek to kill the dark."

The entire conversation was surreal. It made me leery of learning anything else, especially since it didn't release any of my former life from the cursed prison of my lost memories. But fear was a poor excuse for running from the truth. "What do you mean, I'm different?"

Kościuszko paused before answering. "There is much we know not of what they can do. But you was not seeking my people. You make *Votum Fecerit* with Captain Wythe, *oui*?"

"We have a pact not to hurt each other."

"The Seekers would not make." He stopped to weigh his words again before adding, "I know not one can change the *Iskra Stworzenia* as you have. If you is Seeker, and there are many that can do as you, then my people are in greater danger."

Jonathan's surprised remarks at Mr. Cloet's house, about my unique ability to free myself from being cursed, rang through my mind. "Is it possible I'm something different? Not like you, but not a Seeker either—?"

I stopped the spoken thought, realizing, "But that wouldn't explain Lieutenant Sharpe."

"Mm. Captain Wythe give me the warning that the lieutenant is Seeker, what he call, 'Hunter.' What is not for explain?"

"That I had a feeling I'm like him," I whispered.

"Ah."

The throbbing had returned with force. Pinching the bridge of my nose was useless against the assault. Reinforced by every heartbeat, it infiltrated my sinuses, charging toward my temples until it overwhelmed me. I groaned in despair.

Its near victory was short-lived, though. An odd, inky scent—unusual because it was enhanced by a faint impression of pure, unadulterated chocolate—preceded the gentle addition of Kościuszko's hand onto my forehead. Evening sunlight brightened the decimated landscape behind my eyelids, and its flames rippled across my skin. At their touch, the tension eased, taking the pain with it.

"Thank you." I practically melted with relief.

"It was not of the *Votum Fecerit*," he shrugged, then apologized for keeping me from resting for so long and suggested a nearby hill as my place of repose. Warmth radiated from the sunny patch, promising to soothe my sore back. Perhaps not the height of luxury, like the guest quarters of a Mount Vernon or Monticello, but with some improvised outdoor bedding fashioned from my cloak, it sufficed as an idyllic setting for a full afternoon of some much-needed horizontal time.

Once our surroundings resumed a more stationary posture, I opened my eyes to discover the colonel had swung the lid to his traveling desk open. A distracted finger traced the aged, green leather of the writing surface inside. His thoughts didn't appear to follow his empty gaze to the eastern cove, across the river.

"Captain Brott is correct," he eventually said. "Humans fear us. Seekers fear us. Many call us the names of fear and would kill us. So, we keep to the secret. But there is more. Our people do not see Seekers. We know not who is and is not the Seeker."

"How do you protect yourselves, if you don't know who the Seekers…Hunters are?"

"That is the danger."

A blank sheath of paper was retrieved by sliding the bottom portion of the desk's frame outward, revealing the storage compartment within. "It may be I am the fool…" He sighed. "But I believe all can live in happiness."

Kościuszko paused, his personal philosophy lingering in the air between us, two parties quite possibly from opposite shores of a foreign war. "There is more *raison* to tell Captain Wythe. What you say of the smell and the walk of the *Bestia Żywiołów*, it has means for understand from where it comes. That, if no other *raison*, is for tell him."

I closed my eyes, wishing I could just as easily shut out the conundrum he'd placed before me. Here was my own personal gambit, a sacrifice from which the whole of my future might fall. Jonathan wasn't king of the Best Listeners' Tournament. Let's face it—he'd bolted when the tentative discussion of my marital status arose. Explanations about my unsettling discovery of our potential yet previously unrealized rivalry? He'd be "check please," out the door, long gone before I could draw breath to shout my pleadings after him for a truce.

Pawning the task off onto the colonel might delay the inevitable, but I was the one who experienced the best-ya thing in some meaningful way, perhaps beyond what they could perceive yet still interpret. To hide what I knew was the same as allying myself with evil. There was a long game at play, it seemed, and if the task of the Mystical Boys Club truly was to protect us lesser human…ish-types, Jonathan needed to know.

"Would it be okay if maybe I don't tell him everything right away?" Boy, I hoped there wasn't a clock ticking toward any upcoming matches with the supernatural. "I'd like to wrap my brain around the idea myself, first. Try to make some sense of it before I confess to something I don't really understand."

"Is it not truth that is best?"

The colonel let the challenge remain unanswered and focused on his desk to complete his preparations. Ink was extracted from the upper half and deposited into a carved holder in the wood panel. I tensed when he withdrew a knife from the same compartment, but in realizing it was meant to prep a feather for more literary endeavors, I decided it was time to chill and make good on my promise to nap. Soon, the delicate scratching of his new quill across the page crossed into the stirring of my thoughts.

Jonathan was a sidekick during my quest for home, a place believed to be beyond the reach of the American Colonies. If I was so different from Seekers or Hunters or any other—you-pick-'em—awful term that might get callously slapped on me, then was there any harm in maintaining my assumed role among the countless members of humanity's chorus? Let him chase the monsters amid the windmills, blissfully ignorant of how close to the enemy he'd come. A fact that, I had no doubt, would plague him. Whatever impossible dreams for us had come before and were broken, I didn't want to be another Cordelia to him, someone he lost and forever regretted, especially not if the regret would be flavored with hate.

Seekers had never made themselves known to me, other than the redcoat. No way did I want to fall in, rank and file, with Lieutenant Sharpe. He terrified me. Though I had to consider what my culpability was if I kept betraying my secret abilities, if men like Captain Carnage used my careless tips to slaughter people like me. If my family was alive and among their number, those memories hadn't escaped the forbidden recesses of my mind, but that didn't mean such a reality was the work of fiction.

"I believe it is for best," Kościuszko suggested without looking up from his letter, "that you rest. Worry is for another time."

Easy for you to say.

Because what if Jonathan could unilaterally break our pact and kill me anyway, if he was motivated enough?

Chapter Fifty

Playful barking gathering speed from the distance, closing in, stirred me from the luxurious realm of a dreamless sleep, especially once Bose dive-bombed onto my tummy. "Oof! You furry, little monster. Aren't you a furry, little…bear?"

I liked "bear" better than "monster."

Content with any descriptor that accompanied petting, my squishy torpedo padded his way up my chest and splatted, paws drooping over my sides. That didn't prevent a wash of puppy kisses being swept across my face. I laughed, sucked into the lovefest, and continued to baby talk him and ruffle his fur, which he lapped up. His tail was on par for a new world record in happiness.

"He has missed you." Jonathan's laughter boomed throughout the open expanse.

A branch ripe with yellow blossoms leaped into the air as he swung it over his head and passed underneath. Delicate petals tumbled onto the pathway as it bobbed, a couple snagging on his sleeve. Oblivious to the anxiety his sudden appearance triggered, he eased onto the grass next to me and leaned back on his elbows, humming a satisfied exhale while he admired the scenery. A pair of chipmunks chasing one another across the otherwise empty southern route back to West Point was the sight that relaxed me.

Colonel Kościuszko encouraged me with a silent nod before he wandered to the water's edge.

Yeah, okay. Where to start? *Did your bloodthirsty bestie have a nice Goodbye-Now-Go-to-Hell Party?* Or *Guess what? I might be your enhanced-human enemy, but don't worry, I can sniff out deadly beasties too.*

Before I could land on a decent opening for what promised to be a killer conversation, Jonathan interrupted my dilemma. "I was disp-displeased that you did leave without word. It is sno matter. Little Bear found you." He scratched behind the puppy's ear, sending it flapping like a flag in a gale, then called in the direction of the riverbank, "Did she sleep?"

Kościuszko turned from his inspection of a flock of gulls lazing on the current to answer, "For much of the day."

Not wanting to disturb my yawning chest warmer, I tipped my head toward the mountains behind us. The sun was hugging the treetops.

"Good, woman. But look here," Jonathan exclaimed. "You have been in the sun too long. How red you are." Without warning, he grasped my jaw to get a better view of the far side. His forefinger squeezed right smack in the middle of the hidden bruise. I gasped at the incredible pain that shot across the entire left side of my face. It spooked Bose out of his doze, and he slid off my chest onto the grass next to me and started barking.

"Oh! Oh, Miss Smoore. I am sorry. I am so, ssso, very sorry," Jonathan fretted.

"You're drunk." I knocked his hand away, appalled, as he sought to cup my cheek with his fingers, his face inches from mine.

"Nay, of course not." He sounded shocked that I could accuse him of such a thing, then he rolled onto his back to confess to the skies, "Oooh-only, aye. But a little." He chuckled to himself. "You did not tell me that it wasss General Arnold that was svisiting," he accused. Noticing the finger he'd waggled in my direction, he chuckled some more. "You should have been there. They have renamed the fort after him. That should give Gates sa bit of wood under his snail."

Annoyed, I turned to Kościuszko, since Jonathan had taken to scrutinizing his own fingernails. The colonel misinterpreted my silent cry for help and answered, "It was called Fort Clinton."

"Oh, aye. Fort Clinton. Major DeForest kept hiss word and wrote of his slocation, you must know. I's suppose I am to apologize… But the general! Arnold built a navy. An entire navy, mind you. And trained the men in a single summer. The regulars smay have won the waters, yet they dared not dess-scend from the North until the next campaign…

"He was the *true* hero of Saratoga," Jonathan continued his verbal meandering. "To ride into the cannon's sfire! Such courage. Would that I had such courage. Ah, you should have been there. Such stories swould have lifted your spirits. Certainly, Colonel Greaton did need you to give him a lift. What a Friday Face he did have."

Petting time went on pause. Would that Jonathan's actions were otherwise, but the word "giggled" applied. Bose nudged my fingertips, nose first, then dampened them further with his prickly tongue.

I knew better than to mind a drunken man's ramblings. Still…limp mind, loose lips. The uninhibited swipe at my friendship with Greaton was galling. I stumbled to my feet, trying to snatch my cloak from where it was pressed into the grass. At least Kościuszko had remained on active duty. He caught my arm that'd shot out when the concussion threatened to take me ass over teakettle, down the incline.

Assured Vertical and I were back on speaking terms, he brushed debris from the wool of my cloak for me. Bose took a pass at catching the edge that danced in front of him, snagging only a stern look laced with a Polish rebuke. The Furry King of Mischief cocked his head in reply and jumped again at the hem when Kościuszko whirled it around my shoulders. "It seem you have your wish. The telling will be for another time," he acknowledged.

"What iss stelling?" Jonathan slurred from his position in the grass.

"Tomorrow is for best," Kościuszko gently insisted.

"Let's see what kind of shape he's in first, huh?" I said.

"It not last long with my people."

We studied our sauced companion, whose feeble attempt to pet Bose resembled a struggling fish flopping over the dog's eyes. His own, he covered with an arm draped across his pasty brow. The colonel pressed his lips together as we exchanged another look. Any super sobriety-inducing reflexes appeared to be inebriated, as well.

"Did the general leave for headquarters?" I called down to Jonathan's body.

"Aye, aye, indeed." He waved a hand dismissively in the air. It flumped onto Bose. At least it struck the dog's shoulders this time instead of braining the poor animal. As it was, Bose still grunted at the contact. *Thump…thump.* His tail engaged in a slow, steady wag as Jonathan fingered his fur.

Dogs.

Pawing at the ground, he slid forward until he was a puddle of useless fur in the matted grass I'd being warming all afternoon. For him, I guess. A mighty yawn and ear shaking later, he toppled over, rivaling the gods of laziness with his back nestled into Jonathan's armpit. The puppy's familiar huff foretold of sleeping on the horizon.

Watching Jonathan's arm drift from where it'd hung in the air, like the gradual fall of an autumn leaf, I worried about leaving them unguarded. "I'm sorry to ask." I turned to the colonel. "But I can't carry him. Would—?"

"Captain Wythe is good there. I go with you to the Red House," Kościuszko insisted. A first-class escort of heroic proportions, at least to me, he supported my weight more than was typically required. Bose perked up at the sound of crunching gravel and trotted after us, barking.

"Here now. Where are you go-oh-ing?" Jonathan groaned from behind us while rolling onto his stomach and sort of crawling uphill on all fours until he could push himself upright. Kościuszko encouraged me to keep walking.

Unbalanced or not, Jonathan's long legs closed the distance quickly until he was blocking the pathway. "Have I said the wrong thing? I have said the wrong thing. I always ss-say the wrong thing. Nay, I have done the wrong thing. You wished to be at dinner, is sthat it?"

"Jonathan." The horror at his words soured my mouth.

"Why were you not at dinner?"

Seriously? Several sheets to the wind had blown any recognition that he'd been dining with my determined executioner. What else had he let slip from his numbskull?

He refused to let us pass when we tried to circle around him; his body pressed closer, seeking an answer that felt less and less like the one his words had suggested.

"Where is Captain Brott?" Kościuszko distracted him.

"He journeys swith General Arnold."

Warning bells, loud and painfully strong, clanged through my head with the realization. "*Benedict* Arnold?"

Too early, my mind whispered without further explanation.

"Who else swould he be? Now Alexander is gone, and I am to be left alone once more." A look of longing filled Jonathan's eyes. Although they only stroked the empty air, the memory of his fingertips caressed my cheek. His lips sought to close the physical distance. I shied from the stink of stale wine on his breath.

"You must be hungry." Jonathan's sudden revelation startled me. "That is swhat I have done wrong. The day grows sold. I shall fetch you something to eat."

"No, thank you," I said. "I can—"

"God's teeth, woman. What must I do to have my peace swith you? I sacrificed everything. My country, my family, my fortune, my brotherhood… And yet you left me."

"Jonathan."

His head jerked up from where it drooped. Tears poured down his face when it did. The sight almost choked off my reminder to him that, "I'm not Cordelia."

"Oh." He blinked, then leaned closer to focus on my eyes.

Scared by their draw, I stared at his vest instead. The dark neckcloth was shifted out of place. It spilled over in an unruly tidal wave, breaking against his top buttons.

"Savannah?"

"Yeah," I whispered.
"Why did you have to die too?"

Chapter Fifty-One

Jonathan stumbled away, unaware of the destruction he was leaving behind. The fog of his pickled brain drove him to who knew what. Colonel Kościuszko cut off what surely would've been an epic panic attack by reminding me, "You is not dead." He gripped my hands, ensuring I felt their presence there. Stormy-gray eyes held mine without forcing me in, giving me the additional reassurance I needed when he said, "You know this. You is of the living."

It might seem silly that I had to be reminded, but having not died yet, I didn't know what it felt like for my soul to sever ties to my physical form, what my awareness from the Great Beyond would be. My entire memorable life from Before, I'd been oblivious to this sixth sense crap and the cloak-and-dagger laws surrounding it. Now, a whole new reality had sprung upon me. So yeah, in that swift and bizarre moment, it seemed like a distinct possibility that my continued existence could've been bred solely out of denial and the guys were awaiting this dead woman's realization of her own twisted ending.

As reason worked its magic, however, I admitted the colonel was right. "But…why would he say…?"

"Captain Wythe's head is with drink."

"Yeah, but—"

"But…" Kościuszko silenced me by placing a finger near my lips, then he tapped my forehead. "Too much thinking is all together for him. Hmm?"

Which invited another fear to take hold. "Captain Brott—"

The colonel seemed to follow because he interrupted, saying, "It is not meaning he know you is alive."

"We don't know that."

"Then we ask one who know, *oui*?"

"Yeah. All right, yeah."

Just the idea was reassuring. Wonder and Worry didn't have to walk hand in hand. If Jonathan's tongue had spilled something that made our contrived story smell fishy, an entire roomful of officers, plus their more sober aides, bore witness to it.

"How could he do that?" Wrong question to ask, because my amped-up emotions took a hard right down Anger Alley. "How could he risk my life like that? Get drunk when so much was at risk? How could he be so selfish?"

"Do not be bad on him," the colonel patiently chastised.

"Bad on *him*?"

"He sacrifice much for you."

"All that stuff he was rambling about, that was Cordelia. He gave up his country and blah, blah, blah for her. Not me."

"Every one of my people know of Miss Wilkin and Captain Wythe. He did not sacrifice his brotherhood for her. It was for you."

"No. That's…no."

"You did not read the letter," he reminded me. "Captain Wythe write dead for you was very bad conduct. He could no longer be brother to him that demand a lady to die."

A swell rose through my chest. It captured my breath, my thoughts, and swept away the world around me in its whirlwind.

However many minutes later, Bose materialized—seemingly out of thin air—dragging a stick into my lap, where I was huddled on the ground. I'd forgotten he was even with us. Chucking his latest toy led to paws and claws scrambling over my legs to retrieve it. Kościuszko indulged him in his enthusiastic plea to play fetch, while I struggled to understand why. Why—when our future, my entire purpose in journeying with Jonathan, was centered around my home, worlds forever apart—would he cast aside his long-standing fraternity with Brott?

"There was more in the letter," the colonel informed me between throws. "That is for Captain Wythe to say."

"Would…?" Heartless to ask, I knew, but revenge was meted out from both ice and fire. Their relationship's severance could forge a cold and calculated blow upon Jonathan years later, or it might be enough—in and of itself—to spark an immediate storm. Whether by flame or winter's fury, Brott's wrath was surely coming, and through Jonathan, I feared it could reach me. "Would Captain Brott have had a pact with him, like I do?"

"Only he of the brotherhood know what promises are made. Such is not for asking. *D'accord?*" He knelt next to me and insisted, "Brothers do not tell."

"So, my secret that he might kill me for…I should share, but *his* secret that could also kill me, he gets to keep? That is very not excellent for me."

"Remember what is for best."

Bose engaged in a wobbly circuit atop my folded legs, managing to stab me only once with his gooey stick, then outright plopped and made fast work of shredding his prized possession. My pants were soon coated with splinter paste.

Kościuszko took note of the sun dissolving between the trees, then asked, "Who of the officers is you trust? Colonel Greaton?"

Man, I was the blunder he would never live down.

Ignoring my embarrassed frustration at yet another social commentator drawing attention to his attraction, I pointed out, "He's one of the few people who knows the truth about me still being here."

"It is of course." Kościuszko smiled. "Let us go."

"Assuming he attended the whole meeting…"

"I will seek for him to speak with you."

Since our afternoon siesta hadn't included snacks, thank goodness his heart had remained happy even though he must've been ravenous. He offered to delay, although not until closer to the Red House, to conceal us again. At least the human and human-plus threats wouldn't see us.

Monster Vision—what use was it if I lacked the power to save myself from them? More like a curse than an ability.

After he helped me stand, which was somehow accomplished without dropping Bose when the puppy tried to tumble after the stick's remains to the ground, I paused to quietly ask, "How did Cordelia die?"

He wrinkled his nose in disgust. "She was called the 'witch' and burned."

"Damn." A shudder coursed through me. "Having to watch someone you love die is… To see her murdered like that."

Kościuszko shook his head. "Captain Wythe was not there."

"What do you mean? I thought he loved her."

"The Blood—" He couldn't remember their morbidly apt nickname until I supplied it. "Some of the Bloodsuckers was at the burning."

"And Jonathan was part of the Sixty-Third, wasn't he? When he first got to the Colonies?" Forget our tumultuous history. I refused to associate that moniker with him.

"He was their captain." Kościuszko rubbed the tip of my dozing fur muff's ear between his fingers. "The men would know of him if they see him at the burning."

An above-average level of dirty-dog stink clung to Bose's fur. I buried my nose in it anyway. "No wonder her death haunts him."

We continued along the river road in silence. An army of frogs croaked and squabbled around us, concerned with their own seasonal affairs and mindless of our passage.

Still a fair distance from the boundaries of Moore's Folly, I wondered aloud, "It's so sad. Drunk or not, how Jonathan could see me standing there, talking to him and everything, and think *I* was the one who'd died. But I guess… He said once every woman reminds him of Cordelia."

Including me, it seemed. Our friendship was so fractured, I was just another nameless body to walk around, wearing his guilt. The lament that he never did or said the right thing made me realize I'd also become a ceaseless burden, like Brott had predicted. I'd outstayed my welcome. It truly was time to find my way home.

"And yours," Kościuszko said.

"My…?"

He searched my eyes. "Is it you not remember?"

"I, uh, what?"

"Ah, it is not for fear. It is for understand… Miss Ludwika Sosnowska." He raised a hand at my confused look. An old longing filled his voice when he turned away and spoke to the river. "She was to be my wife. Ludwika…was…beauty. Beauty here." His palm circled the flat of his face as he described her, then he touched a finger to his temple. "And beauty here. And in here." His heart.

"She had no fear to take the carriage and go with me," he continued. "I was tutor and soldier to her. Her father promise her to a prince, yet it was me she love. There was the priest waiting, you see. We was betrayed by the man who I had give my trust and say what I do."

Sadness filled his eyes when he checked to see if I was listening to his tale. The determination of Ludwika's father to see her better-matched had interrupted their flight. Surrounded by her father and his soldiers, Kościuszko had drawn his sword, ready to fight for his love, but when he faced his desired bride to declare his intensions, he discovered in her tears that he could not shed the blood of a single one of her father's men. Not even to be with her. Because if he had, and they'd escaped, she would still have been lost to him forever. So, he sheathed his weapon, rather than slay her esteem in him, and allowed himself to be beaten unconscious.

Kościuszko withdrew a white, lacy handkerchief from a breast pocket. That was all that was left of her when he awoke, he told me. He brought it to his nose and inhaled the delicate fabric. A thumb trailed sadly along the turn of the stitching. "It is no more the bearer of the smell she wear."

"Her perfume?"

"As you say, her perfume." Unashamed of the emotion welling up in his expression, he faced me to say, "The feeling I have when I wake, when I know I never will have in my arms my love—it was very, very bad pain. Here." He raised his fingers to indicate the place in my chest where my heart resided. "It never be good again. Always is the pain. Sometimes, it is more. Sometimes, less."

"Cordelia—"

"For Captain Wythe, only he know what is pain more: that night, when you lay as the dead on the ground or the words you did say."

Perhaps knowing the truth wasn't such a good idea anymore. My mind forbade these riverside memories for a reason.

He told me anyway. "You beg him to be quick."

"Be quick?"

Kościuszko stared me down when he answered, "Be quick when he kill you." He lifted my chin so I couldn't look away. "Captain Wythe's pain was pain like when I lose Ludwika. It was so very bad here…" He pointed again to my heart. "…that it was for feel here also."

He laid a hand flat against his own.

Chapter Fifty-Two

Colonel Greaton did us the great and unintentional favor of meeting us on the river road, having seen Jonathan visibly upset while stumbling back to West Point. Suspicion had been driving the colonel in our direction, we learned, though not before Colonel Kościuszko yanked me into the bushes, during Greaton's initial flyby, for our grand reentrance to the visible world.

Astounded by our sudden appearance behind him, coming from the pathway he'd just traversed, he dismissed it anyway—as all the uninitiated to the extraordinary did when confronted with it, I realized—and declared himself relieved to see me in such good health. Of course, a complete report confirming his supposing so was required, which was rewarded with an unguarded grimace as he seconded the notion respecting my excessively sunny exterior.

"It is disgraceful that your…" He fumed, struggling for an appropriate word. "…*guardian* should intoxicate himself when you are in need of his services."

Good, it wasn't just me. Let the Frustration Convention commence, which he obliged me by continuing its opening remarks. "I cannot fathom where he acquired such liquors. Does he keep his own stock?"

"Weren't you at the officers' meeting when Captain Brott was sent away?" I asked.

"Of course, I was there! *I* would not fail you. To be sure, there was barely enough rum to raise a sufficient glass to General Arnold's return to duty. The stores have run dry. Captain Wythe has taken his drink from another source."

Three cheers for serendipity and loyal friends!

Kościuszko smiled a polite *I-told-you-so*.

Far from clear of those troublesome woods of proverb, I realized Greaton was owed some serious pacifying first. "I'm sorry. I didn't actually doubt—"

"No." He sighed. "I am the one to seek your forgiveness. It vexes me tremendously that you have been so vulgarly treated. Yet, I have done you no better. You deserve the finer considerations that polite society would offer you."

"It seems to me, we all suffer from a lack of the 'finer things' while we help protect the polite society we hope to return to someday."

"Well spoken." Hand to his chest, he offered a humble bow. "I am in your debt, Miss Phillips."

How much simpler life might've been if the pleasant warmth our exchanged smiles ignited ran a little hotter in me.

"Oh, Mr. Kościuszko." Greaton noted him as if just discovering my amused escort was there. "You should hurry, sir. General McDougall wanted a word with you and is in quite an ill temper."

The unexpected news caught him off guard. "Why is this?"

"I know of no particular reason." Greaton shrugged. "Other than you were sent for, several times, to no avail.

Kościuszko shuffled his auburn curls, ahem'ed, then smoothed and reshuffled. "Beg pardon." After a fleeting pass of his lips upon my hand, saying, "I had better see to the general's business," he hurried to the principal's office.

Present number of magical protectors against dark and terrible things: zero.

Humans: two.

Well, two-and-some-change.

Plus, negative on the satisfaction scale regarding the permanent expulsion of Brott-worst.

"You are offended?" Greaton misinterpreted my concern about the math that didn't add up to a positive outcome just yet.

"Can we go in? I want to apologize to the general. Colonel Kościuszko doesn't deserve to be in trouble because of me."

"Dear lady, you need not worry about him. He has the approval of His Excellency and the other officers. I dare say, he shall weather the general's displeasure, whatever it may be." Drawing my hand onto his arm, he asked, "Are you tired? It looks to be a fine evening. We could take a turn about the Plain."

"Would tomorrow, during your inspection, be all right? I haven't eaten since breakfast, and I'm kinda hungry."

"Gracious. How ever have you managed? Of course, you must take supper. Let us see if it is ready."

"Did everything go as planned?" I tugged on his arm to delay our return, wanting at least some reassurance the coast was clear, even if it might be illusory. "Is Captain Brott really gone?"

"It all went very well, I dare say. He was greatly pleased at the prospect of journeying with General Arnold. It is ungentlemanly of me to say it, but he is not deserving of such attentions as the general did bestow upon him. They seemed as childhood mates ere they did go. These are far finer rewards than your grievances against him would have him deserve."

"Just so long as he's gone." And stayed that way. "What about when he got Captain Wythe's letter? Did he say anything then?"

"Truth be told…" Greaton's thoughtfulness negated the minimal relief he'd previously supplied. "…other than a moment's surprise in the reading of it, he did not acknowledge Captain Wythe for the remainder of dinner. Perhaps a moment of anger, but I cannot be certain. Know you what was in the letter?"

"I didn't read it. Bose?"

Mischief Mutt was happily distracted by the gathering of frogs that popped into the water whenever he tried to pounce on them. They waddled onto the shore, reforming their line after he hopped past, beginning the cycle of his playful siege anew once he'd reached the end. He caught up once we were underway.

"Not trying to ruin Captain Brott's reputation, or anything…" Were there an option to erase him from my reality, instead of all this nonsense, I would've paid any price. "But he seems like a revenge kinda—"

"He has ruined his own reputation, from all accounts, by his own misdeeds. Now, worry not." He patted my hand. "The Watch are ordered not to admit him, unless it be bound for the barracks prison. Understood?"

Never, ever, would he warn us mere mortals about how he served his vengeance. It would be an unseen blade for me, my corpse dumped into oblivion, once he uncovered the truth.

Perhaps, rather than submit to Fate—were she binding the threads of my life toward such an inevitability—it was high time I admitted my abilities expanded beyond visions of creepy-crawlies and glowing men. Experimenting with what power was locked in the silver key might…crap. Might announce to Jonathan I was draining what magic he kept there.

Clasping the front of my shirt, I realized the hollow between my breasts was empty. It was missing.

Dumb ass.

I'd chucked my sole power source for heightening my senses at Jonathan during my tantrum. Now, it was lost amid the attic's dust bunnies, which meant seeking wandering magical misfortune using my own limited abilities.

"You are made to suffer too much," Greaton grumbled.

Unscrunching my eyes, I regretted the concern I saw screwing up his brow. "Despite my whining, I'll be fine. I'm better than this," I reminded the both of us.

"Nevertheless, I should like to renew my proposal." Greaton glanced at me sheepishly. "My wife, you see…"

The truth aims for our sorest spots, doesn't it?

"Asking about the mail is a daily pastime for you," I said. "I figured it had to be a girlfriend or a wife."

"Then, you understand why I cannot offer marriage. But if you would consider: Sara is much alone. Had she the companionship of a lady such as yourself, it would be a blessing upon my family, and I…should find myself greatly comforted to know I had not failed to act when I should have."

A life as a lady's companion—or worse, her servant—hidden from nightmarish ghouls and a sentence of death for knowing about them. Was returning to a quiet, human existence so terrible, even if it meant being an accessory to another woman's family?

He clasped my hand. "I do not mean to imply—"

"It's a generous offer." I squeezed his arm in return, recognizing an additional mouth to feed out of a pocket bled dry by the army was an exceptional hardship that he was willing to endure. "I just want to go home—to my home, wherever it is—and put all this behind me. The bad stuff, I mean. Not the friends I've made."

"It is a friendship I hope you call upon, should you ever find yourself in need."

In reaching the house, a private—whose weary expression painted him as the biggest martyr from the western world—was ordered over to attend us. He brightened when overseeing puppy-chow time became his assigned task, nor did he mind my request for the addition of a bath. Apparently, the Massachusetts lines were envious of the Connecticut's favor in receiving the desirable duty of Bose sitting.

The generals were preoccupied with preparations for the transfer of command, so my explanation to the backroom boys was dismissed. Greaton found a cramped corner for us by the parlor's fire, away from the whirling storm of harried aides. One informed us that Jonathan had taken refuge in the attic.

Together, we enjoyed a plate of something he called *salmagundy*, which was a fancy word for a bunch of leftovers mixed into a salad of sorts. Still, the mutton was delicious and improved the collection of limp vegetable bits he'd found. It was even better when dressed with the colorful stories of his life back in Roxbury, Massachusetts, which he felt at liberty to share more thoroughly, now his family situation was out in the open.

Those were my last peaceful moments at West Point.

Chapter Fifty-Three

The sun pierced the canopy of leaves in a twisted haze of stormy yellow, shifting and broken as it rode along the arch of the sky, rushing into the horizon to meet the death of another day. A malicious wind howled, its frostiness clawing at my skin. The man in red was staring at the agitated branches overhead, his black curls still as the grave, untouched by the tempest. Then it rushed past us in a gust and fell silent.

Frail wisps of muddy-rose bled from between the fingers clutching his chest. Once loose, the tendrils wormed above his shoulders, straining to reach me. He leaned forward to whisper a phrase into his fist that skittered across the empty air. *"Life is but a walking shadow."* Flecks of ash peeled from the withered tendrils and tumbled from their dying light.

One leg rising, then the other following, he casually stepped over a lump protruding from the weeds and strolled deeper into the cluster of towering oaks, as if it was a bright summer's day.

Unbidden, my pace fell in time with his, my soul lured by the same temptation that carried him forward. Blood drooled from the redcoat's hand along the edge of his outstretched sword. The silver cords dangling from the hilt glinted where clumps collected then sloughed off.

A twig snapped.

That'd never happened before.

The noise cascaded in deafening waves throughout the darkened woods. Dirt, bark, weeds—even the air—shifted in its wake, and a brief glow from inside them trembled, knocked askew from their physical form, naked and ripe for the taking. An overwhelming reek from the remains that crumbled at my feet caught in my throat, their debris vile on my tongue. I gagged, and a chill coursed through me.

Fierce as Hell's scorn, the wind raged from the bleak horizon, shattering the trees like glass, and exploded over the man. Somehow, he remained untouched, yet it swallowed the world around him, everything wrenched apart into nothingness as it bore down on me.

A voice in my mind urged, too late, *Wake, you must wake.*

My nightmare fractured, and creeping across the divide, from the finality of time, a forbidden shade seeped into our realm and touched me.

The Darkness was vicious as it consumed me. Imprisoned by its fury, I was helpless as its fire fed on my body, bit by ruined bit. Screams erupted in my throat, then suffocated without breaking free from my lips. My limbs shrank into my torso, as if wishing they could disappear. Blackened flakes flew into the swirling maelstrom as my skin lifted away. Muscle peeled from bone, the sinew snapping before shriveling, then catching and burning.

Excruciating pain rent my body, and yet, a deeper awareness of what it was doing grew. It was searching—furious, desperate—tearing me apart to uncover what'd been secreted inside. But by reaching so far into me, it also rendered itself vulnerable, and I peered past the void, into the Darkness. Its heart wasn't cast from a black loathing, like I'd thought. The presence there—vengeful, yes, but also in torment, lost, afraid, and as a result, murderous—was a prisoner, as well, to something else. Someone else, who commanded the Darkness.

Whispered words, from a life I couldn't remember, awakened the sleeping fragments of my being. He called my name, and I begged him to come to me.

Brilliance from a silver flame surged from my chest, emblazoning me with light. I was awash in it. Its tender caresses enveloped me, soothed my spirit, gathered the damaged pieces of me, and—drawing from the elements around me—restored me within its embrace.

"Savannah!"

I gasped as Jonathan's face burst into focus in front of me. Fingers dug into my hair as he struggled to pull my spirit back to him, anchored in the waking world. A current from his eyes sought to mingle with the churning tide inside me. Were I to give myself over, it suggested, drift into those welcoming depths, a safe haven would be mine, where I might find release from what haunted me and know unconditional love. I shoved aside doubt and surrendered. Relief flooded through me, and a long and terrible journey subsided, sparking a familiar sensation, one of peace and the surety of home.

Moonlight streaming through the attic window warmed the corrupted forest around me until it, too, faded. The last remnant of the vision lost its hold on me as Jonathan moved within me, his power flowing through me, ensuring the Darkness had been banished. The silver flame quieted, leaving me shivering once his spirit withdrew from my body.

Jonathan paled. His grasp on the back of my head loosened, and he eased me onto the straw mattress, imploring, "Forgive me."

"Yeah," I breathed.

"I-I know you have told me not to…"

"All right."

"…but I could not wake you. You were in distress, and…"

"I know."

"You…?"

He met my eyes, studied how I held his gaze, my forced intent on confronting its gravity, the life within its color. Our unspoken truce stilled his worrying, and the fine lines between his brows vanished.

Knowing he was there, fighting to protect me—it helped. It couldn't cure all my residual fear, what the riverside had done to us, but it did lessen its grip on my heart.

Gentle as thistledown uniting with the earth, his fingers settled onto my hair. The tiny glimmer of hope wanted to return. I could see it in his eyes, as one hesitant moment after another, the uncertain stroke of his touch dove deeper into the tangled waves clinging to my dampened skin. Time held still. His breath caught in his chest, as if afraid a single exhale might collapse the bridge between the horrible state of our transgressions and forgiveness.

What if Kościuszko was right?

"You are fevered." He cupped a palm to my forehead. "Your skin burns."

"Yeah, well. The rest of me is freezing."

"You feel cold?"

"Jonathan." I clasped his hand. "I dreamed of the Darkness."

"What?"

Memories of my former encounter with that ominous presence featured foremost in my mind, the curse unable to restrain them after this unfortunate sequel. "It's the same thing that attacked Cleophes and me."

"Byrlady." He stared, uncertain. "You remember the night by the pond?"

"Yeah. And…" *Don't chicken out now,* I chastised myself, then tripped over my words as I blurted, "Colonel Kościuszko insists I tell you about… He calls it a best-ya something."

"The…?"

"You said it was possessed."

Jonathan's fingers flew to my lips, compressing them. "You must not—"

With that sudden act—although devoid of anything other than human reaction—he startled me and bound my body to the core. Locked in a stone temple, my claustrophobic thoughts panicked, begging for rescue.

"Forgive me. Shh," he hushed me. "I did not intend to…"

Oh, this was a path trod too soon.

"It is dangerous to… Please, understand." He eased his hand from my mouth. "I promise, I will hear all that you and the colonel would have me know. Let us not speak of it until the light returns."

"Light? What light?"

"The light of day." He whispered his warning, "Do not take notice of such things in the night, or it may come to pass that they shall take notice of you."

"Damn it. You and your monsters and your secret—"

"Keep to your courage, Miss." Rather than assault my face again, he squeezed my hands. "If you are to remain with me, it is imperative that you understand. If only it did not frighten, as well." An unseen weight dragged between my breasts as Jonathan lifted a pale ribbon from my neckline. "Please accept this token that I offer you once more." The silver key. "It carries a simple blessing that protects you," he promised.

Whoever signed me up for this magic carpet ride deserved to be tarred and feathered, and drawn and quartered, then shot. A lot.

He'd dressed me with the key while I slept, while the Darkness infested—

It's fine. Nothing scary. Just a personal battery pack to power up my own disturbing abilities. Or attract dark and terrible things. Awesome, right?

I unwound it from my neck. "It does more than that."

"It cannot. I swear, it—"

A mix of confusion and perhaps suspicion drained from his face. A sickly pallor mushroomed in its place. Bandaging his injured rib with his palm, he tilted, dangerously close to collapsing.

"Jonathan?"

"The flask, there." He nodded in the direction of his bag. A concerning wheeze hindered his next effort to pull in air. "There was…something not right…about the dream that held you."

"This smells rancid." I hurried back and pressed the wooden flask into his hands.

A sizeable swallow had him grasping his side tighter. "Linseed oil."

"In wine?"

"The surgeon's restorative."

What an idiot I was. He was self-medicating. That's why he'd been drunk.

Pushing a second round from the flask away, he said, "Nay, I shall not take…so much."

"You're not going to go chasing down unmentionable trespassers tonight, are you?"

He managed a single exhaled laugh. "Heaven will send another."

Okay, great. Yeah.

While they might never know it, Colonel Greaton and Jonathan had found common ground—brushing aside and ignoring midnight mysteriousness. Fantastic strategy.

"Perfect. Well, then." Since a silent night was the plan anyway… "Bottoms up. I insist."

The gratitude in his eyes as he complied stung. As did the truth in his words. Whatever had crossed the rift between life and dusty death, I felt its shadowy sting rooted in the fracture of my soul. The spark that'd blazed alive to protect me, heal me, may've fleshed out that jagged bit of salt from the irritated wound, but I was far from healed. There was a real possibility it'd scarred me, because through my ignorance and fear, I'd made myself defenseless.

Was it so terrible what I was? Perhaps whatever abilities I had were only a curse because I was afraid of the consequences of acknowledging them and so had denied myself the chance to explore them. Granted, Lieutenant Sharpe was freaking weird and not top of my chart for ideal role models. But I'd used the power residing in the key to perform the miraculous, like enhancing my senses to search the forest road for Jonathan's return or lighting the redoubt's cove to find Bose. And it was just as true that I'd felt Jonathan reach into me at my invitation, because I wanted him there to assist me in my battle against the Darkness.

Which made me what kind of accessory to normality? One that hated the idea of fending for herself unarmed, that's for sure.

"All right." I grasped his shoulders, which had crumpled into an awkward, semi-reverse child's pose, and lowered him onto his good side. "I'll wear the key. For protection, like you said. But if I ever find out you're using it to manipulate me or control me—"

"Never. You shall never discover such a thing." Then, he quickly added, "It cannot do anything but protect you. That is the only blessing it has been given."

I don't know whether he intended to, but as I drew my blanket over him, his hand landed on my wrist. Swift as a lover's heartbeat, his fingers interlaced with mine, and he clasped my hand to his chest. As the minutes passed, his clenched jaw relaxed. The strain in his muscles eased, and his breathing became less labored.

Although he'd swept through my body without permission by the riverside, it would've been unfair to accuse him of having broken any similar promises he'd made to that effect before. All the other experiences had been done with my consent. Plus, his portion of the pact obligated him to protect me, and ill-informed of what the taint from…Horrors-That-Shall-Not-Be-Named-in-the-Night might do, had I been infected…well, educating myself about supernatural medical emergencies was a tomorrow problem.

So, I prepared myself for the road to forgiveness by returning the key to its hiding place under my shirt.

I didn't want to disturb him. Not after he'd calmed by holding my hand. Fine, and a heavy dose of Pinot Linseed Oil. Gross. Lying on the floor next to him, I stared at the flickering hues of firelight dancing along his beard, his brow, his paled cheeks, for what felt like an eternity. The hypocrisy of expecting honesty from him while hiding my own nature was the thorn that kept me from sleeping.

"Jonathan? What if I'm the one who doesn't deserve your friendship? What if I'm the enemy, and I just don't remember?"

The steady, though limited, rise and collapse of his chest didn't offer any insight.

Coward, that obnoxious pest named Guilt nagged me. *You wouldn't have asked if he was still awake.*

"Oh, Miss." His unexpected sigh startled me. "I have no fear of you. What you forget is: I have seen within you. Goodness abounds there. I pray, one day, to see the trust that you once had in me restored, that you may never hesitate to call me friend."

Then he truly fell asleep, because his breathing remained unchanged when I admitted, "I do feel safer with you than without."

But what if he was wrong about me?

Chapter Fifty-Four

Breakfast arrived with a knock that echoed through the empty attic. From the moment Colonel Greaton's cheerful "hallo" sounded, it was every paw on alert. Bose yipped and bounded and hopscotched, entangling himself in Greaton's legs. When Pandemonium Pup wasn't recklessly seeking to reduce the colonel to all fours, he was stretched low, preparing to pounce, his butt waggling. Never had he known any love or affection…ever.

"Your porridge, dear lady." Greaton held the bowl aloft, in my general direction, while he risked his free hand to a nippy fate, via overeager puppy teeth, by waving it around to tease Bose. Moments later, he actually said, "Ah, ah. Sit now."

All wound up, Bose missed the change of subject and jumped at his pointer finger.

"I order you to sit."

About as effective in his command of canine corporals as a maestro instructing a goldfish to fiddle. A scampering between us in circles, as I accepted yet another bowl of Purgatory's Pudding—with gratitude—arrested once Greaton lowered an offering of dried meat. "And yours."

Lap, snort, and burp. It was devoured, and Bose's dizzying display of playfulness resumed.

So many revelations in the last twenty-four hours. I felt destined to become an enlightened woman before May's flowers had succumbed to summer's heat. Watching the colonel take a knee to ruffle the spot on Bose's back, this necessity was the saddest. "Do you think you could find Bose a home for me?" I asked.

"Will you not take him with you?"

Blasted puppy powers and their adorable ways. The puzzled expression on his fuzzy, little face as he cocked his head, first at Greaton, then at me, as if he understood farewells were coming, just about ended me.

"Perhaps, a happy alternative, Miss Phillips? Afterall, he was a gift to you," he reminded me. "There are several of the Connecticut who are particularly fond of Bose. Let him remain here, under their care, in the hopes you might return."

Before they were transferred elsewhere, that is. Brilliant solution, otherwise, and I stifled an emotional sniffle as I thanked him. It would've cast the morning in a glorious light, except…a trip to the Necessary and back should've ended by now.

"Where's Captain Wythe?" I asked.

"Well, now. He is attending to his duties with the other men. As any man of honor would do," he responded with bravado.

"But he has a cracked rib."

"Captain Wythe is injured?"

"Yeah, and I think it's getting worse. He could barely breathe last night."

His shock rang as sincere, in his eyes and voice, as he swore, "'Nation."

"Where did you send him?"

"T-to the Chain Redoubt."

"You ordered him to go build a wall when there're hundreds of other guys here to do it?"

"When I saw his name on the surgeon's returns for the day, I assumed it did appear there because he stood as your guardian."

Dedicated to crossing that uncertain path toward reconciliation, my independent heart caused me to beg, "Please, Colonel. He is a man of honor, I swear. That's why he's been trying to hide how much pain he's in, why he would never argue with you about—"

"If you will… The treatment of our soldiers has long frustrated myself and the other officers." Years' worth of growing anger, as he explained his feelings of impotence, reddened his cheeks. "We have not the supplies, funds, or numbers we were promised. Now, you have justifiably informed me that I have done no better by Captain Wythe in my treatment of him. For that, I am deeply ashamed."

I placed a friendly hand on his arm. Traces of his yellowed shirt peeked between the thinned weave of his linen uniform sleeve. "I know how much you care for the men's well-being. It wears on you. I can see it."

Greaton's gaze returned to mine. "Thank you for your words, Miss…Moore."

Huh. I didn't think he even remembered my married name; he'd been so dedicated to ignoring it.

"And for reminding me that I must not fail to act when the need and opportunity arises," he said. "For every man."

Potty-run plea or else psychic puppy announcing readiness to rescue Jonathan, it all amounted to the same yipping and prancing by the door.

Greaton chuckled. "Will you lead the way so matters might be set to right?"

Chapter Fifty-Five

Warring sensations zeroed in on me as we neared the copse. Dazzling sunlight charmed the trees' shadows, arousing from them the flush of nature's devastating beauty. Comforting sounds of humanity cheered the industrious clamor inside, yet the ghostly reminder of arms ensnaring my body and dragging me toward a demanded death encapsulated me.

"Miss Moore, are you…?"

Greaton's face blurred.

Backing from the maw of that feral place…agitation, jealousy…rising, it was rising; drawn by a vindictive judge, a knife readying to—

Voices echoed through my head. "Captain Wythe!"

No, it was Greaton who'd shouted. His orders to fetch Jonathan were repeated through the cove by the laboring soldiers.

"We are returning to the house." The colonel yanked me from where a solid mass was supporting me. The cliff's wall.

"Captain—"

"He can follow us there."

Below us, where the craggy shore dared me to join it, swirling water encircled a branch caked in loose vegetation. At my back, laughter.

"No." Enough secrets, enough hiding. I flung aside the imaginary battle of wills and demanded, "Don't take this from me." Another determined breath later—though I think Jonathan would've called it "stubborn-fueled"—gave me the fortitude to tell the colonel, "If I don't conquer this now—"

"You said he was a man of honor."

"Captain. Brott."

Fury engulfed his face. "I understand you too well."

Clenching my arm against his side, he guided me toward the base of the redoubt, my footsteps reluctant at first, surer with each step pounding softer yet faster in my ears. Bose was already leap years ahead of us. The sight of Jonathan drove me the rest of the way.

A faltering oak in the wind, he swayed. His eyes squeezed shut, and a hand clutching his ribcage, he was unaware of the several concerned soldiers slowed in their work while they debated whether they should assist him. He was unresponsive to the browncoat bent forward, peering into his dipped face.

I rushed over to grasp his arms, the back of his head, and pressed my forehead to his. Hell. His skin was clammy as death. A hand reached out, I think to stop me from peeling the dampened locks from his temple, but it landed on my shoulder, and an extensive weight was unloaded onto me.

"Come on." I patted his face, reviving him. "You're done for the day."

The man was more mulish than I was, insisting, "I shall not shirk orders given."

Jonathan's formal nod to the colonel was a precursor to his efforts to restore himself to full height. His saturated gasp drew uneasy grumbling from the men around him.

A browncoat took a hesitant step toward us. "Reckon I could have your assistance in measuring the soil, Captain? Be it enough?"

"Thank you, Private, but Captain Wythe has new orders," Greaton said. "Sir, it has come to my attention that the lady has already resumed her journey homeward…should any ask." Multiple heads raised from their work at his pointed declaration. "I expect a full report before nightfall as to the foodstuffs and any other supplies you require so you might be reunited. If you have need of an armed escort, you are to send such requests with your report for my review."

It took several moments for the shock to fade from Jonathan's expression. "Aye, sir." Except then, his eyelids lowered, and the weight on my shoulder increased.

A concerned look shot my way. "Well, waste not a moment, Captain."

Which perked Jonathan up enough to start him trudging in the direction of the Red House. He was lilting to the side.

One of the workers directed me to where Jonathan had deposited his coat and weapons. After I'd retrieved them, the same soldier snagged my arm. "We did what we could, Lady."

My recovery was not as quick as I would've liked. Taller than some of the others, strongly built, plain featured—it aided her disguise. "I know you did," I thanked the woman.

From the short distance between the redoubt and where Greaton had blocked the path, his double-palmed, layered arms grasp on Jonathan gave a decent impression of some manly, celebratory kind of hand clasping rather than assistance in keeping him upright. "Captain Wythe, we suffer enough injuries without having to inflict more upon one another. I should never have ordered you to the Works today had I realized you were injured." His cheeks reddened as he said with humility, "Please forgive my foolishness in neglecting to see what is so obvious to me now. You have performed your duties with honor, sir."

These were uncertain times, made better by two former rivals shaking hands amicably.

With the appropriately softened tone for the lady he supposed I was, the colonel ordered, "Miss Moore, you are to escort Captain Wythe to the hospital. I insist he take more spirits, such as the physician would prescribe. Is that clear?"

"You got it, sir." I smiled.

"It may take several days, mind you, to meet your needs, Captain." Greaton snuck another glance at me. "Send along your requests. It shall be done."

No one needed to remind me to be grateful this time. "Thank you," I answered for the both of us.

While we navigated the river path, the commanding tone retired to make way for his hopeful request to Jonathan, "Might I invite the lady to accompany me during the daily inspection?"

The choice was left to me.

As much as my heart was vying for promotion from aide to head-of-the-charge, the hospital tent was a sadly familiar place after so many visits during Jonathan's disappearance, where I was jostled around the cramped quarters while I searched the wounded and dead. It would've been selfish to remain attached to his hip, clutching his hand like an invalid, for the sake of my comfort. And he would've hated it. So, the colonel's suggestion promised to be a pleasant distraction while he was being treated.

Jonathan stumbled. The wretched climb to the Plain was merciless to friends and foe.

"You should not have done that." Other whispered protests, as I ducked under his arm to support him, died on his lips. He was cut off by his own groans.

Our generous ally claimed some business on the Plain that needed attending and asked if he might go ahead. I shooed Greaton and Bose along, which gave the human obstruction a chance to stop for a breather.

"Don't even, Jonathan," I warned. "He allowed you to save face."

"I would labor—"

"Everyone knows that." Then I applied a lighter touch. "As a guy I know once told me—when someone does something nice for you here, you should be grateful. Otherwise, you might insult entire regiments." I brushed aside a wilting strand of his hair as he stared, and teased, "The whole Continental Army even."

It turned out the work crew had refused Jonathan the ability to fulfill his assigned duty. Oh, they deferred to him for his opinion, asked him to stop before his hands closed around a single pebble, wanting him to examine some portion of the stonework. Was it laid correctly? Did he think there should be more earth packed in first? So went Jonathan's complaint when he later told me about his final day of service at West Point. Hardship yet kindness abounded in this place.

Jonathan often worried that if he didn't endure the same hardships as the other men—especially the enlisted—then their natural suspicion of him would be the greater. He never seemed to feel he had done enough, constantly driven to prove himself.

But on this day, it was hard to understand what he was feeling when he instead whispered, "You are incorrigible."

"Always and forever."

Chapter Fifty-Six

Colonel Kościuszko was directing bales of sticks at the base of the Plain's redoubt. His lips took an extended vacay upon seeing us. Being proven a skillful predictor of Jonathan's desire to join the hospital queue alone—issued in a pretty resolute way, so I wouldn't keep Colonel Greaton waiting—lacked a whole lot of satisfaction, so far as my internal nagging aide was concerned. The length of his coat tumbled loose as he shifted it from our joined arms, without any efforts to avoid its being dragged. He held out a hand for the return of his weapons. Deferring to his pride, I unwound the sword and pistol holster from where they were slung over my shoulder and draped them, and his wayward coat, across his arm.

"Hey," I called as he plodded toward the hospital entrance. "No hurry, okay?"

His shoulders drooped heavily, just like the sigh that answered me. An oppressive burst of suffering-ridden air escaped with the movement of the tent's flaps.

A stiff-lipped officer congregation, held during the camp's famine, had debated with the chief surgeon whether if it might be best to send some of the wounded to New Windsor, where their Presbyterian church was temping as a hospital. An ultimate no-go, since another batch of fresh recruits had recently embarked there under General Washington's orders to receive their smallpox inoculations. Community members had delivered an earful about it, which suggested it was overrun with the afflicted still bedridden. An unholy refuge for a man already in misery, with such compliments as the Royal Army had paid in shot.

"What you do here?" Kościuszko drew me away from the tent. "All is not good with Captain Wythe?"

"He can barely breathe." Excellent. I caught myself engaging in a new nervous habit—sawing my chest raw with the leather strap from my bag. "Can it really get worse? If he's not actually injured, why does it seem like it's getting worse?"

"It is for him as it would be for you."

"So, if I was bleeding internally this whole time…he could die?"

"Let us hope such is not what is." Spoken with a grave countenance, no less. A restructuring of his curls accomplished, he supposed, "You have not told him."

Recognizing he meant notifying Jonathan that he might want to amend my friend status to foe, I one-shouldered it. "There hasn't been time. Would you help me? I feel like he'd accept it better if you were there to support me."

"Have not you heard my words of the esteem Captain Wythe have for you?"

Words? Sure, they were swimming around in my head. My heart may've sallied forth to the rescue, but a more-than-insignificant part of me was considering circling back, since my feelings had already been jumbled prior to our riverside escapade. It made me a bad judge of him and what his feelings could be. How could I possibly see into the future and know whether his belief in my good nature would survive the revelation of what I was?

"Worry is for when bad has happened, *d'accord*?" Kościuszko's hallmark positivity was lovely, but…

"Your conjugation of future versus past tense and mine don't sync up. You know that, right?"

He laughed.

"How now, Mr. Kościuszko? Is all in order?" began Greaton's inspection.

Kościuszko continued to smile at me until I nodded my agreement, then he addressed the colonel. Greaton followed the path of his hand, which directed our attention to the progress of the earthy bank of the redoubt. It was shored up with fascines—those giant bundles of sticks, stacked one atop the other. Boards would separate the two layers once everything was finished, and the entire structure packed with dirt.

"There is still the need for lime." Kościuszko's polite reminder rang a familiar tune.

"Once the funds for such purchases are received," Greaton agreed.

Lime was the glue necessary to strengthen the redoubt with stone walls and better protect those encamped on the Plain from a river assault.

Sticks, not stones, will break my bones when the cannon seeks to hurt me. Unbelievable.

Fort Arnold née Clinton, as the official fortification, had been given preferential treatment to supply usage over the enlisted men's Camp Hut. That was where Private Salem was laboring, though he paused and returned my greeting, voice chock-full of relief. "I had heard tales of a mysterious woman attacked. When word reached me that Captain Wythe's lady had vanished into the night… Well now, I am not afraid of confessing, I have lost many an hour of sleep thinking I had done wrong by deserting you."

His knit brows weren't convinced when I spun the yarn about Jonathan guarding me, as promised. In the end, he wished, "Lor' keep watch over you, lady."

I wished him the same.

The breeze tickled the plants gracing the entrance to Kościuszko's Garden as our tour of the grounds continued. Greaton didn't slow. Perhaps he hadn't been introduced to the Works beautification project yet.

Wonder of wonders, Felaróf was scratching his face on the gatepost of the livestock's enclosure, from freedom's side of the pen, probably for the added pleasure of galling the private whose duty it was to tend to the animals. I was permitted the privilege of issuing him a rubdown. While Greaton was distracted with news of a deserter from his ranks, I issued my own whispered update into the horse's ear about Jonathan's condition.

Once finished, the colonel apologized for the delay, unaware of the amusing antics of the naïve, would-be wrangler of tingly horses who was foolish enough to chase after his beastly tormentor. Felaróf danced around the private's attempt to seize his mane and was head-in, ass-out of the hospital tent in no time.

Rather than report the equine victory over the poor bluecoat—whose befuddled efforts to rope his responsibility's neck were blocked by its speckled rump—I continued along the circumference of the Plain with Greaton so he could speak with the Watch.

By this point, it was dinnertime. There was sufficient food from the scouting parties that the men were granted breaks in shifts to take rations. An unruly group of messmates had snuck past the quartermaster with a generous portion of medicinal wine to complement the flavor of their mutton stew. The contraband, completely drunk, inspired singing that grew louder as others on the Plain joined in:

Come join hand in hand, brave Americans all,
And rouse your bold hearts at fair Liberty's call;
No tyrannous acts shall suppress your just claim,
Or stain with dishonor America's name.

In Freedom we're born, and in Freedom we'll live,
Our purses are ready,
Steady, friends, Steady.

Not as slaves, but as Freemen our money we'll give.

Our worthy Forefathers—Let's give them a cheer,
To climates unknown did courageously steer;
Thro' Oceans, to deserts, for freedom they came,
And dying bequeath'd us their freedom and Fame.

Their rousing refrain of *In Freedom we're born…*died. Heads snapped up. Weapons were grabbed, and shouts to "make to the wall" repeated, because rising to greet their song came a warring chorus from the woods. They countered the same tune, picking up the verse with their own lyrics:

We ne'er see our foes, but we wish them to stay,
They never see us, but they wish us away;
If they run, why we follow, and run them ashore,
For if they won't fight us, what can we do more?

Heart of Oak are our ships,
Jolly Tars are our men,
We always are ready:
Steady, boys, steady!
We'll fight, and we'll conquer, again and again.

The enemy voices surrounded us.

Greaton snagged a nearby soldier in blue. "Get the lady to safety." With his free hand, he steered me toward the bluecoat and snatched a pistol from his waist.

I eyed the kid, then the rows upon rows upon rows of dilapidated huts and tents between us and the devil's drop to the river. We were on the wrong side of the Plain.

The entrance guards urged the Watch to "hurry, hurry, hurry!" inside the boundaries of the wall. We dodged bodies as every capable hand dropped their tools and rushed to find a place along the makeshift barrier of sticks and mud. The metal snapping of hundreds of muskets' hammers echoed in the sudden silence. Nervous whispers—

Firearms thundered at us in incomprehensible numbers, plumes of burnt gunpowder choking the woodland air. The bluecoat dashed with me to huddle against the wall, our nearest cover from the hailstorm of bullets coming from the woods. An explosion of sawdust soared above us as the top erupted into chunks that rained down on us.

Two of the guards, who'd been rushing to interlock the *chevaux-de-frise* and close the Plain's entrance, fell with the volley. Several brave souls bolted to seal the gap while the Continentals fired their first wave in return. Another man lost his life in the effort.

"Lady, the colonel said to get you to safety," Boy Bluecoat shouted over the deafening noise.

"Yeah? Where the fuck is that? You want to die here? Start shooting the guys in red!"

I found a big enough crevice in the branches to thrust my steel pistol into and aimed for the likeliest source of enemy gunfire. With so much smoke, it was a crapshoot no matter what.

Crouching low, I fished the tin box of paper cartridges from my leather bag. Jonathan's absence may've been two weeks of fornicating nightmares, but I wasn't entirely useless. The soldiers drilled daily, and I'd paid attention. So, it was with some practice that I ripped open a cartridge to reload. My next shot found its mark—or at least someone's did—because the bloody back was felled from behind a tree.

A close call drove me face-first into the dirt before I could deliver a third piss-off potshot. A soldier crumbled at my side. My courage failed me as the hailstorm of bullets seemed to thicken, and I cowered against the base of the makeshift wall.

Screaming at myself to freak out on somebody else's time, I counted to three…and *c'mon, five*, then slammed my pistol between the logs to *just fire at something!*

Focusing on the daily training I'd surreptitiously followed, the monotonous steps to reload and take aim kept my muscles moving until my cartridge tin emptied.

My personal bluecoat had one left to offer me. I did my best to put it to good use, then Hell's Waiting Room left us flattened on the ground. The damn panic found its opening in my concentration and seized onto my breathing.

"Cease fire. Cease fire!" was yelled down the line. The noise let up, other than an oppressive ringing in my ears.

Bluecoat shook his head; he didn't understand what was happening any more than I did. We exchanged a round of, "Are you injured?" Everything was minor. Minor might be livable, if one didn't succumb to infection.

I risked peeking between the wall's splintered layers. A red sleeve was poking a stick into the clearing from where he was hiding in the woods. A white cloth dangled from its end. Relieved, I crawled to sitting upright against the wall and released a shuddery exhale.

"Bose?"

The body at my feet was pale as snow, skin to hair to everything. It was the homesick teen, the one who had a puppy just like Bose. A bullet had torn through the edge of his eye socket. It'd been enough.

But I didn't see Bose. I yelled his name again, searching through the haze toward the campgrounds.

"Miss Moore?" Kościuszko crouched low as he hurried over to me. "You is here?"

"Where's my puppy? I can't find my puppy!"

Shock. That was why Camp Hut was unstable. It was me that couldn't stop shaking.

I gasped and flew my pistol into action, aiming behind Kościuszko's shoulder, toward West Point's interior. He grabbed the barrel and jerked it skyward, just as the hammer snapped forward. "*Nie!*"

"But he's a redcoat."

Useless pistol, my frantic brain reminded me. *Out of balls, out of order.*

"He is Webb's men," the colonel insisted. "See the yellow facing?"

"Captain Wythe," singsonged from the woods. I froze at the sound of Lieutenant Sharpe calling, "Will you not speak with us, Captain Wythe?"

Kościuszko grabbed the dead teenager. His hand returned with a cartridge bag. "You would stay? It is not finished."

"Colonel Greaton ordered the lady to safety," Bluecoat told him.

"Party's here," I said, because fleeing down the death drop to the river path on rubbery legs, guided by a wobbly, ringing skull seemed crazier.

"Come now, man," Sharpe continued to mock Jonathan. "Have you grown so cold to those who served you faithfully? There is one who wishes very much to treat with you."

Kościuszko passed cartridges to me and Bluecoat. Another soldier leaned over to take a share. Opening what felt like a fistful translated to two shots.

Load up or fork them over to those who will.

Murmuring filtered through the ringing. Whisking around to see what was happening outside the wall, I nearly emptied my cartridge into the grass instead of the pistol's flash pan. Jonathan exited the forest's edge to approach West Point. I stared and stared harder, my mind struggling to understand. It couldn't be him. I'd left him in the hospital tent. Yet, there he was, dressed in a British uniform. A white handkerchief fluttered from a clutched fist.

He appeared uncertain at first. As he should. Why should the Americans honor a cease fire at *his* advance?

Kościuszko's face betrayed surprise but not confusion, like those around him. His brows dropped, and he pressed his lips together. Another round of hammers clicking back joined mine as we prepared to enact justice by firing squad. The collective sound stalled the redcoat's progression. A gamebird staring at the moment that lies before flight and fight, he floated his open palm to the extent of his reach, showing he was unarmed. The white handkerchief was held aloft.

About midfield, he paused—possibly to puke—then recovered and resumed surveying the wall. "Jonathan? Are you there?"

Voices grew louder around us. Men strained their necks to see something within our number. Homing in on the cause of their consternation, I caught sight of Jonathan—the real Jonathan—rising from the mass of Continentals to lumber toward the entrance. He hadn't been that far away from me. Kościuszko grabbed my arm, preventing me from following. "You would kill him if you is killed."

Literally? Note to self: no more pacts without understanding the terms and conditions effing over the parties.

A bareheaded General Parsons emerged from the cluster nearest the entrance to exchange words with Jonathan. Whatever the explanation, the general waved the *chevaux-de-frise* aside. Almost as one, our less-than-merry band returned to peering through the newly acquired windows of Fort Splinter and tracked Jonathan's progress toward the mysterious doppelgänger waiting for him. Our weapons kept a tight watch on the pair.

The residual ringing torturing my ears could increase, decrease—didn't matter. Center stage was too far from either camp for their words to be heard. Based on their stiff demeanors and frequent glances at their backdrop, they were very much aware of their audience's anticipation for a hyped-up resolution.

For one breathtaking instance of nothing else mattering, they shared a small laugh, and the world stood on the brink of rotating backward, toward a time and place that was good and right and whole. Fragile like life itself, though, it fell apart.

A flash of white tumbled to the ground. False Jonathan was a split-second slower retrieving his pistol. It made the difference.

"Hold," he yelled.

A trio of hands raised into the air. Flagbearer of the cease fire, it became Redcoat Wythe's duty to encourage their armed onlookers to back down by displaying his splayed, empty fingers. They were fortunate both sides valued honor, if not them. Turning back to Jonathan, he touched the fist buried in Jonathan's middle. Damn cracked rib. Its untimely bite almost ended him.

Their parley at an apparent end, my Jonathan offered to shake a peaceful farewell. Instead, his doppelgänger wrapped himself around Jonathan's shoulders. The affectionate gesture was tenderly returned.

"Have you a happy embrace for your lieutenant?" One leg rising, then the other following, Sharpe casually stepped out of the woods, over a deceased redcoat, and sauntered into the arena.

The steel pistol rattled in my hands. I leveled it against our pathetic rampart.

"Was I not the perfect subordinate to your will?"

Because this precariously balanced moment can't get awesomer without his sneering remarks.

An exchange of increased rumbling between the two officers warned how the infernal ringing was destined for some aggressive accompaniment. Meanwhile, Redcoat Wythe was the dead meat in the middle once things went south.

Sharpe's face twisted, and he delivered a final verbal blow. If the pain made Jonathan flinch as he straightened to full height, it wasn't visible from where I watched.

He stormed towards the Plain's enclosure. Several browncoats opened the *chevaux-de-frise* gates for him, while Sharpe, likewise, turned to rejoin his troops in the woods, leaving the mystery redcoat staring at Jonathan's receding back. He bent over to reach into the grass. When he rose, the white handkerchief was in his hand.

Maybe it was because so many of my memories were still imprisoned by the curse, or maybe people just suppose wrong, but my life didn't flash before my eyes like everyone says. Instead, time slowed to an impossible crawl during what happened next.

Sharpe pinwheeled around with his pistol. A look of surprise, then fear, flooded Redcoat Wythe's face. From my perspective, the target was unclear, but hey—shoot for the stars, Sharpe, because when the smoke cleared, we'd be flying flags at half-mast for both Wythes caught in the open, Team Red and Blue.

"No!" My voice was unrecognizable as I screamed; it was wild with fury.

Flick of metal, and a detonation.

Through the smolder, I swear I could see the bullet release from the muzzle of the steel pistol and cross the distance. Despite how far it was, Sharpe's gaze locked onto me, and I wondered if, somehow, he could ensnare me the way Jonathan had. Without apparent fear, as if daring the ball to find purchase, Sharpe turned his chest to meet it. A flash of muddied-rose when it struck made it clear why. It ricocheted off him, as if he were untouchable.

Time continued to drag, but I was swift to realize my shot had reversed course. Like in every bad dream, my body was frozen, and fear left me dumb. The bullet parted the air and tore straight toward me. I gasped what I thought was going to be my last breath.

A flash of silver burst from my chest. The ball fled in response. Its contact with Jonathan's protection spell flung me backward, nonetheless, as if an invisible fist had slammed into me, and I fell forever and then some. Through it all, I saw where it eventually imbedded itself. Or, I should say, *in whom.*

Time sped up, faster than before, as if to make up for the pacing it'd lost by accommodating me in—what should've been—me clocking out for good. I landed hard on the ground, and the Plain thundered alive again as the two sides pummeled each other. Clouds of gunpowder clogged the air that'd only just started to clear.

Kościuszko waved off Boy Bluecoat, who was probably thinking some variation of "oh shit!" Greaton would string him up if I died there. Enormous relief broke across his face as I gave him an undead thumbs-up, though he went a little buggy while staring.

Take a number, kid.

The continued gunfire interrupted his frightened fascination.

Uh, wait a minute. The sky was down, and the grass gone sideways, and partly processed porridge was being relocated from my stomach. My noggin went on strike after that latest blow, and the rest of my corporal form refused to be the scab crossing the wellness line.

"Stay there." Kościuszko pressed my shoulder to the ground before resuming fire. Millimeters. I'd managed maybe millimeters.

I grasped the silver key at my neck, hoping for a solid anchor to stall the rocking, lunging, staggering motion. Its metal was icy cold to the touch. I wouldn't be given a second chance.

One shot left. I'd stashed the colonel's cartridge at the base of the wall. For all I knew, it'd been snatched by someone else. There was every excuse to stay and obey. But for some unfathomable reason that aggravated even me—the stubborn, incorrigible nature Jonathan accused me of, I suppose—I refused to lie in the grass while around me, men were fighting, screaming, bleeding, dying.

Moore's Folly kept circling, unwilling to let me focus on the woods. Fine. If my sight wouldn't get me there, my sense of touch was on reserve. I patted the ground, eyes squeezed shut until they were ready to answer the call to duty.

No one had found the cartridge, so I loaded my final shot. It didn't go to waste. Only then did I surrender.

There were corpses aplenty piled around me. Locating more ammunition was a distinct possibility. But the sway of the earth's hammock was tempting me to just…

Another volley of voices shouting, "Cease fire!" roused me.

Several minutes of intense breath holding led to the realization that it was truly over.

Chapter Fifty-Seven

My relative position to the hospital made me one of the first pit stops for the clean-up crew, since remaining grounded felt like a really stellar idea. Colonel Kościuszko thanked the doctor and—was my character that transparent, he'd figured me out, start to finish?—urged the man along, on my behalf, to the seriously wounded. A professional eye still flew over the length of my body. Bose's former friend didn't elicit more than a glance.

One of the many women assisting with the recovery efforts suspended a leaky rod above my mouth. Shouldering the bulk of the burden, the colonel helped me return to an upright position, and the dripping rod—which transformed into a ladle, once my brain landed on reality—was placed into my hands. It was made of sterner stuff than I, which meant it could handle me clutching it to my chest without breaking, while I sought a reasonable rate for my heart to pursue.

Kościuszko startled me, insisting, "Drink."

A second round was spoon-fed to me; the initial ladleful dampened my shirt more than my tongue.

Boy Bluecoat butted to the front of the beverage line for a share. He became all ice-cream-*and*-a-pony, thanks to Kościuszko claiming responsibility for my future well-being and thus ending the delay in him getting a shot. The boy escaped across camp—skipping, of all things— before Colonel Greaton could spot either of us.

A gift for me too?

And it was better than sugared dairy products. Bose's typical chewing out the force that'd disturbed us was coming from inside Camp Hut.

"There." Kościuszko smiled. "It is your brave dog. Let us seek for him."

A fantastic excuse to escape the splatter zone by the wall. My pride had fallen so many stories, it could remain buried at ground zero, thank you. I reached for his proffered assistance and—

Fire burst through my hand.

Hell and a half.

Plus all its territories, had left me a souvenir. Our recent violent activities were branded across my trigger finger and thumb, where caked gunpowder had melted into my charred skin. Seems the price for cheating Death came with interest.

No one was paying attention to us, so Kościuszko obtained my permission to shelter my injured hand inside his palms. Chestnut swirls and a sigh-inducing suggestion of a chocolatey aroma flowed at the behest of his Latin prayer. Their warmth, the light, and his good intentions coursed over the infernal wound and lessened its sting, which had the lovely but inconvenient side effect of fatigue liquefying my body. Naptime was necessary to outright heal my extra-crispy digits. Or maybe it was just the result of the adrenaline rush ebbing. Either way, it calmed the cannonade in my ribcage too.

As my muscles were coaxed into relaxing, each and every shadow of a cut, scrape, and bruise bellied up to the bar, demanding free servings of the sweet stuff my fingers had enjoyed. Worst was an irritation battling the coarseness of my linen shirt. I separated the neckline and uncovered a mark that was screaming with some pretty intense shades of *ouch!*, roughly the shape and size of the silver key.

The normally easygoing colonel—whose courage slew unmentionable, not to mention unpronounceable, evil manifestations—recoiled from the wound between my breasts. "Er, Captain Wythe should do the healing, *oui*? *Oui*. It is for best."

"Oh no. Jonathan."

Last I saw, right as the return serve of that single ball between me and Lieutenant Sharpe flattened me, there were yards separating him from the safety of West Point's enclosure. What if he hadn't made it? Ignoring the dizzying protests in my head, I crawled to the crevices of Fort Splinter.

Browncoats, blue, and a few red, surveyed their slaughtered companions littering the ground. Legit British soldiers were escorted by Continental guards to the outer entrance, where a trio of women did what they could for the bloodied prisoners. But with so many bodies in motion—living and the carried dead—I couldn't spot Jonathan among the masses.

"Wha fired their weapon?" General McDougall shouted.

Traffic on the Plain came to a standstill. Sequestered from their business, the wild, wounded, and weary were made to shut it down and listen up. Kościuszko hoisted me to my feet. Here was the man whose orders could terminate lives or transfer them to greater misery, and he was issuing his demand again, louder.

"I did, sir."

Was my mouth not paying attention a second ago?

A multitude of curious gazes searched me out. Those closest receded from us, opening a clear pathway between me and the general, and exposing all the dastardly plans that frightful bitch, Fate, had concocted. And she'd been aided by my own misguided mush-for-brains. What a fantastic betrayal.

"Miss Moore." Colonel Greaton separated from the convening officers to warn, "Now is not the time for—"

The general yanked him out of his way. "Under a flag of truce?"

Vast and varied expressions fixating on me were…whatever. Those of fear on my behalf, or the eyes imbued with pity—they were another story.

Kościuszko whispered, "Say nothing."

But, as our British ancestors advised with their cliché, "in for a penny, in for a pound."

"Lieutenant Sharpe was aiming for Captain Wythe's back," I yelled. "That wasn't gonna happen on my watch."

Because I was Misfortune's Maiden. I would hold my damned chin toward the skies, defying the lightning to strike, while the ship was swallowed by a merciless ocean. It was my journey to take.

"*Dobry Boże,*" the colonel cursed the ground.

Which, really. Men who subscribed to an honor system believed in repaying the debt of a life saved, and why couldn't I have whipped that revelation out of my pudding head sooner?

"My general," he said. "I love peace and to be on good terms with all the world, if possible. I would choose rather to leave all, return home, and plant cabbages than give you *raison* of complaint." He met McDougall's glare, and my grateful, foolish heart knew his courage couldn't be silenced, not by me or time itself. "But I would be a scoundrel and a coward if I did not say the truth. The British officer drew his pistol upon Captain Wythe."

Opinions buzzed among our onlookers. Officer deliberations began with General Parsons counseling McDougall from behind his shoulder, then the rest fell in. Through the continuous stare of McDougall, I witnessed bitter Fate reminding him of all the hardships my selfish acts had wrought upon an already troubled people, including a number who now were fertilizer for the ground.

Jonathan took advantage of the conferencing to emerge from a cluster of bluecoats. Alive with silver sparks crackling in his wake, he charged toward me with a look so severe, I wondered if Sharpe had enlightened him about whose side my abilities pledged allegiance to. He latched onto my elbow in place of the colonel. "Be silent."

Our battle of wills getting us nowhere, he turned his back on me and shouted, "Sirs, I shall accept whatever punishment the general deems appropriate."

"No." I bolted around him to confront the officers. "I did it to save Captain Wythe's life. If that means being whipped or…worse, I'd do it again."

"The woman is my responsibility."

"I'll take my own punishment."

"General—"

"Jonathan, please—"

"For once in your life, will you not obey me and be silent?"

"Friends don't *obey* one another, they—"

"Then I wish you were my wife, so you might!"

"Never. That will ne…"

Hello, what?

He refused to meet my confused stare, instead defying the world ahead of him and the ambassadors of our grim destiny. Nor would he relent, I knew. I'd matched his courage, attacked his pride, but he would never forgive being stripped of his honor and denied this opportunity to protect me. I felt tears well up as several emotions crashed through me.

Okay, smarty-pants, my infuriated heart challenged. *Which are you refusing him—the cherish or obey?*

Assuming I hadn't ruined everything and robbed us of the choice.

The tears won. They trickled at first and kept on flowing, forming sticky paths down my cheeks, then cutting through the caked gunpowder and shreds of a would-be fortress that smeared onto the back of my hand when I rubbed them aside. But the stream kept rolling, straight into the gash in my soul. Its increasing ache, that squeezed the air from my lungs, hurt so much, I think the pain spanned beyond the confines of my humbled body.

As Jonathan gathered me into his arms, the last of his harsh demeanor subsided. Scraped knuckles wiped the dampened debris from my face, and I was helpless, unable to fight anymore demons, from the war or the extraordinary. For some reason, with my life and his caught on the edge of a precipice, a word away from a fall, he still hadn't used his power to suppress my wishes. I buried myself into him and wished for a do-over.

"General?" A blond-haired man stepped forward from the crowd, the soldier whose shyness whenever I was around stifled him. His discovered voice carried above the officers' impromptu meeting in a rich baritone, drawing their attention. "I did see the cowardly act. The regular raised his pistol in preparation to fire."

Boy Bluecoat hadn't skipped town, after all, because he added, "The British officer broke the truce first, General."

Several others chimed in with their agreement. Someone even felt bold enough to remark, "The lobster has got no whirlygigs, I reckon."

The multitude laughed, issuing a hearty concurrence regarding Sharpe's testicular deficiency.

Another round of gratitude for Kościuszko, who stuck his neck out again, saying, "The lady make honor, fighting with the men."

"Here, here—"

"What is this haver?" McDougall snapped, and the Plain hushed. A united, bated breath waited for the pronouncement of our fate. "Of course, the regular is a scabby feartie. Now, see tae yer duties."

The breach of peace having come to a conclusion, he circled back to the officers' conference. Another momentary skirmish, like countless before, not worth the ink to fill a single line in the camp's journal. So, the men and women of West Point shrugged and resumed their work of seeing to the wounded, collecting supplies from the fallen, and eventually, rebuilding the fortifications for the next anticipated attack.

And nothing more was ever said on the matter.

Chapter Fifty-Eight

Disoriented by the terrible high that'd nearly been our destruction, I stumbled backward, unsteady as a toddler struggling to stand on her own yet aching for the security of those who love her. While everyone else had moved on, my courage was spent. Theirs was a world apart from mine, and I longed to know home again.

"Miss?"

A presence hovering at the small of my back warmed my skin. His touch grew braver, surer, as Jonathan steered me around to face him. Sparks danced in his eyes, the moisture in them catching the light, then relinquishing it. Our thoughts were just as jumbled, judging by the way he stared, taking me in.

"Savannah," I whispered, to which he smiled, slow and relieved.

"Walk with me?"

I nodded. "There's a lot I need to tell you."

Clutching his arm as we crossed the Plain, away from the carnage at our backs, a storm inside brewed. Look at everything we'd survived: monsters, jealousy, contrivances, suspicion, and now this. Why couldn't we cast it all back? Let others fight the war without us and claim some quiet stake for ourselves somewhere else, somewhere peaceful, where we could just be two normal people, wanting a little company from each other. Because what if this thing, his enemy's abilities made flesh in me, was more than he could bear?

"Here now." Jonathan drew us to a stop so he could examine me again. "Are you injured?"

"No… Yes. I…" Please, not yet. Not this. "Are you?"

"Nothing that shall last the night." His careful gathering of my cheeks in his hands reduced me to tears again. "Tell me."

How the winds did blow, knocking me off course.

"You are impassioned from the battle. Many find themselves as you do." He brushed, then picked at, what felt like a splinter imbedded in my forehead. A gentle summer wave washed its sting away. "Nevertheless, I need you to tell me where you are injured, so I might assist you."

"That man…"

Trust him, my heart begged. *He knows you, who you really are.*

I swear, I wanted to.

"…The one who spoke with you."

"Colonel," he called past my shoulder. "Do you know where the lady is injured?"

His hope for a more rational source of information, Kościuszko, joined us, adding his respective shock to Jonathan's as I whipped the key from around my neck and pressed it into Jonathan's hands. "Lieutenant Sharpe has a protection like I do."

The dull and tarnished metal trembled in his palm.

"The lady fired her pistol, being the only one." Kościuszko told him. "But the British Seeker did not fall. She did."

"God's teeth." A hint of panic entered his voice. "Where did the ball strike you?"

It caught the attention of a nearby private, who questioned whether we needed the surgeon.

Get it together, Savvy.

"I was just saying how *close* I came to being shot," I said, interrupting the man from snagging Doctor Hart.

Kościuszko took it upon himself to distract the encroaching private. Doc. Sunshine was oblivious to us, anyway, since he was actively lecturing another patient. Jonathan, meanwhile, guided us to a lonely pocket in Camp Hut, hidden from the ongoing hullabaloo. "Please tell me what ails you."

Time wasn't our ally in this, and those final precious moments weren't mine to waste, should they still exist. I swallowed hard and, in a less colorful confession than what I actually saw, spouted the story of the ricocheting bullet. "…and…Jonathan, I'm so sorry. It bounced off me and hit the man you were talking with. The redcoat, who looks like you."

Death's calling card drained the flush from his face. "Heaven…this cannot…"

Kościuszko found us prior to my apology and clamped a hand onto his shoulder, head bowed. In a sudden flurry, Jonathan physically passed me off to the colonel, running toward West Point's end, shouting, "Thomas!"

My knees buckled as the grim confirmation was delivered to me: "Thomas Wythe. He was brother of Captain Jonathan Wythe."

Retribution for cheating in life's game didn't come with interest, Guilt explained. Just a cost. Death had found a substitute.

If I'd been stronger, if I'd stood by my decision to deny every connection to magic, the key would've remained with Jonathan, and his brother would still be alive. He was dead because of me.

But…there was another figure in this equation.

Disgust at what Sharpe had done burned in my throat. Without recourse or means to refuse, Jonathan's brother had been ordered to walk into that field, into the peril's very epicenter, and when Jonathan had turned his back on Sharpe's words, the bastard raised his pistol, knowing he couldn't be hurt but Thomas could. For all I knew, his target was Thomas himself.

Had I magic of my own, my wrath would've been endless. Redcoats would litter the entire Hudson Valley until he…

"I'm nothing like Lieutenant Sharpe." I yanked the ties of my shirt collar tight, locking its folds in place, so no one could discover the evidence that magic was a fire that could burn me. Then I made the mistake of turning my anger on Kościuszko. "If that's what it means to be a Seeker, a Hunter, then I refuse to be one."

"You can choose what you *do*, not what you is."

"Never. I will never be what they are." I backed away, desperate to find Jonathan. If he believed I was a simple human, nothing flashy or special, with goodness abundant in me, then that was all I ever would be. "And I forbid you from telling him what I am."

Which meant I ignored Kościuszko's reminder that, "Truth is always for best."

I should've listened.

Chapter Fifty-Nine

We searched the dead for hours, outside the camp's entrance, through the woods, among the wounded prisoners huddled in the barracks' prison and the temporary piles by the roadway awaiting completion of a mass grave. Thomas wasn't there.

"Well, this is good." I grabbed Jonathan's arm, stilling him from sifting through the bloodied faces he'd already examined. "If he's just injured, he'll be healed by morning, right?"

Filth snagged in his hair as he ran a distressed hand over his head. Before I could pluck it free, he bolted from the mound of corpses. "We are not of the same cloth."

Oh hell. Why did we ever come here?

It was an all too familiar scene, seeing him there—staring down the forest road, wishing to cross whatever distance to know the other person was all right. There wasn't an appropriate eulogy for something like this, nor any spell that could strip his particular ache.

Once, at the start of a beautiful day during his absence, I'd witnessed a slip of a man's knife. It cut him down before the sun had reached the mountains. Infection in camp was a vicious ally to our enemies. His fear was forgivable.

So, I kept watch with him. There was enough turmoil in my own head to keep me occupied.

"Have ye done, Captain?" a soldier asked from behind us.

Jonathan didn't stir from his post. I answered for him, "We are."

The heavy *thwomp* of the bodies being dumped in the newly constructed moat replaced the sound of shoveling that'd died off some time ago. It all suddenly became too much—the stench, the sorrow, the plague on my own well-being. I couldn't stand there anymore. Lacking anything else I could do for him, I touched his hand to let him know I was going inside. It startled him, and he jerked away, grasping his dagger.

Here it comes.

For him, I steadied myself and vowed the storm could rage, strike with whatever vitriol or chastisements he needed. It wouldn't hear my voice.

Yet, none of the blame for his brother's unknown predicament was laid at my feet. Not once. Instead, his alarm dissolved into quiet defeat. Pain chased through his body as it sunk wearily in on itself, its effect as visible as the residual gunpowder staining the breeze.

"You seemed better before." The dulling of the silver haze surrounding him worried me. It was almost gray. "Did you injure yourself more?"

"The spirits the surgeon gave me earlier helped."

For a limited time only, Kościuszko had said.

"I'll go get you more."

"Nay, would you…?" Jonathan shook his head, as if he thought better of the request, and opted aloud to accept my suggestion.

"Tell me what you really want."

"It…" He cleared his throat. "It is not right, how I treat you."

"You're upset about your brother."

"Nay, that is not…" Gaze landlocked, he mumbled, "It is so, that I should not speak to you harshly. What I mean to say is that I should not ask of you what…"

"Ask me." I folded his hand into mine to remind him, "'Nope' and 'not happening' are expressions I'm super okay using when I want to."

Relief flowed over him, and he chuckled. "Indeed."

A peacefulness found its way to our little spot in the woods, even with the aftermath of the battle hanging around. Energy played throughout our entwined fingers, amid the tracing of his thumb along the blue crisscrossing of my veins. He paused at the remnants of the burn from the steel pistol, then, sighing, returned to his tender ministrations of my palm.

Why can't every moment feel like this?

There was regret in his voice when he suggested we return to the Red House. It became important to him when he learned breakfast had been my last meal, as well.

"But you didn't tell me what it was you wanted," I said.

"You have already given it." His thieving, bashful smile left me breathless. "There is something in your touch. The feel of you…it is difficult to put it into words. It quiets a restlessness in me that I did not know I possessed. With you… Forgive me. I have upset you."

"No." In truth, he had. My grip on his hands had stiffened. What if it was *what* I was that made him feel that way, not who? Born from this inner desire, this hunger in me for magic, I'd drained it from the key for my own purposes, without fully understanding how. What if the tingling sensation that warmed our touch was *me*, stealing his power?

"Colonel Kościuszko said I should…" If I inadvertently took what he perceived as a restlessness, would there come a point where it was too much and our embraces hurt him? "There are things he wants me to tell you. But I—"

"Ah. Hold a moment. We must keep our words to ourselves." Jonathan clasped our joined hands to his chest and whispered into them, *"Nos ex Deo sumus non qui non est ex Deo non audit nos."*

What if my carelessness killed him?

Resisting the silver strands weaving around my arms built a sort of friction against my skin. They fractured, and barbs jutted from the cracks, catching onto my limbs. Jonathan's brows furrowed. If I didn't calm the heck down, their intensifying heat might leave a visible burn. Marks he could see and question.

Some added space between us helped. The strands' fire relaxed into a sultry warmth, and the effect of Jonathan's prayer flowed easier. All the many sounds around us became acute, while we were muted to the rest of the world.

"We have a little time before the light is gone," he said. "Do not fear to tell me what you learned of the Possessed. None shall hear us, so long as you keep hold of me." An attempt to stroke my cheek caused me to flinch. "W-would you prefer that I speak with Colonel Kościuszko in your stead?"

"No!"

Dial it down, or he won't need the colonel to put the pieces together.

Deep breath. "If you have questions, I'm the only one who can answer."

Your words might be true, but that doesn't make you honest, my supposed goodness scolded.

It could take a hike…honestly.

"Savannah." Jonathan's fingertips glided over my wrists, to smooth a silky pathway along my sleeves, then caressed the curve of my shoulders.

"You're hurt." I started to slide away from him. "We shouldn't—"

"I am asking you."

His undoing me didn't require magic. It was him alone that melted me into his chest, had me burying my face into the rising heat of our bodies, both hands clasping onto his coat collar, as if the scent of him was pure oxygen. The rhythm of his breathing anchored me. Here was where I belonged, for however long he could sustain me.

I lost all sense of time with him.

"We should speak soon," he eventually whispered into my hair, "or it shall have to wait another day."

"I don't ever want to speak again."

An amused hum rumbled through his chest. A gentle sweep lifted a strand of hair caught on my eyelashes. He tucked it behind my ear. Deliberate like a wanderer in a sacred space, his touch explored the corridor of my temple, leading to the valley of my cheek, until it reached its destination. The length of his forefinger tipped my chin so our eyes could meet.

"Sadly," he said, "I must insist. If you know from whence the Possessed came, it is important that I hear of it."

"I don't know where it came from. Colonel Kościuszko thought what I saw might…"

"Will you speak of it?"

"I'm not hurting you?"

"Hurt—? You may stay as long as you wish." He smiled.

The steady strength of his heartbeat encouraged me. I described the false soldier's crumbling uniform, its stiff and uneven movements, our encounter and its interest in the Chain, its roar, and—in a tiny fit of courage, since Kościuszko mentioned its importance—its metallic stench. The one piece I withheld was the description of the dark entity that bound its earthen husk together, the detail I knew would betray me.

"This is important news," Jonathan informed me once I'd finished. "The colonel and I simply thought the Possessed was attracted to the Chain. What you described—its uneven movements and the smell of blood— suggests that it was conjured."

"Like, a spell?"

"Blood casting, though the witch attempting to control the demon is not very skilled. A demon, free of any hindrances, would have the ability to move without detection when it possesses an element. What you saw meant it was not there of its own accord."

"Does…" Fearful curiosity was a human trait, right? Nothing to read into it. "…that mean if it wasn't controlled, you wouldn't know it was there?"

A spark of hope presented itself as he said, "My people are tasked with protecting mankind from such evil. We know when a demon is near, although it cannot be seen without the Blessed Sight."

"So, your people *can* see magic and stuff?"

"There is a blessing that can be performed. It enables us to see the forces at work around us, but it is short-lived and costly to the one who seeks it."

But what if it wasn't short-lived? What if, somehow, I'd undergone this blessing, and that's why it hadn't faded? What if the *she* in my mind that I was fighting was Me, and my memories were the cost?

"I wish to thank you."

My racing mind ground to a halt. I stared at him, overwhelmed. "For what?"

"You cannot know what it is to be able to speak freely of oneself when you have lived your entire life in secret, for fear of what might occur should your true nature be discovered."

Oh, fickle Fortune. The opening was there. Providence was willing me to change course and tell him the truth…

But I hesitated too long. The sight of Jonathan at ease unlocked a memory of another time—Mr. Cloet's house, though I couldn't envision the exact circumstances, just a parlor and Jonathan's expression as he sat next to me by the fire. My head ached, but the gift of seeing him at peace elsewhere, because of me, was worth it.

Through some thread of incomplete memories, Jonathan's words about the Chain connected with Mr. Cloet's house, as well. Excruciating pain swallowed me whole, forcing me to my knees, and my vision went blank.

A voice boomed across the distance. I felt Jonathan release his power, how its heat swept out of me, and the resultant chill carried the rest of my awareness back to the real world.

"Send for the surgeon," one of the Watch yelled.

"Open the *chevaux-de-frise*," Jonathan answered. "I shall need to carry her."

"Don't," I breathed.

"Savannah."

"I've got this stupid, stubborn pride thing to maintain."

"God's teeth. You mad, incorrigible woman."

Allspice? It was a member of the holiday dessert family.

"Enough has been said this day, understood?" The press of his forehead against mine vanished. "As you wish. We shall walk when you are able."

"That's what you were doing that night." I was struck by the realization with such an intense clarity, it shattered my prior distrust of him. "You weren't sabotaging the Chain. You were protecting it."

Jonathan sighed. "We did wonder if you had seen us."

"It wasn't just you?" I gasped at the latest wildfire tearing through my skull.

"Please, do not seek to remember. I would restore your memories to you, if I could. I swear it." Maybe it was to keep me from wondering anymore so the curse would keep silent, or perhaps it was the relief of being at liberty to share with me, but his story flew from his lips: "It has been my mission, since before we did meet. A special blessing was prepared from relics that needed to be collected. Now, my mission is complete, though…I needs must write to the general to inform him of what we have learned."

Fantastic change of subject. "Then what?"

"I must uncover whomever is attempting to control demons and what their purpose may be. His Excellency will wish to know. And I should like to learn the fate of my brother. First…" Gray weather dampened his expression. "It is time I honored my vow to restore you to your home."

"But, demons? That sounds kinda like an emergency that shouldn't wait."

"I cannot in good conscience place you in any more danger. Something is at work here. Something I cannot yet see but must. We leave in the morning for the Landing in New Cornwall. Let us pray that the answers you believed to be there will present themselves to us. Can you stand?"

The Watch appeared anxious for our return, so we tabled the conversation. At my ready-set-walk, Jonathan supported my weight, though with his temperamental rib, we were more of a mutual aid society. We sought supper together, arm in arm.

Chapter Sixty

Our morning farewell to Officer Central was brief. General Gates was due to descend upon West Point any day, and General McDougall was itching to dump command on his power-hungry lap and ride the path of freedom. Several days' leave was his due, and McDougall had a massive hangover to get cracking on. So, the backroom had a vibe of "Hey," "God speed," and "bye."

Except for Colonel Greaton, who fancied a stroll anyhow.

Felaróf was saddled and waiting for us, stamping crevices into the river road. One last would-be caretaker to escape—the anxious private was gripping the reins like a lifeline, dodging eager-to-depart hooves between pleading, "Steady, Old Man"—and our equine friend would be rid of the insulting treatment as just another barn animal.

True to his word, Jonathan and I had plotted our future course together. Our choices weren't knock-your-socks-off fabulous, since both were scenic routes with possible action-packed additives available. A forest road return over Butter Hill would provide better cover; however, cruising along the Hudson roadway could be accomplished in a single day, barring any diverting land activities.

The temptation to draw out our journey, for the sake of torturing ourselves with a lengthier farewell, rated third-class stupid, considering how Sharpe had arrived with his musical numbers via that same woodland passage. Their baggage was probably stashed partway during their march, and their retrieval of it would delay their pillaging and accomplice recruiting, and therefore increase the likelihood of our renewed acquaintance.

As much as the means to discovering Brother Wythe's fate traveled with them, if the news was bad, I worried notions of honorable vengeance might muddy Jonathan's focus. With his cracked rib, he needed fighting Sharpe—or any number of redcoats, for that matter—like I longed for the Shakespeare-spouting freak to murder Jonathan in my dreams some more. Never, not at all, forget it. Better to slip by unnoticed along the river, using the blessings of invisibility, if necessary.

Greaton gave a cordial bow, saying, "May Providence see you safely home, my dear Miss Moore."

A final opportunity to take charge of my fortune presented itself, to change my mind and steer my path onto another road. It might not lead toward my home, supposing I still had one. It's not like I could remember it. So, I permitted an image of remaking myself in Roxbury, Massachusetts, a life with friends as their family—a human family—to breeze through my imagination.

"Thank you, sir." It was an idyllic picture, made for another's living room, not mine. "And you."

"Ah now." He flashed a relieved smile at me. "Here they are."

"Bose!"

Several privates from the Connecticut line were escorting him while engaged in an animated retelling of the Marquis de Lafayette's grand escape, having gone with over two thousand to scout the British farewell celebration in Philadelphia for their commander-in-chief. Sir William Howe was destined to leave American shores and face possible censure in London for his failure to suppress the rebellion. Under cover of the fireworks roar, seven thousand regulars had ridden out and sought to surround Washington's favorite Frenchman, but they took fright at the war cries of our Indian troops and excellent display of American arms—so the news reported—thus allowing Lafayette's men to slip through Britain's oily grasp.

A redcoat—fully welcomed within their discussion—argued that those whose tables overflowed with British suppers had no place among true Americans once the city emptied, a sentiment shared by the others.

Throughout their gossiping, Bose ran amok. I caught a lone swipe of fur prior to his rebound leap toward the soldiers, adding his opinions to their debate. They shooed him over to me and tried offering bribes of tasty somethings for his cooperation, but he wasn't interested in me. Stick hunting for his new friends was a matter of urgency.

The breath that whispered along my cheek spoke of a successful visit with the doctor. "If you wish it," Jonathan said, "we can take your Little Bear with us. I am certain, were I to ask it of him—"

"No." I squeezed the hand resting comfortingly on my shoulder. "He's happy."

They say home is where the heart is. Our history together would always reside in mine, but here was Bose's forever, with these men. So, I thanked them for bringing him to say goodbye, such as it was.

Raising their hands in salute to us, they answered, "Captain Wythe. Lady Captain."

Their momentary tribute to fine manners and good society paid, they returned to the service of their new country, Bose bounding in step with them.

Greaton laughed. "'Lady Captain.' You have received a notable promotion. The day before, you were 'Private Molly.'"

It was a little much for me; the lump in my throat overwhelmed me.

Seeing me settled in the saddle first, a handkerchief secreted into my hand, Jonathan then turned to Greaton. "Our thanks, Colonel, for the hospitality shown to us and the many kindnesses paid to the lady in my absence."

Greaton accepted his extended hand readily. "It may have taken a little brute force from Miss Moore, but she was correct in helping me to realize that it is an honor to serve alongside of you. Fare you well, Captain Wythe."

An uneasiness crept over Jonathan's face as he eyed the steep climb into the great horse's saddle, an exercise that would require some serious cracked-rib crunching. In a wordless agreement, it was decided between us that he should walk.

We passed several local ships out on the water, conducting their business as best they could with the changes in the river's free passage. Covert runs to Manhattan required more skill and land travel than before, but the construction of West Point provided a larger number of potential customers too. Word that a commission of gunboats from Albany was due to arrive later in the month meant more mouths needing to be fed. With such circumstances as these, the people of the Hudson Valley faced their new situation with as much courage as their ancestors, who had hacked a living out of the wilderness and expected their progeny to thrive there.

"Colonel Kościuszko didn't say goodbye," I realized as we reached the sunny hill where we'd hidden ourselves.

Jonathan continued his careful watch of our lush surroundings. "The colonel and I spoke this morning."

"You did? About what?"

"He bade me give his regards, and I am to tell you to 'remember what is best.'" A curious glance in my direction was the endnote of that subject.

Miles stretched forward, our steady clopping on the rocky pathway marking the seconds of a day's long journey ahead. Our quiet procession enticed an unforgiving replay of my final exchange with the colonel in my head. I hoped he would forgive me and think of our better moments together.

A flurry of feathers spirited from a nearby branch, claiming a perch closer to the road. I offered a relieved smile to our little friend, glad to see Cleophes was still with us. He darted behind the trunk. After a decent number of trees stretched between us, I caught a snippet of him poking his head into view, but when I twisted in the saddle to point him out, it was westward skies rather than visit Jonathan's raised hand.

Which was salt in Jonathan's anxious wounds, I realized. With the bird's eyes and perhaps ears searching the entire region—a swift and sure scouring of mountains, wilderness, campsites, and beyond, from the heights above musket fire, in far less ticking of the clock—Cleophes could easily seek out Thomas and tell us how he was. What a glorious possibility had just taken wing and abandoned us, for reasons I couldn't fathom.

But I didn't want Jonathan dwelling for long on similar thoughts as we resumed course, so instead, I voiced a niggling frustration: "Why red? What a stupid color for a Continental uniform. How are we supposed to tell the difference between them and the bad guys?"

Jonathan's serious expression stopped my rant. His brother wasn't a bad guy, and neither was he because he once donned the same uniform. A little sting lingered behind his words when brushing aside my apology. Because whatever their opinions of the King's policies, honoring the obligations of service to their home country entailed distasteful duties here and there, including the slaughter of their own countrymen. For all our beliefs in the self-evident truths of divinely granted freedom, that led us to do the same, which brother could honestly be said to have chosen the nobler course?

"You and the general are of the same mind," he said, cutting into my thoughts. "With so many, from so many different places, each in their own colors, how can His Excellency lead us when we are divided amongst ourselves? We are dependent on each man for our liberty. As such, we should be stronger were we to unite under one banner."

"But red?"

"If a regiment cannot afford their own uniforms, they make do with what they have. The men of Webb's Auxiliary took the uniforms of those that they defeated."

Absolutely revolting. It placed Webb's men in danger. Hardly a fitting tribute for a colonel reported to be suffering in a British prison ship, while his men toiled without him.

A subtle shift in the wind warmed my cheek. In its passage, a scent of blossoms tickled my nose and stirred something in me, like nature's version of coffee to my senses. And then I felt it—the call that'd been absent for weeks, a tugging at a broken part of me, urged me north. Rattling the prison door in my mind, a glimpse of my father squeezing my mother's shoulders begged to be seen, a look of pride on my brother's face as his wife presented me with a cake, chocolate swirls reminding me of my dreaded thirtieth birthday on the horizon. Its vague sweetness—although recently endured, the memory whispered through the splintering door—was even greater from our inexplicable absence in one another's lives.

But now, at last, I was going home. I would rediscover them and all the rest of myself that I'd forgotten.

"Would that you could grant me more time."

And like an arm sweeping a stack of books from a table, Jonathan's lament knocked aside the joyful image and the hope it had awakened in me, to send my world crashing into a devastating disarray. Just last night, in the darkest of hours, as I'd cowered in his arms and he sought to ease my panic, stroking my hair and promising me, "All is well. It was but a dream," I saw my fear manifest in his eyes. Lieutenant Sharpe had invaded my nightmares again, though for this new and improved horror show sequel, upon screaming and discovering myself in the attic bedroom, the smoothness of his fingertips still slipped over the length of my throat.

Demons being summoned, both of us hampered by injuries, and now a Hunter—who, Jonathan paled while declaring, should be powerless to invoke such forbidden acts—had willed himself through the realm of dreams to discover who I was. It'd become too dangerous, Jonathan had said, to protect me. He would serve me best if he saw me safely restored to my family, a family that moments earlier had welcomed me from across an unknown expanse to return to them. The forces of war, Hell, and whatever aspects of humanity resided within us, were all working against us, and he was asking me to stay.

So, whose voice was insisting I was abandoning my forever and always?

Thank You

Casie Bazay, author, for your fantastic consultations via Twitter DMs regarding all things horseback riding. Although I might know which way is forward, you saved my characters from betraying how little else I was prepared to throw at them.

J. L. Bell, author and self-proclaimed provider of "history, analysis & unabashed gossip about the American Revolution." I can always count on you for the deep-dives into primaries and the obscure (to this mere amateur historian, anyway) yet rocking details of the eighteenth century. In gratitude, by your humble servant.

Jodi Christensen, my most wonderful editor and sister from another life. Thank you for the gift of your friendship, sympathetic ear, and brilliant feedback. You took me by the hand and led me out of the Battlefields of Yorktown to set off on this incredible adventure together. And what a journey it has been. I am so grateful and relieved to have you by my side.

Daughters of the American Revolution, Schenectada (and all our local) Chapter(s). You ladies are the best. History thrives in all our lives today, in no small part to your dedication, service to others, and some good ole fashioned grave-cleaning elbow grease. Huzzay!

Marie Glowacki, officer of the Albany Polish Community Center, for your enthusiasm in my scribblings about the extraordinary Thaddeus Kościuszko and guiding me to someone more fluent in Polish than my Google search. Waiting in great anticipation for the first official Kościuszko Day in New York!

Stephen Gottlieb, professor and author, for introducing me to George Wythe and the authors of this crazy but great nation of ours. My history nerd heart cannot imagine a more intoxicating realm in which to play.

Lars D. H. Hedbor, author and publisher, for oh so much—sympathy in our joint grief, inspiration taken by gaping at the impressive size of your

RevWar catalog and enviable author table, and oodles of good and practical advice regarding this newest mission of mine. Hoping our next dinner together is not far away.

Shira Love for reading my gobbledygook in early drafts and asking all the important questions that make me scratch my head…then go get a fresh cup of coffee while I mull things over for a slurp, days, etc. This series could not have been possible without you and the zillion hours you have generously donated to the cause. May all your own artistic adventures be amazing and rewarding.

Olivia Marine for explaining to this landlubber how ships do not simply wind in a happy, simple path through an S-bend in the river. Not to mention the endless hours of navigating through the weeds of my early drafts and ensuring things such as statues and not statutes survive the cut. Tea, sandwiches, and gossip soon.

Peter Scagnelli, attorney, for the unpleasant task of schooling me in divorce proceedings for this book and the far-more pleasant task of sharing stories with one another.

Sevannah Storm, cover artist and author, who whipped together my bizarre, nit-picky requests through SKYPE and magically transformed them into a masterpiece on the page, spanning front AND back cover. You are brilliance in artform. How I miss our weekly banter.

Ela Tyler, author, for sifting through my mess of good intensions and translating it into actual Polish. *Bardzo dziękuję.*

Titania, my furry co-author, who relocated from my footstool to my lap for this sequel, despite whatever history book was balanced there…at least I was warmer that way.

The Media Relations staff of the United States Military Academy at West Point, for granting me access to the most amazing hike into the past a historical author could hope for.

Keith Willis, author and wrangler of dragons. From your first sympathetic apology upon learning the writing bug had nibbled on my gray matter to every supportive moment beyond, you make the hard parts easier to slay and the joyful ones even more magical.

The Husband and Sons—you are my everything and my all. Yes, even when I am drooling over paintings of dead guys or their gravestones. This adventure would be incomplete, and my joy in it insufficient, without you.

To all my friends and family here unnamed—you make the world a marvelous place, even when I am tucked away from it, typing furiously to escape. Thank you for always being somewhere in the background, supporting me.

~

Thank you for taking the time to read *The General's Watch*.

If you enjoyed it, please tell your friends and take a moment to write a quick review on your favorite site. Even a single sentence helps authors tremendously.

Additional Thank You

to everyone who supported us through our Kickstarter campaign

Believes in the Cause
Kay & Ben deGonzague
David & Janet Marcil
Marc Kristel
Jillian & Greg Bennett

~

Book Congress
Christina Rizkallah

~

Bring in the Cavalry
Brief Candle Press
Megan Kell
Jean Petrucelli
Scott & Julie Van Alstine

~

The General's Box
Sorrel & Neilson Barnard
Jessna Woods

~

New Recruit
Rachel & Jeff Klauser

~

Stick to the Cause
Anne Winchell

~

Express Rider
Matt Murphy

~

The Creative Fund by BackerKit

Traitors

~

The Enlightened series, book three

*How do you choose between protecting the ones you love
and betraying your country?*

Still wounded from the events by the river, Savannah and Jonathan must rebuild their trust if they are to uncover who is summoning the Possessed. Their mission returns them to the militia's camp, a breath away from the redcoats. Shadowing them is the enigmatic Lieutenant Sharpe, who haunts Savannah's nightmares yet holds the answer to what she truly is.

Scared to reveal her connection to the enemy, Savannah must recover her memories before her ties to her forgotten family and all hope of returning home fade forever.

An Author & Adventurer into History, **Kiersten Marcil** is the ambassador of a fantastical ride through the hidden deer paths of the American Revolutionary War in her book series, The Enlightened. The first book, *Witness to the Revolution*, was an American Fiction Awards finalist, a "Recommended Read" by Author Shout Reader Ready Awards, and received the bronze medal for historical fantasy by The Historical Fiction Company Awards in 2023.

Growing up, the Battlefields of Saratoga were her backyard and tourist sites like Fort Ticonderoga were an easy day trip, and Kiersten couldn't have cared less. It wasn't until journeying into adulthood that she grew to love books, and even then, not until she became a museum educator that she discovered the fascinating world of history.

Kiersten currently lives in Upstate New York with her family: The Husband, Useful Son, and Second in Line for the Throne, as they are affectionately known on social media, along with her two furry children, her co-author and research assistant.

However, you can find her at: www.kierstenmarcil.com

www.ingramcontent.com/pod-product-compliance
Lightning Source LLC
Chambersburg PA
CBHW070613300726
48975CB00006B/1809